NO LASTING
BURIAL

ALSO BY STANT LITORE

The Zombie Bible Series:

Death Has Come Up into Our Windows

What Our Eyes Have Witnessed

Strangers in the Land

Other Works:

The Dark Need (The Dead Man #20)

NO LASTING BURIAL

BASED LOOSELY ON THE GOPSEL OF LUKE
AND ON THE LEGEND OF THE HARROWING OF HELL
FIRST CENTURY AD

THE ZOMBIE BIBLE
FIRST BOOK OF YESHUA

STANT LITORE

Originally published as a Kindle Serial, November 2013

Published by 47North, Seattle

www.apub.com

ISBN-13: 9781477818053
ISBN-10: 1477818057

Cover design by Jeroen ten Berge

Library of Congress Control Number: 2013953969

Printed in the United States of America

for Inara, my fierce Inara

CONTENTS

6

7

8

9

PART 1

AD 26—Present Day.
Kfar Nahum, in the Roman Province of Galilee.

OUR FATHERS' SEA

SHIMON TOOK precautions. He asked the town's *nagar* to reinforce the door of his house with strong pine. And every evening at sundown, Shimon gave his crippled brother a curt nod and made sure that his mother bolted the door behind him with heavy planks of wood; through the door, he could hear her breathing hard with the effort. Then he walked out through the storm-battered houses of the fishers and hurried down the grassy tideline to the boats, to join Yohanna and Yakob, his uncle's sons, in readying the boat that had been his father's for their night's long battle with the sea.

The fish they brought back, a few dancing in wide nets, were just enough to keep them all alive—never enough for them to buy another boat or gather any wealth. The sea had been plentiful once, so much so that the fathers had told them that their fathers had been able to walk across the water from one shore to the next in calm weather without getting more than the soles of their feet wet—the fish had been so thick, they had just walked on their backs. The sea had been that full of the blessings of God.

But Shimon knew, with an ache of grief and old guilt as he pulled the oars and they went out to sea—Shimon knew the dead had poisoned the water. In the old stories, the lurching dead had blighted farm and field. Men and women who had been strong and hale sickened and perished. Perhaps it was the same with the fish. Sometimes in his dreams, while he shivered in his threadbare blanket, he thought he heard the emptiness of the sea, a kind of silent cry, like the cry the womb makes in a young woman who longs for a child and has none. The sea, once so full, longed for fish.

And some nights, out on the sea, they would haul up one of their too-empty nets and feel some weight in it, and looking down they would see rising out of the deep one of the dead tangled in the net, its face lifted toward them, eyes pale and white like those of a dead fish. Already reaching a hand toward the surface, its jaw opening.

Shimon hadn't slept well in years.

Often, as he lay in his bedding in the morning hours while Rahel and his brother moved quietly about the house, he would wake, shaking, remembering. He recalled the eyes most. It was never the lurching walk or the low moaning from a dead throat that stirred him from his sleep; it was the eyes, for wherever Shimon hid in the dream country, those eyes were waiting there for him. He might be dreaming of having a great house of sunbaked clay, cool inside with many carpets—like the houses that men of the Law had, in Yerushalayim far away. He would dream of holding a great banquet there, and many men would come in clothes so fine that Shimon's eyes ached seeing them. But always, when Shimon looked up from his food, he found his banquet guests staring back at him with those dead eyes. Those terrible eyes, in all their faces.

Or he might be dreaming of a woman, her body soft and scented beneath him. He would slide into her as smoothly as he might slip into the sea, and feel her clasp him, feel her arms about him, holding him to her; feel her breasts and her thighs against his body, damp with sweat. Yet as he began to move in her, she would not moan or cry out, and he would glance down at her face and see her looking up at him with those same eyes. Those eyes that held no life.

And he'd wake, his sweat cold on his face and back. He'd bite his lip and lie without tears, gazing at the open sky over the atrium where he and his family slept in the summer—or at the ceiling over his head in his cramped little side room if it were winter. In those months, the cold light from the atrium revealed the stone slabs of the roof laid over stout wooden beams, but though that wall between him and the vast unanswerable sky was familiar, it brought him no comfort. Shelter for the body, never for the heart.

———

Tonight Yakob rowed them quietly out into the dusk, and Shimon and Yohanna stood in the boat casting the nets again, the ropes cold and wet in Shimon's numb hands, a damp that he could feel even through his thick fishing gloves. The nets were woven flax and weighted, and one had to hurl them out over the water; it took a lot of strength and precision to cast one, and it could take two grown men to pull up a net if it was full—but the nets had not come up full in a long time.

The boat creaked beneath them; it was old. In his father's time, that boat would have been recognized anywhere on the Sea of Galilee. Now its sand-red paint was almost entirely gone; the boat had been skinned white by the water, like driftwood and sea wrack. Shimon and the others toiled on it like survivors scrambling for food in a ruin, as though they were three brothers who were the last remnant of their town. But the true brother of Shimon's own blood sat broken at home in a broken house, his absence a bitter core in Shimon's heart. Above the shore behind him, *all* the houses of Kfar Nahum were broken, each house a wounded body, burned and scarred and in some cases empty and boarded up, so many structures of memory and stone maimed years ago by men, living and dead, who had taken out their anguish, their rage, their grief and hopelessness on the bodies of others.

They knew their work, these three. Yohanna had the best eyes, and he watched the water. Yakob could endure at the oars the longest. And Shimon could sense the smallest shift in the wind; he knew when to let the sail fly or when to furl it up tight against the sudden rages of the *shedim* howling over the water.

"Maybe today," Yohanna said, as he always did at the casting of the nets. He was a man who liked to hope. Shimon might have resented that, but Yohanna's hands on the nets were strong, and in any case Shimon found it difficult to stir the ashes of his anger these nights. He felt emptied out, like his father's house. He swung one of the nets, feeling the pull of its weight in the sinews of his arm. As it came around he lifted it high and cast it out into the wet dark, letting the rope pay out through his gloved hands, the cold sound of the water swallowing it. Shimon began the count.

"Maybe today." Yohanna glanced at Shimon's face, and his own fell. He added in a low voice, "There are blessings left in this sea. We just haven't found them yet. We have to keep trying. Until the *navi* heals the land."

Shimon ignored Yohanna's optimism, as he always did, and Yakob changed the subject, as *he* always did. His hard eyes softened as he looked at his brother. "Tell us again about your *navi*," he said. Yohanna had been one of the town's self-chosen exiles, leaving two years past to seek out the wild caves in the cliffs above the Tumbling Water, where Yohanna ha Matbil, the baptist, whom some men called *navi*, or prophet, lived in defiance of the moaning *shedim*, forsaking town and city, living on locusts and camel's milk and leading men and women down into the water to wash away their evil.

Shimon's count reached twenty and he tightened his grasp on the rope, stopping its slide. He sat quickly on one of the boat's two benches—the one nearest the stern—and knotted the rope around one of the iron hooks set between his feet. The original hooks had long since needed replacing, and it had cost him severely. The iron came from Threshing, and the men and women of Threshing wanted nothing to do with those surviving families who wrestled their hunger in the emptied houses of Kfar Nahum.

Yohanna cast his own net and told his story as he knotted the rope. Shimon took up another net and swung it out into the night as he listened.

"He brings everyone up from the water with his own hands; he won't let any of his followers do that. He will look into the eyes of a man he's lifted from the river, and say things that I still hear in my heart though my mind doesn't understand. He would look in your eyes and say, *Prepare yourself, God is very near.* Or he would say, *We are all kin. All tossed together by God into this world.*"

"We are all kin," Yakob repeated quietly.

"I asked him about that," Yohanna said. "One night when the stars were out and all the baptized slept in their tents by the riverbank. I went to him and I said, *Rabboni, my teacher, my master.* I said, *Who are my kin?* And he just looked at me as though I should know the answer without asking. He is like that. He doesn't talk much, Yohanna ha Matbil—unlike me, though we have the same name. He hardly ever says anything, really, and so he teaches us all to listen."

"We are not all kin." Shimon's voice was gravelly, as he hadn't used it yet that night, and it startled him to find himself speaking now. "The Romans are not my kin. Those Greek-loving Hebrews in Threshing and Tower, they are not my kin." Something flickered inside him, then settled, and he sat back on the row bench, silent and heavy. The others didn't answer or challenge his silence, and after a few moments he ceased to be a man and became a part of the boat again.

———

Then there was only the silence and the sea and the starlight. A few times, the men pulled up the nets for a look, and the few small, lean musht they caught soon lay glistening in the bottom of the boat. Perhaps enough to feed the three of them and their families for one meal. When the nets were back down, they slit the fish open and gutted them and then wrapped them in sheaves of lake-weed that they kept in a bin behind Shimon's bench, a bin filled with water to keep them fresh. Shimon watched the wrapped fish for a while, numbly; then he lifted his eyes and watched the dark surface of the lake, that watery mirror of his own heart. There was no wind tonight; years before, when Shimon hadn't yet learned despair, he would have been thankful for that. The wind was to be feared; demons rode it, the *shedim* that wandered in the desert places until witches called them out of the dark or until the wind picked them up and swept them into the towns and the stone houses of the People. Sometimes one heard them howling and keening in the rocks high on the hill of tombs, and if a man did not live a good life and keep the words of the Law often on his lips, if he opened his mouth too often to speak blasphemies or untruths, the wind might blow a demon into his mouth. The demon would inhabit his body as a man inhabits a house, but would damage the house it dwelled in, casting the man to the earth in fits or tormenting his mind and making him shriek and curse at people who weren't there. Zebadyah the priest claimed that these same demons inhabited the corpses of the unburied dead and the unclean and half-eaten, that it was these *shedim* that drove those corpses stumbling to their feet and made them pursue and feed on their living kin.

So when there was a cold wind over the water—as there often was, chopping the surface of the sea and cutting even through his water-coat—Shimon shivered amid his numbness and his grief, and drew his coat more closely about his body, as though by keeping covered, he could keep the demons from slipping inside him. And when the night's catch brought up a few fish, he was always careful when he gutted them to take out the heart and wrap it in a bit of lake-weed, tucking it into his coat. Before sleeping for the day in the empty house that had been his father's, he would hand the heart to his mother, who lay it on the coals of the smaller firepit in their atrium, the one they didn't use for cooking. The smoke from the fish's heart would keep even the most malicious of the *shedim* away, for their fathers had taught that the fish were God's gift to the People, to make them strong and virile and prosperous.

But now it was rare to smell the heart-smoke of the fish, and Shimon feared that each wind brought more *shedim* into the town, and that even the water itself had become a house for the demons, a dark mirror of the air that was their usual home. Somewhere down under that dark, placid surface were many pale corpses, some buried perhaps in the sediment, some drifting in the water. A soft glow on the far edge of the sea signaled the coming dawn, yet Shimon felt cold.

"Do you never think of what waits beneath our boat?" he asked suddenly.

The others turned to look at him.

After a few moments, Yohanna cleared his throat. "Fish, I hope. Somewhere." He was pale.

"I never stop thinking of it," Shimon said. He kept staring at that still, deceitful surface. "You think you can forget everything in this silence over the water. You think you can leave your dead beneath the waves. But there is no lasting burial."

They took up their oars and rowed slowly, letting the nets trail behind in the water, in no hurry to return to their surviving kin with news of another night lost. Shimon sat in the middle of his despair like a hard gray stone. But then he glanced up from his oar and saw a single white seabird, the morning's first. It skimmed low over the sea with a swiftness that was holy. His gaze followed the bird's long glide, and for a few moments the sight of it made his numbness almost pleasant, the way that the last slide into sleep is pleasant, when a man loses all feeling but that soft weight of drowsiness.

Even as the bird lifted into the sky, the sun burst over the water behind them like the sounding of a shofar, lighting the bird's wings and the water beneath it, and blazing against the white walls of Beth Tsaida, the fishers' houses by the tideline below Kfar Nahum town. Those were houses of stone built to withstand the strong winds from the sea. Houses built to last; only the people inhabiting them had not.

As if in answer to the sun's arrival, an eerie cry sounded over the water. A high, wavering cry, a wail. Shimon stiffened; for a moment he didn't know what creature was uttering that scream, though he thought there were words in it.

"What was that?" Yohanna gasped.

"A man," Yakob said, looking over his shoulder. "There's a man on the shore."

Shimon glanced where Yakob gestured, even as the cry died away, leaving his heart beating fast. They were close enough to the shore now that if Shimon had held up his arm and tried to cover the man with his hand, he would have needed to use nearly his entire palm.

He squinted against the sun's glare on the water. One of the boat people, maybe, though the man was standing with his feet in the sea. Why one of the vagrants would walk out into the breakers and risk the touch of the waterlogged dead, Shimon couldn't imagine. The man wore a wool robe the color of sand, though it was torn, dirtied. There were bruises on his face and arms. A vagrant, maybe one of those men with a demon that made him shriek in the night until the fishers of Kfar Nahum drove him away.

Yet that cry, that terrible cry.

Shimon could not slow the thumping of his heart. The oars slipped in and out of the water, and the boat moved smoothly toward the shore and the man.

The man on the shore lifted his hands to his mouth and called out again, and the cry carried loud and far. Yakob cursed and made the sign against the evil eye. That high wail as though he were the God of their fathers in the desert, calling the People to Har Sinai, the mountain that touched the clouds. Shimon made out one word in old Hebrew, strangely ululated: the word for *fish*.

"God, I wish he'd stop that," Yakob whispered, pale.

The very air seemed to quiver as the cry went on, and on. Then the boat lurched hard to the larboard, tilting, nearly tossing Shimon into the sea. He grasped the bench and his feet scrabbled against the side of the boat as the gunwale nearly touched the surface. The boat—they were tipping! With a bellow, Shimon threw himself across and up against the highside. Yakob and Yohanna did so, too, shouting over the cry from the shore.

"Did we strike something?"

"I don't know!"

"Right the boat!" Shimon roared. He knew from the boat's tilt that the keel was coming dangerously near the surface, and he heard water lapping over the low gunwale as the boat fought for balance. Glancing down, he saw dark water coming over the gunwale and the nets trailing in the sea, and gasped.

There the nets were, some way below the surface, and he could see that they were full, in fact perilously full, of teeming, squirming fish. Musht and barbels and sardines caught in the tight weave of the nets. The fish were blue-silver and they flashed in the dawn, like pieces of living iron. Their thousand mouths opened and closed helplessly, their eyes dark and glassy as if with shock at their sudden birth and capture, as if tossed in one slippery instant from God's hand into the waiting nets.

"*Fish*," Yakob whispered. "*Fish*."

"*Fish*," Yohanna whispered.

Then Shimon was whispering it, too. The word fell from their mouths like a sigh of awe, like an invitation to wake from an evil dream. *Fish . . . fish . . .* Their sigh went out over the water until that word and the slosh of the waves against the boat and the slapping of the wet scales of fish against each other's bodies and against the straining nets became one sound, one hope.

FACES IN THE WATER

EVERY MAN older than a boy knows this, and likely every woman, too: You cast out your nets and catch some flash of new life. Then your dead rise from the waves of your past to wrest it from your hands.

The boat began to right itself, but only barely. Even as Shimon looked down into the water, he saw a pale corpse clinging to the bottom of the net and trying, clumsily, to climb it; its face tilted back, and its small, lifeless eyes gazed up at the water's surface and at Shimon above it. Shimon gazed back at those empty eyes for one terrible instant, his heart violent in his chest, his body cold with horror that this ruin of a human being, its insides perhaps crawling with *shedim*, might seize his flesh, might *eat* him.

Great strips of flesh trailed from the thing's cheek, where fish and the water itself had been at it. Shimon reached for one of the small spears stowed beneath his bench for incidents such as this, and he took the spear in his gloved hand and began thrusting it down into the water, cautiously but quickly, knowing he mustn't cut the net. Knowing also that the corpse must not come up *with* the net.

The face emerged from the water and its mouth opened as though to moan or hiss, but water poured out instead of sound; the corpse reached one maggot-white waterlogged arm toward him. With a wild cry, Shimon drove his spear into its face; his hook tore through the thing's scalp as easily as through a fish. In a moment it hung limp from Shimon's spear, its eyes still dead and unseeing.

Then it slid away and sank into the deep. Its face still gazing lifelessly up, it faded to a dim white form far beneath the water, and then could no longer be seen.

Shimon threw his weight back against the far gunwale, fearing the tilt of the boat. He was breathing hard. He felt a hand clap his shoulder, and Yakob's breath near his ear. "It's all right, Shimon. It's all right."

But his hands were clenched so tightly around the spear that he couldn't loosen them. He just kept staring at the surface of the sea. And then he saw them. Faint in the murk, clinging to the bottom of the nets, beneath the flashing silver of the fish, other pale figures. The corpses of the sea of Galilee.

In the next moment, Yakob and Yohanna glimpsed them, too.

"Holy God," Yohanna breathed.

"We've brought them up with the fish," Yakob whispered.

"Spears," Shimon cried hoarsely, his body so shaken with fear he felt that if he let go of the spear he held, he might retch and fall into the sea.

But then the boat tipped harder, tugged down by the weight of the dead crawling up the ropes from the nets. The mast swung down, dangerously near the surface. Yakob and Yohanna didn't spare a moment to grab spears; they threw themselves hard against the highside gunwale, fighting to balance the weight of the dead. Gazing down with his spear still clutched in his hands, Shimon saw the nets and the fish beneath him, and the dead breaking the water, reaching with their long gray fingers for the gunwale and the warm bodies above it. Their eyes pale stones glistening with seawater. Shimon stabbed down at them. But one grasped his fishing spear and pulled, nearly wrenching Shimon out of the boat and into the lethal water. Such strength. For just a moment the corpse's face was only an arm's length from his, with its dead eyes and torn flesh hanging loose from white bone. Its jaws opened, spewing water.

And then, in the dawn light on that dying sea, Shimon did something that he could never afterward truly believe he had done. Something in him roared awake, like a lion springing from a cave. So many nights he had failed to bring home fish for his family, failed though his father had been a boatman envied on every coast of the Sea of Galilee. So many mornings he had come home to see his brother's skin stretched too tight over his ribs, to hear their mother's voice shrill with the bitterness that hunger breeds in the heart. How often he had heard weeping by day in the house nearest his as he tried to sleep despite the growl of his belly, or seen beggars listless in the shade of derelict boats just above the tideline, their eyes vague with the nearness of death and their faces gray as the faces in the water. So many silent nights on the water, so many empty nets. But not this time. This time, nothing living or dead would keep him from bringing the fish home.

Shimon took up an oar and leapt on the gunwale and spun the wooden blade in his hands to give it momentum and force. He slammed the blunt wood into one of the pale faces. The corpse lost its hold on the net and was hurled aside into the waves, where it sank as swiftly from sight as a dream upon waking. Then, roaring as though furious at the dead and at the sea and the sky and Mighty God himself, Shimon spun the oar, slamming it into one face after another, dislodging the dead, in one case crushing the corpse's skull so that its body went limp as he sent it back to the sea.

The last of the dead grasped the gunwale with one hand and with the other, the haft of the oar, just above Shimon's own hand. Hissing. Shimon lifted the oar in both hands, drawing up the dead, water streaming from the corpse. Shimon caught a brief glimpse of its eyes near his, white gums drawn back from its teeth, water trickling out from a great gash in its cheek. All his nightmares made real. His memories given flesh. With a shout he swung the oar over the water away from the nets and shoved it out into the air; oar and corpse fell back, attacking the surface of the sea in a fierce splash. The corpse clung to the oar, but the waves bore it away from the boat, its dead eyes still watching Shimon. Still hungering. After a moment its wavering moan called out across the water.

Shimon fell back into the boat, his chest heaving. Yakob and Yohanna tried to haul up the nets, heaving on the ropes, hand over hand. Doubtless, if they could get the fish into the center of the boat, they could keep the craft from trying to pitch itself into the sea. But after a moment they gave up, faces pale with strain, and let the nets fall back into the water. They gave the ropes a little slack and tied new knots, letting the nets sink deep, and at last the boat righted itself, its slender mast swinging slowly back toward the sky.

Yakob collapsed onto the other row bench. "Can't haul up those nets," he gasped. "We'll go under. We have to drag them in nearer the sand."

"Only one oar." Shimon had caught his breath.

"Two," Yohanna said. "I stowed a spare beneath the bench before the last Sabbath."

"Then row," Shimon growled, forcing himself up and onto the bench.

The others grabbed up the oars and swung them out and began to row fiercely, rowing backward so that they could keep their eyes on the shore. Shimon sat with his hands empty, his face dark and brooding. He could hear the man on the shore calling to them, but didn't heed the words. He heeded only the low moan of that corpse being carried out on the tide, riding its oar back toward the empty heart of the sea. Its voice was like another he'd heard, fifteen years before. All those years his past had lurched after him, threatening to swallow him. Moaning for him. He had hidden his heart in cold numbness and now that numbness had broken open, revealing blood and fury inside. Even as the boat lurched on the water, each stroke of the oars bringing the fish-heavy craft near to foundering, Shimon kept his gaze fixed on the stranger on the shore. This man who had called the fish, and called the dead up with them.

15 Years Past.
The Fall of Kfar Nahum.

THINGS DYING AND BEING BORN

THE DEAD feasted in the town that night, devouring Roman and Hebrew alike. Before they came, Rome's mercenaries had set up their tents in a half-moon around the town's north, as though all the birds of prey around the Middle Sea had settled here, ravenous, with blades for talons. They all wore Roman armor but their features were those of an entire world: faces dark-skinned and white, black hair and golden, short men and giants. The conscripts of an Empire, come to punish the town that had hurled a Roman tax collector into a house filled with the dead. All day they had plundered Kfar Nahum, and with the fall of dark, they reveled, peeling the town and its people open like fruit to be enjoyed and devoured.

But they had not come alone.

Something more ravenous even than they had followed them down out of the dry hills, perhaps attracted from old battlefields where they'd stood silent and waiting by the loud clink and clank of strange armor. The moaning dead fell upon the tents and the houses, and the town filled with shrieks.

Soldiers who only moments before had been slaking their hungers with wine or rape were tugged beneath growling, grasping corpses even as they reached for their swords. The natives of Kfar Nahum were bewildered at this judgment that fell upon both oppressors and oppressed; some ran to grab up fishing hooks to use for spears; others ran for the shore and the boats and the safety of the dark waters of the Sea of Galilee, that freshwater lake of storms; others tried to get back to their houses.

Shimon bar Yonah was only thirteen, short, and as yet unacquainted with despair. He peered out through a chink in the window of his father's house, but could see only dark silhouettes against the fires the Romans had kindled at the edge of town to light their carousing earlier that night. He heard screams, heard the wavering moans of the dead. His urine ran hot down the inside of his leg, and the reek of it filled his nose. He was never afterward able to forget the shame of his terror in that moment.

The outer door slammed open, startling a cry from him, but when Shimon turned to see the man who came to stand at the entrance to his small room, dark in the doorway, his chest heaving, he was not one of the dead nor any Roman but his own father. Yonah, the man other fishermen in the village looked up to. A man who seemed a giant to his son, as perhaps all fathers do, a man who towered over him and could surely carry a boat out of the sea on his shoulders.

Yonah was clutching his left arm near the shoulder. He dropped to one knee and looked into his son's face. His voice was raw with pain. "Son, listen to me. Your mother—I hid her in the *kokhim*. The tomb of our family. The one place the Romans would not look. You must go there. Go there now. Run. Don't let the dead follow you. Go to your mother. Go *now*, son!"

He grasped Shimon's arm and thrust him toward the door. Shimon glanced back wildly at his father. In one dizzying instant, he saw blood seeping between his father's fingers where he clasped his left arm. Shimon hesitated; he felt the slow crawl of panic into his chest.

"I'll be behind you," Yonah cried. "Run, boy!"

And Shimon ran.

Shimon's heart was a wild, desperate thing in his chest; his side burned as he tore through the narrow streets of the town, ducking as screaming figures darted or fell past or tried to clutch at him. Dying men and women lay writhing in the dust behind him as he ran, and other shapes fell on them with snarls. Once, Shimon saw ahead of him, at the doorway of a house, a woman screaming in the street, her belly torn open. He saw her face—the town's midwife. A man with only one eye glanced up from the ravaged body with entrails clutched in his hands, and his eye was white and had no life in it.

Shimon screamed and veered to the left, ducking as two corpses in the street hissed and snatched at him; one caught hold of his sleeve at the wrist but the fabric tore and Shimon stumbled and ran on, with the corpses pursuing. Ahead he saw the door to the weaver's house, where the Roman mercenaries had herded all of the town's small children. An oil lamp still burned within, and Shimon had a brief glimpse of adult shapes bent over small, still bodies, large hands pulling entrails and red organs from their bellies. One of the feasting corpses glanced up and its eyes shone like cat's eyes in the light of the lamp. Shimon ran past, sobbing, but the corpses pursuing him ducked within the broken door and joined the feeding.

Everything after that was a confusion of snarls and moans and hands grasping for him, and a man in Roman armor lying in the street, his legs torn away, two of the dead bending over him, sucking greedily at his insides. His screams as he begged for help. Shimon covered his ears. He couldn't stop. He had to get out of the town and find his mother. He couldn't stop. Crying, he ran, and ran, and *ran*.

Then he was through the houses, and his small legs carried him up the rocky slopes of the hill west of the town. A wind was picking up, and he could hear the *shedim* screeching and howling among the stones and crags. He hurried for the refuge of the tombs, where no demons could enter and where the dead were always silent. The family *kokhim*, and those of the other fishing families of Kfar Nahum, were chambers dug out of the side of the hill. On shelves carved into their interior walls were laid the bodies of their ancestors. Once, centuries ago, the People had piled mere cairns of stone over their dead; now they gave them beds inside the earth and often left the tombs open to the air so that God could look in and see the dead, and remember them.

But these walking dead that had lurched into their town during the night, interrupting the carousal of the Roman legionaries, were not the dead of Kfar Nahum. Shimon didn't know where they had come from, only that their faces were unfamiliar and twisted in savage hunger. Perhaps they had come down, as a few dead did each year, from the great battlefields left neglected in wild places. He didn't know.

Behind him, the light of flames rushing before the wind. Parts of the town were dying in heat and fire and screams. His body went cold with panic as he panted and forced himself uphill toward those dark tombs. Suddenly, he heard a thin, faint cry—from ahead, not behind. An infant's cry. Shimon froze, listening. Then he bolted, running up the slope to the tomb of his family.

The *kokh* was open and dark, the dead inside silent on their shelves. Shimon leaned into the opening, the cool of the tomb on his face, and called out, "*Amma, amma,* mother, mother!" into the cool, dry night within.

"*Shimon?*"

"I'm here. Father sent me." He was shaking.

"Shimon—" Almost a moan, and Shimon caught his breath, fearing for her and fearing the dark. He stepped in, stumbled over loose pebbles, and caught himself on his hands, there at the very lip of the tomb's round chamber. Even as he picked himself up, his eyes adjusted and in the faint starlight and the dim glow of the town's burning he saw his mother lying on her back near the wall. Her body was flushed and damp with sweat; the distant glow from the fires in her eyes. She lay naked on a blanket, her legs parted, the knees lifted, and Shimon averted his eyes. She was clutching something small to her breast; he could hear suckling. The woman glanced up at Shimon, her face twisted in fear and exhaustion—her son stood there and not his father.

Shimon stood in the door, not knowing what to do. His face flushed as he watched the small life suckling at his mother.

"Your brother," Rahel said after a moment. She sounded hoarse and breathless, as though she had been weeping. "This is your brother."

Rahel bat Eleazar had given birth alone, without any midwife to assist her, and though she had been blessed with a clean birth and a living baby, she was left weak and shaken. Obeying the words she whispered there in the shadows of the tomb, Shimon took up a fold of the blanket she lay on and pressed it between her thighs to stanch the blood. Weakly she touched his hand with hers, pressing slightly, and Shimon held the cloth to her. He listened to the sounds his brother made. He listened to Rahel's breathing, heavy in the dark. And he listened to the cries and moans from the town below. Whatever entered his heart as he listened to these things, as he sat where no man or boy was ever permitted to sit, between the knees of his mother at the place of birth—whatever this moment did to his heart, there was always a quietness in him, for all his life afterward.

When his mother slept and Shimon was sure that no blood had soaked through the blanket, he left the cloth bunched up and pressed to her as best he could, then took up the waterskin his father had left there for her—it was empty now—and slipped out of the tomb. He knew his mother would thirst when she woke, and he knew there was a spring farther up the hill, where he and the other boys used to go and watch the moon rise over the sea. Standing on the slope, he glanced once at Kfar Nahum's stone houses and the dark murmur of the sea behind. Some of the fire had been put out, though it still raged near the synagogue. He could just see dark shapes against it. Somewhere a man was screaming, high-pitched and desperate, in Latin, words Shimon didn't know. He heard moaning still, but thought there was less of it.

Shivering, he turned his back and crept up the hill, bending low so that his silhouette would not be seen against the stars. Halfway to the water, he stopped—not because he had seen or heard anything, but because something had coursed through his body, cold and sharp, a shock of instinct that he could not have described or understood. He dropped and pressed his belly to the dirt, breathing in small gasps of fear.

A moment passed. Then another.

The man far below was still shrieking his incoherent Latin words.

Then, somewhere near, the slide of a foot over the soil. Shimon tensed.

Now a step. Then another slide, the sound of a foot dragged across the dirt.

Shimon's heart set up a panic beat in his chest. He lay trembling.

A dark shape slouched by perhaps a stone's throw from where he lay, just a moving patch of night where no stars shone, a man's shape or a woman's, hunched forward, one arm hanging uselessly at its side. Shimon held his breath, and his heart was like all the shouting since the world began, ready to give him away. Yet the corpse didn't hear it; it just dragged that one foot behind it, swaying as it walked downhill. The reek of it reached Shimon and he gagged; he covered his mouth and nose and fought with himself to stay silent.

The screams in the town seemed faint now, drowned beneath the roar of blood in Shimon's ears, but he could still hear them. He could see again the midwife being eaten, the midwife who might have helped his mother. He could see again the blood on his father's hand. A mad urge seized him, to leap to his feet and shout and throw himself at that corpse, perhaps with a stone in his hand. To make that shambling, violent corpse *know* that this town it meant to consume had people in it, men and women like Shimon's father and mother, people who lived and loved and breathed. To smash the stone into its face, if that's what it took to make it see.

But he didn't leap up.

He held still. He clenched his fist about blades of the coarse grass, as though holding himself to the ground.

The corpse was moving down the slope now. It tilted its head back, drew in a long breath that Shimon could hear in the dark, and then it *moaned*. A low wail of need and demand that wrenched at him. It was the sound of a man whose tongue had been cut away, and then his mind, and then he had been left on the shore of the sea with no sight or sound of his wife and children and all his kin, but only the need to find them and clasp them, crushing them to his body with strong, stiff arms and consuming them in his need. That low moan of a man who didn't know where they might be found or how he might come to them again. Such profound and despairing need as Shimon had never heard in a human voice. He shivered in the grass.

The moan went on and *on*, far too long. Longer than a living man would utter any cry, long past when the lungs would burn, for the corpse voicing it felt no pain or anguish of the body. Or if it did, that was as the bite of a flea beside the pain of its solitude and hunger.

Then the moan fell and the corpse passed on down the hill. The sounds of its feet faded into the noise from the town and the chill breeze carrying the unbodied *shedim* through the grass. Its shape was distant now but dark against the glow of flame and easily seen.

Shimon lay breathing a while, recovering. He knew he had to be brave. Brave for his mother and her baby. All at once, he got up and ran forward at a crouch. He rushed; he had to get the water and get back into the tomb before any other corpse appeared on the hill. The momentary urge for battle had faded; after hearing that moan so near, he dreaded any further encounter with the dead.

And he wanted to be there when Rahel stirred. He could not let her wake alone in the dark.

PART 2

"I AM ALIVE"

RAHEL WAS already awake when Shimon returned; he heard her breath catch when his shape filled the opening to the tomb. Then heard her relax when he called, "Amma," softly. For a moment he hesitated, glanced over his shoulder at a night filled with stars and the sound of the sea and the glow of flame, the houses of his father's town burning far below at the edge of the water. Distant moaning, screams. Fewer now. Anything might be happening in the world outside the tomb. The Romans and the people of the town might be spearing the last of the dead, or the dead might be eating the last of the living. No way to know.

He felt vulnerable and exposed. He ducked into the tomb. Went to his mother and knelt by her, held the waterskin to her lips and listened as she drank. She did so in small swallows, and took a long time. Then her fingers touched his hand weakly, and he pulled the skin away, set it aside.

"Your father," she said hoarsely. "Where is he?"

"I don't know." He couldn't tell her. He couldn't tell her about the blood he'd seen on Yonah's hand, the raggedness of his father's breathing. His throat closed against the words. To speak it would be to make it real, to make his fears become truth.

Rahel shut her eyes tightly and clutched her infant closer to her, and a tiny, almost inaudible sound of misery came from her throat. Shimon closed his eyes, too, not wanting to see her pain, not knowing what to do.

After a while, Rahel whispered in the dark:

> *Though the fig tree does not flower,*
> *And no grapes are on the vines,*
> *The olives give no oil*
> *And the fields no barley*
> *The flock does not come home to the fold*
> *Nor the herd home from the field,*
> *Yet I will cry out in joy.*

Her voice trembled, yet she did not allow the silence of the tomb to swallow her song. The song of Habakkuk, a *navi* of their People in years past, one of those blessed or cursed with the gift of seeing things that usually only God saw. A song he'd made at a time of war.

> *I will cry out in joy,*
> *I will take joy in my God.*
>
> *God is my strength;*
> *He makes my feet like the deer's;*
> *He makes me walk in high places.*

"How can you sing that?" Shimon said suddenly. "How can you?" His hands were shaking. "Everyone's dying. I saw— They're being torn *apart*."

Rahel looked at him in the dark. "Oh, Shimon, Shimon. I am alive, I am alive, I am alive, and my sons are alive."

And she began whispering the words again. Shimon turned his back, overwhelmed with the night's horror. He glanced up, saw the round openings in the tomb wall into which the ancestral dead had been slid feetfirst onto their shelves in the dark and the silence. There were corpses there, many. His father's father and his wife, and their parents, and theirs. And many of their brothers and sisters whose faces had been forgotten but whose names remained, chipped into the stone beneath their places of rest. He reached up to the lowest of these shelves, ran his fingers across the deep Hebrew letters, worn by time yet still readable if there were only enough light. His hand still shook a little at the memory of the corpse walking down the hill, at the memory of its cry of hunger, yet the silent dead on their shelves above him and all around him did not frighten him. Their silence and their presence was strangely comforting. Death had visited the People again and again over the long weeping of the centuries, yet the People lived.

"Would you like to hold him, Shimon?"

His mother was lifting the small baby in her hands, holding him out.

"It's all right," Rahel said, seeing him hesitate.

Swallowing, Shimon took the boy in his arms as gently as he might a sacred scroll, terribly aware of his brother's fragility. Yet as Shimon felt the small weight of his brother's body, the warmth of him, something blossomed open inside his heart. Settling the boy into the crook of his arm, he freed one hand and touched the child's face, first the tiny brow, then the soft cheeks, feeling his brother's warm vitality in the dark. His throat tightened and he wished to squeeze his brother to his chest, but he didn't for he feared hurting him. After the horrors he had seen this night, this warm body in his arms was a miracle, as though God had reached through the door of the cave and touched the world, in this one place, at this one moment.

He ran two fingers over the boy's hair, which was fine and sparse. Then he touched the boy's left arm, marveling at its smallness. He found the boy's hand and felt the small fingers close around his; he drew in his breath. That firm grip, and the soft glint of the eyes in the dark. Shimon wished his father was here, that he might hand him the baby and see the two of them together, but also he was glad that it was he who held the child and who got to look into the little boy's eyes. Those eyes were as bright with life as though they were God's eyes, looking out of that tiny face at a darkened world.

Solemnly, Shimon touched the boy's right arm, and gasped. That other arm was so thin, and the boy didn't move it at Shimon's touch. The arm hung limp at the baby's side.

"Amma," Shimon whispered in the dark.

She looked at him. Shimon saw her eyes and the faint glow of distant fire on one side of her face.

"He's broken," Shimon whispered.

"Hand him back to me, Shimon." No urgency or surprise in her voice.

Gently, his hands shaking from the fear that he would drop the boy or break him further, Shimon handed his brother back. Their mother held the baby to her breast, and Shimon looked away. A sense of crushing disappointment settled over him, a fierce pressure on his heart. To have a new life, a new hope offered in one moment and then torn away in the next, to find that his brother, like everything else this night, was maimed and broken—

"He is your brother," Rahel said quietly. The baby made no sound of suckling, just soft breathing; perhaps he was falling asleep, pressed to the warmth of his mother, his whole world her living flesh, unknowing of any dead outside or of any hunger but his own. "Whether he is broken or not, he is your brother. Shimon, never forget that."

Shimon didn't move; he just stared into the dark.

"Shimon?"

A moment later: "Shimon?"

He glanced at his mother. She had suffered this night. Though his insides burned with wrath, he leaned over her and pressed his lips to the baby's head, felt the softness of the infant's skin. He did not even hear the distant cries in the houses burning by the sea. Rahel turned the baby toward him, and after a hesitation Shimon felt for his brother's heartbeat. Found it, so much faster than his own, and in all the lethal night there was no other sound.

ZEBADYAH

DAWN FOUND the last men and women of Kfar Nahum laying the bodies of the dead outside the town in long rows, both Hebrew and Roman, and shrouding them in white linens. When the linens ran out, they used blankets, or coats, or whatever they could find. Most of the legionaries had perished, and those that hadn't had fled into the hills—that left many, many dead. The charred and broken houses of the town reeked of them.

A few of the living women took ashes that were still warm from the ruins of the houses and the Roman tents, and put the ashes in their hair. Then they knelt by the corpses and keened, as other women had done before them on many battlefields and in many burned cities throughout the long centuries of their time in this land. Zebadyah the priest ignored them at first, searching the dead for the face of his father. As he passed, men and women lowered their heads in weary reverence, but Zebadyah turned his gaze away from them. There was sand in his graying hair and his white robe had been torn and soiled by his flight when the Romans broke the door of his synagogue and by the long night hours he had waited hidden beneath one of the boats out above the tideline. There, with the boat's keel for his roof, Zebadyah had covered his ears against the screams of his people and the wailing of the dead in their hunger. He recalled, as in a nightmare, a whisper in his ear out of the air, when the Romans first began pulling people from their homes: *Go. Go quick. Hide.* And the same whisper as he hid beneath the boat: *Stay here.* Now shame smothered his heart.

His father Yesse had suffered during the night; one of the others among the grieving had told him of it, his voice shaken, as soon as Zebadyah had walked into town from the shore. In the hours of their drunkenness before the dead came lurching out of the hills, and while Zebadyah trembled beneath the boat, the mercenaries had stripped and beaten and mocked his father, for no better reason than that he was old and weak and Hebrew. The legionaries had dragged him from his house. This was a man with white hair and a long beard, who had served in his youth as a priest and who stood ready still to serve as one, if he should ever be called again to the *lev ha-olam*, the heart of the world, the Temple in distant Yerushalayim. Yesse had outlived two wives and had survived the deaths of three of his five sons, who had drowned in a storm at sea. He was revered by the town, and Zebadyah, the oldest of his two living heirs, brought fish for him and sat with him each evening as he ate. The drunken legionaries pulled this old man from his house and made him dance in the open ground before the synagogue, and then at swordpoint they forced him to strip away his garments and stand naked. He wept as they made crude jokes about his circumcision, as they asked him if he found he could still give pleasure to women, or whether he had lost some piece of his manhood and grown so white-haired searching to find it again. Perhaps they would have humiliated him further, but at that moment the moans had broken out, and the famished dead from the hills had fallen on them with their lethal hunger.

When Zebadyah found old Yesse at last, groaning in pain and grief where he sat against the side of a stone house near the edge of the town, the elder rebuked his son. "Tend to the People first," he rasped, "and let God tend to me, Zebadyah."

Zebadyah carried his father to the synagogue, feeling by instinct rather than conscious thought that it was the town's safest place, though he grieved to see the door broken from its hinges, blood smeared across the letters from the Law that his father's father had carved, with great labor, into the lintel and doorposts. He could hear the other survivors groaning within. The usually dim, cool interior was now lit with candles and stuffy from the smoke and the heat of the bodies smothered together beneath the low roof. The tiny flames shone strangely on the polished cedar of the cupboard against the east wall where the Torah was kept. The menorah had been knocked over and lay flat on its table and the shofar that used to be beside it was missing, but at the time Zebadyah hardly noticed.

Yakob and Yohanna were already there, with Leah bat Natan and several other women, carrying waterskins among the suffering and the feverish, or pressing wet cloths to hot faces. When Zebadyah's sons saw him, they hurried to lay out bedding for Yesse.

"There are many here who are unclean, father," Yakob whispered as Zebadyah laid his father down. His eyes showed their whites. By *unclean* he meant *touched by the dead. Bitten.*

Zebadyah nodded wearily, whispering words of praise in his heart that his sons were both alive, however haggard they might look.

"Was grandfather bitten?"

"I am fine, boy." Yesse opened his eyes.

"He is fine," Zebadyah repeated numbly. He sat for a moment, just to catch his breath. Gray-eyed Yohanna, his face become overnight that of a man and not a boy, crouched beside Yesse and lowered the waterskin to his grandfather's parched lips.

Zebadyah heard a raised voice behind him and glanced over his shoulder. He saw Benayahu, the town's *nagar*, the woodworker, repairer of houses and boats, with his back to the synagogue wall. His face twisted in rage and horror. "Snatched her," he was crying. "Snatched her from my hands. My wife. They took her from my hands; they *ate* her!" Beside him stood a boy whose dirt-darkened face was streaked with pale rivers left by his tears, and the boy—who was not Benayahu's—held the *nagar*'s yearling daughter in his arms, asleep.

But Benayahu did not glance up at either the boy or his child. He had torn away the right sleeve of his tunic and he held the ragged, rolled-up cloth tightly to his upper arm. Zebadyah didn't know if the bandage covered a bite or a wound from a Roman blade, but at this moment he did not have the strength either to care or to fear.

The priest worked his mouth a moment, to get enough spit to speak clearly. He looked to his sons' gaunt faces. "Where are Yonah and Rahel? And their boy?"

"We haven't seen them, father," Yakob said.

Zebadyah squeezed his eyes shut. If they were not here . . .

He forced his head up, looked around at the refugees of their town. More than forty lay on the clothes and blankets that had been tossed across the synagogue's stone floor for bedding, some of them shaking, some of them still. Some with horrible wounds, and their kin huddled over them, praying or giving them water or pressing wool against their limbs or their bellies to staunch the bleeding. Feverish faces in the candlelight—all these men and women waiting for death and for what nightmare might come after. A few of the unbitten stood solitary or sat against the wall, their heads down. None of them would ever sleep well again, ever trust the night again or the strength of their doors. A few looked his way, but Zebadyah lowered his eyes. He had hidden during the night while they suffered. He hadn't known the dead would come. He had hidden from the *living*. The Romans. But he hadn't been here—that was the accusation he believed he'd see if he faced them. He hadn't been here. He, their priest.

He realized Yakob was speaking to him. Perhaps had been for a while. His son's words rushed toward him from some distance like a flash flood down a river channel.

"—never got in the synagogue. It was Bar Nahemyah, father. He held the door against them during the night, and the corpses piled about his feet."

He glanced up at his son, whose face was drawn. He tried to understand. Bar Nahemyah—but he was only a youth, hardly older than Yohanna.

"Then he took some of the others and left. Yohanna and I stayed because people started bringing their wounded here, and they needed water and help."

"Have to find them," Zebadyah muttered, rising to his feet.

Yakob caught his arm to steady him, but he shrugged away his son's grip and the look he turned on his son must have been grim and desperate and near madness, for Yakob stepped back quickly.

"The old altar," Zebadyah rasped. "Past the grain caches, between the tanner's house and the ruin of the old wall. That one. Burn an *olah* there, while I find Yonah."

"We have no goats, no doves, father," Yakob said hesitantly. The altar hadn't been used since the days of the Makkaba; instead, Zebadyah went to Yerushalayim once a year to atone for the sins of the town, buying a goat to sacrifice from the market in the great city.

He muttered, "Perhaps God will accept a few fish. This one time."

He bent quickly to grip Yesse's shoulder and whisper, "My sons will look after you." Breathing raggedly, Yesse didn't open his eyes, and after a few beats of his heart Zebadyah left him and staggered toward the door of the synagogue.

———

He stumbled on through the death-reek of the town, seeking his brother Yonah. He stepped through the broken doors of houses and peered into emptied, unlit rooms with bloodstained walls. At the door of one house he heard low growls and he ducked away quickly, shaking.

He even strode out among the legionaries' tents beyond the north end of the town, but searching there he found at first only dead Romans and dead women and corpses whose heads had been split by Roman blades. Too many of the bodies were known to him. He saw Asher lying dead across the body of his wife, where he had perhaps died defending her from either the living or the dead. He saw Nahemyah's two sisters, their bellies torn open, entrails spilled messily about them where the dead had feasted. Their eyes glassy with death. But Zebadyah noticed one of the women's fingers twitching. He gasped and hurried by.

Nowhere did he see Yonah, or Yonah's wife or his son. Yet it was unthinkable to him that Yonah had perished. Yonah the iron-hearted, Yonah the furious. He recalled the rage in his brother's eyes that autumn as he cast the tax collector the Romans had sent into a house at the edge of town, a house empty except for the corpse that had wandered inside and been trapped. The man had shrieked and pounded on the door from the dark interior, and Yonah had not flinched, though Zebadyah's own palms had gone slick with sweat. He tried to remember that tax collector's name, and in a moment it came to him: Matityahu, a Hebrew from the Greek city of Many Birds to the west.

Reaching the end of the Roman tents and finding still no sign of his kin, Zebadyah glanced back and was struck to the heart by the sight of his smoking town and the shore and the wide, wide sea. For a moment he couldn't breathe. When he was a boy, he used to stand on this shore beside his father, near this very place, once a week, welcoming the Sabbath Bride with song, with shouting and praise and the slapping of his hands against his thighs. The Bride would tread lightly over the water with the dusk from the eastern shore, hurrying toward them from God's house in the heavens to bring rest to God's People.

When he was a boy.

Now beside the beauty of the waves his town lay crumbled and reduced to charred stone, like a withered old corpse seated beside a lovely woman, a woman who has not yet consented to bury him, though she can no longer feed him bread or fish.

Zebadyah closed his eyes and pressed a fist to his breast, as though he must hold in the anguish or it would burst him open. "What evil have we done, O God?" he moaned. "How have we broken your Law?" His voice gathered strength, as it had so many times as he prayed on the synagogue steps. "Lord and judge of the earth, for what do we stand judged? Was it our violence against Matityahu, who was Hebrew as we are? Was it that we took goods from the heathen traders, the pig-eaters, that we defiled our town? Was it for the Grief of Ezra? For what, Adonai?" He sank to his knees, the hard earth. "Why? Why have you made a wasteland of us?"

At that moment he heard a cry. A hoarse voice, a small voice, a child's, calling out for help. Zebadyah opened his eyes and looked to the tents.

There it was again.

Staggering to his feet, the priest followed the sound. After a moment, he stopped, called out: "Where are you?"

The cry that answered was inarticulate and without words, but it led Zebadyah to a great tent crimson as the insides of the eaten.

The centurion's tent. It was cut open on one side, doubtless by the slash of the centurion's sword as he made his escape from the dead lurching through the tent's door.

Inside, Zebadyah found a corpse with a cloven head and heard gasping breath from beneath the centurion's overturned desk, a heavy thing of no wood the priest could recognize, one of those ostentations the Roman military brought with them on their galleys from other shores across the world.

Pinned beneath the desk was a boy of eight years, his eyes glassy in a gray face. Zebadyah knew the child, for he had circumcised him and given him the name his father Cheleph had chosen for him: *Yakob*, a name Zebadyah's own eldest son shared. But Zebadyah had not seen the boy's parents at the synagogue.

"Yakob," he breathed. He bent quickly to feel for the boy's pulse. It was fast but steady. "Oh, Yakob."

The boy's gaze wandered a moment, then met his.

Zebadyah felt weary as the land itself. "I am going to get you out of here." He drew in a quick breath and got his hands under the edge of the desk and pulled, prying it off the boy. It was much heavier than he'd expected. He strained against it, gasped a prayer, heaved again. A surge of strength surprised him; it had been years since he had set his hand to an oar or heaved up a net from the clinging water. But he would *not* leave this boy to die in a heathen tent. The boy made no move to wriggle out as Zebadyah raised the desk, but the priest pulled at it until he had the desk high enough to thrust it to the side with his hip and shove it away, thudding into the dirt.

Breathing hard, he bent over the boy again. Yakob bar Cheleph was naked but for a thin night-tunic, and he had soiled his legs during the night, for his underclothes were gone. With a bit of nausea, Zebadyah wondered suddenly if the boy had been raped by the centurion, and the desk thrown against him on purpose, in hopes that the dead would bend over it and feed on the boy while the Roman escaped. This had not happened, clearly; the corpses must have followed the centurion out. The desk had lain across the boy's hip, and he was bruised there, badly. Running his fingers quickly over the boy's hip, Zebadyah didn't feel any bones broken. Yet when he got his arms under the child and lifted him, the boy cried out and nearly fainted.

"Father," the boy gasped as Zebadyah regained his feet with the child in his arms, "father—"

"He's gone, boy," Zebadyah said. His voice hoarse. "He's gone."

The boy shook; even to be held must have been a torment, his body was so bruised. Zebadyah blinked, forbidding his tears, and held the boy gently to his chest. The boy's eyes were glazed with pain and shock, the need in them louder in Zebadyah's heart than the roar of his own shame. Zebadyah looked to the door of the tent, where a wind from the sea tugged at the canvas. At that moment, he made a vow, and he made it without sacrifice and without ritual. He made it as a man, not a priest—the first time he had ever approached the God of his fathers so nakedly. He vowed to raise the boy with his own two sons. Little could Zebadyah do to repair the shattered houses and shattered lives of his town—he had not even been there to protect his own father—but he could shelter this one small boy. Surely he could do that.

THE GRIEF OF EZRA

THE DEAD must be buried: that was the one most important condition of their Covenant with God. Generations before, the Makkaba had left so many fallen in empty places in the hills with their eyes open to the sky. Furious to drive out both the Greeks and those Hebrews who wished to be like the Greeks, the Makkaba had rushed from battlefield to battlefield, striking hard like the hammer after which he was named, not pausing either for burial or for tending the wounded. Kfar Nahum had paid the price of that neglect of the Law during the night. Many of their people now were bitten and feverish. Those few still on their feet would invite no new disaster. By midmorning, Zebadyah led some forty of the survivors of Kfar Nahum in carrying the dead up the slope to the tombs. All the dead, not only those who were Hebrew.

The tombs nearest the town were long since filled with their ancestors; farther up the hill were those of the living families, with some shelves occupied and some vacant and waiting. And highest on the hill, three new *kokhim* that had been dug in the past few years at Yonah bar Yesse's request, in anticipation of good harvests from the sea and growth for Kfar Nahum. "Who is born, dies," Yonah had said with a cold smile. "Will we have no houses waiting for them?"

Zebadyah and the others brought the hastily shrouded dead to these new and empty *kokhim* and there they set the Hebrew corpses on shelves, and in heaps against the wall they lay the corpses of the legionaries, some of them still in their armor. Though most of the tombs stood open to the air, that God might look in and see the dead and sing them to restful, unwaking sleep, each of the caves holding these dead would be sealed behind a great stone. These dead, whether Hebrew or Roman, would lie forever in the dark.

Zebadyah bent and took up a handful of dirt, dry and grainy, and rubbed it on his hands. He was grim. His father would live, but many down in the synagogue would not. And those who did—*how* would they live, after what had happened? Most of the town's women were dead, because most of them had been forced to the Roman tents before the dead came, and the dead had reached the tents first.

He glanced down the slope, found the winter-bared sycamore that stood by the entrance to his own family tomb. In it, his wife, taken by death while bearing his third child, the one who hadn't lived. The girl. This morning he felt no pang, staring down at her tomb. Only dull relief. She had been spared the brutality of the Romans and the coming of the dead. She had been spared this day.

Yakob bar Zebadyah stepped from one of the *kokhim* to get another body to bear within, saw where his father was looking, and walked over to stand beside him, his own face drawn with weariness and fear. He had left Yohanna in the synagogue tending Yesse and Bar Cheleph; of their kin, only he and his father were here on the hill.

"She was a good woman," Zebadyah said to him after a few

moments. "She lived by the Law. Never a Greek garment in our house, never an uncleanness on her lips. I loved her."

They stood by each other, in silence.

Not heeding the priest and his son, the other men worked quickly, carrying bodies into the hill. They shelved the dead, then hurried back out into the pale sun, not pausing even to chisel or scratch the words of Ezra into the stone beneath the burial shelves, as was usually done: *For you God are holy and we who are flesh lie before you; who can stand before your face?*

A gust of wind across the hill, and Zebadyah stiffened against it, his lips closed tightly. Only when the wind died away did he speak. "God has withdrawn from us, Yakob." He gestured at Kfar Nahum below them by the bleak sea. "Look at the town. Our houses are built like Greek houses. Look at the women grieving, look at their dresses. Look at the decorative designs along the hem, designs that are not Hebrew." He thought of those he'd never see again, and of his brother, whose body he hadn't found. His heart grew small and cold. "God has turned his face. We were unworthy of his protection. The Grief of Ezra, my son."

Yakob only looked at his father with eyes that had seen too much suffering in one night to know or care how that suffering might be interpreted. But Zebadyah bent over one of the bodies, gripping beneath its arms to lift it, his anguish violent in his breast.

The Grief of Ezra.

That was what their People called the words of Ezra the Scribe, who centuries past had led the People home over the desert from their captivity beneath the walls of Shushan and the other cities among the mountain forests and wide plains of the east. Returning to the holy land after long exile, they had found their fathers' country ravaged by the hungry dead. They'd hastened to rebuild the long-crumbled wall about the great city, Yerushalayim, and those towers whose names their fathers had sung to them when they were young—names beautiful as the names of rivers: the tower of Meah, the tower of Chananel.

Every man toiling at the stones kept his spear beside him, where he could grasp it quickly if the dead lurched out of the olives on the mountain and came at them. When the dead came, hissing in the dark, many men who sealed the gaps in the wall with their bodies and their spears died, torn apart by hands that were without warmth, devoured by bodies in which there beat no heart. And as darkness ate the sky or as dawn bled into the heavens above the eastern ridge, more dead would stumble down from the high olive groves. Always more dead.

At sunset on the nineteenth day while the wall was still low and half-finished in some places, Ezra the Scribe stood before the People with his back to the stones and demanded of them that they stand and look out at the corpses. *Our land that God gave to our fathers is defiled,* he cried, *and you can smell the reek of it. Yet after all the evil that our fathers did, God has delivered us, patient as a father, and given us back our city. Yet even this day we do not keep his Law. Many of you have taken heathen daughters to your beds, and dress in the clothing of the east, and burn gifts of berries or small fruit to the gods who are not ours. And now we may be devoured. And this day, this night, will we still fail our God, until he turns his back again and no remnant of our People remains on the earth, and there is never again a return home? For God is holy and we are flesh before him.*

Then Ezra gave his fatal command, that the strange wives must be cast outside the wall and given no home within the city. *We must wall out what is unclean,* he shouted. *We must be clean and Hebrew again. Or this very night we will be eaten, and perish.*

Some of the men in the city refused, and some were slain. Ezra's speech had filled those at the walls with fear—the men who had gazed night and day into the eyes of the dead, men who'd taken up their spears and fought for the wall with their lives. At Ezra's word, many of these turned against their brothers in the city, tore their wives from their arms, and threw them over the low wall. Some of the women beat on the stones of the wall and screamed the names of their husbands. Others ran in search of crevasses in the rock or shrubs under which they might hide from the corpses that already lurched toward them.

While the dead ate, some of the men threw down their spears, set their backs to the wall, and covered their faces, shaking. Others toiled furiously at the stone and mortar, but did not look to the ground below. Ezra alone stood on the unfinished wall that night, watching by starlight and by the light of a torch he held as the screeching dead devoured the women. It was said afterward that he did not look away or blink or cover his ears against the screams and the cries for help. That he watched silently without tears as the women the men of his People had loved were caught and eaten, one after another, shrieking as they died.

Only when dawn came and there were at last no screams but only the moaning of the *shedim* through the mouths of the old dead and the new dead—the heathen wives risen in hunger, with horrible wounds that did not bleed—only then did Ezra come down from the now-finished wall. As he walked through the streets of Yerushalayim, such was the horror in his face that any who looked on him fell stricken to the ground, and died.

Ezra did not halt. Passing through the gates of their ancient city, he walked out alone into the wilderness above the Tumbling Water, speaking to no one. And he was never seen by the living again.

———

That was how Yesse his father had told the story.

Now, after the night of the dead, the Grief of Ezra held a new horror for Zebadyah.

"We must wall out what is unclean," he said quietly as he and his son carried another corpse into one of the crowded tombs. The reek was in their clothes now, in their hair. Though they both wore heavy fishing gloves and though the dead were shrouded to protect the living against any accidental touch, both men stank of rot. Zebadyah imagined that even if he were to swim in the sea, as the Greeks did, he would not be free of that smell. "We must wall out every heathen influence, every heathen word, every *thing* in our homes that was made by heathen hands and brought from outside, anything that may have tempted God to look away when the dead came last night. We must scrub every bit of rot from our doorsteps and our walls. We must bury and seal away these dead. We must be clean again. Until the *navi* comes. We must be Hebrew and faithful, so that God's gaze will be drawn to us again. To bless us, not to curse us. God gives and God takes away." He glanced at his son, whose face was pale with horror, and said, "Blessed be the name of our God."

"*Selah*," Yakob whispered. *Always.* His face was still gaunt with shock, his motions stiff as the two of them carried another body in. This one was a beardless mercenary in Roman gear, one of the heathen polluting their land. He had paid for that, and Kfar Nahum had paid with him.

After they threw the body down among the corpses in the chamber, Zebadyah put his arm around his son and drew him close, held him as Yakob shook with silent cries. Just held him. The others bringing in bodies stepped around them without speaking.

At the sound of song, Zebadyah and his son stirred and stepped from the tomb into the chill air. The surviving women of the town—thirteen of them—had formed a line before the tombs and were singing the Words of Going that were as old as the People, words of lament for those who were lost and could not be recovered. That cold morning, their traditions and their memories were all they had left. No help had come from Threshing beyond the hill or from Rich Garden or Tower south along the shore, though a few from Kfar Nahum had fled to those towns during the night.

After the women fell silent, Zebadyah lifted his own voice. His eyes were dry, his back stiff and straight. In his deep baritone, joined after a few moments by the other men, he sang the cries of Iyobh whom God had tested, words of grief that in the long years of exile and then return had become the words of their People, the essential song of a tribe whose first duty was to endure:

> Man that is born of woman is of few days, and full of trouble.
> He comes forth like a flower, he is cut down.
> Yet there is hope for a tree, if it be cut;
> At the scent of water it will bud, and bring forth boughs.
>
> But man dies, and wastes away;
> Yes, man gives up his breath.
>
> The waters wear away the stones:
> Washing away the things that grow out of the earth,
> All the hopes of man.

Then they closed the tombs.

———

Even as the last of the great stones slammed into place, as some of the People knelt in their grief and others turned their faces again toward the town below, a strange and unexpected sound rang out, echoing against the slope of the hill and out over the sea. A horn call clear and deep as the voice of God himself.

The men and women glanced at each other's faces in wonder. The call of the shofar.

GOD WEEPING IN THE GRASSES

SHIMON BAR Nahemyah, the town's *other* Shimon, held the horn to his lips, the ram's horn he had taken from the synagogue. In his other hand, a heavy stone. His shoulders bore a fisher's thick storm-coat, snatched up from his house during the screaming cold night. Other young men stood to his left and his right, their faces pale and shining with cold sweat. Bar Nahemyah put all his breath and all his fury into the cry of the horn. He blew the *t'qiah*, the challenge that meant: *God is here! This place is his!* On how many battlefields of his ancestors and at the start of how many holy feasts had that same call gathered the People in strength?

Letting the horn fall to hang about his neck on its tough bull-hide cord, Bar Nahemyah lifted the stone, his hands shaking in his cold fury. He and the other youths were a short walk up the shoreline from the last houses of Beth Tsaida, and before them, in a great pit into which each day's incoming tide poured cleansing water, was the town midden, the feasting place of gulls, where the poor left unwanted girl-babies before their eighth day and their naming, and where food that had been defiled and could not be eaten was left for the birds.

It was low tide, but there were no birds there now. Only the dead, both the quiet dead and the ravenous. The bodies of bruised, naked women lay across the heap, where the Roman revelers had tossed those who had collapsed during the repetitive rapes of the night. Three of the wakeful dead crouched over the women, tearing their flesh, their shoulders hunched, reminding Bar Nahemyah strangely of town elders gathered about the scroll of Torah, heads bent, peering into it for some sign of God's purpose.

There was an old man in the pit also, and though his face had been chewed away by the dead, Bar Nahemyah thought it was Asa the tanner. He was clothed and there were no bruises on his body from being beaten, no visible wounds except where the dead had been at his face, their groping fingers digging out his eyes and their teeth tearing away the soft meat of his cheeks. He had not been thrown there by the Romans. Doubtless he had taken refuge beneath the refuse, witnessed the women hurled into the pit over him, lain shaking with his eyes clenched shut, hoping the Romans would not notice him there. Devoured from within by his terror.

But though the Romans must have hurried away quickly, shunning the midden after tossing in those they'd used and killed, there were no places shunned by the dead. The dead knew neither fear nor shame nor disgust at any stench. Only hunger. Perhaps Asa had screamed when he heard the corpses hissing at him from above the midden pit, dark silhouettes against the stars. Screams that were utterly lost amid the death-cries of the town. Or perhaps he had lain silent and still while they fed on the dead or dying women, until one of the corpses found him, too.

Bar Nahemyah and the others had kept silent in their approach; until the call of the shofar the dead hadn't looked up as they lifted red flesh and entrails to their gaping mouths. Watching them, Bar Nahemyah had stood cold, as though he had swallowed the winter wind and given it a place to lie still and icy inside his chest. When he had left the synagogue with the shofar, he had not taken time to wash away the dried blood on his hands and arms from the two Romans he had killed during the night, nor the filth that had spattered across his coat as he drove a hammer into the heads of the groaning corpses that sought to surge through him into the synagogue.

He was fifteen and only recently a man. He had watched skulls burst apart beneath his hammer, had seen the meat and bone inside the human body. Had seen the girl who had given herself to him in an hour of gasping and heat on the night of their betrothal torn apart before his eyes, screaming for a few brief moments as the dead ripped out the insides of her belly, hollowing her until she lay still. He had seen all that. Now Bar Nahemyah was cold, everything in him cold. The shaking that had taken him after the violence had subsided before the rising of the sun, leaving behind only this heatless fury. No messenger or messiah of God had arrived during the night to halt the slaughter, no Makkaba riding from the cities of the south with vengeful, armed priests on dark horses behind. No miracle, no deliverance. There had been only the hammer held in his hand.

He had cast away the hammer in disgust and wrath once there were only bodies before the synagogue door, and he had not stopped to retrieve it as he strode out to check for other dead. Only after he came down to the shore had he realized his hands were empty; he'd stooped then to take up the stone he held now.

As the notes of the shofar faded, he lifted that stone and gazed down at the dead in the midden. "Heard that, did you?" he called to them.

The dead hissed and lurched to their feet, their jaws opening to reveal bloodied teeth.

"Don't get too close," Bar Nahemyah said to the others.

Then he hurled the stone.

For the briefest of moments it spun in the air like a ball in one of those games the pig-eating Greeks favored.

Then it smacked one of the corpses in the left shoulder. The corpse spun about and crumpled to its knee. The other two shambled past it. But even as Bar Nahemyah's companions threw their own rocks down at the dead, the first corpse looked over its shoulder at them and growled like a beast as it staggered to its feet.

Then the men were hurling stones down at the midden, to the cracking of bones and the growling of the dead. One of the corpses toppled and lay still, its head crushed in. The others lurched on up the shallow sides of the pit, reeking of death and offal and salt water. A stone crushed one's thigh—a corpse that, in life, must have been a girl nearly old enough to bear a child, her hair long and lank about her gray shoulders, one of her breasts chewed half away. Still she dragged herself across the shore with her hands, hissing and snarling.

Their bodies broke beneath the rocks, yet they kept coming.

And coming.

"Fall back," Bar Nahemyah snapped. "More stones."

The young men retreated at a stumbling run toward the grasses at the tideline, and along the way they lifted from the sand and shingle what they could: rocks smoothed and tossed landward by the sea, gnarled driftwood, shells of sea creatures blind and deep and strange as the world's beginning, anything that could be thrown at the dead to do damage.

Another corpse fell, a large-bellied man, most of whose face had been eaten away before he rose. The sharp edge of a broken shell lodged between his eyes like Dawid's slingstone, and he toppled backward and did not get up.

The last corpse still growled and lunged toward the living with uneven steps. It was the girl; she had risen up on one foot and was coming after them at a crouch, dragging her bad leg behind her. It was nearly on them now, and Bar Nahemyah's companions fell back into the grasses. Bar Nahemyah himself stood his ground.

"Be still, you unclean *tameh*," he cried, wrenching a long branch of driftwood free of the sand. Lifting it like a club, he waited for the corpse to stumble nearer. Its eyes were fixed on him, those gray, scratched eyes. Its jaw worked, opening and closing.

With a shout, Bar Nahemyah swung the branch, slamming it hard into the side of the corpse's head, knocking it to the sand. He leapt over the fallen girl, spearing the end of the branch toward its head even as it hissed and tried to get up. The side of its head gave, yet it spat, and the thing's hand clutched the end of Bar Nahemyah's coat. Then he was slamming the branch down against its head, again and again.

Until it was still.

Bar Nahemyah stood over the body, panting. The other young men drew back in mute horror at both the dead and the man who had fought. The corpse's fingers were still curled about the hem of Bar Nahemyah's coat. Bar Nahemyah roared, shouting all of his rage and impotent grief at the thing's dead face, and lifting one foot he drove the heel of his sandal against the clutching hand and broke its grip.

The hand fell back limp against the grit of the shore.

Bar Nahemyah gazed down at it for a long moment, breathing heavily. Then glanced up at the other pale-faced youths. At the midden and the stinking dead lying on the offal. Heard the sigh of the waves and behind him, at the tideline, the rush of the wind in the grasses like the sound of God weeping. He cast the branch aside into the sand. Though his lips moved, no words came. He swayed on his feet. Then he tilted to the left and vomited.

STANDING AT THE SHORE

BEFORE SUNUP, Shimon had walked to his father's house in Beth Tsaida, that long line of fishers' homes just above the tideline. He found the house empty and in disarray, its atrium open to the sky and silent but for a few of his mother's chickens, the small, enclosed rooms around the outer wall dark. No one was there. The ewer his mother used for water had been shattered, and there were streaks of blood across the atrium's dirt floor. For several long moments, Shimon stood staring at those dark stains, hardly breathing. All he could think of was the blood on his father's hand. Was this more of his blood, or had others entered the house and struggled during the long night's fight with the hungry dead?

But his father clearly was not here, whether this was his blood or not. And that meant this day was up to him.

Hastily, Shimon scooped up an armful of blankets and ran with them back up the hill to the tomb. He ignored the weeping he heard in the town and ignored the fear in his breast, knowing that if he stopped moving, that would be it. He would be too exhausted and too panicked to get up again.

When he reached the tomb, he wrapped Rahel and the maimed baby in blankets. He put his mother's arm about his shoulders and, supporting her weight, he helped her slowly down the hill. Rahel looked about with bloodshot eyes, her face paling with horror as she smelled the smoke and witnessed the ruin of their town, the crumbled houses, the bodies in the streets.

A few survivors were already moving, shrouding the corpses or simply walking in listless circles, their faces bloodied or tear-streaked. No one called out to Rahel and her sons; no one challenged them, not one.

His heart beating fast, Shimon lay his mother down on her bedding in the small winter room she'd shared with his father, and handed her the baby, that small, crippled baby, that shattered hope. He covered them both with blankets. Rahel was shaking, but her son didn't know if it was with cold or fear or grief or shock. He rubbed his hands together a moment, trying to think. Swallowed against his own fear. This was too big for him. They needed his father. Where was his father?

"Shimon," Rahel whispered. "There." She lifted a trembling hand, pointed.

He looked. It was his father's white *tallit*, the four-cornered prayer shawl he wore to the synagogue, still folded over its peg in the wall, miraculously undisturbed by whatever chaos had struck their small house.

"Bring that here, please."

When Shimon pressed the *tallit* into her hand, Rahel took the folded shawl and brought it to her lips, kissing the rough fabric.

Glancing toward the roof, she whispered fiercely, "Adonai, find him, bring him home to us. Please. Let him be breathing. We need him. The boys and I. We need him. Bring him home."

Her voice wavered. She kissed the *tallit* again, her eyes shining. She sang softly:

> *Though the fig tree does not flower,*
> *And no grapes are on the vines . . .*

She closed her eyes, fell silent. After a moment, she ended her prayer as prayers were always ended in Kfar Nahum: "Bless us and keep us, O God. Until the *navi* comes."

———

At those words, Shimon straightened. He recalled the rough way his father had shoved him to the door, uncaring of his own safety. If God were watching, he would not bless him or his town for shaking in the dark. He heard the soft sounds of his crippled brother mouthing, reaching for a breast.

He went to the bin in the atrium beneath his mother's olive tree, took up a clay bowl from the stack beside it, and scooped some of the last of their grain from its bin. He brought the bowl back to his mother and saw the relief in her eyes. He realized from the way her hands shook as she accepted it how fatigued and hungry she actually was. He glanced about, made sure the waterskin was within her reach. Then he met her gaze.

"You are safe," he said. "I'll go find father."

Rahel nodded, her eyes closing. "The boats, my son. The boats. He would have gone to the boats. Gone out on the water, to get to some other shore where there were no dead. So he could circle into the hills and come back to us. See if his boat is here."

Shimon took his mother's hand quickly and kissed it, his eyes filling with tears that he blinked back. Then he turned and hurried to the door and flung it open, nearly ran across the packed dirt of the narrow street outside before stopping himself and turning to shut the door, putting his weight against it. Again he saw the blood on his father's hand. Breathing raggedly, he leaned a moment against the door, gathering his courage. Then he hurried through the battered houses and out to the wild grass. He saw the sea, open and vast with its horizon of far hills, and he ran for the line of boats, the long row of wide-beamed fishers moored above the tideline.

It took him only a moment to be sure. Some of the boats were missing. His father's boat, others. The tide had come and was now receding, and had washed away whatever track Yonah's boat had left in the sand when his father dragged it out to the water, a task that normally took two men. It was not a small boat, and his father never brought in small catches.

Swallowing, Shimon straightened and looked out over the waves. A few cranes glided low over the water, but he could see no dark shape of a boat out there, nothing but the blindness of the sun's fire on the sea.

A fear took him then, and he walked out onto the sand and planted his feet there among the shells and lake-weed the tide had left behind like memories the sea refused to carry. For no reason he could have given, Shimon was certain in his heart that if he went back to his mother now, he would never see his father again. That he must wait here, faithfully. Watching the sea. Awaiting the rock and pitch of the boat's return on the waves. His mother had water and grain. He had found her and brought her and his brother safely home; he'd done his father's command. Now his duty was here, at the edge of the sea.

Once, while he waited, he heard the call of a shofar and lifted his face. The call was very beautiful, and it carried over the water, and the hills across the Sea of Galilee gave it back. Shimon looked to the sea with fresh hope. Perhaps his father would hear the call and row toward it or run toward it along the shore if he was already on the land and not on the water. But there was still nothing on the sea, neither boat nor bird.

When Bar Nahemyah and other young men, ten or twelve, began bringing bodies down to the shore and laying them out in a long line on the sand, Shimon watched without speaking. The sight of the corpses was horrible, yet he neither flinched nor looked away; he felt detached, as though this were happening on some other shore and not here. He could see the rise and fall of their chests; these bodies still breathed. Their faces were flushed with fever, and they bore terrible wounds on their faces or their arms. Bites. Some had been torn open, and those were pale as though emptied out. Shimon bar Yonah knew some of them. There were old men and young, old women and young women, nearly a hundred. And among them, a few mercenaries, some dark-skinned, some olive, some white. Hired swords from every part of the Roman world, broken away from their brothers and then reassembled into a unit that could be put to the use of Empire, fighting for coin and glory rather than any bonds of blood or kin or covenant. Shimon did not understand how such a thing could be.

"*Shalom*, Bar Yonah. Will you aid me?" Bar Nahemyah called to him. He had the eyes of a man who did not remember sleep or rest, and so would not seek either. Gore had spattered his storm-coat.

"I have to wait for father," Shimon said, his voice distant. "He'll need me."

"All Kfar Nahum needs you, every man who still breathes." Bar Nahemyah's voice was low and intense. He swept out his arm, indicating the line of unconscious bodies. "By noon all of these will be dead, and some will have risen, and they will hunger. They will want to *eat* our People, what is left of our People, our kin. Look at them. Romans and heathen, and our own brothers, our own sisters gone from us. *Every one* of these will kill. But that is *not* going to happen. Let us have justice. I will see that these unclean monsters suffer for all time, for what they have done this night. For Ahava my beloved. For our fathers and our children dead."

But Shimon had turned his head back to the sea, whose waves were louder in his ears than Bar Nahemyah's impassioned words.

When he said nothing, the other man's eyes flashed hot with anger. "Your father understood justice," he cried. "He would have helped me."

Shimon felt no guilt. His whole heart was pulled by the emptiness of the sea, and he felt tugged beneath waves of dark terror. He gazed out desperately for some sight of his father's boat that he could cling to.

Bar Nahemyah's face hardened. He turned away.

There was the sound of Bar Nahemyah exhorting the other youths, a drone in Shimon's ears. Then cries as other young men came down to the shore. Yakob the priest's son was with them, and he exchanged harsh words with Bar Nahemyah. Heated voices. A fight broke out, men beating each other, some to protect their ill, others to seek vengeance for the eaten. For a few beats of the heart, men fought on the sand over the bodies of the dying. Still Shimon ignored them.

In the end, a few ran back to the town, led by the priest's son. The others turned the bodies onto their bellies and bound their ankles. They took cloths and filled these with stones from the shore, then knotted up the cloths and bound those to the ankles of the bitten. One after another they lifted the feverish bodies, one youth at the head and one at the feet, and carried them into the boats, piling them atop each other like fish. And when there were no more, the boats slipped from the shore, each with two youths at the oars, their eyes hot. Shimon felt a dull horror as he watched the boats grow smaller on the waves.

Those in the boats were not dead. They lived. They breathed . . . though none of them were awake or aware, and none would survive the morning. Dimly, Shimon understood that Bar Nahemyah meant to toss them into the sea, that there would be no tombs on the hill for these. Yet the horror of it was something outside of him, like water beating against a rock; the horror *inside* of him, the memory of the blood on his father's hand, the frantic look in his father's eyes—that was far more personal and overwhelming.

Behind him, the priest's son came running back with Zebadyah his father panting behind him. Perhaps the priest had been searching again among the tents and ruins for survivors; it had taken Yakob a while to find him.

And now it was too late.

When Zebadyah reached the shore, he broke to his knees in the sand, his eyes wild. He screamed at the retreating boats: "No! Come back! Bar Nahemyah, come back! The dead must be buried! They must be buried! The Law! Come back!"

But no answer was called back over the water, and none of the boats turned its bow.

———

Shimon felt someone beside him, and though he didn't turn, he knew by the sound of the youth's breathing that Yakob was there.

"Amma is in the house," Shimon said. He kept his eyes on the water.

"Yohanna and I will bring her water," Yakob promised. He stood by Shimon a moment, seeming to understand why his friend was here, and whether because he could not think of something to say or because he knew that there wasn't anything to say, he spoke no word but only gripped Shimon's shoulder. Then he turned and went to help his father up from the sand. The strength seemed gone from Zebadyah's limbs; his face glistened with tears.

Numb inside, Shimon gazed always past the boats out across the empty sea, looking for one boat, one boat that had set out in the dark and not returned.

Somewhere out in the middle of the water, as the sun rose hot over the sea, the youths set aside their oars and stood, their legs spread wide for balance as the boats rocked. They lifted the bodies over the gunwales and slid them, one after the other, into the cool womb of the sea. The wrath Shimon had seen in the youths' eyes as they set out made the reason for their act clear. The young men knew the bodies would rise, and the memory of the dead devouring their village during the night was bitter in their minds and hot in their hearts. They needed someone to suffer for what had been done, for the kin who had been eaten, for the kin who were dying now. They needed to take an eye for an eye, a tooth for a tooth. They could not make the Romans suffer; the Romans were gone, eaten or fled. They could not make the dead who'd attacked suffer, for they had been destroyed during the night and the dawn that followed, by Roman swords or Hebrew fishing spears or by Bar Nahemyah's hammer and stone. But these bodies that lay now in their boats would become eaters, too. Unless speared through the brow or burned with fire, they would walk and moan for years, feeding on the People.

Or—dropped into the sea, their ankles bound, these new dead would writhe in the water, without food, without breath, their moans heard only by the fish. They could be made to suffer. The youths hoped this fiercely, and like the heathen tribes from whom their fathers had wrested the land many centuries before, they gave their dead to the sea. Not in reverence but in fury and a longing to forget. A punishment meted out, justice done, and the pain of that night would lie beneath the waves, never to be spoken of.

Afterward, as they beached the boats and walked back to the town, each of the young men spoke quietly to himself.

My father died in a storm at sea, one man whispered.
My brother perished in his boat, another said.
My wife was drowned.
My sisters were taken by the waves.
My friend, my beautiful friend, perished in a fishing accident.
It was easier that way.

All those whispers of fear and forgetting. Even a century later, travelers along that shore would claim that they could hear those whispers on the wind among the tombs.

———

But on the shore, Shimon still stood on the sand. He stood there throughout the day, unmoving, thinking neither of food nor rest. Just watching the sea. When the tide came up to his feet, he looked at the water's edge lapping his sandals and realized his throat was scorched with thirst. Crouching, he cupped his hands in the water and lifted some to his mouth, but he kept his eyes on the sea, like Gideon's men drinking while watching the far ridge for the coming of the dead in the old story.

Afterward he walked above the tideline where the boats were moored. After the violence of the previous night, many of these boats no longer had owners, and their nets lay in them unused and unnoticed like dry leaves. Shimon stood among the derelicts and watched the sun set on the water, a fire as though God had seen that the land was defiled and had decided to burn it away and start anew.

Then the sun was gone and it was dark and there were stars, and no moon rose. Yet, by starlight, Shimon could see one boat coming back, a dark, low shape on the water. No splash of the oars. Just drifting in on the tide. Yet Shimon knew whose boat it was. The youths' boats had all returned in the late morning after giving their cargo to the sea, and no fishers had set out with their nets this night. As the boat neared, Shimon could see that a single figure sat on the bench, its hands in its lap. A dark silhouette.

"Abba!" he called softly. "Father!"

The figure rose unsteadily to its feet, making the boat rock on the tide. Shimon heard its low moan of longing and hunger, loud over the water.

After a moment he covered his ears, his cheeks moist with tears or mist from the sea, but he could still hear it, he could still see that boat sliding in.

PART 3

AN EVENING VISITOR

RAHEL'S HUSBAND had been dead four nights when there came a knock at her door.

A knock at the door, a strong fist, but the knocking was too urgent, as though the man demanding entrance was uneasy, uncertain of himself. Rahel lifted her face from where she knelt in the atrium with her husband's *tallit* across her knees and the baby sleeping in his basket beside her, and for a moment she considered not answering.

Again the knocking, insistent.

She pressed the heels of her hands to her eyes, breathed deeply a moment, then folded the prayer shawl carefully and rose to her feet, the *tallit* still in her hand. She moved toward the door.

There were too few of them left to ignore each other.

That, and she couldn't quite escape the candle-flicker of hope in her heart. She had seen her husband's corpse, had confronted him on the sands. It couldn't be him at the door.

And yet.

She found that she was running. She leapt from the atrium into the antechamber at the old door, and quickly tugged at the bolt. Unlatching the door and letting it creak open, she found herself confronting the priest. Zebadyah's face was strained and pale—he hadn't slept in several nights, perhaps—but his eyes were hard with purpose.

"*Shalom*," he said.

"*Shalom*," Rahel whispered.

They stared at each other, one of those silences that are both uncomfortable to keep and uncomfortable to break. *Shalom* had always been their traditional greeting in Kfar Nahum, a wish for peace and a plea for peace. Not a Roman peace, not *pax* or order, the absence of conflict. No, Hebrew peace, wholeness, a community living and thriving together.

How empty that wish now seemed.

"Do you want to come in, Bar Yesse?" Rahel said at last. A week ago it would have been unthinkable to her to open her door to a man who was not her husband when no one else was home. But the pain in Zebadyah's eyes called to her, and he was at least a survival of her husband, in some small part. And the days were brutal on her heart, alone in her house with her children. The house was strange to her now, for it had too many empty and silent spaces.

Zebadyah's face became stern. "I have come to offer you my home."

"I don't understand."

"You were my brother's wife."

Her eyes burned and she blinked quickly. It would be unbearable, weeping when her door was open and her face visible to the street.

"Now you are alone and you have a son—"

"I have two sons." Rahel's throat tightened. Such had been her grief that she'd had little time to fear, either for herself or Koach. Now all the fears came rushing in.

"You were my brother's wife, now his widow. You have a son who is too young for the boats. When a man dies and his sons are not old enough to feed his house, the Law tells us his brother's duty is to take his wife and provide for her, and to take her gladly to his bed to give her more sons in his brother's name, so that his brother's line might not die out from our land. All my life I have kept the Law. I will not fail to keep it now." His voice turned gentle. "I had not planned to seek a second wife, but if I had, I could not have hoped to find one lovelier. My brother chose well."

"No," Rahel whispered. "This can't be."

Zebadyah's face darkened. "Don't make this harder than it is, woman. I grieve for him, too. But the winter is on us, and there isn't much time."

Rahel shook her head and began to swing the door shut, but Zebadyah blocked it with his hand and leaned into it, holding it open against her. She took a step back, but he followed, and then his hands were gripping her arms just below the shoulders, firmly. An echo of her husband's strength. She gazed up at his face with wide eyes. She felt small and caught—by him, by the Law, by her bereavement. As though it were not his hands that held her but God's, pitiless and demanding. God's hands that demanded that she live a certain way, fulfill commitments that were made before her grandmothers' grandmothers were born, and always without any sure promise from God beneath her feet, only shifting sand, pulled out from under her by the vanishing tide.

"I will treat you and Shimon well, and Cheleph's son also," he said quietly. "I loved Yonah. I will not let his widow starve alone in this house."

"What about the baby?" She just managed to get the words out.

Pain in his eyes. "You know what has to be done."

"No."

"We will talk about it later. Come to my house. There are witnesses there already. You will eat well tonight, and you will have a warm bed."

"Your bed," she choked.

He gave a small nod.

"And my son? Will you have someone just take him out to the midden, leave him there? To die?" Her voice rose, shrill.

He was quiet a moment and she tried to twist away, but he held her fast.

"We tried to follow only those parts of the Law that were easy. And look what happened. You have duties, Rahel, even as I do."

"Don't call me that." Her heart beat a panic drum against her breast.

"I am trying to help, woman! You are my responsibility—I am trying to help." He pulled her to him quickly and kissed her. She stiffened as his mouth covered hers. Warm and moist and so different from Yonah's. The kiss was rough yet there was something tentative in it, as though he were a man never completely sure of himself. For a heartbeat or two she permitted it, still in shock. Then her stomach turned and she shoved her hands against his chest, turning her head away. "No," she gasped.

"Rahel," Zebadyah said quietly.

"I was his, and I will die his," she said.

"*Rahel.*"

"You will call me Bat Eleazar. You have no right to my name." She tried to pull away but he held her. Her eyes went dark with fury. She was shaking, though she didn't know it. "I will wall my door against you and starve first." Her voice rose in pitch. The panic was not so much that he would touch her, but that he would take from her the memories of Yonah and of her life here, in this house. The thought of sleeping beneath his roof was almost worse than the thought of sleeping in his arms. She drew back into the shadow beneath the arch leading to the atrium. From his basket by the olive press, her infant began to cry.

"Please go," Rahel said.

Zebadyah glanced in the direction of the cries, and seeing the hard purpose in his face, Rahel went white. "This is your brother's son," she pleaded, her voice low and intense.

Zebadyah turned his face back to her. The gentleness was gone from him and his eyes had become hard as small stones. "Ezra cast even the wives, the heathen wives, over the wall," he said quietly. "What is unclean, what isn't whole—we must cast that out of our homes, out of our hearts."

Zebadyah thrust her to the side firmly and made to step by her, but she caught at his arm and threw her small body back between him and the atrium and her son.

His face darkened. "Step aside, woman," he growled.

"Get out!" she cried. "Get away from my son!"

He struck her.

Her vision white, she felt the wall against her back. Her head rang. She dug her fingers against the wall, desperate to stay upright. Panic in her heart like cattle breaking through long grass, trampling it, crushing everything in their way. Yonah had never, *never* struck her.

Her vision cleared.

Zebadyah stood silent, hesitating, as if startled by his own violence.

The baby's cries broke her panic. She screamed and leapt at him, but the priest caught her wrists and held her as she kicked at him, still with that look of dawning horror on his face.

"*What* is going on?"

A young man's shout.

The priest had left the outer door open. Shimon stood there, his face full of thunder—looking suddenly very like his father.

Yakob, the priest's son, stood beside him on the doorstep, his face shocked.

"Shimon!" Rahel cried, almost faint with relief.

Zebadyah released her quickly, as though his hands burned. He looked at his son and nephew, and his face darkened slowly with shame. "Bar Yonah," he said, his voice a little hoarse, "I need to make sure your family is provided for."

Shimon's eyes were cold. They took everything in: the screaming baby in the atrium, the bruise developing over Rahel's cheekbone, the priest's slightly hunched stance. "They will be," he said quietly. "Your son and I have reached an agreement. I am taking my father's boat out tonight, to fish where he cannot. Yakob will help me, for a while." He glanced at Rahel. "I'll be able to feed us, mother. I am sure of it."

For a moment, no one moved. Rahel drew in a sobbing breath, looked at her son carefully, and at Yakob. She saw in their eyes that Shimon had known she would not accept the protection of Yakob's father. Shimon had *known* this. He had done this—taken on this responsibility—for her, and to honor his father. Knowing what it meant. Shimon's *bar 'onshin* had come and gone; in announcing his intent to feed the house of his father, he claimed that house and all within it. What was to be done with his brother, what was to be done with his father's widow—this was all up to him now, and to no other. Rahel's breast warmed with pride and gratitude. Shimon was his father's son. He was *her* son.

Rahel straightened, smoothed down her garments, grateful none of them were torn. She wanted to touch her face where it hurt and burned, but she did not. Her hands were shaking, and she clutched her skirt until they were still. She stood with dignity, and though her voice quivered, it was not weak. She faced the priest. "God will provide for my sons and for me, Bar Yesse."

He glanced back at her, his eyes full of so many things that he must have wanted to say and couldn't. Then he looked at her son, and Shimon met the priest's gaze with quiet resolve. It was as though a weathered old tree were facing a tall rock.

The priest looked away first. "It is your house, Bar Yonah," Zebadyah said quietly. His shoulders tensed. Then he stepped past him to the door, Yakob moving aside to let him past.

Rahel's heartbeat did not slow until the sound of the priest's footsteps, and then his son's after him, had faded in the street. Not until she held the baby in her arms, holding in tears that she would not shed where her son could see. Not until she felt the cool cloth against her cheek and Shimon's words soft by her ear, promising that he would care for her and for his crippled brother both, whatever might come. That she would never be hungry. That she would never need to go to the priest if she didn't wish it. That she was his mother and he loved her. And then she did cry, and it was a long time before she was done.

FIRE ON THE WATER

THE STONE steps leading to her roof were cold under her bare feet, but for once Rahel didn't mind that; the shock of sensation each time she set her foot carefully down—so carefully, because she was sore, and carrying her child in her arms—reminded her she was alive.

It was after dark now; the first panic of Zebadyah's visit had dulled, to be replaced with a throng of small, sharp fears, each of them nipping at her like wolves harrying deer. She felt that each step might send her body crashing to her knees in fatigue, yet her mind was fiercely wakeful. In any case, she couldn't bear finding a place to sleep in her open atrium or in the small winter rooms around the inner walls of her house. The house was too empty; the family they had once shared it with had not survived the night of the dead. Shimon had succeeded in scrubbing most of the blood out of the walls, but Rahel thought she could still smell it. And Shimon had also boarded up the outward-looking windows of their house, which made it worse. She understood why he had done it; many had died that night because the dead had climbed through open windows. Other houses throughout the town were boarding up, too. But in seasons past, she had often leaned out of those windows and talked with the town's other women as they passed by. Now those other women were gone, no one left to sit *shiva* with her and mourn with her for her husband, and even her windows were gone. This no longer felt like her home.

Only the rooftop felt the same.

Reaching it, she stood still for a few moments, just breathing. The wind from the sea was chill against her face, but she didn't fear the *shedim*. Let them come. What more could they take from her?

She gazed out at that sea, where she could see the white chop of the waves and a few dark shapes rocking on them: the boats moving out to gather the night's fish. They looked so few, so few. Only a week before, the boats had set out like a flock of great birds, fast over the water. Now she could count only ten. In one of them, with Yakob and young Yohanna, was her older son, setting out in his father's boat, on the sea without him for the first time. Tears burned her eyes. She blinked them back and made her way to the little bed of cushions Yonah had made for her during the early months of her pregnancy, knowing how much she loved the open air and the sky and the scent of the sea.

Her infant stirred slightly as she settled with a groan and a sharp ache where she had torn in birthing him, but she held him close and drew the shawl in which she'd wrapped him up over his head until he fell asleep again. She held him to her, kissing the top of his head with the softest brush of her lips, again and again. She smelled baby, and she smelled her husband, for the shawl she'd swaddled him in was Yonah's *tallit*. It was wrong, perhaps terribly wrong, to swaddle a baby in a prayer shawl, but the cloth carried

Yonah's scent and her heart knew the shawl would protect her son, as Yonah himself would if he were here.

Her heart beat a little faster. She tried to think of whether Yonah would have lifted this child into his hands and accepted him as his own son, if he'd lived. She felt certain he would have. Yes, she was certain of it. The man who had held her after that storm on the sea would never have turned away any life that came from her body.

She glanced out at the sea again, its wind in her hair, and could not remember ever having felt so alone. "What do I do?" she whispered, pressing her nose to the *tallit*. "What do I do?"

But her husband was not there to answer her. There was only her, making decisions to stand between her children and the hungry grave. Shimon would bring home fish, and perhaps . . . perhaps he would not grow to resent her for not going to the priest's bed, for risking her children in the winter.

It was not too late, she knew. She could run from the house, up the street, knock on the door of Zebadyah's house, endure the staring eyes of the few other surviving women from the windows and rooftops of their own homes. She could give herself to him, undress for him, and whisper after he lay in her, "Please, feed my sons." Many women of her People had done so before.

But her belly twisted at the thought, and her face throbbed where her husband's brother had struck her. She clutched her baby closer, shivering.

She didn't know if Shimon would be able to bring enough food for the three of them. She didn't know if Zebadyah would be harsh with her, if she went to him, if he would often strike her. But she knew he would never feed *both* her sons. He would not take her second son into his house.

As though hearing her thoughts, the infant stirred and began to cry. She lifted him to her breast. Seeing the way he kneaded her flesh with only one hand while the other hung lifeless at his side,

Rahel closed her eyes, forbidding herself tears. A feeling of warm sleep stole over her as often happened when the baby fed. For a while her fear for him pierced through it.

Yet somewhere between one breath and the next, she slipped into the dream country. And it was water, all water, dark waves covering all the world and nowhere any shore. It closed over her, taking away sound and light. Then she flailed about and found herself facing Yonah, her husband's face stern yet his eyes turning gentle when he saw her, as they always had.

She had wedded Yonah when she was fourteen, had wanted to believe he would be a shelter and a strong place for her in this uneasy world. Once, when she was still young, he had rowed her out onto the water, uncaring that the sea was for fishermen, not their wives. That one night, he had gone without nets or spear, just rowing out with his wife until they were far from shore and no other boats could be seen dark on the water. The waves rolled them with a motion that was soothing and sure. There he made love to her, while the stars moved slowly across the sky. She remembered the sound of his breathing, his face above hers, his touch. Afterward, a storm had fallen on the sea. He bound her to the row bench, then cast his coat over her, while she watched the surge and growl of the sea and the heavy dark of the sky with wide eyes. She watched her husband fight the waves, and the sea tossed them and spun them. Water came over the gunwale and tried to slam her from the boat, but her husband's ropes held her fast.

Then the sea was quiet, as suddenly as though the storm had been a candle snuffed out. The clouds broke open, revealing the moon. Yonah cut his wife loose from the bench even as she sobbed and gasped in great gulps of air no longer laden with water. She shivered with cold as he clutched her to him, tearing away his soaked tunic and then tearing away hers, so that her body and his were pressed naked to each other, and she could feel the fire in him and his heart loud against hers, as when they had made love. His rough hands rubbed life into her arms and back. She shook and clung to him and sobbed, and heard him sobbing in her ear, too.

The moon had set while they made love, before the tempest; but now there was a moon in the sky. The storm had lasted all of a day and it was now the next night, the Sabbath night, and as they warmed each other, Yonah started to murmur the words of a song in her ear, words he might sing to greet the Sabbath Bride as she came over the water.

> *Though the fig tree does not flower,*
> *And no grapes are on the vines . . .*

Rahel woke with a start, her infant asleep at her breast. She heard shouting in the distance. Blinking quickly, she looked about and her first impression was that the sea was on fire. But as her eyes focused, she realized that men had built a great blaze on the shore among the wrack left by the outgoing tide. She could see their shapes dark against the glow of it, and hear their voices, most of them indistinct but one calling louder than the rest and carrying to her on the sea wind.

Zebadyah.

He was reciting passages from the Grief of Ezra. Catching the words, she shivered and clutched her infant tightly. She watched with wide eyes as the men on the sands tossed items into the flames, and she heard the roar and rush of the fire as it fed. She couldn't see what they were burning, but she could guess.

The remains of the Roman tents. Any clothing of Greek weave or any ornaments from other towns that the Romans had looted from their homes, or any they had left. Anything that was not Hebrew. Anything that was unclean, or broken, or suspect. Anything that might tempt God to look away from the town when the dead lurched near.

They were cleansing Kfar Nahum.

Perhaps it was only that she had just risen out of the waters of sleep. Perhaps it was only the stress and anguish of the past few days. Whatever the reason, Rahel had a vivid, brutal vision of Zebadyah lifting her infant up and casting his small, wailing body into the flames.

She shivered. Pressing her lips to the baby's head, she whispered, "It's all right. It's all right."

But she could not look away from those flames, or from the dark silhouette of the priest standing so near them, nor shut her ears against Zebadyah's harsh, grieving cries. And she did not sleep again that night.

ONE OF OUR TRIBE

SHIMON'S FIRST nights at sea exhausted him. After he and Zebadyah's sons pulled the boat up to the tideline, gutted their fish by the predawn light, and stumbled back into the town with their catch, it was all he could do to embrace Yakob at the door of his house and offer a tired grunt of thanks—though if he'd been able to summon more words, he would have called him *brother*. Then he'd enter with a weary nod toward his mother and her infant, tumble into his bedding in the olive's shade in the atrium, and snore until long after the noon heat. He had been out on the sea with his father a few times, but it had never been like this— *his* hand casting the nets, and no midnight nap while his father fished. You didn't nap when you were one of the men in the boat, when it was your hand that must keep the tiller or the oars if a storm came up.

On one of these first mornings, he stepped through the heavy cedar door of his father's house and heard his infant brother shrieking. Not a hunger cry but a pain cry, a thin, desperate wailing that tore through Shimon's body, making his blood run cold. There was a hoarse note in the cries, as though the boy had been wailing for a while.

His heart sped up. Where was his mother? Was she all right? Why hadn't she come at her infant's cry? He burst through into the atrium, not even pausing to toss away his coat or peel off his gloves that reeked of fish and were slippery with oil.

And he stopped, shocked.

Rahel knelt on a rug she had unrolled across the atrium's dirt floor, a rug that had belonged to one of Yonah's kin, now dead. She was holding her baby tightly to her, her own eyes squeezed shut; she must not have heard Shimon come in, not over the baby's screams. A stone knife lay discarded by her left knee, and in the early dawn light blood shone on the blade. Her hands were bloody, too.

Shimon took it all in at a glance, and realized it was his brother's eighth day. The stone knife—stone, not iron—was used for circumcision. He didn't know where Rahel had found the knife or from where she'd taken it.

"Where's Zebadyah bar Yesse?" he asked hoarsely.

Rahel gave a start, glanced up at him, her eyes red from weeping.

Not knowing what else to do, Shimon came and sat by her. The baby's cries were deafening.

"He thinks my child is unclean." Rahel's voice quivered. "Do you think I'd trust him with a knife?"

Shimon knelt by her. Without speaking, he took his infant brother and held him, that small, squalling, misshapen thing that had brought such anxiety into their house. Rahel put her face in her hands, shaking silently, staining her face with blood.

The baby kept wailing. Shimon swallowed. For days he had tried not to look at his brother. Now he couldn't look away. Uncomfortably, he held him, uncertain of what to do. The boy's wound had been cleaned and bandaged.

After a few moments, Rahel drew a shuddering breath and rose unsteadily to her feet. She left, then came back with a cloth and pushed one corner of it, which she'd dampened, into the baby's small mouth. One hand pressed to her left breast as though it pained her. For a few moments the baby still shrieked; then his mouth closed around the cloth and he sucked at it vigorously, making small, muffled whimpers.

"He is Koach. Koach bar Yonah," she said.

"Koach?"

"Koach." Her face was wet with tears. Tears for her child's pain, tears for her own. Tears reddened by the blood on her face.

On the eighth day of a boy's life, he is circumcised and gifted with a name and a blessing that tell him what he will be. This was always a rite performed by the priest, but today, by the morning's light in her own house, Rahel had laid the boy on this rug and taken up the knife and had done it herself.

She had named him Koach.

The word for "strong."

Silently, Shimon and Rahel knelt beside each other, gazing down at that small, anguished face. A bent child, but the only child Rahel would ever have again. The three of them were the only family they had left.

Gently, Rahel drew her fingertips along the curve of the boy's cheek. "You will grow strong," she promised him. "Strong." Her voice low and fierce with that tone that only mothers use, the tone that over the cruel years of history has made even emperors kneel before those who birthed them, has made even kings seek the embrace of their mothers' arms.

Fourteen Years Later—AD 25.

BARABBA

THE MAN was Barabba the Outlaw, the Roman-killer, and he rode one morning out of the hills and out of the wilderness and walked his horse through the streets of Kfar Nahum as though he owned the town. His beard was dark and there were small twigs in it as though, like a prophet of old, he had neither time nor attention to spare it. His face was brown with dust. From the right side of his saddle hung two heads with their hair cut in the Roman style, and to the left side he'd roped three more heads, these torn with strips of flesh missing as though they'd been savaged by beasts. Each with a puncture wound in its brow. Their faces those of the unclean dead, the dead that hunger.

Men and women drew back into their doors as Barabba passed, not wanting to be near the unburied heads. Barabba himself was a forbidding figure, a giant on a black horse larger than any they had ever seen. It was as though God had turned a bear into a man and sent him into their narrow streets. Every town in the land had heard of this man, even ruined towns. In the dead-haunted hills above the Tumbling Water, this man and others like him, men who knew the use of curved blades and of poisons, waited in caves or lurked by the high pass called the Red Way. They set themselves against the living and the dead alike. *Bar Abba*, their leader called himself, "son of a father," to hide his kin and his home from the Romans. None knew where he had come from, but they said he had not seen his brothers, his sisters, his mother in long years. They said he had never been seen to weep. Or laugh. That he had once ridden his horse into a Roman centurion's house and killed the man with a blow of his steed's hoof, then swept his wife and daughter up into the saddle—and that they had later been sold from the block in Yoppa, to be slaves in far provinces across the sea. They said that he had once left a Greek idolater flayed alive and hanging from the gates of Beth Anya as a warning to any who might defile the holy places of their People. That he had abducted a levite who had informed the Romans about his movements, and had taken the man up to a cave in the hills and forced him to eat a poisoned loaf.

In the cities of stone several days to the south, some hoped in him. Some feared him. But in Kfar Nahum's crumbling houses, he had been only a story. Until this day.

Barabba didn't speak until he had reached the open space before Kfar Nahum's synagogue, a massive basalt edifice. The synagogue was the only building in this town that was still well-kept; the others had fallen into a dilapidation and a weariness that conveyed the town's poverty as starkly as the gaunt faces and thin, brittle-looking arms of its inhabitants. But if Kfar Nahum's poverty affected Barabba, he revealed no sign of it. He looked at the faces of those who had gathered, but without pity.

Before the polished steps of the synagogue—polished only because aging Zebadyah made the washing of them his religious duty each day, a duty performed with his own hands and his own cloth and water he had carried up from the sea himself, for the only slave he had owned had died on that night he refused to remember—before those clean, white steps, Barabba sat his saddle and glowered at the crowd that was gathering, men and women who had slipped from their doors to follow his horse—at a safe distance—through the streets. In fact, by the time the hoofbeats fell still, most of the people who still lived and breathed in Kfar Nahum stood in that public space or filled the alleys that emptied into it. Their faces were pale; they couldn't look away from the corpse-heads that hung from the stranger's saddle, moving a little as the horse breathed.

Koach stood there with Rahel, apart from the others, occasionally lifting his one good hand to scratch at his cheek, at the first fuzz of beard on his young face. Shimon stood near, blinking in the sun, called from his rest after a night at sea by the hoofbeats and the shouts in the town. Yet Shimon stood with his back to his younger brother. Koach used to try to draw his attention, to help him clumsily with small tasks. Now he knew better.

Small and weighing less than a milk-goat, Koach was unobtrusive at his mother's side, yet he felt how the others standing in this open space looked away from him or past him, as though despite his size he were so obvious and so visible that it took great labor *not* to see him.

All but a few, like Bar Cheleph, who watched him in open hostility, his eyes hot with the capacity for violence; once, Koach had been set upon and beaten in the street. Vividly he recalled Bar Cheleph forcing his hand open, tearing a small carving from his fingers and tossing it into the grass. Vividly he recalled the blows falling on his back. To many of the ragged survivors in Kfar Nahum, Koach was an unwelcome reminder of the night of tombs, and all their grief. Of sorrows they'd rather bury and forget. *Hebel*, the men called him, "useless." Rahel had sewn his right sleeve longer than the left to help him conceal his deformed right hand, and she had padded the sleeve with wool to hide the thinness of his withered right arm, yet it made no difference.

He cast a resentful glance at that synagogue door, with its old Hebrew letters carved into the lintel and the doorposts—words of the Law. He was barred from entering; he should have stood before the men of Kfar Nahum and recited from the Torah, a year since. But the priest would not allow him his *bar 'onshin*.

Koach stared up at the stranger with sudden heat in his eyes. Barabba was so different from him—a strong man on a giant horse, with muscled arms and a scarred, cold face. No one would ever deny *him* anything; he would never be helpless or useless.

Barabba turned his horse slowly and made a disgusted sound in his throat. "I came here looking for men!" His voice was low but strangely clipped. His was not a Galilean accent, but it had none of the softness of the Greek in it either. "I came looking for men, but all your faces are pale and your mouths gape like fish. Tell me this is Kfar Nahum, the town of Yonah bar Yesse."

"This *is* the town of Yonah bar Yesse," a tired voice said from the door of the synagogue.

Zebadyah stood there, his *tallit* over his head, having just come from his prayers within. He stepped out and stood in the whiteness of the sun and the whiteness of the synagogue steps, the whiteness of a world long since drained of color.

"Good! This is what I've come to say." Barabba leaned a little from his saddle, addressing the priest, though all the others could see his face and hear his voice, which carried. "If there are true men of Yehuda tribe in this town, they are needed. Each year there are more dead in the hills, and they are in the cities now, too. And what's more—" His voice rose hot with hate. "There are Romans! Always more of those, too. They mock our ways, they starve us, they spit in the face of our God. Beth Anya would not pay their pig-tax, so the Romans broke the doors of their synagogue and burned their Torah. In our Yerushalayim they've hung Roman eagles of gold and silver on the walls of the Temple. Graven *images*, in the places where we *worship*! While you in the north sleep, Rome has come into our house like a thief, to take our bread and defile our women and hang their foul gods on our walls."

Koach heard the stirring of the men and women of Kfar Nahum, indrawn breaths and muttered curses. A few hands flickered in the sign against the evil eye. The corpse-heads at Barabba's saddle stared sightlessly.

"For two generations the Romans have done so with us," Zebadyah said quietly. "Why ride all the way here to tell us what we already know?"

"Because it is getting worse." Barabba stroked his horse's neck, then dropped his hand to his side. "I know your kind in the south, priest. Pharisees. Appeasers. Most of our People cower and shrink back from Romans who pass in the street, but you—the Romans own you already."

With a quick move of his wrist, he unhooked one of the heads—one of the unclean heads—from the right of his saddle and hurled it into the center of the square. It rolled a moment, then stopped with its dead eyes gazing up, as if to accuse God in his sky of crimes of violence that its lips had never been able to reveal in words—only in a long moan of anguish silenced by Barabba's knife.

Everyone drew back.

Koach swallowed against the tightness of his throat. The dead. The dead that were in the water, the dead that were in the past, the dead no one talked about.

But this severed head was here, and terribly close, and could not be ignored.

"Look at it." Barabba's voice was a whip crack in the dawn air. "*Look at it!* Can you appease *that*? When our People returned out of exile—the only one of the twelve tribes to come back, the only one true to our Covenant—we found our land crawling with these. Teeming like ants. Because the heathen have never cared for our land as we do. Have never cared for the dead as we do. But we took back our land, built walls against the dead, lit the sacred fire in a new Temple. We carried out the Law until no moan could be heard in our land. We did that, because we are a People whose faith cannot be bent and whose teeth cannot be drawn. We are a People of lions." He turned in his saddle, his gaze sweeping the crowd. "Well, that is how we have always been. Exile in Susa did not tame us. The Greeks did not beat us. And now, now, will you let the *Romans* take your teeth? The Romans are good at stilling the dead—that's what I hear the children of Israel say, wherever I ride. There have never been men with swords like those the Romans breed or hire. They may walk on us and ravish us and starve us, but they keep our land safe. That is what I hear. But our Roman masters, they take our teeth, our claws. Until we are sheep. And then what? What then? What happens one day when the Romans tire of us, or are busy defending some other shore? Will we sit about like a flock of sheep, waiting to be eaten by the dead?"

"God will send us a *navi* to deliver us," one of the younger men called out. "A messiah!" After a moment, Koach realized that was Bar Cheleph's voice.

"*Navi!*" Barabba turned his horse about and walked it toward Bar Cheleph, staring him down. "We make our own *navi*, our own messiah. God waits too long; let God affirm whom we anoint, or speak from heaven with his own voice if he dissents. Follow me, men of Kfar Nahum. We will make this land Hebrew again."

"What can you do?" That was Shimon bar Nahemyah's voice. He stepped forward to face Barabba. "The Romans are strong. What can you do, Barabba?"

"A strong man can still die with a knife in his back. Even a Roman." He leaned nearer. "There are many of us—in the south.

Not so many in the north. But there, about the Mount of Olives, we harry the Romans wherever we find them. Another year, boy, and we will make the Romans *beg* to leave Israel."

They held each other's gazes, each measuring the other.

"What is your name?"

"Shimon bar Nahemyah."

"Ride with me, Bar Nahemyah. I see the shofar about your throat. It's time for the ram's horn to be heard in our cities again. I tire of the braying of Roman trumpets and the din of Roman drums."

Bar Nahemyah watched him a moment; the others watched him. Shimon frowned. Bar Nahemyah's yearning was naked in his face. In a moment, perhaps his old rage would return, that rage with which he had once faced the dead at the synagogue door. He still wore that night's shofar about his throat, having refused to relinquish it to the priest after the battle with the dead fourteen years before.

"You were hiding," he had accused Zebadyah in the days that followed, when they met at the door of the synagogue.

The priest had looked stricken. "It is not my sin that I am here to discuss," he said hoarsely, "but yours. The dead unburied, the dead you threw in the sea."

"The Romans came, and you hid. The dead came, and you hid. You weren't there at the synagogue. You didn't blow the shofar when it was needed," Bar Nahemyah had told the priest coldly. "*I* will carry the safety of this town, and do what needs to be done."

And he had left the synagogue steps that day and had never again stepped within it, not even for the Sabbath. Bar Nahemyah had no surviving kin, no wife, no children. It was said that Bar Nahemyah lived and ate alone in the atrium of his father's empty house, with only his bitterness and anger for company. And in Kfar Nahum, only he and Koach did not go to meet God with the other men.

The thought that he might leave the town struck Koach with sudden fear. Unlike his own brother Shimon, Shimon bar Nahemyah had never been ashamed to speak with him, had never looked away from him.

Bar Nahemyah never looked away from anyone.

It was he who had driven away Bar Cheleph and the other young men who had knocked Koach to the ground, that one hot morning. Often Bar Nahemyah would pace the unkept streets of Kfar Nahum, his eyes fierce, the lines of his body taut like a ship running before the storm. Years ago, some had left Kfar Nahum, fleeing to other towns along the shore, but any who encountered Bar Nahemyah as they slipped from their houses stopped, looked down, and quietly went back within their doors and unpacked. There was a fury in Bar Nahemyah's face that none could ignore. While he, *he*, remained in Kfar Nahum, who else would dare abandon it?

"I want to," Bar Nahemyah said at last. "I want to come with you. My heart demands it. But my head hears the screaming of our People in your smooth words."

"Maybe it is the Romans you hear screaming." Barabba's face darkened with anger, but his voice was steady.

"Maybe."

"Go with him!" Bar Cheleph cried out. His face bore that same fear that Koach felt. As he always did, Bar Cheleph was lashing out before he could be hurt. "And others with you! We'll have fewer fish. And fewer mouths."

"Be quiet, son," Zebadyah said.

Bar Nahemyah was staring coldly at the corpse's head, where it lay defiling the earth near the priest's feet. "I trust my own hands and anything I hold in them," he said. "I do not trust you, Barabba. I've fought my fight. I am done."

"Go, stranger." Shimon bar Yonah lifted his head and faced the horseman, his voice bitter, his shoulders hunched as with remembered pain. "We are men who grieve, and this is all that is left of our home. We will not leave it for you or anyone else."

"Pray the Romans don't take it from you," Barabba snapped.

"We have little left for them," Shimon said. "If they want it, let them try. But you, leave us be, as you've been asked."

Koach stared at Shimon in wonder, never having heard his taciturn brother speak so many words at once.

Barabba wheeled his horse about in a cold fury. "Why are the rest of you silent?" he cried. "Rise up! I call you, rise up! What is wrong with you? Maybe you are all half Roman or Roman-lovers." Suddenly he caught sight of Koach, where he'd shrunk back against his mother's side. "There! That boy! What is wrong with his arm? Why haven't you cast him out? What kind of Hebrews are you?" His voice rose in a shout. "He is probably a Roman's child! A rape child!—"

"He is *not*!" Rahel shrieked, and her small hand thrust Koach behind her.

"The Outlaw is right!" Bar Cheleph cried. "God does not bless us or feed us. We are starving! We have let such a boy live!"

"Starving!" someone else shrieked. "We're starving!"

"Stone the boy!" He recognized Mordecai's voice.

"Stone the boy!" others shouted. "Stone the boy!"

It was as though all the griefs and terrors of fourteen years had been poured into a wineskin and sealed, and the wineskin had held them contained and out of sight. But over the years, the skin had grown brittle, and now Barabba with his words and his hurling of severed heads to their feet had dashed the skin against the earth, and everything this town had refused to look at was gushing out. It was gushing out ugly and sharp as vinegar. These angry faces no longer seemed those of men and women whom Koach knew. They stared at him with dead eyes and opening mouths, like the mouths of the dead.

Several stooped to lift stones from the side of the street.

Koach took a step back, blanching, but the stones did not fly. Not yet. Shimon stood between Koach and the crowd, his body tensed. Some of them wavered. Bar Nahemyah and Benayahu—the town's *nagar*, the woodworker and repairer of boats whose house stood by theirs—took their stand by Yonah's son. Zebadyah looked on in horror.

Rahel gripped Koach's good arm, her face rigid with fear. "If they throw," she whispered, "you run."

"Amma . . ." he whispered.

"You *run*, Koach. Your brother and I, they will not throw at *us*. They will *not*." There was a savage edge to her voice.

At that moment, Barabba wheeled his horse, and his long knife rang from its sheath. "I will take care of this for you," he shouted, and kicked his heels in. But even as his gelding sprang forward, Shimon tore the heavy fishing coat from his shoulders and flung it over the animal's head. The horse reared, hooves striking the air. Cursing, Barabba fought for balance.

"Run, Koach!" Rahel cried.

Koach stumbled back, then fled, the slap of his sandaled feet against the dry, packed earth before the synagogue. Someone grabbed for him and missed; others sprang out of his way. Glancing over his shoulder, Koach caught a glimpse of Barabba tearing the coat free and hurling it aside. A spray of red in the air as his knife took Benayahu across the face; the *nagar* had tried to grab at the bridle, and now fell back with a gurgled cry. Zebadyah was shouting, and there were screams, and Rahel stood before Barabba's horse.

Then a turn in the narrow streets hid the synagogue and the Outlaw from view, and Koach panted as he ran. More screams— terrible screams—but he didn't dare stop. Panic beat an overpowering drumbeat in his chest, and in his ears he heard his mother's voice: *Run, Koach, run. Run. Run.*

He ran. Gasping for breath, he leapt as far with each stride as he could, down the slope of the land toward the sea. He began ducking through the narrower spaces between houses. Behind him, hooves like battle-drums against the packed earth of Kfar Nahum's streets, and in his ears the rush and roar of his blood. Without thought, Koach ran to where the small houses were packed thickest, nearest the water where his mother and his brother and the surviving fishers lived. Barabba bellowed somewhere behind him, but he ran on, panting. He had the confused impression that if he could get to his mother's house, he might hide somewhere within. But already his sides burned, and he ran half hunched over.

Then he could see his mother's house ahead, that small stone structure, its walls whitened by the sea, and the hooves were louder behind him. He ran past the last few houses, and the door to the house ahead of him—the door of the last house before his mother's, the *nagar's* door, in better repair than most—was thrown open. A girl stood there, one his own age, a girl with a strange face and a frightened look.

"Inside!" she cried. "Quickly!"

Koach had only half a breath in which to make up his mind. Home was before him, but he would be alone there, in an empty house, with a furious man and a blade coming for him. He could hear the hoofbeats behind, just around the corner. He didn't trust others in the town, none but his mother and perhaps Shimon his brother and perhaps Bar Nahemyah who was alone, as he was.

"Come on!" the girl cried.

Something in her eyes told him what he needed to know.

With a gasp he flung himself toward the girl and her door.

PART 4

THE CARPENTER'S DAUGHTER

THE GIRL caught Koach's hand—her fingers so warm around his—and pulled him up against her side and into the house; her other hand caught the latch of the door and swung it shut against the sound of hooves. Her eyes were wide in the soft dark. Koach could hear her breathing and his. He could also feel her body, the softness of it, pressed to him. It made places low in his body heat in a way that astonished him.

She put her lips to his ear and whispered, "Come on. I'll hide you."

She led him quickly across the atrium of her father's house, beneath the open sky. Koach looked at her in wonder. There were few young women in Kfar Nahum, and few young men, but Koach did not remember having seen her before. There were finger-shaped bruises just below her sleeve, as though someone had gripped her arm hard enough to drag her across the atrium and fling her to the ground or into a room. But at that moment, with Barabba's hoofbeats still loud in his ears, Koach barely noticed them. She had a strange face. Her eyes were wide apart—too wide—but they were fierce with the fire of her heart, and for a moment he found it difficult to look away from them.

She did not look at him with the horror he was used to seeing in girls' eyes.

She pulled hard at his wrist. "Come on!" she whispered.

Outside, the hoofbeats went still.

"God of Hosts," she whispered. She pulled him out of the atrium into one of the small rooms along the wall, drew him in, and let the great rug that served for a curtain fall closed across the door. Within, shards of light speared toward the floor from a window long boarded up against the dead, in lines as sharp as though a man had drawn them there. Koach could see motes of dust flashing into existence as they drifted into the light, and then fading out of existence again, each one lit up briefly with fire from the sun. Despite the terror in his heart, it startled him; it was so beautiful. As the girl stepped through the light and into the shadows behind it, Koach caught the briefest glimpse of hair the color of rich earth.

A clatter as his heel struck a pile of clay bowls.

"Hide!" the girl gasped, and her small hands shoved him down into a heap of bedding. She began reaching for blankets to pile over him.

"Why?" Koach panted. "Why are you helping me?"

A small scream, muffled against her closed lips. "Don't ask questions!" she whispered fiercely. "Hide!"

A horse's whicker at the door. Koach stiffened.

In another moment, there was a hard rap against the wood, as if something blunt had struck against it. The Outlaw's sword-hilt, perhaps.

Another rap.

Then two more.

In the moments that followed, Koach could hear his breathing like a wind over the sea. He hadn't known breathing could be so loud.

"Come out! If you're in there, boy, come out!" A pause. "That's how you want to die? Hiding? You come out, I'll let you run."

Shamed, Koach began to get up, only to feel the girl's hand pressing him back.

"Don't," she whispered.

He shook his head, tried to get up again.

Her hands pinned his shoulders. "No, he won't break the door." Her mouth barely made any sound, just the movement of her lips. "He won't. He won't defile another's house!"

There was a harder pounding at the door, and a great crack. The girl's face went white. Koach peered past her, through the tiny gap between the rug and the wall. He saw the outer door half fall to the side, the wood splintered about its rusted bronze hinge.

Barabba stood with his hand still on the ruined door, his expression lethal. For a moment, Koach's heart clamored in his ears; he was sure the Outlaw would kick the door the rest of the way open and come for him with knife or stone, tearing aside the rugs to reveal the inner rooms, until Koach was found.

Yet the girl had been right: even as the door broke, Barabba hesitated. To violate the sanctity of another man's house, a man of your own People, to stride in boldly as though you owned the house and all within, that would invite the wrath of holy God. That gave even Barabba pause.

The Outlaw's eyes burned. As Koach and the girl held their breath, Barabba visibly struggled with himself. Then he turned partly away with a snarl. "Hide, then, in the house of good men!" he called, his voice thick with a fury that had been building perhaps for years, like a storm piling hot above the sea.

"Hide, little rat! But it doesn't matter how deep you burrow. One day soon, when we've thrown the Romans into the sea, good men will rip you out of your hole, you and every heathen and every *hebel* and every unclean weakling, and drag you out to be stoned in the open before the eyes of God. Hide and shiver."

"He's right," Koach whispered, barely moving his lips. "I'm not just *hebel*; I'm a coward." He was shaking. Too well he remembered the pain from Bar Cheleph's fists. Barabba would be worse.

"Shh! He'll *hear* you!"

But he knew that he had to get up. Shimon his brother had stood before the Outlaw without fear in his face. Koach had not been permitted to stand before the other men in the synagogue; if he couldn't stand like them now, or if Barabba did burst in and this lovely girl who'd hidden him was hurt in his place . . .

Koach took one of the girl's hands in his, dislodging it from his shoulder. He opened his mouth to call out to the Roman-killer, who still stood furious in the door. The girl hissed in frustration, and then suddenly her small weight was pressed down on him and her lips found his and they were warm and soft, and his heart pounded in alarm. Any intent he might have had to call out or rise and stride to the door washed away like sand on the tide. After a moment, his lips parted around her upper lip and he kissed her. His one good hand still clasped her wrist captive, for he did not know whether to let go or to put his arm around her. It took his entire being just to manage the kiss. He did not even hear the Outlaw's boot strike the ruin of the door, or his steps retreating, or the whicker of his horse as he reined it about outside. Koach heard nothing but his own heart and her soft breathing through her nose as her own lips parted and the kiss became something new and different and overwhelming, something much more than just a frustrated girl silencing him the only way she could think of, something so warm and real and moist that it was painful.

"I'm sorry," he gasped when the kiss ended.

Silence thickened between them.

Then she whispered, "I'm not."

Startled, he looked into her eyes, which shone in the light from the window. There was a look in them he had never seen before. It scared him and excited him.

"What is your name?" he whispered.

"Tamar," she said. "Tamar bat Benayahu."

"Bat Benayahu," he whispered. He had no idea what to say, or how to say it. So instead he touched her face with his fingertips. "You are so graceful," he said.

She shook her head. "No. I know that's not true." She looked pale. "I'm not . . . not what you said. Graceful."

"You are."

Her eyes glistened. Her voice dropped to nearly a whisper. "He keeps me shut in here, mostly. Forbids me to step outside the door. Because I am ugly. Because . . ." She lowered her head so that her hair hid her face. "My father is ashamed that no one has asked for me."

"You are not ugly," Koach whispered. "You are beautiful."

She shook her head sharply.

He put his hands on her shoulders. "You are *beautiful*," he said again. "Beautiful as the moon on the sea and the shells on the shore."

"You are kind," she whispered, a catch in her voice. "I knew that. The last time father let me out, I saw you walking with your mother. My father says terrible things about you, and I know others do, too. I know that your arm is weak. But you are Yonah's son. They say that, too. And I—I've seen how you help her. Your mother. Her face—you can tell that she cries often. You're what she stays on her feet for. You're not *hebel*. You're kind."

She glanced up at him through her hair, and her eyes were wet. They caught at his heart.

"Is this what it's like to be kissed?" she whispered. "You press your lips to a boy's, and your heart falls out? And suddenly you're saying things you didn't mean to?"

"Yes," he whispered back. "Or . . . I don't know. I haven't kissed anyone before." For Koach, it wasn't like his heart spilling from him in a rush of words. It was more like all the words in the whole word getting stuck in your throat, and being unable to get any of them out.

Suddenly he remembered.

"Your father—your father is hurt," Koach gasped.

She gave him a wild look.

"I don't think he's hurt badly. But Barabba was striking at people by the synagogue."

She glanced at the broken door, and her eyes held terror and dread. "I have to find out what's happening."

He grabbed her arm, but she shook her head.

"Wait here. Quietly. I won't be here to hush you," she added, blushing.

"If I shout, will you kiss me again?"

"I might," she whispered after a moment.

Her face was a deep red now, and Koach felt a flash of anger at her father. How could he have told her she was ugly? He cupped his hand behind her neck and drew her face to his, quickly, before he could change his mind, and kissed her, open-mouthed and anxious.

When the kiss ended, she rushed to her feet and darted across the atrium, swift as a deer. Koach sat dazed.

Then she was gone.

Koach lay beneath the wool bedding, which smelled like Tamar—a scent of sawdust and wood and clear water and long-held fear that seeps into the skin so deeply that it becomes a scent, too. The warmth of her lips remained with him, new and bewildering, as though God had touched him and changed something inside him, forever. He didn't know *what* had changed. He only knew that he was not the same youth he had been an hour earlier.

He wanted to know her, know everything about her. Did she climb to her roof sometimes and gaze at the moon over the sea, as he did? Did she like to sing softly in the evening? Did she have a secret place, a place God had shared only with her, where she went to think? He wanted to listen to her talk of herself, as no one had ever done with him, and he wanted to kiss her again.

There was a shout at the broken door, and Koach tensed. He'd heard no hoofbeats. Wood creaked as the remains of the door were yanked open. Then steps and loud breathing. He peered out at the atrium from under the corner of his blanket. A thin, wiry man with a dark shock of beard was moving quickly from one room to the next, glancing through the inner doors. Benayahu. He held one hand clutched to his right eye, and there was blood seeping through his fingers. A gash opened his cheek below his hand and it gaped red and dark in the dim light. His mouth was curved in a snarl of rage, his face flushed; the way he moved, the aggression and violence latent in his body, made Koach hold his breath.

"Tamar!" her father roared. "Tamar!"

When there was no answer, he made a low feral sound—a sound Koach had never heard a man make before—and he stooped over a basket in the atrium and tore out a cloth, pressing it to his face. He swayed on his feet a moment. Then he glanced across the atrium at the small chamber where Koach lay. Koach drew the blanket entirely over his head, tried to make himself as small as possible beneath it, and lay very still.

Benayahu strode near, seized the rug over the door, and tore it aside, letting in a flood of sunlight. He stood there looking in, breathing hard.

Koach didn't move. He began to count silently.

He made it to four.

Then the *nagar*'s breath hissed out between his teeth. He let the rug fall back.

Benayahu strode to another room without speaking. Koach heard the flapping sound of another rug pulled aside. Then another. When Benayahu stepped back into the atrium, Koach shivered at his glimpse of his face. He had seen such a face before. He remembered the way Bar Cheleph had stood over him in the grasses, beating him. In a dull horror he remembered the bruises he'd seen on Tamar's arm. He swallowed and lay very still, hardly daring to breathe.

He remembered the small carving he'd made, a fish, torn from his hand, though he'd tried desperately to hold on to it. And the scent of the grasses, the way a few wild blades had brushed his face as he shielded his head with his good arm. The sharp, violent pain that came with each blow of Bar Cheleph's feet. The shouts of "*Hebel! Hebel! Hebel!*"

And that terrible moment when he wondered if he was going to die, if Bar Cheleph and the other young men were going to beat him to death there on the tideline.

Then Bar Cheleph's strangled yell.

The blows stopped.

Startled voices, then running feet. Running away from him.

Koach lay still. His back and left side were one dull burn of pain.

A hand on his shoulder made him tense. He was rolled onto his back. He found Bar Nahemyah's face above his, stern but concerned. The shofar hung about the man's neck, and the knuckles on his right hand were bloodied.

"On your feet, Bar Yonah," he said.

Koach just looked at him, dazed, trying to breathe.

"I said get up. Yonah would have been ashamed of you. He would have wanted you to fight."

Bar Nahemyah grasped Koach's arms and pulled him up until he was sitting. Then he took a closer look. "God of our fathers, your face is a mess," he muttered.

"Don't hit me anymore," Koach whispered. "Don't."

"No one is going to hit you. But put away your wood and your knife. This is a town of Yehuda tribe, not a settlement of pig-eating Greeks, worshippers of wood and stone."

"The fish—"

Bar Nahemyah glanced about, his lips in a thin line. "Bar Cheleph took it when he ran, I think."

Koach moaned softly. A terrible sense of loss.

"Be thankful. It can curse his house instead of yours. What were you thinking, making such a thing?"

"It was beautiful."

"So is a blade, or a woman's body. But there are times when it is evil to hold one."

Koach didn't understand. He groaned when Bar Nahemyah lifted him to his feet.

"Damn," Bar Nahemyah whispered. "You can't stand, can you?"

Koach tried, but the world seemed to tip; Bar Nahemyah caught him and lifted the boy into his arms with a grunt. "I'd better take you to your mother," he said grimly, carrying the youth as he began walking through the grass toward the houses, his body lean and wiry against Koach's. "If your brother finds you here, like this, he may kill Bar Cheleph. He is Yonah's son."

Rahel had already been awake when Koach returned to his brother's house. She'd listened with fierce eyes as he told her what had happened and hissed through her teeth at his bruises. Then she swept him into her arms and crushed him to her. "My son! Oh my son. My son, my son."

She cleaned his face with a damp cloth and lay him in his

bedding, and for a while she sat beside him singing to him softly, though her eyes burned dark with fury.

The ruined outer door shut with a crack, and then Benayahu was gone. Koach let out his breath. Now that the danger was past, he thought of Tamar. The bruise he'd seen on her arm.

He wished he had some way to warn her that her father knew she was gone from the house and was searching for her. His own body felt sore with remembered blows, and he thought: *Tamar and I are the same.*

Except that he had been beaten *once*, while she lived under her father's roof and might be beaten many times. Bitterness twined about his heart like a thorny weed, and the hurt of it was far more cruel than anything he had felt before.

People often think that violence, though it causes pain, is something that can be shrugged away, or healed, or walked away from afterward. But it isn't. The violence of a man's fists on a boy's body, or of a man's sex forced into a woman's body or a girl's, doesn't just inflict pain. It tears away another person's security, their ownership of their own body, their faith in their ability to direct and protect themselves. However briefly, they become another's property, another person's thing to beat or destroy, and when it is done, it is a long work, a fierce work, to convince themselves entirely that they are their own again.

"He's gone."

Koach opened his eyes blearily. Tamar's face was inches from his, her breath soft and warm on his cheeks. It was pleasant.

She straightened, smiling, and he rose to his elbow. His eyes were dry with sleep. The exhaustion and adrenaline of this morning had been too much for him.

"He's gone, Koach," she said again.

"Is my mother all right?" The words rushed from him.

She nodded. "She's hurt, but others are helping her." She saw his face and added quickly: "Not badly hurt. The horse—its hoof struck her hip. The priest says the bone is broken but he thinks she will heal. Seeing her struck—a mother of Israel—it made everyone furious. When Barabba rode back to the synagogue and saw it, even he looked ashamed. Then everyone started lifting stones; they were going to kill him, Koach. They were going to try."

"What happened?" he breathed.

Her eyes were bright. "They made him go away. Out along the north track, toward Threshing. He was yelling and screaming over his shoulder. I've never seen anyone look so angry, not even—" She blanched.

"Not even your father," Koach said softly.

She gave a tight nod.

Koach reached out to her with his left hand, gripped her arm just below the bruise, but he let her go quickly when he saw her wince. She looked at him.

"He shouldn't do that to you." His voice hoarse with emotion.

They sat silently for a while. Then she whispered, "I have to get you out of here. Before my father comes."

"He came while you were gone."

She flinched.

"Come to my mother's house," Koach said suddenly.

"What?" Her eyes widened. "But—I am my father's. I'm not betrothed to your brother, or . . . or you. I'd be stoned. Father would think I was in your bed, or Shimon's."

"You hid me," Koach said quickly. "I want to hide you, from whoever would hurt you. I want to keep you safe."

He couldn't believe the words that were rushing from his heart to his lips, but neither could he stop them. The urge to protect her, to do *something*, rushed through him like wind and fire.

"I— You have to go." She tugged the blankets from him, and Koach got carefully to his feet. Tamar grasped him by his sleeve and led him quickly through the atrium, glancing at him over her shoulder.

Koach stopped by the outer door. "Wait—"

Her eyes were round and dark.

"Thank you," Koach said after a moment. "For hiding me."

He could hear the beating of his heart.

"Go," she whispered. And unlatched the door. "Go."

He leaned in quickly and brushed his lips over her eyelid, everything in him suddenly tender. He heard her breath catch. Then the battered door creaked open, and her hand between his shoulder blades pushed him through. He stumbled out, caught himself. The door rattled shut behind. He stood blinking in the sun in the empty street, and in the direction of the synagogue there were many voices shouting.

For a moment he stood dazed. He stared at the cracks in Benayahu's door, reluctant to leave. Everything in him was a rush of feeling and want and hope and fear. Then he recalled the danger to Tamar if she was caught with him, and he turned and ran the few steps to his mother's door.

WHERE GOD TOUCHED THE WORLD

TAMAR HAD spoken the truth. The Outlaw had returned to the synagogue to find grim and furious faces. By then, Rahel had been carried to the steps, her face white with pain. Another fisher's wife knelt by her, pressing a warm cloth to Rahel's hip and talking with her softly, Rahel's dress drawn up about her waist. Shimon and Zebadyah stood with their backs to her, facing the oncoming hooves, and men and youths of their town stood beside them.

No one remembered later who hurled the first rock, but the stone was a large one and it smacked against Barabba's left shoulder, nearly knocking him from his horse. Then there were many stones, the men and women before the synagogue stooping swiftly and then straightening to hurl the rocks with cries of rage. Barabba wheeled his horse in a circle, screaming curses on the town, calling them Roman-lovers and hiders of the misbegotten and unclean.

The air filled with stones, hurled wildly. One struck the back of Bar Nahemyah's head, and as he stumbled, stunned, Barabba rode at him in a rush. Leaning out, the Roman-killer caught him as he fell and hauled him up over his saddle.

"One recruit, at least, I'll take from this ruined town!" Barabba shouted. He drove his knees into his horse's sides. The steed screamed as rocks struck its flanks.

"Stop!" Zebadyah yelled to the others. "Stop! You'll hit our own!"

Then the horse was galloping down the streets with screaming men and women rushing after, but Barabba was quickly out of their reach and riding hard along the shore like a leaf before a storm wind, with Bar Nahemyah stretched dazed and unmoving across his saddle, taken from them swiftly and without farewell.

When Koach heard of that, he said nothing for an hour. It was as though his brother had been torn from him.

———

Shimon carried Rahel back to his house, lifting her in his arms as though she were a child. He lay her in her bedding beneath the olive in the atrium and gave her wine to dull the pain. He shouted for Koach to bring water, and Koach carried it to him in a small bowl—because he could not manage a ewer with only one hand. Rahel was no longer pale; she was flushed with wine, but she looked so frail where she lay, her face twisted in pain, that Koach stumbled in shock, dropping the bowl and spilling the water. Shimon turned on him with a look of rage. "You're useless!" he roared. "Get out of here."

Koach left the atrium with what dignity he could, blinking back hot tears. He had seen the whites around his brother's eyes, knew it was fear and worry for his family that fed his brother's anger, but the words hurt deeply nonetheless. He sought out one of the rooms along the outer wall of his mother's house. Not the room in which he slept during the cold winter, but a quiet, unused room where he hid his secrets.

He sat with his back to the wall and shut his eyes. He could still feel Tamar's kiss warm on his lips. After a while, he turned and slid out the loose stone at the bottom of the wall at his back, the one that concealed his secret place. It took a lot of work to slide the stone out one-handed, but he was practiced at it.

In the small, concealed space, he kept his carving knife. In another corner of the room lay pieces of driftwood like a pile of kindling, some as small as his thumb, others nearly the length of his arm. He took up one of the pieces now, a scrap the size of his hand. The wood had been cedar once, perhaps a tree on some mountain slope in White Cedars to the north, washed down the Tumbling Water to their sea. Koach clasped the wood securely between his knees and stared at it for a while, searching for the beauty in the heart of the driftwood. Then he found it, and began working the knife with his left hand, carving, cutting away the pieces that weren't needed, working slowly, calming the beating of his heart. Losing himself in it. Ceasing for a few moments to think of Barabba and his rearing, terrifying horse, or of the girl with earth-dark hair who had hidden him and kissed him.

The carving was Koach's secret, and it was his commerce, too. His creations might be unclean—in fact, in the Law, the Second of the Ten declared, *You shall carve no image in wood or stone*—but they were also beautiful. He had learned that, the evening Bar Cheleph had beaten him to the earth and taken from his hands the first carving Koach had ever made—a small, simple replica of a fish. He had seen Bar Cheleph's eyes. Not just his hate but his desire for the object Koach held. The people of Kfar Nahum were a severe people, but they were also people of the sea. And that meant they were lovers of beauty, though compared to their Greek neighbors in other towns of the Galilee, they loved it quietly.

Seeing that, Koach had not cast aside his knife after carving that little, forbidden fish. He had kept making things. He carved little boats. In time, the boats even had oars and nets, delicate traceries of wood that took him days to complete.

And because Koach lived most of his hours alone in the house with his mother, he listened. Whenever he heard his mother lamenting for some lack, he would slip away quietly when she wasn't looking, a wood-carving stowed within the long coat he wore. He would go to knock softly on one of his neighbors' doors. He did this usually in the late evening, after the fishers went down to the sea, and a fisherman's wife would open the door at his knock.

After the Romans' raid on the village and the fires that had scorched the town, the houses of Beth Tsaida were sparsely furnished and sparsely decorated, and even what pottery the village had was simple and unadorned. Koach's wood-carvings were unique in all the town, its one bit of beauty. It was not difficult to barter them for things his mother needed—salt, or oil for her lamp, or a bowl of dates or figs. Not difficult . . . as long as he chose carefully which fishermen's wives to approach. And as long as he bore with patience the way they avoided any accidental touch, any brush of their fingers against his. The way they avoided looking at his right arm. They took the carving as often as not, and handed him the little pouch of salt or the spare needle or the thimble of fine thread, but they did not look him in the eyes. They did not speak his name. In fact, they rarely spoke to him at all.

He never went to Zebadyah's door. And there were other doors he avoided, too. Doors where he would be greeted with a kick. Or where not even a love of beauty could turn the house's occupants from a strict observance of the Law.

Yet Koach felt little shame as he whittled at the driftwood he held between his knees. In a cruel world, a boy or a man must find beauty where he can, or hunt after it until he does. Or else the hard edges of life will gut him as a man guts a fish, and toss him wriggling to die in the sand.

———

The day passed. Long ago, when Koach was small, the atrium would have been loud with his mother's chickens, but those hens had long since been eaten or bartered away. Now the house was quiet. A few times Koach heard Rahel cry out in pain, and he peeked around the door of the small room. His mother still lay beneath the olive tree, her face white. Shimon, tall as a bear, brought her a fresh wineskin. Another time, there was a knock at the door. Koach heard the door open, a murmur of words, then heard it slam shut. A few moments later, he heard his brother and his mother talking in low voices. He could make out most of what was said.

"Who was it?"

"The *nagar*."

"How is he?"

"He'll keep his eye."

"God. Oh, God."

"It's all right. It's all right."

Shimon sounded numb again, the way he usually sounded. The rage that had leapt up like fire taking a cedar was gone, and he stood in his ashes.

Silence fell over the house.

Koach slipped the half-carved wood and the knife back into their place in the wall. Then he settled back, his lids heavy. The carving had brought him quiet without bringing him peace: he couldn't recall ever having felt so fatigued, so overwhelmed. All of it was too much. The horseman's fury, the fear for his mother, the unexpected, impossible warmth of Tamar's lips against his own, the dread of her father's barely restrained violence, the screams in the town, the dead eyes of the townspeople as they lifted rocks from the dirt; the hoofbeats, hoofbeats in his ears, in the earth beneath his feet, hooves louder and louder, riding him down, riding him down, riding him . . .

He woke to the slam of the door in the early dusk: his brother leaving to fish. It took him a moment to breathe evenly again. As his heartbeat settled he stirred, and realized there was a pillow beneath his head, a small, sewn square stuffed with crow's feathers. It was his mother's pillow; she must have come while he slept, despite her pain, and tucked it beneath his head. He hugged it to his cheek with his good arm, overwhelmed with a sudden tenderness toward her. It was a feeling he hadn't experienced before— not a boy's clear-hearted awe but a man's love for his mother, his acknowledgment of her sacrifices and her truth.

After a few moments, he stepped softly from the room and found his mother beneath the olive, asleep with her mouth open, her face still flushed. He watched her breathe for a few moments, his heart in turmoil. She had been hurt today, because of him. Because he was useless. Because he was *hebel.*

Though he couldn't have said why, he walked quietly to the stone steps in the opposite wall that led up to the rooftop. The stones were cool beneath his feet; he hadn't spared a moment to put on sandals. Once up there, he glanced first to Benayahu's house. The *nagar*'s house was separated from his mother's only by the narrowest of alleys, and its roof was lower, so that he could see into a part of the atrium and into the small rooms on the far side of the house if the rugs that covered the doors of those rooms were drawn aside. The few he could see into now were empty.

He sighed and turned toward the sea. There was a breeze against his face, but only a light one. Boats were setting out on the water. His brother was out there, he knew. And Yakob the priest's son and many others. All young men of Beth Tsaida who'd had their *bar 'onshin* in the synagogue and had learned to handle the oar and the net. All but he.

"I want to be of use." A whispered prayer. "To my family. To Tamar. To someone." It had always seemed to him as though the night he was born God had turned his back on him and on the town, had walked away across the water and never looked back and never returned. Now God seemed far away, hardly relevant. But who else was there to talk to?

Suddenly he heard footsteps approaching, a man's steps, heavy though muffled and slow, as if he were trying to be silent. The man came through the narrow clutter of fishermen's houses until he passed by Benayahu's. Koach slipped to the edge of the roof, lay down on his belly, and peered over it, his heart racing.

The man was Zebadyah bar Yesse.

The priest stopped before Rahel's door, close enough that Koach could have spat on him. The boy covered his mouth and nose with his hand to hide the sound of his breathing.

The priest stood before the door for a while. Then he called out Rahel's name in a low voice that he clearly hoped wouldn't carry.

There was no answer.

"Bat Eleazar," Zebadyah called again, just above a whisper, and he gave the door a tentative rap with his hand, just enough that someone inside might hear it.

"Bat Eleazar . . . Rahel, come to your door. Please. We need to talk about your son. And we need to do so now, while others sleep. Please."

The door rattled quietly and then swung half open. The pale oval of Rahel's face appeared in the dark. Her eyes were dilated and black.

"I am grateful for what you did today, *kohen*," she said. "But I know you are no friend of my son's." There was a quality to her voice that made Koach realize, with a start, that his mother had been weeping.

For a moment, heat flickered in Zebadyah's eyes. Then he sighed. "I am tired," he said. "That man left those heads on our soil. Yakob has taken them up the hill to bury, but Bar Cheleph and I have been all day washing the uncleanness from our earth." His gaze was direct. "I stood by your sons because we cannot allow our town to be trampled ever again by outsiders." He nearly spat the word. "But we must talk. You know what your son has been doing." His voice sank to a whisper. "Those . . . those *images*."

"It is the only thing that makes him happy," Rahel said. "The only thing that makes him feel useful."

Koach blinked back moisture from his eyes.

"It has to stop," the priest said. "It has to . . . Look, I do not think as Barabba does, not any longer. Your son is a good boy, and you love him; I can see that . . ."

"Then let my son have his *bar 'onshin*!"

"I *can't*!" Zebadyah cried. "I am thinking only of what is best for the town."

A soft hiss of breath. "*I* am thinking of what is best for my son."

The priest glanced about quickly, as though concerned that the rising of his voice might have drawn listeners. "Take him, then," he said, his voice trembling with the effort of holding back what he felt. "You, Shimon, your crippled boy. Take him from the town. I will send goods with you, what I can. You can go to Rich Garden or Threshing." His face clenched in pain, as though it were a great sacrifice to wrench these words from his heart. "Find some new home. But the boy cannot stay here."

"He is Yonah's son." Her voice fierce.

"I know!" Zebadyah cried, with a sharp gesture of his hands. Rahel shrank back into the doorway. A few faces peered through the windows of nearby houses. "I know! Do you think I do what I do lightly? You damned, unreasonable . . . *woman*! Is your son more important than every life in this town? Would you imperil us all with your grief, your pride? He cannot stay here; I have overlooked him for too long because I loved my brother, because I love you." He nearly shouted the last, and then stopped abruptly, as if shocked at what he'd said.

An uncomfortable silence. The woman at her door, the priest outside it.

Zebadyah breathed, "I am sorry."

"I am your brother's wife," Rahel said coldly. "Not yours. And you have no authority within the walls of this house."

Zebadyah's voice was muted now, pleading. "Bat Eleazar, just listen to me."

"I am done listening."

"He is broken, unclean, and he carves images in defiance of everything we believe in, everything we are. He has to go. It is God's Law."

"If God had had a mother, his Law might have been less cruel."

"Blasphemy," Zebadyah gasped, drawing back a step, a hand raised as though her words were something physical that he could ward away. "I can't . . . I can't hear this!"

"Then don't." Rahel's voice was sharp and it began to carry; Koach could see doors of nearby houses cracked open. His mother's voice was fire; Koach was certain that if she had addressed *him* in that tone, he would have withered like a vine in the sun's heat.

"This is my husband's house," Rahel hissed. "My husband's. The first man of this town. The man who stood against the Romans when you would not. A man who gave his *life*. So that my son could be born in a Hebrew town. And how *dare* you come to his door and talk to me of God? My husband knew God. Do you? Was it God who told you to hide shaking by the boats? The night they beat and crippled your father, the night my husband *died*, was it God who told you to bow and scrape before our heathen masters? Was it?"

Zebadyah went pale. Utterly pale. "Remember yourself, woman," he rasped.

But she shut the door on him.

For a few moments Zebadyah stood very still. "I paid for my sins," he whispered at last. "I pay for them every night. Every night until I die."

Then it seemed to occur to him that he was speaking merely to a door of wood, and not to Rahel or to her dead husband. He turned and walked away with his head bowed. A few faces watched the priest from nearby doors. Zebadyah strode by without looking at them. Then the doors shut again, closing each family once more within the hungry gloom of its own house.

Koach was breathing hard, as though he had run to the *kokhim* and back. He just lay there on the roof, trying to take in all he had heard. No one had ever spoken to him of his father's death, or been willing to. His mother looked sad when he was mentioned. Shimon's face just went cold and hard. Koach only knew his father's name because everyone in town spoke it reverently when they addressed his brother. *Bar Yonah*, they said, *Bar Yonah*, as though Yonah had been some hero out of old stories, whose death had left a hole not only in Koach's life, but in Kfar Nahum itself. Koach tried to imagine him, a man he'd never seen, standing with a fishing spear in his hand, or an oar, or a knife, as Roman soldiers or the lurching dead came at him.

Koach suddenly wanted to run down the steps into the atrium to his mother and demand stories from her. Stories of Yonah that might tell him who his father had been, and who *he* might be. But sounds from the *nagar*'s house broke the moment, snapping his thoughts like kindling. He froze, listening: the murmur of a voice in anger and a faint sound like a sob.

He got to his feet and returned to the edge of the roof facing that house, and looked down into it. The rug over one of the far rooms had been drawn aside, and there was a light, a small candle burning on a table. Tamar was sitting on the floor beside it, hugging herself and rocking back and forth. Her head was down, her hair covering her face, but Koach could see that she was shaking and that she was naked to the waist. He blushed hotly for just a moment, but the tingling in his loins disappeared as quickly as it came, for everything about the way Tamar held her body spoke of terrible pain. Koach had the impulse to leave the roof and go unbar the door of his house, slip out into the street, and run to Benayahu's door and knock and call out to her, make sure she was all right. But just at that moment, a dark shape cut off the candlelight, and he knew that a man was standing between the candle and the door. His voice was raised harshly, but his words were muffled by the room he stood in, and Koach couldn't be sure what was said. After a moment there was movement against the light and a quiet crack, as of a hand striking flesh, and a small, strangled sob. Koach sucked in his breath. He was beating her, and the crack of his hand sounded again. And again. And *again*. Koach's hand became a fist.

The shadow moved, and he glimpsed the man grasping Tamar's hair, holding her still as he hit her. But at that moment her gaze flicked up in pain, and she saw him.

They saw each other. From the rooftop to the small room.

Had Koach been able to think past the shock and the fury in his heart, he might have expected to see anger in the girl's eyes, or shame. Shame that he would see her like this. But Koach didn't see those things in her eyes. Only recognition. Then her eyes glistened in the light of the candle, as though filling with tears that she had forbid herself until that moment.

And her face relaxed. Like letting go of a burden too heavy for her. Like glancing down and seeing warm bedding before you when you are tired. Like relief.

Relief that one other person knew she was suffering, and cared.

He took a step back, but her gaze held him. A silent demand in her eyes: *Don't go. Don't leave me alone.*

So he stayed.

Something in him died and something else was born, something dark and furious, as he watched the blows fall on this young and beautiful woman. He did not turn his head; he would not betray her. He witnessed all of it. And when Benayahu had left his daughter sobbing on her bedding, Koach longed to go to her, to tend her bruises with a damp cloth or to hold her. But he didn't know how. He could not call out to his mother. Rahel was not a man; she could not interfere in the doings in Benayahu's house. There was no one to go to, no one who would listen to a one-armed boy, or care. His brother, maybe, a strong man, could leap from this roof to the other. But Koach was not his brother. If he tried that leap, he would only break his body on the stones between their houses. He might go down to Benayahu's door, but why should the *nagar* open up his house to him?

He did the only thing he could: he waited with her while she cried, though a gulf of air separated them. Finally she lifted her face from the bedding, and the misery in her eyes smote his heart. Quickly she brought her blanket up to her face and dried her tears. Then Tamar rose and slipped from her room, disappearing from his sight.

Koach stood still on the rooftop. He felt emptied of all feeling. He counted the beats of his heart. Somewhere around two hundred, he saw Tamar emerge onto her own rooftop, stepping onto it from unseen stone steps. At first she didn't look at him. She just stood there with her head down, in her blanket, the moon on her hair. As lovely as Batsheva must have looked to Dawid the king. Like Dawid, Koach had seen her naked, but unlike Dawid, the sight moved him to a desire to protect her, not possess her. He had seen her bruised and now, as she lifted her head and their gazes met, he saw her heart in her eyes. Her solitude and pain.

Neither of them looked away.

Neither dared call out, for fear of alerting Benayahu or breaking the intimacy and peril of this moment.

They stood like that a long time, seeing so much hurt in each other's hearts.

Finally, he mouthed the words in his heart, keeping them silent but exaggerating the movements of his mouth, to be certain she would know what he said:

I want to help.

I know, she mouthed back. Then: *You didn't leave me. That is help.*

A shake of his head. *I will help.*

They considered each other. Then she did something he did not expect. She let the blanket slip from her shoulders, let it settle to her feet, gently as feathers. For a moment, she held her arms across her breasts, then let them fall to her sides. She lifted her chin, though her face burned. She let him see her, all of her, her beauty and her bruises. This gift of herself. Her father might strip her or beat her, but he could not take this from her: her right to open her heart and her body to one whose heart called to hers. Koach held his breath. All his life, he would remember this moment. His first sight of her. The memory would be holy to him. As though her rooftop were the place where God touched the world and created beauty.

His loins stirred for her, yet his face was wet.

Whether he wept for her, for himself, or for them both, he couldn't have said. His hand trembled as he lifted his fingers to the clasp of his own tunic. He kept himself fully clothed at most times, even in his mother's house; he couldn't bear the way others looked at him when his deformity was visible. But he could not hide it now, could not conceal it when this young woman had unclothed all of her bruises, risked everything to be seen by one other.

He kept his movements slow, his heart loud with his fear. It took some work, with only his one hand and not his mother's to aid him. But at last his clothes were in a heap beside him, and he stood naked on the roof, the air cool on his skin. There was mercifully no wind to chill him or carry to his ears the voices of the *shedim*. He stood as straight as he could; his phallus had stiffened and grown so that it stood hard, as he had found it lately in the mornings when he woke, but for once it did not embarrass him.

He wanted to give her what she had given him: a sight of all of him. Even, no longer concealed in its long sleeve, his withered arm and deformed right hand, the hand that could never touch her face or bring her pleasure or work to feed her. Never having felt so naked, he looked to her eyes anxiously. Saw them tearful. But she was also smiling.

He felt warm through every part of his body. Whatever the days ahead brought—whether hunger or ill dreams or riders out of the south with heads tied to their saddles, or stones hurled at him, or dead lurching up from the waves—whatever the days brought, for the first time he was certain he would not face those days alone.

One Year Later.
AD 26—Present Day.

THE STRANGER

SHIMON'S BOAT approached the shore, riding low in the water and almost tipping into the sea from the weight of its nets. Even as the fishers breathed in the fecund scent of kelp and dead shellfish, the stranger came wading out toward them, the lake water about his knees, his eyes wild. "Your nets!" the man cried, an edge to his words, a hill-country accent Shimon couldn't place. "Your nets!"

Shimon stared at him as he heaved at the oar, uneasy. The man's clothes were strange—not a tunic and cloak but a long robe of brown wool. His arms and legs were smeared with dirt, as though he truly had walked here out of the deserts in the south. His hair was lank about his bruised face. His right arm bore bruises also, as though he had tried to shield himself from blows. With him came the reek of a man who had spent long days without a roof or clean water.

Even as they heard the scraping welcome of the shingle against the keel, the stranger took the gunwale in his hands. "So many!" he gasped, gesturing at the nets, staring wide-eyed at the fish. His face was wild with shock. "So many! And they're . . . they're *beautiful*! I didn't know this would happen, I just cried out, I cried out, I cried out!" His gaze shot to Shimon's face, and in his eyes there was sudden joy, like a man who has walked all his life in the dark and for the first time sees firelight burning away the shadows. Shimon just stared back, the others silent behind him in the boat, startled at this raving man.

"Don't you understand? I *heard* you!" the man cried. "I could hear all of you, all last night, all of you moaning . . . your hunger, I couldn't bear it, couldn't bear it, couldn't . . . and I heard the father, I heard the father weeping for you, and don't you see, don't you *see*, he must have heard *me*, he must have heard me, too, he must have heard me, the father heard *me*!" His hands tightened at the gunwale, as though he were going to pull himself into the boat, his voice rising. His eyes shone with tears. "Do you understand! Do you understand! It was too great to bear, the hunger and the father's cries and the screaming and the screaming and the screaming"— his voice was now a wild shriek of joy, so that Shimon leaned back away from the man—"and I cried out and *he heard me*!"

The stranger's eyes rolled back and he pitched to the side, crashing into the water.

Shimon swore and cast his oar aside, leaping to his feet. He sprang over the gunwale as Yakob and Yohanna looked on, their eyes wide. He felt the water about his shins, the cold shock of it against his toes, and pebbles shifting beneath his sandaled feet. The boat scraped past him and he plunged his arms into the water, groping. Shimon found the man and hauled him up. The stranger's head lolled back and his mouth fell open.

"We'll get the boat up!" Yohanna cried behind him.

Shimon didn't answer. He slapped the man's cheek to rouse him.

Yohanna and Yakob leapt from the boat, the familiar sound of their sandaled feet sinking into the sand. Their hands gripped the gunwale and they began sliding the boat up the shingle. Though large, the boats of Kfar Nahum were lightly built; yet it was a great labor dragging the craft up toward the tideline.

After a moment, Shimon dragged the man out of the sea and lay him on the sand. Life came back to the stranger's eyes, and he gasped, "Water."

Shimon got to his feet and ran to the boat, exchanging a bewildered look with Yakob. Reaching in, he snatched up one of their waterskins, then ran back to where the stranger lay.

He held the waterskin to the man's lips, saw his throat move in great gulps. Then the stranger choked a little, and Shimon lifted the waterskin and set it aside. Even as he did, the man's hand grasped his wrist with a fierce strength. His eyes were intense. For a moment the stranger fought for breath. Then he gasped: "Cephas!"

Shimon didn't understand. Cephas was the Aramaic word for *rock*.

"Cephas," the man said, swallowing, getting more moisture into his voice. His gaze held Shimon's with an insistent, desperate demand. "Somewhere I have to be. Something I have to do."

Shimon shook his head. He didn't know whether that was a question or how to answer.

"Cephas, Cephas." The man fell back, his eyes turning toward the sky. "Something, something I have to do. I knew it, I knew it so clearly, so clearly only a moment ago. Like my father had spoken it right into my ear. Right *into my ear*, Cephas. When the fish came, I knew what it was, this thing I have to do. For just a moment, a breath, I knew it, Cephas. I knew it." He seemed to be fighting to catch his breath. "Now it's gone, gone, like . . . like leaves blown into the desert."

"Who are you?" Shimon gasped.

But the man closed his eyes and his grip on Shimon's hand weakened. Then his chest rose and fell as though he were asleep. Shimon slipped his wrist from the man's grip and stood, a little shakily. He gazed down at the man's battered body in its ragged brown robe. If Shimon had not heard the man's eerie cries, calling the fish, he would have thought him one of the boat people, the beggars and outcasts wandering up and down the shoreline of the Galilee who had become stuck here at their shore, too sick or too weak to move on. They often slept under the derelict boats just above the tide's reach. Shimon glanced uneasily up at those boats where they lay rotting in the tall grasses, but there was no sound or sign of movement. Yet there were always beggars there.

His hands shook. Had this man's cries—his eerie calling for fish over the water—filled the nets? The man's words were like raving. Like the words of a witch who had called the *shedim* into his body to inhabit it. The body was a house: What was living in this man's house?

Yet the nets had been empty, and now they were not.

"Yohanna!" he called.

In a moment, the son of Zebadyah was at his side. "Who is he, Shimon?"

Shimon only stepped back, making the sign against the evil eye.

"Wait." Yohanna gave the man a closer look and drew in a breath. "I know this man."

Shimon looked to him quickly, but Yohanna only frowned. "I don't know who he is. But I've seen him. I'm certain of that. I have seen this man before."

"He must be one of the boat people, one of the unclean," Yakob called behind them. Glancing over his shoulder, Shimon saw the boat half up the shingle with Yakob trying to pull it up alone, the veins standing out against his forehead. The nets were still in the water. Cursing, Shimon sprinted for the boat and lent his own arms, gripping the hooks beneath the gunwale and lifting the boat as he dragged it. In a moment, Yohanna was with them, leaving the stranger behind on the sand.

"He's not one of the boat people," Yohanna gasped, as they pulled the boat up the sand.

"He *looks* like one of the boat people," Yakob grunted.

"Didn't you see his robe? Fine wool. Pattern at the hem. Not rags. Not boat people. Essene, I think."

"Essene," Yakob wondered. "What is an Essene doing here?"

"I don't know."

"But his face—he's Galilean. He's one of us. Not from Kfar Nahum, but he's from here."

"I know."

Shimon took a steadying breath and turned his back on the stranger with the bruised arms and face. "Talk later," he said. "Nets won't wait."

———

A few moments of struggle, and they had the boat up into the tall grass above the tideline. Yakob took the prow, guiding the boat into place in the line of fishing vessels. Those still in use were at the end of the line nearest the town; those farther down were long derelict, decaying and spattered with gull feces, wooden corpses of themselves waiting for time to eat away their last timbers.

Then they ran back for the nets. Shimon glanced at the man lying in the sand, but he didn't have time to stand about wondering. They needed to be quick, for the oncoming tide was tugging at the nets, and the flashing silver of the fish, tails wriggling against the nets, was drawing down out of the sky white birds, swooping low.

They ran down the sand, which was wet and packed beneath the slap of their sandals. They took up the casting ropes and strained to pull up the nets, fearing the nets would break and spill this miracle catch back into the sea, the way a broken body spills back into the dark the life God once breathed into it. Shimon sucked in air through his nose and breathed out through his mouth, pulling hard on the ropes on each inhale.. He kept his eyes on the water and the wild flopping of the fish, fearing that they might yet haul another corpse out with the catch. His forehead was clammy with sweat.

Then two hands grasped the rope beside his and pulled, and the net came half out of the water. Shimon glanced to the side; the stranger stood there. The sea had washed most of the smell of the hills from him; water still trickled from his hair, making dark streaks down his robe. He returned Shimon's look, then heaved at the rope again.

"What are you?" Shimon panted. He wanted to pull away from this strange beggar man, but he didn't want to let go of the rope. The nets were heavy. He could not remember them ever being so heavy.

"A friend," the man said. He was calmer now, though his voice was strained.

"You've been in the desert." Shimon glanced at the man's brown robe.

"I have," he said.

"Are you an Essene?"

He shook his head. Not one of the desert hermits, then, who lived in their small communities hiding in caves from the dead and teaching their bodies to endure any hardship, that they might draw nearer to God.

"You're tattered and bruised." Shimon's voice was thick with his distrust of outsiders. "Are you unclean?"

The question appeared to startle him. "No," he said, and heaved at the rope. "No, I don't . . . I don't think so. Not unclean."

"I don't know what you are, who you are, but you called the fish," Shimon said, struggling to understand. "What *are* you? I *heard* you call them."

The man's eyes were dark and he stared past Shimon and over the water, intently, at some far other place. His voice changed, going quiet and intense, burning with terrible clarity. "Something is happening, Cephas. And whatever is happening, it will be like sword and like fire and like bread in the mouths of a thousand, thousand children, and nothing will ever, ever be the same way again."

Shimon stared at him, uneasy.

The stranger's attention returned to the rope they were straining at. "I cried out, and they came," he gasped. "Barbels, musht. No catfish, nothing unclean to throw back. How many will they feed?"

"The town," Shimon said. Hoarse. "The entire town. For two weeks, maybe three." He heaved at the net, and suddenly it broke open, spilling fish over the sand, flopping and wet.

The stranger gasped.

Shimon caught his breath also. There, where the water met the land, where the net had broken open at their pull, their last heave had pulled a white corpse half up onto the sand. Its hand was caught in the netting, with the fish flopping about it as though in panic at the unclean touch. The corpse itself was still, a gash in its brow where Shimon's fishing spear had caught it.

"No," the stranger whispered, his face white with horror, as though the appearance of the corpse was some intimate betrayal. "No."

CEPHAS

THE THING'S jaw was open in gaping, eternal hunger, its eyes sightless. Gazing down at it now, Shimon felt none of the rage that had surged in him, hot and violent, when he'd defended his nets on the sea. Only dread, cold in his belly. One thing to encounter the dead out on the sea, or in the dark waters of the dream country. Quite another to see one wash up on his shore.

It seemed to him that if he were to take his eyes from the corpse for even a moment, its hands might twitch and it might lurch again to its feet.

But it didn't move.

The corpse just lay there on the shingle like a stain of blood on a garment, one that could never be cleansed, never be entirely hidden or forgotten.

"El Shaddai," Shimon whispered, stepping back. There had

always been one or two that would walk out of the waves and feed on the vagrants under the boats until they were discovered and stoned. But there had been three already this year.

And then this.

He tore his gaze from the dead thing and looked out at the cold waves, at that sea older than humanity that could hold so many dead concealed within it. The dread in his belly hardened, like a heavy stone to crush him to his knees.

The stranger was pale. "That . . . that's what you were beating at, with spear and oar, when you stood in your boat."

"Didn't you hear them moan?" Shimon said.

"I heard them moan," the stranger said. "Every moment I'm awake, I hear them moan." He let the rope fall from his hands and walked down to crouch beside the corpse.

Torn between watching the raving stranger and watching the corpse, Shimon stepped near and took the net itself in his hands, his muscles bunching, pulling it away from the hungry tide. For an instant the corpse dragged over the sand. The stranger gripped the tattered remnants of its tunic in his hand as though to pull it from the net, but the water-drenched garment peeled away from the corpse like an old blister, leaving the stranger crouching with it in his hand and the corpse dragging nakedly after Shimon, the sand sloughing some of its skin away as though its skin were only a second and equally decayed garment.

The stranger's face was so full of pain that Shimon had to look away. He kicked the corpse's hand a few times, knocking it loose from the net. Then he left the stranger and the corpse there, pulling the net with him, leaking fish. The corpse would have to be buried, in accordance with the Law—under earth or hard rock, so the uncleanness of it wouldn't spread to blight the plants that grow in the open air. But that could wait until the fish were brought in. It would have to.

———

Soon the other nets were half up the shore. Shimon, Yakob, and Yohanna ran back to gather up the spilled fish in their arms and carry those up, too, before the tide could take them. They had to work fast. There were other boats approaching the shore but still a ways out. Yakob ran to their own boat up above the tideline, snatched out an oar and an armful of the sheaves of lake-weed for binding the fish, then ran back. He tossed the sheaves into the sand at the others' feet, then veered and ran down the shore to a great white rock that was always above the tide and could be seen from some distance out. He leapt up on the rock and waved the oar, shouting at the far boats. Out on the water, men stood up against the rock and sway of their craft and called back to him, their voices thin in the dawn.

Yohanna and Shimon opened the unbroken nets, and the fish rivered out onto the sand in a flood of flashing scales. Still breathing hard, Shimon clapped Yohanna's shoulder. "Get help from the town. Bring bins, baskets, anything you have."

"What about him?" Yohanna nodded to the man still crouching at the water with that garment in his hand.

"Never mind him. Don't you see the gulls? Be quick!" Overhead, the sky was filling already with white birds, swooping down in wheeling circles, screaming their hunger. Shimon's blood roared in his ears. No time, no time.

"There won't be much help. We came back earlier than most," Yohanna said.

"Then bring the women!" Shimon roared. "We are *not* losing these fish! Not to the dead. Not to the sea. And not to the birds. Get me some hands!"

Yohanna nodded, clapped Shimon's shoulder in return, and then sprinted for the tideline grass and the low, crumbling houses beyond. He was the fastest runner in Kfar Nahum, a man with long legs as though he had Greek blood, but even if he had been short and slow, Shimon would not have left the nets himself.

Swiftly, Shimon crouched beside one of the opened nets and began wrapping the fish in sheaves of lake-weed. Even as he worked, the fish slick and wriggling in his hands, the air about him filled with beating wings and hoarse shrieks, and the gulls descended on him like the host of God. Some dove at Shimon's face and he beat them off with an arm; others settled on the nets or on the spill of fish on the sand, digging in with their sharp beaks. Then Yakob leapt in front of him and swung his oar about, slamming the hard wooden blade against the birds. There was a grate of other boats on the shingle, and then running feet, and other men sprang over the fish with oars in their hands.

A man knelt by him; Shimon glanced to his side and saw the stranger, his eyes still haunted. His dousing in the sea had washed away his stink but it could not wash away his bruises or his desert-tangled hair. Shimon shrank back. The stranger looked so much like one of the under-the-boat beggars, only he *moved* nothing like them. He took up a fish and wrapped it swiftly. His man's hands were free of rope burns and the straight scars that came of cuts from a slipped fish knife, but they were calloused and rough. He was a man who worked with his hands, then. Only not with fish. His feet were raw and scarred and bare, as though he had walked long on this shore or in the hills without sandals.

He looked . . . unclean.

The stranger reached for a second fish, and Shimon's breath hissed in through his teeth.

The stranger stopped. Hurt flashed in his eyes, but he concealed it quickly.

His own movements quick, tense, Shimon knotted a bit of cord about a sheaf of fish, baring his teeth against the storm of feathers about him.

"I'd like to help," the stranger said.

Shimon ignored him. The stranger watched as he bound a few more musht. The scent of the fish maddened Shimon's belly; he yearned to abandon the nets and gather up one armful of musht, just one, and run with them over the sand and through the grasses to the stone fishers' houses, to his mother and brother whom he'd often left ravenous, as his father never, *ever* had. He longed to cry out at the door for Rahel to light the firepit in the atrium. Or he might not even gather up that armful, might not even leave the shore; he might lift the fish raw to his teeth, even as he crouched here near the water.

The stranger reached again for a fish—with his bruised, unclean hands—and Shimon turned on him, his eyes fierce. "Stranger," he said.

The man crouched, very still. Watching him.

"Your accent," Shimon said roughly. "Are you half Greek? From Many Birds?"

"Natzeret. Both my parents are Hebrew."

Natzeret was a small town high on the hill on the road west, above the Greek colony city that the Hebrews called Tzippori, or Many Birds, because of the brightly feathered creatures that the Greeks had brought from many parts of the world to sing among the town's well-watered trees and marble pillars.

"Those bruises on your face, your arms . . . ?"

"Stoning," the stranger said.

"What?" Shimon shot him a look of horror. "What were you stoned for?" His voice was little more than a gasp. This man might be a killer, or a seducer of men's wives, a blasphemer, or a witch.

"I . . . I don't know." The stranger's eyes were full of raw pain and bewilderment.

That was hardly reassuring.

"I'm . . ." The man glanced down at the fish. "I'm having trouble, trouble remembering. There are all these rooms, these rooms in my mind. Some have people in them, people I've known, people I grew up with . . . mother, father, brothers, priests, and weavers. Children running and laughing and singing. And others are empty and cold, as though whoever was there packed and left and is not there anymore. And there is one roo—" He took a breath. "There is one room with a rug hung over the door, and that room burns with light and I can't see in." The man looked away. "Maybe that's where my . . . my missing memories are, Cephas."

Shimon swallowed. That was not the answer he'd expected. No sin confessed or evaded . . . only these mad words that made little sense.

The man gazed fixedly at nothing. Perhaps he was walking through that house in his mind, checking the empty rooms.

"The gulls," the stranger said. "And the tide. You don't have much time. May I help you?"

Shimon tossed three more fish into a sheaf, bound it, and muttered, "Why do you call me that?"

"Call you what?"

Shimon met his gaze, boldly, intending to stare him down. But the stranger's own gaze was intense, and for just a moment, Shimon thought he was gazing into a mirror, a dark mirror, where he saw the inside of his heart and the inside of his gut reflected, and everything he regretted and everything he'd given up. The stranger's gaze was direct and unguarded and piercing, uncaring that they were strangers and might share no kin, uncaring that they might be different.

It rattled him.

"Cephas," he muttered, trying to recover. "You keep calling me Cephas."

The stranger just looked at him.

"I am Shimon bar Yonah." The anger rose in his voice. "Everyone here knows my name and my father's. He was the greatest fisher on this sea. I am Shimon his son."

"I am Yeshua bar Yosef," he said, "and I *know* you. You are Cephas, the rock. We have met before. Or . . ." The man looked just past him, his eyes going cold and clear, as though he were gazing far out over the wooded ridges and high peaks of Ramat ha-Golan. ". . . Or we *will* meet. I know this," he whispered. "How do I know this? It's your voice, isn't it? I heard your voice . . . when I was in the desert. I am certain of it. It was your voice."

Shimon watched Yeshua out of the corner of his eye. The desert. If this ragged man had spent long nights out there, *alone*, in the wilderness of the Essenes, where the wind screamed almost without cease and the *shedim* moaned in their hundreds on neglected battlefields, what uncleanness might he have brought back with him or within him?

Yet, whatever his misgivings, the tide was coming in. The shrieking gulls were swooping low now in numbers that might be too much for Yakob's swinging of the oar to keep back. Shimon needed help, and quickly. "Fine," he said. "Whoever you are, help."

The stranger nodded and bent quickly to the work.

Other boats slid up onto the shingle, escaping the night hunger of the sea. Men leapt out, Mordecai and Natan El and others, bringing armfuls of lake-weed to use in wrapping the fish. Some ran to stand sentinel with Yakob, oars lifted in challenge to the screaming gulls. One—Natan El—began searching the shoreline for stones large enough for a cairn, to bury the corpse they'd dragged up. The water had destroyed the thing's face, and it was impossible to tell who that corpse had been, whose kin. No tomb for the waterlogged dead, only a pile of rock. Other such cairns stood at places along the shore, sun-bleached and stained with the leavings of gulls.

Some of the fishers joined Shimon and the stranger at their work, not speaking but gazing about at the heaps of fish with wild eyes. A few cast wary glances at the corpse where it lay lifeless on the sand and lifted their fingers in the sign against the evil eye.

Then, with a shout, Yohanna came running down toward the shore from the stone houses. Others ran beside him, women and old men carrying empty baskets. Glancing up, Shimon saw his mother Rahel, and Bar Cheleph with his bad hip. And, running behind, his gray hair wild in a gust of wind, Zebadyah the *kohen*, Kfar Nahum's priest.

"What has happened?" the *kohen* cried out against the wind. "What has happened?"

"Fish!" Yakob shouted, and swung his oar against a bird that had swept too low; the gull wheeled quickly out of the way. "Fish!"

"Fish!" Bar Cheleph cried.

"My son!" Rahel cried, and her eyes glistened. "Oh, my son!"

Yeshua looked up at her, and for a moment a sad smile transfigured his face.

Soon the sand and shingle was littered with baskets and lids and rolls of cloth and bits of cord, and half the town crouched with the sea lapping at their feet, working swiftly to gut the fish and bind them or basket them. Several women, their eyes shining, began carrying baskets and sheaves of musht in a line up the shore toward the stone houses. Bar Cheleph—whose limp seemed to be bothering him—hung back. Perhaps because Shimon glared at him. The younger man had beaten Shimon's brother once, and Shimon hadn't forgotten it. Yet his anger was not as strong as his guilt, for when he gazed at Koach with his useless arm, he saw what Bar Cheleph saw: a body twisted and unclean, a broken oar on a boat that needed all its oars. But Koach was his mother's last child, the last she would ever have. And no one would lift their hand against anyone his mother loved, not while he stood near.

Bar Cheleph moved down the shore a little way, gathering up bits of wood and other drift as if for a fire. As if he meant to begin roasting some of the fish *right here*. On the shore, this very morning. That changed Shimon's mood quick as a sea wind.

There hadn't been a fire for cooking fish on the shore since he had been a boy. Since before that night . . . He swallowed back some of the saliva filling his mouth, wiped sweat from his brow with the back of his hand. He felt suddenly faint.

The priest stood on the shore looking about with startled eyes. His gaze moved over the sand as though he were looking for the footprints of God, looking for some reason why this blessing had been visited on ruined Kfar Nahum so unexpectedly.

Then his gaze settled on the stranger. Yeshua had risen to his feet and stood over one of the baskets, lifting wrapped fish quickly into it.

"Who are you?" Zebadyah said bluntly, without any note of welcome.

"He is the one I told you of, abba," Yohanna said. "He says he called the fish."

"He has a mouth. He can speak." He raised his voice. "Who are you and who are your kin, beggar?"

Yeshua glanced up, his face still drawn with memory of pain. He opened his mouth as though to answer, but at that moment there was a cry from farther down the shore.

"Look! Look!"

They all swung about to look.

Some way to the south, a man was walking up the shore, coming toward them. That was strange, both because few walked beside the sea—most took their boats to move from one town to another—and because hardly anyone ever, *ever* came to Kfar Nahum.

But he did not walk like one of the boat people. He strode along that shore like one accustomed to long travel and unafraid of it, though not unwearied by it.

"Who *is* that?" Shimon murmured.

Yeshua straightened from the basket, and his shoulders lifted as though whatever pain he had brought with him was abruptly gone. He stood tall and still. His eyes had that intense, elsewhere gaze again, as though he were staring intently past them all at something only he could see. "I remember this," he whispered. "Father, I remember this. When the father needs a thing done, he calls us together, all of us, all those he needs." He shook his head slightly, as though in wonder. Then he cupped his hands to either side of his mouth and called out: "*Shalom!*"

The distant walker lifted his hand in response, and it was clear that he carried some object in it. He brought it to his face, and suddenly a loud blast rang out against the hills. A horn call, deep and resonant. Shimon could feel the call even in his bones.

"My God," he whispered.

Yakob and Yohanna both gazed at the far traveler without speaking, their faces struck with wonder.

Zebadyah scowled. "It can't be," he muttered.

After more than a year following the Roman-killer through the streets of the cities of their People and into wild places in the hills, Bar Nahemyah had come back.

PART 5

THE CARVED MAN

THE NEWCOMER strode with purpose up the shore. Yet his eyes held not just the fatigue of a man who has walked through the night along the sands, but the weariness of a man who has walked a year and found no place to rest in all that time. His shofar was still slung about his neck; he wore a tattered but heavy cloak, and his clothing was simple and plain though of southern weaving. His beard had grown long; his hair he wore in a braid down his back. Girded about his waist was a cracked leather scabbard the length of his forearm, from which protruded a hilt of polished bone. He carried a waterskin over his shoulder but no pack; he was lean, his face weathered, bitten by the wind and by the stress of things he wished he hadn't seen. He slowed his stride as he reached the men and women standing on the shingle, then stood with his hand lifted in greeting.

Zebadyah spoke first. "Dead have been coming up from the sea. What makes you think you are welcome here, Bar Nahemyah? You who gave our dead no burial?"

Bar Nahemyah's face tightened. He glanced past the priest. "*Shalom*, Bar Yonah."

"*Shalom*," Shimon said hoarsely.

Silence. Bar Nahemyah heard only the gulls' cries and the beating of the oars against feathered bodies. Men stood with fish in their right hands and baskets in their left. All eyes on this man who had saved their town and then destroyed it. This man who'd felled the corpses at the very door of the synagogue, saving the town's last men and women, and then filled the sea with their dead and dying. And who had, a year ago, been taken from them. And who hadn't come back. Like all the town's fathers, like God and Yonah and so many, Bar Nahemyah had abandoned them.

Here, facing his town . . . Bar Nahemyah felt unsettled. He didn't let it show in his face. But even as he and his town watched each other, the wind gusted and tore his cloak aside, baring his left arm. The men at the nets gasped. Zebadyah cried out. Bar Nahemyah braced himself but made no effort to conceal his arm. What they saw there had been dearly bought.

"What have you done?" the priest moaned. "Bar Nahemyah, what have you done?"

Nearly twenty fine scars, white against Bar Nahemyah's sun-darkened skin, had been cut in parallel lines between his left shoulder and his elbow. They were too fine and too close a pattern to be wounds from a battle; anyone looking knew that they were a deliberate scarring of his flesh.

"You've defiled your body," Zebadyah said, his eyes dismayed.

"No." He let his voice ring with cold purpose. "This is a covenant. My body was marked when I was eight days old. That was a covenant with God. This is a covenant with the unclean dead. Nineteen of them I have put in the earth since leaving Kfar Nahum, and nineteen marks I bear in my flesh, to remember." His voice fell. "Though I don't think I could ever forget. I have seen Herod's ghoul pits."

The other men's faces went white.

Even in Kfar Nahum, it was known how the old Herod, that desert king hired by Rome to rule over an enslaved People, had grown old and mad. They had heard how he'd slain even his own kin. How he had filled the Roman baths in his palace with the dead, and thrown first his wife and then his own young daughter into the water to be devoured. How he'd sat on the steps of the baths, watching with tears on his face as his daughter was eaten. How at her shrieks, all the blossoms in Herod's gardens had withered. How he had sealed off the baths afterward with so many layers of stone that the wailing of the dead could no longer be heard. How he'd then sat in his bed reeking, unbathed, for the better part of a month, and anyone who came to him with reminders of affairs of state, he'd had put to death.

When Herod had been a young man, he had built great cities of marble on the coast, cities of Greek design and Roman public spirit, cities to rival any in the world. Caesar's City, and Yoppa rebuilt, and a new Temple in Yerushalayim, far greater in size and beauty than the Temple of the ancients, though this one had been built with unclean hands. The young Herod had sat in his gardens and sang poetry and made love to his wife beneath the stars. The older Herod had slaughtered all the children in Bet Lechem on a whim, and given his family to the dead to devour, because he believed they were plotting to poison or knife him in his sleep. When the moaning *shedim* creep into a man's ears and his mouth and into his heart, no one is safe.

Herod had been entombed for years, and his son, the new king, Herod Antipas, hid from nightmares of the brutalities he remembered, devoting the dark hours of his nights instead to endless revelry, to feasting and wine and the dancing of naked young women before his seat of white marble. But Antipas's bitter-minded wife found the memory of Herod's bath useful; she'd had Greek stonemasons wall up the baths in Antipas's house, though she bid them open up the roofs to the sky. Corpses had been tossed in, and Herod's wife often had dissidents lowered down to them on long ropes.

Bar Nahemyah had seen a man, one of Barabba's, lowered into the stink and the dark, kicking his legs and screaming as the corpses below reached for him with long, grasping fingers.

He had seen *her* watching, standing at the edge of the wall. Herod's wife. Had seen the slight curving of her lip, and her eyes shining in the dusk.

He had turned away and covered his ears against the shrieks.

"I have seen," Bar Nahemyah repeated.

Zebadyah's voice was quieter now, less of a shout, yet thick with dread. "What deeds have you done since Barabba took you? Who have you killed, that you have fled back to us for refuge? Were you pursued? Have you led the Romans upon us?"

"Pursued, yes." His voice was cold. "But I lost them near the Hittim. I have no yearning to witness another night of fire and fear in my own town. No one has followed me, *kohen*." His gaze flicked back to Shimon, who had a desperate look in his face. "Yet the day . . . the last day, when we must rise with knives against Rome's living and its dead or die the slow death ourselves, that day is near. And I do ask you for your help."

"We have none to give," Shimon said.

"We have nothing to do with Barabba's knifemen, or with you," Zebadyah said.

"That isn't for you to say." Bar Nahemyah touched his fingertips to the ram's horn. "I still hold the shofar." The accusation was in his eyes: *coward*. Zebadyah's own eyes went dark with rage. But inside, Bar Nahemyah quailed. He had come back to his own town, his own place, and in their eyes—even in Shimon's eyes—he saw that he had come back like Barabba: stranger, killer, one outside the Law.

Turning away from the aging priest, he approached the gathered people on the shore and saw for the first time what they were gathered *about*. He sucked in a breath at the sight of that once-human corpse the nets had brought up, weeds tangled about its legs. It had been dragged far above the advancing tide, with a mound of stones stacked beside it ready for burial. Near it stood a strange man with lank hair and a bruised face, his eyes watery but intense. He wore a brown robe that clung, soaked, to his body, as though he had walked up out of the sea. And all around him, the nets, *the nets*, the fish on the sand thick as pebbles in the hills.

For a moment he forgot his desperate journey and his dread at the corpse. He walked toward the fish, his mouth open. He couldn't understand it. Couldn't believe it. There were so many.

"The fish," he whispered.

"They've come back," Shimon said hoarsely. "Our fathers' fish have come back."

The pang of guilt and hope was sharp as a knife's twist in Bar Nahemyah's belly. "But the fish were gone. They were dead."

"Nothing's ever really dead," the strange man with the bruised face called out. He stared not at Bar Nahemyah or at the fish but up the shore at the derelict boats by the tall grasses at the tideline. "Not dead, not *really* dead, unless we let it be. I think that is so."

"I am Shimon bar Nahemyah. I do not know you. Who are you?"

"Everything comes back up," the stranger said. "Everything rises, everything rises, sun and rain and sun again, and all our dead, all our dead . . ." His voice fell until it was too quiet to hear.

"The town is beset," Zebadyah cried, "by madmen and heathen!"

"This isn't madness," Bar Nahemyah breathed. "It's prophecy. He's seeing visions." His heart beat a little faster—for he had heard something like this before, had heard holy ones in Yerushalayim city, men whom God had touched. He'd heard them talk in such a way on the Temple steps, while the alley stones behind echoed with the moans of the dead and with the hard footsteps of men in Roman armor. And now here, on this northern shore, he found a miracle of fish spilled across the sand out of some story of his fathers, and man who spoke like a *navi*. Hope lit like a heathen corpse-fire in Bar Nahemyah's heart, burning away decay and despair from his year in Barabba's caves.

"There are no more prophets," Zebadyah said, his tone bitter.

"Ha Matbil is a prophet," Yohanna said quickly.

"No!" The priest's eyes were fierce. "Enough with your Ha Matbil! El Shaddai preserve me, I have no use for sons or kin who follow killers or witches into the desert and leave the rest of us to mourn alone."

"I did not follow Barabba," Bar Nahemyah said quietly, not taking his gaze from the stranger. "I was taken."

"But you did not come back!" Shimon cried.

"Those," the stranger said suddenly, before Bar Nahemyah could reply, "those, those by the boats, who are they? Who are they?"

The stranger took a few slow steps up the sand toward the boats. Bar Nahemyah saw that a few men had emerged from those broken shelters and stood in the tall grasses, gazing down the shore at the fish, some of which still flopped on the sand. The men were ragged and gaunt, their faces gray from illness and lack of food.

"Scavengers, Yeshua bar Yosef," Shimon muttered.

"I don't understand," the stranger, Yeshua, said.

"They are boat people," Bar Nahemyah said. The sight of them there, a terrible reminder of the land's ruin, made Bar Nahemyah feel even more weary . . . and old.

"Other people's poor," Shimon said impatiently. "Other towns'. They come to us hungry like the dead, when there is already so little to eat."

"No," Yeshua whispered. He bent to lift a basket of fish and he nearly fell, but he caught himself, still muttering. "No one goes hungry, no one goes hungry, no one goes hungry, not this day, not this day, not this . . ." One arm around the basket, he took a step toward the old hulls.

"What are you doing?" Shimon cried.

At that moment several of the gulls swooped low, for Yakob and the others, listening, had let their oars fall still. One of the screaming birds flew at Yeshua's head while the others swooped at the basket he held. Yeshua's eyes went hot with anger and he shot his hand out against the bird and shouted, "Enough! *Enough!*"

A rush of heat nearly tumbled Bar Nahemyah from his feet, as though a fire had roared into existence. The gulls tumbled back, screaming and beating their wings, as though knocked aside by a hot wind. Yeshua straightened, one arm about the basket, the other outstretched and emitting heat. His eyes were fierce. His hair lifted, but not with the wind.

Another gull swooped low but veered away from his hand. Then *all* of them veered away, and in a moment they were gone across the water, wailing, gliding away on their white wings low over the waves.

There was silence on the sand.

Bar Nahemyah fell back, as though winded by what he had just witnessed. He stared at the stranger, at his wild eyes and his outstretched hand. The others stared also, standing as still as Lot's wife, translated from flesh to pillars of salt by something they should not have been allowed to see.

SITTING *SHIVA*

SHIMON BAR Yonah stared over the water after the gulls, his face still warm from that rush of heat. Hardly breathing, he glanced back at the stranger. Yeshua lowered his hand, and then his head, his hair falling over his eyes, lank and damp with lake water. He was panting, his hands clutching the basket now as though it might somehow keep him standing.

Zebadyah recovered himself first. "Witchcraft," he gasped. "This is witchcraft! The man has a demon. *Shedim*. Bar Yonah! Yohanna! Get away from him!" He stepped back. "Stones! Sons of Kfar Nahum, sons of Beth Tsaida, bring stones!"

"Wait!" Bar Nahemyah cried.

Yeshua began laughing, a quiet, desperate laughter that carried in the stillness left by the departing gulls. Zebadyah looked on in horror. "Stones," Yeshua said, shaking his head. "Stones. So I haven't left Natzeret after all. Stone me, stone me then. Suffer me not to live." Without looking at the priest, he turned and walked toward the derelict boats.

But the stranger still carried the basket of fish. *Shimon's* fish, fish to feed his town and kin. "What are you doing?" Shimon called after him, his heart beating in sudden alarm. When the stranger didn't answer, he cursed. "Yakob, Yohanna, get the rest of these fish up from the tide!"

He strode after the man from Natzeret, stumbling a little, the wind suddenly fierce at his back, threatening to knock him over onto his belly. He heard Rahel call out his name, and the priest also. He did not stop. The grasses at the tideline bent in waves before the sea wind. Behind him, a rush of talk and shouting as those on the shore demanded to know what was going on, who this stranger was, whether possessed or prophetic. He ignored them. He ignored them all, a sudden fire in his heart. No. This stranger was not going to invite *boat people* to eat his fish. Fish from his sea, his father's sea.

Bar Nahemyah ran up alongside him, and the town's two Shimons went striding up from the sea together, one with a shofar about his neck, the other with fishing gloves tucked into his coat.

"Who is he, this man?" Bar Nahemyah said quickly. "He who speaks like a holy one? He sent those gulls away as easily as a boy might throw a rock."

"I don't care who he is. I don't trust him." Shimon lifted his voice. "Bar Yosef! Those fish came into shore in my boat, my nets. Whatever wonder has been done here, these fish are to feed *my* family!"

But Yeshua didn't turn. Didn't answer. He just walked along the line of the boats with that basket. He seemed to have forgotten that he held it. He looked at the boat people, and his face grew haggard with grief. Shimon hurried after, his alarm louder within him. He tried not to look at the people by the boats, tried just to barrel after the stranger, but the horrors there were such that he could not keep his eyes averted. Nor could Bar Nahemyah.

There were men and women both among the splintering and rotting boats, some lying beneath them, some sitting against the sides of the old hulls. Few were entirely clothed. One woman lay on her back, her eyes lifeless though her breasts rose and fell with her breathing. Her cheeks were hollowed; her rags had been torn from her hips, leaving her legs naked and bruised. They lay apart, where probably one of the other vagrants, or many, had thrust them open; she had not closed them. Perhaps she had not moved for hours.

Shimon and Bar Nahemyah hurried past.

By the next boat, a naked man sat by a pile of broken bones, bones too long to be those of a gull or a crane or a goat of the hills. He lacked the gray look of the other boat people, his face flushed with color as though freshly fed, and his eyes glinted as he noticed Shimon. Shimon's body went cold; there was something in that man's eyes that he had never seen in a man's eyes before, and it made him fear. A fear of the gut, a fear of the hunted.

To those who slept and breathed and died beneath the boats, more emaciated even than he and his mother and brother, any flesh might be food, anything with meat and bone might be sustenance.

Yeshua bar Yosef stopped walking at last and, setting the basket down by his feet, he knelt by two women who sat listlessly against the hull of an overturned boat. One's face was drained of life, her eyes sunken, her breathing ragged. The other—barely more than a girl—watched the first. Her eyes were moist. She held a sharp rock in her hand, dried blood at its tip. She lifted it warily.

"Don't be afraid, *talitha*," Yeshua said softly.

Talitha. Aramaic for "little girl." As a man might call his daughter or his child-sister. The word and the tenderness in it struck Shimon. Why was he claiming kinship with her?

"I will not hurt her," Yeshua said. "I will not . . . not do that. I only want to help."

The girl just watched him silently.

The dying woman beside her stank of urine and sweat; Shimon and Bar Nahemyah hung back. But the stranger knelt by her as though he had no fear that she might touch him. The girl beside her took her hand and gripped it fiercely, and the woman lifted her head slightly and looked at Yeshua. Her face was so covered in grime that it was impossible to tell whether she was old or young, but the shape of her nose and the hue of her skin were Greek, not Hebrew, though the young woman beside her was one of the People. Shimon gazed at the dying woman in dread. She seemed barely human to him. There were footsteps soft in the grasses around them, and glancing up, he saw boat people standing on the other side of the derelict, staring at the basket of fish with desperate eyes. Bar Nahemyah curled his fingers around the hilt of his knife, and the gaunt men approached no nearer.

Yeshua reached for the woman. Her companion's breath hissed softly, but the girl did not move. Only watched him.

"Don't *touch* her, Bar Yosef!" Shimon cried.

"Why?" Yeshua's shoulders quivered. His eyes were dark again with that anger with which he had hurled the gulls out over the sea. "Because everyone else refuses to?"

He parted the woman's rags, baring her breasts and her ribs, which stood out in stark violence against her skin. Shimon drew back another step, and Bar Nahemyah closed his eyes as though against a sudden rush of memories.

"Oh," Yeshua whispered.

"We starve and die." The woman's voice was dry and slow, as though she rarely used it. Her eyes seemed out of focus. "They've been . . . eating the bodies. And the dead come up from the water. We are forgotten."

"You are not," Yeshua said, his voice hoarse with emotion. He covered her again with her rags. She made no move to help him or hinder him, as though her body were no longer a part of her, no longer her concern. Her hands lay beside her like wrinkled, dead things. The young woman who sat with her took her right hand and squeezed it, her face pale. She hadn't put down the sharp rock.

Yeshua watched the dying woman a moment, then seated himself beside her, not touching her, just sitting with her.

Beside Shimon, Bar Nahemyah whispered, "Bar Yonah, the women of our People all look that way, in the alleys of Yerushalayim, the city of our fathers. So many women leaning against walls, breathing, barely alive. Starving. Our own People. They look just like her. And they will go on looking that way until we shove the Romans into the sea."

"We've shoved enough into the sea," Shimon said bitterly, thinking of that terrible, beached corpse. He bent slowly and lifted the basket of fish. He could take it back down to the shore, get away from these starving beggars. The other boat people watched him. Yet he hesitated. Beside him, Bar Nahemyah stepped back and leaned against another boat. Shimon gazed at the woman, unable to look away. She was covered in her rags now, but the sight of her ribs seemed burned into his mind. It was his own nightmare: that the sea might one year yield no fish at all, until his mother and his useless brother were only skin stretched over bone, like this woman.

"Bar Yosef," he whispered.

Yeshua did not look up.

"Bar Yosef, she is not of the People."

No answer.

"Are you going to just sit there?"

Yeshua took a slow breath. "I am in pain, Cephas."

Shimon looked at him, startled.

"Great pain. Not just these . . ." He touched a bruise on his arm and winced. "This," he said, lifting his fingers to his right ear. "It doesn't matter if I wake or if I sleep. Always, always I hear screaming. You and your fathers and your sons yet unborn, all of you screaming, all of you . . . hurting. Sometimes it is so bad I can only stand, stand completely still, like a . . . like a rock, Cephas, like a rock, for hours and hours and hours." His hands began to shake. "And I don't know why, why none of you hear it, why not one of you hears it, why only I, only I am alone, I and the father and the father weeping in the desert. In the . . . She is screaming, this woman here, screaming, both of them, and no one hears. No one hears," he whispered. "If I can comfort just her, just one of you, just *one*, maybe it will stop, maybe the screaming will finally stop."

"She's only a boat woman," Shimon said. His voice subdued.

"What does it matter," Yeshua said wearily. "The father made her and I heard him, I heard him, Cephas, weeping in the desert, and you cannot tell me, you cannot, that he doesn't care. You cannot tell me that." He lifted his face, and his eyes were bloodshot. "I have hungered and thirsted out in the desert, and I have been driven by stones, and I have been alone. So alone. No one should ever, ever be alone, Cephas. She doesn't have to die alone."

Yeshua lowered his head. All around him, Shimon could hear the boat people whispering, "Fish, fish . . ." Shimon clenched his teeth. But Yeshua said nothing more. He was sitting *shiva* with that woman. Sitting in silence, mourning her own death with her.

The woman's breath rasped. Shimon realized she didn't have long, and this *shiva* would be short. He shook his head and stepped away, taking the basket with him. He would not stay to watch her die—that would be too much like his nightmares—and he would leave this man to his madness. There were fish to gut, to fry, to eat and store. A long day. Yet as he walked back down the line of boats with the gaze of the boat people on his back, guilt sat heavy in his chest.

Why should he feel that? These were not his kin.

When he'd been a child and the fish were plentiful and the boat people less near to starvation, some of the fishers had made a custom of tossing a few glistening musht out of their boats onto the sand as they came in to shore. Seeing the beggars fight over the few small fish, some of the fishers had laughed. Still others tossed none at all, but fended the vagrants away from their nets, with the blunt ends of fishing spears if need be.

His father had been one of those.

Shimon's belly growled, and he glanced down at the fish, some of them still opening and closing their mouths. Some of them motionless. The scent of them. His hunger woke like a beast within him. He shuddered; perhaps the whole town was turning into boat people.

He reached the last of the derelicts and leaned against it, breathing hard. He closed his eyes a moment but opened them immediately because in that brief darkness, he'd seen dead faces rising from the water again, dead fingers reaching to grasp him.

Shimon gave the boat a hard kick, needing some way to assuage the storm within him. The long-disused hull gave a little before his foot, and there was a startled cry from under the boat.

Shimon froze.

"Who is that?" he shouted.

This time there was no cry, no sound even of soft breathing. No one slipped out through the tight gap between the gunwale of the tipped boat and the ground.

"Come out!" Shimon dropped the basket to the grass at his feet. "I know it's you."

Again, no answer.

Shimon took the gunwale in his hands and lifted, gasping at the strain. For a moment the boat didn't move, but then he managed to heave it slowly up and tip it, letting it fall back onto its keel with a crash that brought cries from a few of the boat people behind him.

The young man beneath the boat . . . was Koach.

SHIMON'S BROTHER

KOACH HAD begun to dream of horses.

Even now there was a bulge in the left side of his shirt, where his mother had sewn for him that hidden inner pocket. He had concealed a wood-carving there, small enough to hold in his palm. A horse, strong and sleek as Barabba's, carved of cedar. He had dreamed sometimes of Barabba's stern face and the flashing hooves of his steed, but he had also dreamed of the scene Tamar had told him of: Barabba riding furiously from their town, his horse faster than wind or bird. A horse might carry him away from here, he and Tamar together, to some place that did not hate them.

Often, he rode horses in his dreams.

He had taken to visiting the boats on the shore where they were harbored by day. He studied how they were made, and learned which ones were damaged, which ones had fittings that had cracked or were under strain. He spent weeks at this, climbing beneath the overturned boats and reaching up and learning with his fingers. He went early and returned early, feeling his mother's eyes on him as he left the house and fearful of being caught by the town's other youths, now that Bar Nahemyah had been swept away from the town.

He began carving fittings for boats, leaving them, one at a time, on the doorstep of the *nagar*'s shop attached to Benayahu's house. He did this many times. One day, as he approached the door, Benayahu opened it and gave Koach a hard look, then glanced at the fitting Koach held.

"You have a skilled hand."

Koach sucked in his breath and tensed to run, fearing the man's anger at his presumption and his gift, already feeling the blows to come. Benayahu stood in the door a moment more, his silence full with thought. Then he turned and went inside, leaving the door open. An invitation, or a reprieve. Koach wondered which. He gathered what courage he could, then strode to the door and ducked into the shop, into a dim interior rich with the smell of cedar curing.

Benayahu was there, smoothing a long plank by the flickering light of an oil lamp. The shop had a window but it was boarded up so tightly that barely even a chink of sun made it through. He was a man who had lost too much to the dead.

He didn't look up to acknowledge Koach, but with his foot he slid a block of wood and a knife across the floor toward him.

For several beats of his heart, Koach was all but overwhelmed with an urge to take Benayahu's hammer in his one hand and drive it into the man's brow, such was his fury at this man who left bruises on Tamar's body. The man had turned his back to Koach, bent over his work.

Koach forced himself to breathe calmly. He was here to be near Tamar, to find some way to help her. Striking her father and getting himself stoned would not help. His face hard, Koach sat on the floor. He set the block between his knees and got to work.

———

From that day, Koach had assisted Benayahu with his carpentry. He had found a use at last, a wall to build between himself and the name Hebel. And he was good at it. He didn't know how many fishermen in the town realized it, but within the year his craftsmanship had appeared on half the boats on their shore.

Benayahu was a strange man, silent and moody like Koach's own brother, his eyes often dark with guilt and violence barely restrained. He rarely said a word, just gestured to show what he wanted Koach to do. Sometimes he took a tool out of Koach's hand, without touching him, and showed Koach how to use it correctly. There was no affection in his face at those times, only a cold determination. The man had no son, and no other apprentices in his shop. Except for his daughter, he lived alone, and he must have lived with the certainty that when he died, his skill would die with him.

Sometimes, after he put his tools away, the aging *nagar* went to stand by one wall of the shop, where thick Hebrew letters had been carved into the stone. It was a name, a woman's. The *nagar* would just stare at the letters. Then he would turn and pass through the inner door into his house, leaving Koach in the shop. The lock would slide shut with a hard, bronze clack. Koach would stand there, his hand clenched, shaking with helpless anger. Because those were the evenings that ended with Tamar being beaten.

At first, Koach tried to think of some way to speak with Benayahu about his daughter, but he could not find that way. He had also hoped for a chance to speak with Tamar herself, but he caught few glimpses of her by day. The door between the shop and the house was kept shut, and Benayahu did not invite him in. Nor did the man leave his shop; each day he brought a waterskin in with him before Koach even arrived. Once, only once, Koach glanced up to see the door open the smallest crack, and Tamar peering in at him. In the next moment, Benayahu struck the side of his head. Tamar's eyes widened and she shut the door swiftly.

"Look at my daughter again and I'll throw you in the sea with the dead, *hebel* boy," the *nagar* said, his voice quiet and cold. Those were almost the only words he had spoken to Koach since the first day.

Koach lowered his head, nodded. He unclenched his left hand, rage hot in his heart. His face ringing.

The beatings had become worse, so that some nights Tamar did not come to the rooftop but only lay shaking in her bedding in the atrium, where Koach could barely see her.

They could not shout to each other from rooftop to rooftop, but over the nights of that year, they made for each other a secret language of signs and gestures, and with movements of their hands they sang silently to each other of love and need. His need to be useful to one other person, to be *loved* by one other. Her need to be free of her father's house. A hand pressed to the breast meant: *My heart. You touch my heart.* A flapping motion with one hand meant: *How I wish we might fly away like birds.* Fingers pressed to the lips meant: *I wish you could kiss me.*

Having found no way to speak to her father, Koach began to dream, by night and by day, of carrying her away from that house, as Samson or some mighty one of centuries past would have done. But he was not Samson, nor mighty; his very name was a lie.

By day in the shop, he'd glance down at the fittings he was carving, his thoughts feverishly intense. He lacked strength, but he had skill. The *nagar* had seen that; others might also. There were Greek towns across the sea where there was no Law and no priest. He didn't know how the Greeks would look on a cripple, but surely they needed skilled woodworkers. If Tamar would fly away with him, perhaps there was some place, somewhere he could carry her to.

At last, a night came when he stood on his roof, shrugged the concealing wool from his shoulders, and, gazing across at her body, beautiful as the curve of the moon, and at her eyes that were so strangely calm after her pain, he decided he would tell her what he intended to do.

They would meet by the boats, but they would go on foot, the long walk around the shore. He couldn't row a boat, and the town had no horses.

THE BOAT PEOPLE

THE BOAT tipped and the sky opened hot and blue above him. Koach blinked up at his brother's face.

"What are you doing here?" There was nothing polite in Shimon's voice, and something in Koach hardened when he saw the contempt and frustration in his brother's face.

Koach was lying in the sand beneath the boat, wrapped in a heavy water-coat that had been their father's. Rahel had woven Shimon his own coat for the cold nights on the sea and had given this one to Koach, the only protection he had from his dead father. But it was too large for him, and often he felt small and childlike in it.

Koach rose, an ungainly move that involved pushing himself up with his good, left arm and then hopping to his feet.

"I'll go home." He couldn't keep the bitterness from his voice.

"Why are you out here?" Shimon said again.

"I was waiting." He didn't meet Shimon's eyes, concealing the wound in his heart.

He had slipped down to the boats after dark, after his brother had gone out to sea and his mother had given herself to sleep. He had waited, and *waited*, until the day crept beneath the gunwale of the overturned boat and it was too late to slip quietly back. Then he could only lie there while gulls called somewhere above the wooden roof of the boat's keel, their lonely, forlorn cries giving voice to the fears of his heart. And when the shore had echoed with the startled shouts of the town's men, he had lain still and silent beneath the boat, touched by no curiosity.

She hadn't come to him.

Perhaps she'd realized that the young man she'd been dreaming with could never cast a net for her, never catch fish, never bring home food for the fire.

Now he'd been discovered, and his face was dark with shame. A boy with no *bar 'onshin*, no betrothed, with dreams he hadn't earned. A boy who had thought, for one year of longing and desperation, that he could be a man.

"Waiting for what?" Shimon demanded, towering over him, as he always did.

The look Koach turned on him was resentful. "What do you care?" Koach cried.

"*You*." Shimon started to step away but then turned back, every line in his body tense.

"Bar Yonah," a quiet voice said, and with a shock, Koach recognized Bar Nahemyah—Bar Nahemyah who'd been gone so long—walking toward them through the boats.

"Stay out of this," Shimon said. To Koach he said, his voice quiet and cold, "Every night I risk my life and my neck for you, to feed you, and I cannot even keep you safe in my own house! Get out of here. You shouldn't be here. *Raca*—you have never been anything but a dead weight, something I have to look after, house, clothe, protect—and you give *nothing* back. There's no place for you here, among the boats. Run home."

Koach couldn't bear to see any more of that old disappointment in his brother's eyes. As he backed away, he saw the stranger rise to his feet, a few boats down, a look of pain in his bruised face. Slouched against the hull behind him sat a woman as gray as a corpse and a young woman beside her, her shoulders shaking. Koach stared at the girl; she was weeping without sound, the way Tamar did.

"You're always ashamed of me," Koach said. He didn't look at his brother. He just blinked quickly and then walked away from them all. He heard his brother call his name.

"Give him a moment, Bar Yonah." Bar Nahemyah's voice.

Koach walked on unchallenged until he was a little way up into the tall tideline grasses, pale blades that brushed his cheeks in the chill wind.

He was not crying.

He didn't cry anymore.

This moisture on his face was only drops of the sea carried to him by the wind.

Only that.

For a while he gazed bleakly at the cracking, battered houses ahead. He could walk up there now, to Benayahu's shop, as on any other day. He could pretend nothing had happened, draw his shame about him like a coat, growing smaller and smaller inside it. Or he could stand at the door of the house and call for her. But that would shame and endanger her, and himself. And what could she say, what could she tell him that he didn't already know?

The voices behind him grew louder, more heated. "Your brother," the stranger was shouting. "That was your brother, your brother, your own brother. And you call him *hebel* and *raca*? How can you . . . how can you do that? My own brothers . . . my own . . ."

His voice choked, and it took him a moment to speak again. "What is *wrong* with you? Do you even know how blessed, how blessed you are, that you *have* a brother, you have kin in your own house, your own roof, people who sit with you to eat . . ."

Koach glanced over his shoulder, saw the stranger gesture wildly toward the shore. Following the gesture, Koach realized for the first time what was happening there. He walked back through the grasses, aghast. All those fish. All those nets spilled open on the sand. All those *people*, the fishers' wives and their older kin and even a few from Kfar Nahum itself, men who worked in small shops and not in boats. All of them gathering up the fish. Koach stared down at that crowd of baskets and bins, speechless.

"None of you stand *near* each other," the stranger was shouting as Koach approached, "not even brothers! And all your boats . . . all your boats on the water, none of them calling out to the others. Just silence, that silence over the water . . ."

Koach listened. The aloneness in the stranger's voice was familiar to him.

"If you were one of us," Shimon said, "you'd understand—"

"I *want* to understand!"

"—but you aren't one of us."

"I know!" the stranger cried. "I am unhomed! They threw me out. I came back from the desert and told them what I'd heard, *what I'd heard*, what I still hear, what I keep hearing, and what woke me weeping in the night, the truth, the truth, I told them the truth, and they threw me out." The stranger's voice was quiet and nearly choked with pain, yet his words carried. "And I ran, Cephas. I ran. All the way here. And I am exhausted and I am hungry and I am afraid . . ."

He was interrupted by a loud, prolonged rasp, something unlike any other sound Koach had ever heard. An alarming sound. He turned to look. It was the woman with the gray face, the woman sitting against the cracked and beaten hull. Her breast fell once more and then did not rise. Koach saw the light leave her eyes. One moment her eyes were those of a living woman. The next, they were empty. It was like looking to see your reflection in a bowl that has no water in it, no mirror.

She was gone.

The wind in the grass.

The stranger gazed at her body with horror. "No," he whispered.

Even Shimon seemed shaken, as though the *malakh ha-mavet*, the angel of death, had brushed his shoulder as it passed.

"No." The stranger went pale. "I told her she didn't need to die alone."

Shimon murmured, "Yeshua bar Yosef . . ."

"No," Yeshua cried. "No! All of you screaming and screaming and screaming *and none of you hearing*! Do not *talk* to me, Cephas! Just do something about it! Please!"

The stranger bent and lifted the basket of fish from the sand, and thrust it into Shimon's arms. The broad-shouldered fisherman staggered back until he caught his balance.

"*Help* me," the stranger pleaded.

"Bar Yosef, our own families starve."

"No, no one will . . . no one will starve, no one. There will be so *many* fish." He sounded as though tears might come. "*Please*, Cephas. Feed these women and these men, Hebrew or Greek or whatever you see, just *feed them*. Please."

The man backed away, his face still stricken with horror. Then he turned and all but ran through the grasses, away from the boats, his pace desperate, the wind tearing at his hair.

"Wait!" Bar Nahemyah called. He ran after the stranger.

Shimon stood shaken, staring after them, still holding the basket. As though the woman's death rasp was still too loud in his ears, in his heart. Koach could see the horrified recognition in his brother's eyes: The boat people weren't supposed to be like *that*.

Like people. Like men and women who might weep for each other and then die hungry and alone.

Shimon exhaled slowly. "You and I, we will talk later," he muttered, then walked slowly away down the line of boats, the basket in his hands, with some of the boat people shuffling after him or stumbling to their feet as he neared them.

———

With his brother gone, Koach only felt empty. He was *hebel* again, useless as a bit of a driftwood washed up among these grasses.

Numbly, he approached the two women, one alive, one dead. The younger woman glanced up at his approach with grieving, tired eyes. A sharpened rock slipped from her hand to the sandy dirt, as though she simply didn't care anymore. Her face was wet with tears, but her crying was silent and she barely trembled with it. After a moment, she leaned her head on the dead woman's shoulder.

Here was yet another person who was entirely alone, with none to comfort her in her suffering. Another outcast, like himself. Like Tamar.

Without thinking about it, he shrugged off his father's coat. One-handed, he draped it clumsily about the woman's shoulders, then patted it down. His brother would likely be furious at this use of the coat, but Koach didn't care. He took the woman's arm and tried to lift her to her feet. After a moment, she stood, letting him help her. Some of her hair fell across her face, dirty and tangled. She kept her eyes lowered.

"What's your name?" Koach asked softly.

She shook her head weakly.

He frowned. "I am Koach bar Yonah."

She touched her fingertips to her throat in response. The

sound she made was caught somewhere between a grunt and an exhalation.

"You can't speak," Koach whispered. He felt a small thrill of fear. Zebadyah the priest taught that when a man or a woman could not speak, it was because the *shedim* had slipped down their throat into their body, and they could only moan, or make no sound at all, like the dead that walked. But this young woman did not seem that way to Koach. She seemed small, and frightened, and so stricken with hunger and grief that she could hardly stand. And she had remained by her dying friend, so she loved.

Koach tried to think of some comfort for her. He glanced down at the corpse. "The priest will make sure there's a cairn for her. He won't leave her unburied . . ." He trailed off; the woman was still keeping her face hidden, and he realized that it must be terrible for her that her grief was this naked. He considered leaving her there, but his cheeks darkened with shame. He had left Tamar in her father's home for a year, not knowing what to do, and she was still trapped there. He couldn't leave this woman alone in her anguish, too.

He glanced down the shore, and caught his breath. For a moment he just stood with the woman beside him, staring down at all the people from the town and all the fish being gathered into baskets. Some men were dragging boats up toward him, and a few were settling logs of driftwood over small, improvised firepits far above the incoming tide. Bar Cheleph sat at the nearest fire, but Koach didn't even shiver at the sight of the man who'd once beaten him into the grass. He was too swept away by the sight of all those fish and all those people. A gust of wind brought the scent to him, and hunger groaned violent in his belly. He saw the stranger his brother had been talking with striding out now along the shore with Bar Nahemyah following him. He saw his mother walking among the firepits, pausing to speak with the town's other women. He saw Yesse, the priest's crippled father, seated by the nets, lifting fish in his hands and shaking his head. Yesse was *hebel*, too, but was allowed to be, because he was old and had served his tribe for many years. Someone must have carried him out to the sands.

Koach's eyes stung with moisture. His own grief seemed suddenly small. The fish had come back.

"Come on," he said, gripping the woman's arm. He could feel the warmth of her body through the sleeve of his father's coat. "I'll get you to a fire."

The woman cast him a quick glance before lowering her face again. Her eyes, shining with tears, were Hebrew.

Koach helped her down from the grasses onto the shore, her steps small and uncertain. Sand fleas darted from beneath their feet. She was shaking.

"It will be all right," Koach whispered. "It will be all right."

———

Afterward, Shimon could never explain how he came to be walking among the derelict boats with a basket of fish. Yeshua bar Yosef had spoken with such anguish and anger that there had seemed no choice but to respond. Now Shimon moved with quick steps along the boats, tossing fish into the sand. Everything inside him rushed about, as though the stranger had let the wind into his body the way a man might let wind into a house.

He heard the priest's rough voice.

"What are you doing, Bar Yonah?"

Zebadyah stepped between him and the next boat, pointing a gnarled finger at the basket of fish. His eyes were cold. "These," he said, "do not eat with us. They do not grieve with us. They mutter Greek prayers by our sea; they take our food. Sometimes they come up in the night and reach into unboarded windows, or tap at our doors. You know this. What are you *doing*?"

The windows of the house of Shimon's heart clacked shut, and rage boiled within like trapped summer heat. At this moment, he saw no kinship to his father in the priest's face. Zebadyah bar Yesse seemed old, shrunken, his fingers crooked and curled as though he were fighting to grasp sand. And this man, this weak, frightened man, who had once dared to strike his mother, now dared tell *him* how he should manage his nets.

"I am Shimon bar Yonah," he said. "I do what I please. This is my father's town. That is my father's boat. These are my father's fish." His voice hardened. "You . . . are not my father. Get out of my way."

Zebadyah's face flushed as though he'd been struck. He took a step back. "Shimon . . ."

"Get out of my way, old man," he said.

"Ezra," Zebadyah said hoarsely. "Remember Ezra. I tremble, Bar Yonah. There are fish, but all this can be taken away in a few beats of the heart. The waters wear away the stones. You are Yonah's son, and the town will look to *you*. Do not listen to that witch!"

Shimon shoved by the priest and walked on, ignoring everything but the blood in his ears and the rage in his heart. Finally, he threw the basket into the sand by one of the vagrants in disgust and turned away as the emaciated man reached into the basket with terribly thin hands.

Shimon stumbled to the last boat in the line, a boat with its hull stove in and no one sheltering beneath it. He sat down against it, closing his eyes. He could hear his own heartbeat. He breathed raggedly. The sun was growing hotter in the sky, and the insides of his eyelids were red and bright.

After a while he smelled fried musht and felt a cool cloth pressed to his head. "I brought you a musht." It was Yohanna's voice.

He opened his eyes against a blaze of light and then shaded them with his hand, wincing. He could hear the smacking of lips and the moans of the boat people all around him, as the fish both filled and tormented their long-empty bellies. Yohanna was crouching beside him. He handed Shimon the cloth, then passed him a sheaf that had one musht in it.

Yohanna smiled faintly. "They're cooking these, down by the water."

Shimon took it, felt the heat against his hand through the lake-weed. The fish must have just been lifted from the coals and wrapped moments before. His belly snarled within him as all of his hunger woke. He lifted the fish to his mouth, tore into the hot flesh with his teeth. It burned his lips.

He didn't talk until he'd finished the fish, and Yohanna just crouched nearby, watching his face.

"I spoke harshly to your father," Shimon said.

"I know." Yohanna took a slow breath. "He can be a hard man to speak with."

Shimon grunted.

After a silence, he said, "That man. What is wrong with him? He treats the boat people like they are his kin."

Yohanna's eyes widened. "Kin," he whispered. "'We are all kin.' God of Hosts, Shimon. That's where I've seen him. I *knew* I'd seen him."

He frowned. "What are you talking about?"

"The stranger. I saw him once. With Ha Matbil."

SCREAMING IN THE DESERT

YESHUA PACED the edge of the tide, heading up the shore away from the nets and the people gathered about them. His shoulders were tense, his eyes dark. The wind tugged his hair across his bruised face. The bruises did not bother Bar Nahemyah; he'd seen enough men stoned in the south to know that a man finds rocks hurled at him not when he offends God but when he offends other men.

Yeshua had a long, restless stride, and Bar Nahemyah had to strain to keep pace with the man.

"I let her die alone. I shouldn't have let her die like that. How could I let her die like that?" Yeshua stopped to look out over the water, but his tone was as restless and haunted as his stride had been. "I heard this town's hunger in the night, I heard it. I heard all of you. Night and day and night again in the desert. And the father . . . I heard the father weeping, weeping for you." He glanced at his hands, his face raw with grief. "I cried out, and the fish . . . but for what? You are still screaming."

Visions. The man was having visions. Bar Nahemyah trembled. Since the night of Ahava's death, the night he'd held his beloved's body shattered and bloodied in his arms, Bar Nahemyah's yearning for a *navi*, a messiah to save their ravened land, had hardened into cold steel within him. Now that steel was desperate and strong. The yearning for one who would be another Makkaba, riding against those who wounded their People, but who would be a *navi* also, one who saw visions in the desert or struck water from a rock. Some God-sent mighty one out of the stories of his fathers.

Barabba had not been that man.

"The fish and the birds heed you," Bar Nahemyah called to Yeshua. "You are the *navi*, aren't you?"

The stranger turned. "You think I'm a prophet, Zebadyah thinks I'm a witch." Bar Nahemyah forced himself not to look away from the intensity in his gaze. "You should worry less about what I am," Yeshua said, "and more about what I will do." He glanced back toward the nets. "What can't I remember?" He paused. For a few heartbeats, there was only the sigh of the water and the distant calls of the banished gulls. "Those corpses in the water. I can hear them even now. How did they get there?"

"The Romans—"

"The Romans." Yeshua's face tightened. "The Romans! The Romans didn't starve those women by the boats. The Romans didn't throw those dead in the sea and forget them."

"No." Guilt settled cold and heavy in his belly. "I did that."

Yeshua stopped and looked at him. Bar Nahemyah found his voice suddenly hoarse. "Help me make amends, *navi*. Israel is unclean. I would cut the rot out of its body. Barabba would cut off the whole limb, but that cannot be the way. You . . . you *care*. For every one of our People, even those under the boats. I saw that." Quietly, he knelt in the sand.

"No." Yeshua's voice was choked. "You mistake me for the Makkaba, or for your Outlaw. I don't know what I am. I don't know, I don't know, but I am not that."

Bar Nahemyah lifted his head, and he felt the first twinge of doubt. But he was on his knees, the hope in him too sharp to permit any turning back. "Place your hand on my head, *navi*. I will be the first to follow you. Say one word, but one word, and I will lift this shofar to my lips and sound a blast that every Roman in our land will hear. Don't you have eyes to see? Ears to hear? You said you have heard the screaming of our People!"

"I have heard." The pain in his eyes was terrible to see. "I hear them even now. Even now. The part of me that grew up a child in my father's house suffers exile. The part of me that walked out of the desert suffers the exile of all men and women, living and dead." He paused. "I have to get through the door. Where I have to go, what I have to do, it is on the other side of that door. That burning door. That burning, burning, burning . . ."

Bar Nahemyah gasped.

Yeshua's hands and face appeared to blaze with light. Bar Nahemyah felt the heat of it on his own skin, as though he were in the presence of mighty Eliya himself, who had burned the heathen priests from the land and summoned chariots of flame. His hands shook.

Then the heat and the light were gone.

Yeshua lowered himself to the sand and sat with his arms about his knees, his face stricken. "Can't step through," he whispered.

Bar Nahemyah was shocked to see tears on the man's face.

"Please," he said. "I know you are hearing what God hears. That is what the *navi* does. And it terrifies you, and it *should*. I understand your anguish. The things I have seen, *navi*. Things that make me want to cut out my eyes. I have seen Roman eagles on the walls of the Temple, on the walls of the *lev ha-olam*, the heart of the world. Children sitting with their backs to its gate with their ribs showing. I have seen Herod Antipas's hired dogs arrest craftsmen who couldn't pay their last coin to Caesar, and have them tossed into pits of the dead to be eaten. I saw a woman crawl to Barabba's feet and die there in the dust after pleading with him to free our land. She died . . ." He swallowed. "She died from bleeding to death, *navi*. She died because those desert men the Romans hire to do their killing when they've wearied of it had cut away her breasts. They cut out her sheath, then her tongue. And when she begged for help, she could do so only with her eyes.

"That was a Hebrew woman. That was one of my tribe. I saw her and others, strong men and weak, die begging God to send a *navi*, a messiah. I saw—" Bar Nahemyah choked a little. His voice went hoarse. "The earth is drenched in the blood of our People. *Our* People, ground into the dirt by Roman heels. Our wounded, screaming People."

Yeshua looked up at him wearily. "If you think to add more screaming, you are no son of Abraham nor of our father who watches us from above. You are someone else's son, not his." An edge of anger in his voice. "This land has always been taken in violence, but it has . . . it has never been held so. Our fathers did not hold and keep this land safe by violence against either the living or the dead, but by the Law."

"The Law!" Bar Nahemyah cried. He would *not* let this man hide, like Zebadyah, behind the Law. "The Law says a man may take an eye for an eye!"

"What will you do, Kana," Yeshua said slowly, "when you and the Romans have no eyes left?"

Kana.

Bar Nahemyah stopped, watching the man, holding the name in his mind.

"Kana," he breathed. The Hebrew word for *zealous*. "Kana. I will take that name."

"I think it is your name already," Yeshua said. "But put away this thirst for death, put it away, please; death will find us all soon enough."

"I don't understand you," Kana cried. "Are you a coward? Do you want us, all of us, all Hebrew men, to stand with our knives sheathed while Romans walk by and strike us across our faces, knock us to the dirt and take what they will? And you . . . you who hear . . . whatever it is you hear . . . you who speak with a voice of . . . of prophecy . . . what will you do? With your baskets of fish? What, will you feed men in the morning who will be dead by evening?"

"I . . . I don't know what the dusk will bring." Yeshua brushed the bruises on his arm with his fingertips. "I don't know. Only the father knows that."

THE SILENT WOMAN

WITH THE woman from the boats leaning hard on him, Koach approached the small fire Bar Cheleph had kindled in the sand near the tideline. He had dragged driftwood and weeds and grasses to toss into it, and now sat solitary on a log and dug out a few hot coals with a stick to make a smaller firepit, one for cooking. A basket of fish waited in the sand by his hip.

When Koach seated the silent woman across the firepit from him, Bar Cheleph said without looking up: "I made this fire, Hebel. Find another."

"You can't hit me, Bar Cheleph." There was no quiver in his voice. "Not here, where my brother and kin can see."

Bar Cheleph bared his teeth at Koach, but said nothing. He began laying the fish across the coals.

At the scent of the fish roasting, oils bubbling out from the slit in their gullets, Koach's mouth watered. The silent woman, too, stared at the fish.

"You hide behind Shimon bar Yonah as though you are his woman," Bar Cheleph said in a low voice.

Koach bit back his anger and took up a small stick, stabbing one of the fish. Letting out his breath slowly, he turned and lifted the fish to the woman's lips. Her eyes, still reddened from weeping, glanced at him gratefully as she bit in. Koach found the sight sensual, and disquieting: her head leaning forward, her small teeth cutting into the fish, her gaze lifted to his. He was suddenly aware of the woman's body beneath his father's coat, her curves. He swallowed.

She stared back at him a long moment before lowering her eyes. He took a breath. Shaken, he understood. Bereft of her last companion, hungry and alone, she was offering herself for the assurance of food. In the next moment she must have glimpsed his awareness of this, for her eyes dilated briefly—with fear, not with desire.

"You don't have to do that," he said, his throat dry. "The fish is a gift."

The fear in her eyes grew. Perhaps she had never been offered a gift before. Not being able to offer something herself, not knowing what he might want in return, or whether it would be something she had to give—this had to be terrifying to her.

Koach saw all that in her eyes, in one of those flashes of insight that very young men sometimes have.

"No," he said again. "I just want to see you eat."

Bar Cheleph grunted. "Take her up the shore and rut with her, Hebel. Might be the only woman you ever get. That is"—he smiled, his eyes cold—"if you *can* rut."

On any other day, Koach would have fallen silent and hung his head. But not this day. He rose to his feet, his good fist clenched at his side. All the fury and helplessness of the past year—of his whole life—rushed up at once, like a wave of the sea driving a boat before it. "My hand makes fittings," he shouted. "Fittings for the boats! So that they can get out on the water. So that the town won't starve. I am *useful*! What do *your* hands do?"

For a moment, Bar Cheleph kept his eyes on the coals. His face tightened, and Koach knew his words had cut deep, too. Bar Cheleph worked hard at mending nets, always worked hard at them, because his right hip didn't work the way it should, not since that Roman officer had thrown a hard cedar desk onto him in his rushed escape from the dead. Bar Cheleph could not stand easily in a boat, and he did not go out with his adopted brothers and Shimon to wrestle with the sea. Yet his arms were thick with muscle, and he had succeeded in not being *hebel*. Barely.

Now Bar Cheleph looked up, and his eyes were hot with hate. For a moment Koach was sure he meant to stand and strike him. He tensed. Then there was a footstep behind him, and a new voice, a sharp voice: "Will you always trouble my sons, Bar Cheleph?"

Koach glanced up as Bar Cheleph whirled.

Rahel stood behind him, leaning on a stick she'd plucked up from the sand, her eyes cold as winter.

Bar Cheleph's face darkened, even as Koach felt a rush of shame. Was he so *hebel* that he needed his mother to protect him?

"You've made the fire," Rahel said. "They need you at the nets, do they not?"

Bar Cheleph hesitated, grunted, "They do," and got unsteadily to his feet. He gave Rahel another dark look, then slid past her and hobbled down the shore. Rahel made a small noise in her throat and seated herself on the log where the priest's foster son had sat a moment before.

For a while they were silent. Rahel, her son looking down at the coals, and the unknown woman timidly biting at her fish. At last, his mother said, "Why do you share food with her?"

"She's hungry."

Rahel's eyes were cold and keen. "And what about Bat Benayahu?"

Koach's breath caught.

"I am your mother. Do you really think I sleep deeply enough that my son can slip out to the boats without me knowing it?"

Koach took a moment to breathe. Then said, "I meant to give her my pledge."

"I approve. Though Benayahu might not." Rahel turned to the silent woman. "Go. Now."

The woman started to shrink back, but Koach caught her arm in a fierce grip. "No. Stay, please."

"Son!"

"I offered her food and water, and that is father's coat."

Rahel's lips pressed together. "That hospitality was your brother's to give, not yours."

Koach looked aside at the silent woman as she nibbled on that fish. The fire was warm on his back and its warmth got inside him. He wished suddenly that he could know her name. His thoughts were loud within him: *I have fed her, protected her.*

I provided for someone.

For a woman.

For another person. Even a boat person.

To her, to this woman, I am not hebel.

Keeping her eyes averted from Rahel—as though to show that she offered no challenge to her protector's mother—the woman finished her fish, dropped the bones into the fire, and licked her fingers, as though years of hunger had taught her to waste not even the oils.

A shell of resolution hardened over Koach's heart, like ice over water. He felt the wooden horse, solid and reassuring, against his side: a thing he had made, a thing that was more than just a dream of some magnificent steed that would carry him and a woman he loved far from this place. At that moment he decided he would bring the carving to Tamar. He would find some moment when the *nagar* was away and bring this gift to her door. He would ask her why she hadn't come, and find his answer in her eyes.

"I am a man in our house also," he told his mother. "Always you are protecting me, telling me when to hide within the house, when not to step outside our door. I can't row. I can't help with the nets or the casting. But I can carve fittings, I can cook a fish, I can do *something*."

A long silence.

"You are like your father, little Koach." There was no accusation in his mother's voice, only sorrow. Koach glanced at her, and for just a moment, there was a woman in her face he didn't know—not his mother, with her stern hold on the life and future of her family, with her determination and the hard steel of her love for him—but a woman vulnerable and alone, a woman who did not unclothe her heart for anyone. This woman gazed out of Rahel's eyes for the briefest of moments, then was veiled again.

"So much like him," Rahel said, and there was pride and grief in her voice. "More than your brother. He is more like *my* father." She smiled faintly. "I wish you could have known your father. Yonah was a man who did as he pleased. But he also had two strong arms, and the love of all the fishers of Kfar Nahum." She bit her lip slightly, as though struggling to hold back words. Then she said, simply, "She is a stranger. Be careful, my son."

Rahel stood slowly, favoring her left hip. She glanced over Koach's head and her eyes widened. Koach saw the glow of reflected flames in her eyes.

"No," she whispered. "Oh, Bar Yesse, no."

Koach looked quickly over his shoulder. He could see dark smoke roiling over the grasses of the tideline and the dull red flicker of flames in the midday sun.

One of the overturned boats was burning, one of the relics of their fathers. A gust of wind blew the dark smoke toward the town itself. Against it stood a figure in white, a torch in his hand, the air wavering around him in the heat.

Then he heard the roar of his brother's voice, and men and women were leaping up from the cookfires and the nets with loud voices. Koach found himself on his feet, but Rahel was quicker; she was already running across the sand.

WALL OF FIRE

BURN THE shelters under which the boat people took refuge, and they would have nowhere to sleep, nowhere to stay. The unclean and the heathen would have to leave. No longer would they lie like fish on the shore, like so many meals, an invitation to the dead. They might try to take shelter in the emptied, boarded-up houses of Kfar Nahum, but squatters had been driven out before.

With smoke billowing dark all about him and scratching his throat, Zebadyah strode from one boat to the next, setting fire to each in turn. One of the boat people, only one, came at him. It was a wizened man who might have been only twenty, though his face was gnarled as tree bark and his hair gone white from suffering. The man was yelling; Zebadyah thrust his improvised torch in his face, and the man stumbled back, shielding his eyes.

The others just watched the fire from either side of it, standing still as cairns, their faces gray. The sight of them—so many hungering strangers, so many lurkers about his town—chilled Zebadyah. They looked to him like the dead.

The priest had never really stopped reliving that night. Even in the light of day, he often heard and saw those dead about him, felt the clamminess of his palms and the outbreak of cold sweat on his brow. So many times he'd had to stop and stand, breathe for a few minutes, persuade himself that he stood in the cool of his synagogue, his hand still poised over the scroll of Torah. He would gaze down at the scroll and its letters and breathe, and realize that night was long past.

Now he fired another boat, roaring out a song in desert Hebrew, a song of Dawid from centuries past. Never again would he stand by as strangers swarmed into his town, leaving his people starving, dying.

"Stop!" His brother's son was pelting up the shore toward him, a few others behind him. "These are our father's boats!"

"Our town will not become a midden for beggars and heathen!" Zebadyah shouted. "Yonah would not want that."

And, turning, he put another wind-bleached hull to the torch.

"No!" Shimon cried.

Yonah's son threw himself at the priest, his hand shoving hard against Zebadyah's shoulder, nearly knocking him to the grasses. In panic and fury, Zebadyah thrust the torch at Shimon's face. As Shimon staggered back, his hands over his eyes, the priest heard a cry behind him. As Zebadyah turned, Yohanna his son seized the torch just above his grip.

"You," Zebadyah gasped, the sight of his younger son like a physical pain above his heart. Shoving the pain back, he backhanded Yohanna, hard, across his face.

His son sprawled into the sand.

"Craven boy!" Zebadyah stood over him, livid. All the pain of the years tore its way out of him, making his voice savage. "You abandoned our town! You went out to live with unwashed heathen and bandits of the desert! No son of mine! *No son of mine!*"

While Yohanna still lay dazed, Zebadyah stepped away from the boats, out onto the sand where all could see him. He looked out at all their pale faces, his torch held high, cracking and spitting. "Remember the Grief of Ezra! Remember Ezra standing at the wall! Remember. We have no wall of stone or brick to keep out the unclean, either living or dead. But by the Law of El-Shaddai, Mighty God, we will make a wall of fire."

They stared back at him, some grim, some fearful, some bewildered. Yohanna rose slowly to his feet, a bruise already darkening his right temple.

Zebadyah's own eyes were hard. In the silence he could hear, loud as thunder, the cracking of wood beneath the devouring fire. The crackle of his torch. The quiet, dry sound of one of the boat people weeping. The sigh of the tide and the hiss of wind in the grass. Shimon slid to his knees in the sand, his eyes still covered. He moaned in pain. Zebadyah felt a stab of regret that was then eaten away by his anger: that *Yonah's* son, his *brother's* son, should shelter these vagrants and eaters of flesh.

"Bar Yesse . . ."

He stopped.

That was *her* voice.

Rahel bat Eleazar's voice.

"Bar Yesse . . ." She walked toward him across the shore, approaching from the cookfires. He did not answer her. He gave the next boat to the hungry flames.

She stepped past her kneeling son, her fingertips touching Shimon's shoulder briefly. "Bar Yesse," she called, "these boats are all that's left of so many we've buried and so many we couldn't. Bar Yesse . . . *Zebadyah*, please."

He watched the fire lick its way up the hull.

"Please, Zebadyah," she repeated softly.

He had never heard her say his name before.

When he faced her, her eyes held sorrow, sorrow deep as the sea, and even . . . empathy. For him. Looking in the eyes of this woman he'd wanted, this woman his brother had left behind, his shame deepened. The torch he held seemed suddenly repulsive and out of place.

"Zebadyah," she said. She bit her lip. "He would not have wanted this."

No one else on the shore spoke.

He hadn't noticed before how much she had aged, how many lines there were about her eyes, not until this moment—but she was all the more beautiful. The wind caught her hair and blew it across her face like a dark veil, and he could not bear her beauty.

"Bat Eleazar," he whispered.

When he spoke up, there was a note of pleading in his voice. "Everything is broken and unclean. Sons. Walls. Our whole land. Everything is broken."

She only gazed back at him. With those eyes.

The torch fell from his fingers and the sand half-smothered its flames.

He heard Yakob step near, felt his son's arm around his shoulders. "Come, abba," Yakob said against the crack and roar of the flames behind them, "come, let us get some fish. There are fish roasting, abba." His voice was soft, and Zebadyah's heart shrank within him as he recognized it—it was the same tone he used with crippled Yesse, when his own father was being difficult.

Worse still was the pity in Rahel's eyes.

"I am old, son," Zebadyah murmured. "I've grown old, as the Law is old."

He looked away from Rahel's face, his eyes dry though his heart was full of weeping. He let his oldest son lead him down the shore. All around him, men sprang into action, as though awakened abruptly from sleep, and ran to scoop water from the sea to fight the flames, but he didn't spare them a glance.

———

Shimon kept his palms pressed to his eyes, gasping for air. That had *hurt*. God, but that had *hurt*. But the sharp flecks of burning at his eyes did not hurt as much as the sound of fire eating the boats.

More than just old wood was burning.

He wanted to leap to his feet, take up a waterskin or fill his coat with sand that he could hurl over the flames to silence them. But even as he lowered his hands and blinked against the pain, he saw that it was too late. The wood burned quickly, and some of the boats already were mere piles of charred drift. He stared at them, numbly.

A hand gripped his shoulder. "Cephas," a quiet voice said, behind him.

And the sound of that voice was like a torch touched to the dry pine of his heart. This was all Yeshua's fault. He had come and upended *everything*. When had strangers ever brought good to their town? Matityahu the tax collector, who had trailed a Roman legion behind him. The swordsmen the Romans hired. The Outlaw on his dark horse. All of them had brought evil and dismay. Now there was this vagrant from the hills who brought up the quick and the dead.

"If you are of God and not a beggar or a witch, you who call up fish," he said without turning, his voice shaking with anger, "why were you not here ten years ago, fifteen?" His words became a shout. "Why heal us only after we're broken, feed us only after we've starved? Prophet or messiah, where were you *then*?"

The hand squeezed his shoulder. "I don't know. I don't know, I don't know. I don't know how to answer you. I can't see the road I have to walk, the road ahead or the road behind. It is dark and it is dark . . ." Yeshua's voice was thick. "The road is dark, and I don't know what I am. Or what to tell you. I am sorry."

The anger flowed from Shimon like water, leaving only weakness behind, and sobbing. He shook, on his knees in the sand, with the sea at his back and the boats of his People burning before him. He let the stranger hold his shoulder, and he just shook and wept. The pent-up fury and despair of fifteen years rushed through him like a school of fish with sharp teeth, chewing at him as they passed through and over him, leaving him gasping in wordless pleas against the violence of a world in which fathers sought to devour their children or in which some children were born wrong and some children starved.

"I am sorry, Cephas," the stranger kept whispering, over and over. "I am sorry."

Shimon might have wept there for an hour, or a month, or a year, or a year of years, for all he knew. But suddenly there were cries up by the houses of Beth Tsaida, and then shouts from the men at the nets and the fires, and the slap of running feet against the wet sand. Shimon looked away from the boats at last and saw men and women standing against the cookfires, their faces terrified.

A newcomer was running from the direction of Beth Tsaida, and he was Natan El, one of the younger fishers, only a little older than Shimon himself. The man stumbled, caught himself with one hand splayed against the sand, and got back to his feet. Then he was bolting down the shore toward them, his legs pumping. "The dead!" he cried. "The dead!"

Shimon felt all the warmth leave his body.

"It's Benayahu!" Natan El cried. "Benayahu the *nagar*! I saw him running north past the midden, bleeding from his hip. He said he saw the dead! In his house! His house! In the town! He saw the dead in his house! The dead!"

PART 6

KOACH'S BATTLE

KOACH DIDN'T hesitate. He cast the last fish from the coals to the feet of the silent woman who was gazing at him with wide, terrified eyes, and he sprang to his feet. Natan El was still scrambling down the sand toward them, screaming about the dead in Benayahu's house.

The *dead*.

There was shouting all along the shore, Zebadyah demanding to know what was going on, whether Natan El had actually *seen* the dead. Yakob was already striding north along the shore, stooping as he went to lift a large shell from the sea wrack left by the previous tide. The shell had been broken, and it had a jagged edge. "We have to find Benayahu!" he cried. Other men sprinted to catch up with him. To them it was already clear what had happened: Bleeding from his hip, Benayahu had fled Kfar Nahum, fled to the hills perhaps, so that he would not be boarded up within his house for the seven days of uncleanness while the town waited to see if he would die and then rise, moaning, to his feet.

But Koach realized something else.

The dead were in Benayahu's house.

In *Tamar's* house.

Koach cried out her name and broke into a run. The silent woman gasped as he left her by the fire. He'd forgotten her, forgotten Bar Cheleph and Bar Nahemyah, the stranger, even the great sheaves of fish, forgotten his grief beneath the boat, forgotten everything but the way Tamar's shoulders had trembled as her father beat her, and the hot shame in his chest as he watched and could not help. Everything but the warmth of her lips pressing his.

He ran.

———

Koach found the door of the *nagar's* house ajar. He touched it with his fingertips, his heart pounding, and felt the grain of the wood. He pushed slightly. Its hinge was well-oiled, unlike the door to his mother's house, and it swung open as silently as thoughts in the mind of God.

Some instinct older than speech or fire warned Koach not to call out. He slipped through the door. The atrium was empty, as was Benayahu's room across it, but Tamar's room was concealed by a heavy rug drawn over the entrance. The stillness of the house pressed on him, urging silence and slow movement. Hearing the roar of his own blood in his ears, Koach stepped across the atrium beneath a pale sky, leaving the door open behind him. As he neared Tamar's room, his breath seemed loud to him, and he held his hand over his lips. He could see that room in his mind so clearly: the little heap of bedding, a bundle of clothing in the corner, a small pot, a table for an oil lamp. The shadow of Benayahu against the small light. The rise and fall of his arm. Tamar's silent shaking, her silent tears.

He hesitated, then drew aside the rug.

The air behind it was warm and heavy with the scent of recent death. He could see her silhouette against the dim light. She stood on her bedding, with her back to Koach and her face to the boarded-up window, her hair lank and unwashed about her shoulders. Koach stood very still, his belly heaving at the smell. He clamped his jaw shut against the nausea.

Tamar was breathing, but far too slowly, as though she were asleep. He could see her shoulders rise and fall. She was holding her hands behind her at the small of her back—no, they were tied. Coarse fishing rope, the kind used for netting, wound savagely about her wrists. In the dimness, Koach could make out the dark line of it cutting into her skin.

Koach could neither step through nor let the rug fall and walk away. He could not move. His heart beat so fast from his run into the town—like that day Barabba had hunted him and Tamar had pulled him into her father's house, onto that very bedding where she now stood, stinking like fish left to rot on the shore. Koach kept looking at her wrists. He should step forward; he should unbind her. He should hear her whispering to thank him for coming to help her, at last, after the years of being beaten and broken with none to step between her and her father. He should help her now.

But his mind could not grasp the strangeness of this scene. This girl who had kissed him, tied in her own house. Reeking.

He heard a soft footstep behind him, at the outer door. A hoarse whisper: "*Koach?*"

His mother's voice.

The corpse standing on the bedding turned its head slowly, its eyes glinting in the dark. It hissed.

Gasping, Koach lurched backward, tripped on the edge of the rug, and fell, tearing the rug aside, letting in a flood of sunlight. Even as the floor knocked the breath from him, he caught a nightmare glimpse of Tamar's body stumbling toward him, one foot caught in linens, her arms trapped behind her, the dull sheen of her eyes.

Rahel screamed. Her cry held not only fear for her son but anguish, as from some night of grief years past yet horribly present.

The next moments were confused, like things witnessed during a fever. For an instant the dead girl was on top of him, her breath cold as winter on his throat. Her teeth snapped near his skin, her body shaking with a low growl. Then the weight of her was gone and he was rolling to the side and there was another scream from his mother, a scream that cut into his heart.

Koach scrambled to his feet and saw his mother and the girl grappling. They rolled on the floor and his mother was on top of her and drove the heel of her hand down against the corpse's chin, driving her head back. The neck didn't break, and the corpse lunged up, snapping its teeth at her, its jaws closing on her hair. Rahel gasped and fell back, pulling the corpse with her; there was a flash of metal in the sun, a knife in Rahel's hand, pulled from somewhere within her clothes. She pressed her arm to the corpse's throat, keeping it at bay while she sawed swiftly through her hair near the scalp above her right ear. It bit toward her hand and she jerked back, dropping the knife. It rattled across the floor.

Breathing in quick gasps, Rahel scooted backward away from the growling dead, kicking wildly as it lunged at her. Then Koach grasped his mother's arm. With a strength that startled him, he pulled her to her feet, his body hot with adrenaline. For an instant her gaze met his, her eyes wide. Then they *ran*.

They rushed into the atrium, with the corpse right behind them.

"Tamar, *please!*" Koach cried, glancing over his shoulder.

She was stumbling after them, snarling, her arms bound behind her, her hair wild about her face, her eyes glazed with death.

Mother and son ran to the outer door. Koach gasped her name under his breath, over and over again: *"Tamar, Tamar, Tamar—"*

They burst through the door out into the street, and turning, Koach saw the girl staggering after them, lurching across the threshold, her jaw distended in a snarl of hunger.

Rahel stumbled, and Koach tore his hand from her grasp.

"*Koach!*"

"No," he gasped.

He couldn't leave Tamar like that.

Even as he faced her, he heard running footsteps, a few shouts. Men from the shore, and a few women. Bar Cheleph was there, and Yohanna. Their faces were pale.

The dead girl turned its head, taking in all the living, and then lurched toward them. But it stumbled and sprawled on its face.

The townspeople formed a wide semicircle, keeping back while the corpse thrashed in the dirt. It lifted its head and its jaws gaped open, a low groan of hunger.

"Tamar," Koach whispered.

She had torn her dress in her fall, and Koach could see glimpses of her body. He recalled those nights on the rooftop, gazing at each other. His belly heaved and he twisted to the side, falling to his knees and retching into the dirt outside her father's house.

He knelt there, vomiting up everything he could and then vomiting up empty air, uncaring if the body of his love reached him or not, everything coming apart inside him. An arm around him and a murmur in his ear told him Rahel was with him, but he didn't turn to her. He just shook and shook and spewed out his insides.

A sandaled foot stepped past him. Koach glanced up in a haze, saw Bar Cheleph limping toward the corpse where it twisted in the dirt, having rolled onto its back. Bar Cheleph held a hooked fishing spear in his hand, perhaps taken from one of the fishers gathered silently about them. Anger had contorted his face. It was as if, seeing this dead girl bound in the dirt, helpless to seize and devour, he saw a moment at last where he might release his rage. His fury at his parents' deaths, at his town's, at all that had been

taken from his People by the living and the dead. He lifted his foot
and drove it into the corpse's face with a feral cry and a cracking
of bone beneath his sandaled heel.

"These things!" he shouted. "They eat up everything, everything
we have, everyone we love." The crowd watched him and the dead
girl, mute in their horror or in their catharsis. Their eyes glazed with
a particular kind of lust, a need to see violence done. Koach got to
his feet, breathing hard, just as Bar Cheleph bent over the corpse
and drove the spear down through its breast. The dead girl spat and
hissed, one side of her face crushed in, her wrists trapped beneath
her, her body twisting and writhing in the dirt. Her head jerked up
and her jaws snapped, but the fisherman was out of her reach.

Bar Cheleph stared down at her face, his own contorted. He
twisted the spear in her body, his weight on it holding her pinned
to the ground.

"Stop!" Koach cried.

Without thinking, he threw himself at Bar Cheleph, slamming
his small weight into the man's side and grabbing the spear with
his hand to wrest it from him and pull it free of Tamar's corpse.
Bar Cheleph gasped as the breath was driven from him. He backhanded Koach savagely, knocking the boy to his knees. A sigh from
the gathered men and women, as though they were witnessing
violence committed in a drama, as the Greeks do.

"Leave him alone!" Rahel cried, and struggled against two
women who held her back.

It took Koach a moment for his vision to clear. Then he saw
Bar Cheleph looming over him, his face cold. The corpse spat and
twisted on the ground, trying to get at either of them.

"Get back to your mother, Hebel," Bar Cheleph snarled.

But now Koach's body was hot with his own anger, and he
was wild with his own grief, which was no less than Bar Cheleph's.
Koach glanced at the dead girl's face and his eyes were dry. *Hebel.*
Useless. He had not been able to help this lovely girl who had

kissed him, this girl who had protected him from the Outlaw, this girl who had been kind to him. He had not saved her from her father's blows. Nor from this.

Bar Cheleph turned his back to the boy, wrenched free the spear, and drove it in again. The corpse uttered no sound of pain, only frustrated, animal hunger. It threw its small body from one side to the other, but could not free itself of the spear, nor lift its arms to catch at the warm, enticing life above it. Whether it could hear the drumbeat of a living heart or the ocean sound of Bar Cheleph's blood or the wind of his breathing—whatever it sensed that made it yearn for meat and flesh—it could not reach him. The girl's lips gaped wide and it *screeched*, a sound that cut into all who were listening like the crack of a Roman whip. And the screech went on and on, a primal demand for life and food, a demand that could never be satisfied.

That screech wrenched Koach into motion. Maybe he had been *hebel*, but he could not allow himself to be useless to her now. Groping with his hand in the dirt, he found a jagged stone a little larger than his hand.

Koach got shakily to his feet. Bar Cheleph ignored him; he was merely the useless, unclean boy that he had beaten aside. The man's whole attention was on the screeching corpse. Koach looked down through a blur of moisture at the stone he held, something heavy and solid and final.

He had to do this.

There was no one else.

"Forgive me," he whispered.

Koach bent quickly over the corpse, startling a shout from Bar Cheleph. Tamar's body lunged at him, her jaw gaping. With a cry, Koach drove the stone down into her head. He screamed her name once, then fell silent but for a small, choked sound.

WOUNDS FROM THE DEAD

SILENCE IN the street.

"My son," Rahel whispered.

But Koach didn't answer. He just crouched over the body of the young woman he'd loved, the woman who had touched him so often in his dreams as he lay in the quiet hours in his bedding. He squeezed his eyes shut and breathed raggedly. The stone fell from his limp hand, a soft thud into the dirt.

No one spoke. No one moved. Rahel swayed a moment on her feet as though feeling faint, but she didn't approach. Bar Cheleph took a few unsteady steps away, looking on, wild-eyed.

Koach opened his eyes and, against all Law and custom, he pressed his hand to the dead girl's cheek. Her skin was cold. So cold.

His chest clenched in on itself. Pain, a new pain. He had known fear and rejection and grief, but this was a new loss. She was someone he had loved, someone whose heart had mattered to him, someone he had yearned to protect. Gone, torn from her life as savagely and quickly as a fish might be ripped from the sea.

"Tamar," he whispered.

There wasn't much left of her face; he had destroyed her with that blow from the rock. His hands began to shake.

She hadn't forsaken him.

She had never intended to miss their tryst.

While he had been reviling her bitterly in his heart, she had been in that room, dying. He leaned back on his heels and just breathed. Just breathed. Then he took from his pocket the carving he'd made for Tamar, the wooden horse.

He turned it over and over in his hands, feeling the smooth length of its limbs, the intricate carving of its mane, the small roundness of its eyes.

She was dead.

She had tried to *eat* him.

But more than that, she was *gone*. The *shedim* within her corpse had eaten her heart and her soul, leaving only hunger behind, only that.

Koach didn't know how long he sat there, turning that carving in his hands as though it were the only thing real left in the world, the only thing that wouldn't fade away and die. But at last he tucked the carving gently into the bodice of Tamar's nightdress, giving it to her as he'd meant to. Then he rose to his feet, while others around him murmured. He stepped up through Benayahu's door and into his atrium, hardly aware of his own movements. He found the small knife his mother had lost and brought it back to the body. No one took a step toward the corpse; no one bothered Koach as he knelt by Tamar and turned her gently to her side. Then he sawed at her bonds, one-handed. She must have been bound by her father, who had then fled his fevered daughter and his house when she stopped breathing.

Or even *before* she stopped breathing.

But no, there was blood on her mouth; she had risen and bitten him. But how had *she* been bitten? How? Her father had kept her so tightly locked away. Had she started down toward the boats to meet her lover, then been set upon by some corpse out of the sea? Run home then in terror, bleeding? Or had something crawled into their house? Had she eaten a fish that had nibbled at a corpse? Could such a thing make the fish unclean, and the one that ate it unclean? If so, why wasn't the whole town defiled? How had this *happened*?

The cords snapped with a quiet, rasping sound, and Koach set down the knife, his hand trembling. He lay Tamar on her back again and rose to his feet, breathing hard. She had been *bound*. That man—that man who had beaten Tamar, night upon night upon night—he had just tied her like a slave and *left* her here. Clear in his heart he recalled all the times Tamar had walked painfully to the roof after a severe beating. He recalled his own fantasies of killing her father, of driving a fish hook through his breast, of taking a boat and slipping out to the sea by night with her, to seek some far town on the other shore, some place where he would not be shunned for his withered arm, some place where a cripple might find a way to feed and shelter the woman he desired. He recalled the beatings he had seen, how he had seen them—and done nothing. Now it was too late.

There was a bellow, and without turning he knew that his brother was forcing his way through the onlookers. "Koach!" Shimon cried hoarsely. "Koach!"

Koach didn't answer. His fist was clenched at his side, his other hand limp and useless. He felt Rahel's hand on his shoulder, but he shrugged it away.

"Koach!" Shimon shouted again. Then a grunt as he shoved someone out of his path. "Let me by!"

Koach glanced back then and saw his brother break free of the press, all those faces drawn with horror. Bar Cheleph had faded back into the crowd; Koach caught a glimpse of his face, flushed as though with shame.

Shimon stopped; the two brothers faced each other. The rage in Koach's breast went out like a candle at a breath of the *shedim*, a gust of wind in the night. He looked from his brother's face to Tamar's, her lips still pulled back as for a snarl or a screech; her fingers still half-curled into claws, her chest completely still. Koach unclenched his own fist, and fatigue settled over him like heavy mud. His hand began to shake.

"I am not strong enough to carry her to the tombs," he said.

Shimon glanced at the rock that had fallen from his brother's hand and then at Koach's face. This was his younger brother, the feeble one, whose very birth had failed the hopes of his family. Yet what he saw now in Koach's eyes struck him to the heart. This was no boy looking back at him with tears in his eyes; this was a young man. In his face Shimon saw graven both the stubborn strength of his father and the ferocity of his mother, to defend his own. A hot pool of regret settled in his belly—regret for his words earlier, by the boats.

Grimly, Shimon shrugged the heavy water-coat from his shoulders and lay it on the ground beside the girl's corpse. Then he took the fishing gloves from his belt and put them on. He took hold of the body and rolled it into the coat. "I will take her," he said, wrapping the coat about her like a shroud. He pulled the hood over her face, shutting away that feral grimace, that blood-stained mouth.

His brother watched him silently as he lifted the girl into his arms. She was light, as though he held only a few coats. Neither of them said anything. What was there to say?

A hand gripped his shoulder. "I will help, Bar Yonah." That was Bar Nahemyah, his gaze fixed on the dead girl.

"No need, Bar Nahemyah."

"Call me Kana," the man said softly. "It is a long walk—"

He fell still at Shimon's look.

Shimon turned toward the crowd, who stood between him and the walk out of this town to the tombs of his People. He could feel Koach's gaze on his back. The sun overhead seemed too cold. After a moment, those gathered parted to let him pass, standing aside, staring at him as though they were witnessing some holy rite. Bar Cheleph leaned back against the wall of the house opposite Benayahu's, his face lowered. As Shimon passed his mother, whose face was flushed as from exertion, she lifted her voice softly and began to sing the Words of Going, the most ancient of songs, the keening lament for the dead. The sound made Shimon's eyes burn; he could never hear it without recalling the singing on the hill the morning after most of Kfar Nahum died. The grief of the town's women, carried to him on the air as he cared for his mother and infant brother, as he ran down to the sea to watch for his father's boat.

Having passed through the crowd, Shimon looked back. He saw his brother still standing alone where the body had lain, with that haunted look in his face. Then Shimon could not hold back his fury. The last of the day's numbness broke, and all the anger of a fatherless son poured out, and in that moment he knew the breach in the wall of his numb grief could never be repaired, never be shored up again. Though his heart was naked and torn with pain, he faced the men and women of his village. His gaze swept them all, and some of them ducked back as though he had struck at them. Bar Cheleph didn't look up.

"The Romans," he said in a voice cold as the tomb, "say we are a small people. Would you prove them right? Do we defile our dead? This is not worthy of our fathers. It is not worthy of our town. It is not worthy of our People. You are small men, and you shame me."

His face quivered with emotion; then he got it under control. "My brother, who you call *hebel*, he is the only one today who is *koach*, the only one whose heart and will are strong." Shimon spat in the dirt before their feet and glanced at Bar Cheleph, who didn't look up. "I am ashamed of you," he said.

Bar Cheleph's shoulders tensed.

Then Shimon turned and carried that dead girl from his town.

Koach lowered himself to his knees and touched his forehead to the earth, oblivious to his brother's receding footsteps and to the whispers around him. "God," he murmured, "let me sleep and find that this is only the dream country." His shoulders shook, but he did not weep. He heard his mother's voice fall silent. He heard some walk by him and depart. He paid none of them any mind, just pressed his face to the dirt. It was like something deep inside him was lost and he couldn't find it, didn't know what it was, didn't know where to start searching.

He heard Bar Cheleph, his voice anxious. "Bat Eleazar, I meant no offense to your son."

By which he meant Shimon.

Koach didn't hear his mother's reply. He whispered, "You killed her."

Stillness.

"You killed her," Koach said. Louder. Lifting his face from the dirt.

Bar Cheleph looked shaken. "She was already dead, Hebel."

"You *killed* her." His voice a hoarse whisper. "You never even saw she was hurting. That she needed help." His chest went hot. "You all killed her."

Bar Cheleph drew back, as though wishing to flee. Yohanna, who stood near, took his arm and murmured something in his ear.

Around them, a few other faces went ugly. Koach braced himself, every line in his body taut and furious, but before either words or blows could fall on him, he heard a low gasp.

"Koach—"

Turning, he saw his mother swaying on her feet. Her face had gone gray, her eyes a little glazed. She held her right hand pressed to her left arm just below the shoulder, and with a shock Koach saw that her sleeve had darkened beneath her grip.

"Koach . . . I don't . . . I don't . . ."

Her voice was faint.

Then her eyes rolled back, and with a slow, terrible kind of grace, she slumped to the ground as though between one heartbeat and the next her body had been emptied of her spirit.

WHAT HAPPENED AT RAHEL'S HOUSE

KOACH WAS by her side at once. He pressed his left hand to her brow, and paled. She was burning.

"No," Koach whispered.

Slowly, as his heart beat brutally within his chest, he drew Rahel's sleeve up her arm. The underside of the sleeve, between wrist and elbow, had gone dark with blood.

Then he found it: a bite in her arm, just above the elbow. Flesh had been torn out of her arm, and only the thickness of the wool sleeve she'd pressed to the wound had prevented it from spilling her life's blood already to the earth at her feet. Now that she had fainted, it ran down her arm in a rush like red water, darkening the soil beneath her. With a cry, Koach pressed the sleeve quickly against the wound again, holding it there with his one hand. His eyes burned; she had concealed the bite from her sons, had not wanted them to know she was about to die.

About to die.

His legs gave out beneath him; he found himself sitting by her, everything a blur to him but the wound on her arm and the pressure he held against it. *Tamar, Rahel. The waters wear away even the stones, and nothing is left.*

Yohanna crouched by him. His voice came from a great distance. "—*have to get her inside. Make her comfortable. Let me help, Bar Yonah.*"

He glanced up at the older man's face, saw the pity in his eyes, but it was like looking at a reflection in the water rather than at something real.

"*She needs you to be strong, Koach. Strong.*"

Strong. His name, Koach. The word for *strong*.

He heard his breathing, loud in his ears. "Yes," he whispered. "Inside."

Yohanna placed his arms around Rahel and lifted her, his face strained; Koach got his arm around Rahel's legs and did what he could to help carry her; people gave way as the two carried Rahel awkwardly toward the door of her house, so near Benayahu's. At the doorstep, Koach set her legs down and fumbled a moment with the latch on the door, then swung it open, putting his shoulder against the heavy wood. Yohanna carried Rahel through, and Koach followed, his heart pounding, panic rising dark and shrieking in his mind.

As he caught the door with his good hand and began to swing it closed again, he found Bar Cheleph on the doorstep.

"I'll help," Bar Cheleph said quietly, his face dark with shame.

Koach shut the door in his face.

Yohanna carried Rahel into the atrium while Koach ran and gathered up blankets from her room. He made a small bed by the olive tree, then left Yohanna to lay his mother there and hurried for water from her ewer. When he came back, he found Yohanna pacing. Rahel lay with her eyes closed, her fingers moving restlessly over her blanket. Small whimpers came from her throat, each of them like a shock of ice to Koach's heart.

"She's going to die," he whispered. "She's going to die."

"I have to get the *navi*," Yohanna said, his face pale. He bolted toward the door.

Koach heard his steps. Heard the door sway open, heard it slam shut. He sank to his knees by his mother, a bowl of water in his hand. Some beast was clawing its way up his chest, tearing him. An old beast, the helplessness. He was *hebel* again. His mother was dying, dying the worst of deaths—the one where the body staggered, lurching, to its feet once it no longer breathed. His eyes blurred. His brother wasn't here; there was only him. And he could do nothing.

He took her right shoulder and shook her gently. "Amma," he moaned, "amma."

Her breathing was shallow. Her eyes opened at his call, making him gasp, but they didn't focus; they seemed to stare past him, at the open sky.

"My son," she rasped.

He fumbled, found her hand, clutched it fiercely. His throat was dry. "I am here, amma. I'm here."

"My son, your father would have loved you." She began to shake, as though she were terribly cold, though her face shone now with sweat. "I kept you too safe. I was so . . . afraid . . . for you. He would have seen how strong you were. He would have been proud of you."

"Amma," he whispered, pleading.

"*Tzelem elohim*, my son. Your face is God's face; you are his likeness. What does your arm matter. Your face is . . . so beautiful. Tell Shimon . . ."

She fell silent.

"What? What do I tell him?"

But she didn't say anything more. Her breathing was even shallower. Koach watched the tiny rising and falling of her chest, cold with fear.

———

He didn't know how long he sat there watching her die. He didn't care. In all the town only Rahel and Tamar had spoken to him as to one who might be respected and loved. And perhaps Bar Nahemyah. Now he would be alone. He'd thought he was alone before. Now he would truly be alone. What hopes he'd kept secret had been crushed; what people he'd leaned on had been torn from him.

Breathing against the tightness in his chest, Koach tucked Rahel's blanket about her. That took some doing with only one hand, and for a moment he glanced down at his lifeless arm and hate seared through him, self-hate, hot as a furnace. He struck his chest with his left hand, because the pain of that small blow distracted him and jarred him back to the present, to the things that needed to be done. He got up, went to the little room that was Rahel's during the winter, took down his father's *tallit* from its peg, and brought it back to her. He lay it folded beside her, then took her right hand and curled her fingers around its edge. His father could not be here, at his mother's last breath. There was only his son, only one of his sons, the worthless one. His father's shawl was the only small comfort he knew how to provide.

A heavy knock at the outer door startled him.

But he didn't rise until the knock came again, and Yohanna's voice called: "Bar Yonah! Bar Yonah!"

Numb, he went to the door and opened it. Yohanna stood at his doorstep, and with him stood the bruised, haggard beggar-man he'd seen on the shore, the man who was as alone as he.

Yeshua looked past him, toward the atrium. He looked exhausted, his eyes bleary.

"Will you let us enter?" Yohanna said softly.

Koach hesitated. Once you invited someone over the threshold, they were no longer a stranger. They were your guest, as fully under the protection and provision of your roof as your own kin. You were bound to them, and they to you.

But he had strength neither to argue nor to shut the door. He could hear his mother's ragged breathing in the atrium behind him, and that quiet, desperate sound to him was as loud as shakings in the earth. He nodded tensely.

Yeshua stepped by him, without a word. Yohanna followed, gripped Koach's good shoulder, then shut the door for him.

As if in a dream, Koach followed the other men into the atrium. The stranger seated himself by Rahel—gently, as though she were sleeping and he didn't want to wake her. He just sat by her in silence, as Koach had moments before. There was sorrow in his face.

Seeing that, the heat of Koach's fury returned. His mother would not live long. He understood what was coming, as much as any young man could. He didn't want anyone else here, certainly not any stranger to their town. Why had he opened the door?

"Why did you bring him here?"

"He is the *navi*," Yohanna said softly.

For a moment, the word stirred Koach despite his fear. A word of hope from remembered stories. Rahel's stories. Always when the dead had risen to devour the People, there had been a *navi*, one anointed to counsel and preserve their tribe. Elisa, who had called the very *malakhim* of heaven down in chariots of flame to scorch the unclean dead from the earth. Yirmiyahu, who had faced a corrupt king and begged him to shatter the gates that locked in the living with the dead. Daniyyel, who had prayed an entire night unharmed in a cave of walking corpses.

But how could this man, in his ragged brown robe, with those bruises on his face . . . how could he be the *navi*? Koach peered at those livid marks on his skin, and his throat tightened. They were so much like Tamar's bruises. This man had been beaten, like her. He was a man someone had failed to defend.

"I know him now," Yohanna said. "I've seen him before. I couldn't remember where at first. It was last summer, with Yohanna ha Matbil in the wilderness about the Tumbling Water. I was there." He was quiet a moment, and when he spoke, he did so quietly, as though fearing to disturb either Rahel or the stranger. "We light few lamps and we live in the dark and we try to sleep, Bar Yonah. We don't want to remember. Your brother seems content to sit in the silence, to sit *shiva* until his last breath, but this silence grew too heavy for me. So I left. To live with Ha Matbil beneath the open sky. I was there on the Night of Five Hundred *Mikvot*, when so many were immersed in the river to be cleansed. Nothing I've said about that night is an untruth. People's faces shone as they rose from the water. Men, women. And the moon was full and the stars as bright as they were for Moshe in the desert. And I heard the singing, I *heard* it. The *malakhim*, the angels of God, calling to each other in the dark, from one hill to the next. Like something important was happening in the land, a blessing, at last. That night we did not hear the moaning of the dead but the singing of angels."

He fell silent for a moment, but Koach didn't say anything. He was barely listening. He watched the rise and fall of his mother's breathing. In his heart, he stood in a dry, bleak place, where Yohanna's words were little more than the wind in the stones.

"At sunset before the song in the night," Yohanna said slowly, "a man came walking down to the shore. Ha Matbil immersed him in the water. And after, as the man walked from the east bank out into the ravines, Ha Matbil pointed him out to me and to the other men who were with us, and he said—I remember it—*There is the* olah, *the lamb of our God, who takes away the evil and the uncleanness from the world. A* navi *has come like one Israel has never seen, and I am not worthy even to tie his sandal-string.*

"That's what brought the hundreds. It was a mighty sign, Bar Yonah. That night they came to the water. So many. Hundreds. All of them kneeling before Ha Matbil, confessing all they had done and all they had seen and not stopped, every uncleanness they had witnessed or made happen in our land. And Ha Matbil gave them to the water and brought them up again. To each one of them he said, *The time of God is near. Be ready. It is near.* And oh, Bar Yonah, what we heard. What we *heard.* Ha Matbil, he looked at the hills, at the singers none of us could see. He saw what would come—like a *navi.* And he said, *It is near.*" Yohanna looked rapt. "Your brother thinks this man from Natzeret has one of the *shedim* eating him from within. But I think he is of God."

"This." Yeshua spoke suddenly, though he did not lift his gaze from the rise and fall of Rahel's breathing. "This. This is what the father wanted me to see. What he whispered in my ear, out in the wind, in the rocks, in the wind in the rocks. It has to be, it has to be. This. This is what I have to do. This . . ." His voice trailed off. Yohanna stared at him intently.

"She's dying," Koach choked.

"She is dying," Yeshua said. "And I am dying, and you are dying, and those women and men out by the boats are dying. We are all dying, dying, dying . . ." The stranger traced his fingertips over Rahel's arm, over the torn edge of her skin. She didn't stir. "But not today. No more dying today."

With fingers as gentle as though he were touching a lover, Yeshua opened Rahel's right eye and gazed into it a moment. Her eye was very round and very dark, but she gave no sign that she was aware of him. Koach tensed—that a stranger should touch his mother!—yet he found himself waiting, waiting for he didn't know what. Breathless.

Yeshua's voice was soft and distracted, as though he were talking to himself, or to someone who sat right beside him, someone only he could see. Koach held himself back, tense.

"My mother . . . she told me once that our father did not promise a life without pain," Yeshua murmured, closing Rahel's eye. His words were slow and spoken with terrible clarity. "Not without pain. Only that he would weep with us. Only that his heart would break. Only that he would take each moment of suffering, each death, each, and hold it in his hands, and . . . and bring from it something, something even more beautiful than what was lost. A forest of cedar grows from a field of ash, and each seed, every seed must fall to the earth, fall and fall and crack open and die before it can become a barley plant." He touched Rahel's hair, stroked it a moment. His gaze never left her face.

He began singing softly, words in the dialect of old desert Hebrew, and after a while he hummed them, as though he needed his mind elsewhere and could no longer spare any of it to make articulate words. He moved his fingers carefully over Rahel's arm and hummed that quiet desert melody, one Koach had never heard before—though hearing it, he could imagine men and women of his People singing it or playing it on flutes as they stood at the doors of their tents, long before they came to this land.

Koach watched like a man gazing over the brink of a cliff, his heart thunderous inside him.

Then Rahel sighed softly and closed her eyes, and the stranger moved his fingers back and forth over the inflamed bite, kneading her torn skin as though shaping clay with his hands. The bite closed, and then, a moment later, it was gone. Simply gone. The olive skin of her arm was smooth and unbroken as though it had never suffered so much as the press of a thumb.

THE SCENTED FIRE

RAHEL DREW in a shuddering breath, and her eyes opened. For a moment they remained glazed as with fever, and then they cleared. Her eyes focused first on Yeshua, and a light came into them as though she had stepped out of the desert to find her door open and a banquet in her home, with friends waiting for her whom she'd thought long dead. Koach had never seen such a look in her eyes.

"At last," Rahel whispered.

Yeshua didn't speak. There was a sheen of sweat on his face, as though he were the one who had wakened from fever. He lifted his fingers from her arm and sat back, his breathing ragged.

The word "amma" caught in Koach's throat; he sat staring at his mother. What he had just seen could not be; he didn't dare move, didn't dare find out if what he'd seen was real or if he was only sitting in the dream country, deceived in thinking himself awake.

Then Rahel's gaze flicked toward him, and she breathed his name.

Koach let out a cry and flung himself down at her side, putting his good arm around her. "Amma!" he cried. "Amma!"

"My son, my son," she wept.

Yeshua and Yohanna were forgotten. Koach wept openly against her shoulder, enveloped in the scent of his mother's hair and the sharper scent of the blood that was drying on her clothes.

"What happened?" she rasped. "What . . . I was . . . burning up. I was bitten, unclean. Son, what has happened?"

He squeezed his eyes shut and just held her.

"Ah, Rahel." Yeshua's voice. "Rahel, Rahel."

The stranger stood unsteadily. In a moment Yohanna was at his side, offering an arm for him to lean on, but Yeshua pressed his hand against Yohanna's chest and then stepped away on his own. His face had gone white and his eyes were wild like a man staring into the great emptiness of the desert, an emptiness that perhaps not even God could fill, an emptiness that devoured all things, all peoples.

"I need air," he whispered. And he moved out across the atrium, almost stumbling on the way. Yohanna hurried after.

Rahel was shaking. "I was dying," she breathed.

"You're all right, amma. You're all right."

She drew in quick breaths. "Yes. Yes, I am." She lifted herself onto her elbows. "We have a guest, son. Help me up. We need to get him food and water. Help me."

───

Yeshua sank against the wall of the atrium, breathing shallowly. Quickly Yohanna swept up one of the blankets from Rahel's bedding, and drew it about the stranger's shoulders. His voice was a low murmur. "*Rabboni*, it will be all right. Just breathe."

Yeshua coughed. "Water."

Yohanna brought him some in a clay bowl from the ewer at one corner of the atrium. Yeshua's hands shook when he took the bowl, but he drank deeply. A little water trickled from the corner of his mouth, making Yohanna acutely aware of his own thirst.

Yeshua lowered the bowl from his lips; the water sloshed in the bowl, cupped between his calloused hands. "I should've . . . should've asked for . . . for wine, not water."

"You healed my kinswoman, and my friend's mother," Yohanna said softly. "I will bring you all the wine in Kfar Nahum if you ask it."

Yeshua glanced down at his hands. "Healed," he whispered. "How, how did I do that?"

"You sang," Yohanna whispered back.

"I asked," Yeshua said. "I could hear her, hear her hurting, hear her dying. I could hear it so *loudly*. And I asked, I asked, I called out . . . Like with the fish. Like with the gulls. Like with . . ." He groaned. "For just a moment I *remembered*. I remembered *everything*. Everything. All of it, all of it from the desert. Every word, every . . ." His eyes glistened. "What I'm to do, and why, and what I *am*. And now it's gone, all of it gone. Why can't I hold on to it, Yohanna, why?" He squeezed his eyes shut. "All those nights, those nights with my back to a rock, a rock in the desert. All the screams in my ears. And it's hard, so hard, to recall anything else but that moaning, that moaning that won't stop, that will never, ever stop . . ." He swallowed. "Help me, Yohanna. Help me up. Help me stand."

Yohanna reached for his arm, gripped it, and lifted him to his feet. Something nagged at the edge of his mind. Then, as he steadied Yeshua with a hand at his shoulder, the thought burst in on him with a suddenness like a crack in the mast. He gasped.

"I will be back." Releasing the *navi*'s arm, he ran for the door. "I will be back!"

He flung open the door, burst through, and slammed it behind him. In the street, he shoved aside Bar Cheleph and another young man who were laying planks of heavy wood beside Rahel bat Eleazar's doorstep. He hardly noticed them; he broke into a run, and he ran faster than he had ever run in his life, faster even than on the night of the dead when so many young men and women he knew had died. He ran and his heart beat with a hope that was so violent it was like panic.

———

Yeshua leaned against the wall of the atrium, drinking his water, his eyes dark with thought. Having almost forgotten he was there, Koach helped his mother kindle flame above the coals in the cook-pit in the atrium. There was another pit near it, a smaller one, long unused, but Rahel kindled it also, and took a small pouch of spices and herbs and sprinkled them over the coals, and their redolence filled the air. Koach had not smelled that in . . . nearly a year. The scented fire. The coals on which you would lay a fish's heart to keep the *shedim* away.

"I hope it will," Koach whispered, watching the little flames. He should have been the one to carry Tamar to a tomb. It should have been him. But he couldn't have carried her with one arm. He should have gone with Shimon, at least.

"I hope it will too, son." Rahel didn't need to ask what he meant. The scented fire seemed to them small and fragile, but perhaps it meant no one else would be eaten.

"I thought we'd have to bury you, too," Koach whispered, blinking quickly. He looked to the stranger, Yeshua, a surge of gratitude and confusion in his heart.

"Don't tell Shimon," Rahel said. "Your brother has worries enough." She closed the pouch and set it aside. "The Sabbath is coming," she whispered. "This evening. If my sons can rest, really rest, with full bellies . . ." She smiled faintly. "That, I ask for. I feel . . . so weak. Like I might fall over."

Koach said nothing. He was thinking. For the first time since that cry on the shore—"The dead! The dead!"—he was thinking.

Something had fed on Tamar, but hadn't eaten anyone else. It had found her on her way to the shore to meet him, and either she'd . . . *stopped* . . . it, or after wounding her it had pursued someone else, following them away from the town. And the attack must have happened some way up the shore from Koach's own hiding place beneath the boat, because he'd heard no cry from her, nor any moan from the corpse.

He tried to make sense of that.

The corpse might have been missing part of its throat, might have been unable to voice one of the low wails of the dead.

But he should have heard *her*.

Surely he would have heard her scream for help.

Perhaps Tamar had needed to take the long way through the stone houses, to avoid watchful eyes. Or there might be some other reason she had not been near.

Or perhaps she *had* been.

Perhaps the thing had seized her, torn into her before she even knew it was there, and perhaps she—who had learned how to suffer beatings in silence—had swallowed her own cry, to keep him from running out to her.

That thought was more than he could bear.

"There are still dead out there," Koach said.

Rahel's hands paused in their work, but only for an instant. Then she whispered, as though to herself or to God, "I ask only for rest for my sons. And for me."

The dying wasn't over yet.

Koach thought he knew why the corpse that had killed his beloved was not in the town, nor on the shore. Tamar had led it away, in silence, led it away from her lover and her town, before finding some way to slip back unseen by it. And when she had, the fever had already been on her, the fever that would burn her away, leaving her body empty for one of the hungry *shedim* to make its home in. She hadn't come to him to say goodbye. She had run to her father's house, perhaps with dawn already in the sky, to die there.

To protect him.

To protect their town.

She had been the strong one.

Rahel looked at him, and her face softened. "It is all right, my son," she said. "Sometimes you have to weep."

He lifted his hand to his face. His cheeks were wet.

"How do you bear it?" he whispered.

Memory flickered in her eyes. "You just do."

"Does it get better?"

"No. It doesn't." She reached for a small basket lined with cloth, something to place fish in. "But you get stronger. The burden is not less heavy, but you are more able to carry it."

Koach's face crumpled, "I want her back, amma."

Her face crumpled, too. She held out her arms and he threw himself into them, as he had many times when he was a small boy.

"I know," she whispered into his hair, holding him tight. "I know."

———

A heavy slam of wood against wood interrupted them. Koach gave a start and sprang to his feet.

The door. It was the door.

He exchanged a fearful glance with his mother. Her eyes hardened.

Koach ran to the door and pulled it clumsily open. A plank of rough-hewn pine barred the way at the height of his shoulders, and two men—Natan El and Mordecai—held it in place while Bar Cheleph swung his hammer.

He was *nailing* it to the doorposts!

"What?" Koach gasped.

Bar Cheleph's eyes were wide with fear. "Get back, Hebel. All within are unclean. You'll die, and rise," he said. "But we won't let you break loose to devour the town."

The men let go of the board and reached for another.

Heart racing, Koach glanced past the men. The street outside had emptied. A few people watched from the doorways of other houses, eyes showing their whites. He caught sight of the silent woman, standing in the shade cast by the nearest wall of Benayahu's house. She had pressed herself to the wall as though to make herself unseen or unnoticed. Her face was white with terror.

"No one's unclean within," Koach said. His throat tightened. "My mother lives."

"Not for long." The board clacked into place beneath the other, and Bar Cheleph set an iron nail at one end and drove the hammer against it. The sound was fierce and brutal and loud, the board driven against the doorpost and the doorpost driven against the stone wall of the house. Bar Cheleph kept swinging the hammer, rhythmic blows as though the house were being beaten. Koach shrank back, a wild image in his head of the house boarded up for the ritual seven days, he and his mother and Yeshua dying of thirst within, unless they found a way to leap, unseen, from the roof.

Koach drew himself up, his voice high with fear. "This is my brother's house—"

"And when he returns, he'll understand. Seven days to separate the unclean from the living. Then he can go inside and sort out the living and the dead, the clean and the bitten."

"Don't!"

"Get *back*, Hebel." Bar Cheleph lifted the hammer, the whites of his eyes showing. "We *saw* the dead girl touch you, saw you touch her cold flesh. I grieve for your mother, we all will. But she is dead. Or will be in moments. We all saw the wound." He glanced over his shoulder at those who stood at their doors. "Help us! Quickly. Before she rises!"

Mordecai lifted a third board, and he and Bar Cheleph slammed it into place below the others, at waist height. Koach shivered; he was looking now at a wall, a wall of hard wood with chinks of light between the planks.

He ran back into the house's interior, into the open atrium. Rahel was nowhere to be seen. Koach ran to the stranger, who still leaned against the wall with a nearly emptied bowl of water in his hands and one of Rahel's blankets about his shoulders.

"Bar Yosef," he cried.

The man didn't look up. His eyes stared into some other place.

"Bar Yosef . . . *navi* . . . they're boarding up the door. Help me stop them. Please!"

Still he didn't look up.

Koach bit back a shout of frustration. If only he were not *hebel*, if he were a man like any other, *he* would be carrying his lover's body up the hill and Shimon would be here to stop Bar Cheleph. "I have only one arm. *Help* me!"

"They aren't boarding up the door. They've stopped." Yeshua frowned. "Or they will stop. In a moment . . . Can't you hear them, Koach? The dead, all the dead."

Koach felt a chill. But he couldn't think about that now. He looked about the atrium desperately, and then rushed to his secret room. He ducked inside and knelt by the cold wall, his fingers scrabbling at the loose stone. There. He felt the hilt cold in his palm. His carving knife, small but freshly whetted and sharp.

He stepped out of the small room and hesitated, his heart wild in his chest. That hilt in his palm.

Yeshua watched him, his face troubled, but said nothing.

Ice in his heart. "I'll do what I have to," Koach whispered.

Suddenly the rug over the door to Rahel's room was drawn aside, and she stepped out into the atrium and walked with swift purpose toward the outer door. No trace of her earlier struggle, her fever, or her torn and soiled garments remained. Her hair was combed and bound back as though she were preparing to host guests in her home. She wore her cleanest, least tattered gown, one green like the grass by the sea. No kohl for her eyes or adornments for her ears and throat, for she was Hebrew, not Greek. Yet she stood tall and regal. Bar Yonah's wife, once a power in the town in her own right.

Koach fell in at her side, his knuckles white about the knife.

"I am not dead, Bar Cheleph," she called out in a cool, clear voice.

Bar Cheleph looked in over the boards and his eyes widened. "Get back," he said.

"It's all right," Rahel said. "I have no fever. I am well. There is no need to board up my door, or to do any violence to my house. Let it stand as it stood when my husband lived in it."

"Bat Eleazar," Bar Cheleph whispered.

She met his gaze, then drew her sleeve up her arm to the shoulder. "Whatever this stranger from the inland hills might be," Rahel said, "he has washed away my fever as I might wash away dirt from this gown. I am well."

Mordecai gasped and stumbled back.

Bar Cheleph only stared at Rahel's arm, at the smooth skin where a wound had been. The muscles of his throat moved.

"Tear down the boards," he said hoarsely.

When neither of the other men moved, he gasped, "Tear down the boards. Now. As you love my father, move!"

There was a great wrenching of wood and the cry of nails being torn free of the doorposts, and then the men cast the planks aside and the door was again an open space. Koach took a slow breath, let it out. Then he slipped the knife quietly into the pocket inside

230 OF STANT LITORE

his tunic. He hadn't needed it. He shivered. If he'd used it to carve
flesh, he didn't think he would ever again have been able to use it
for carving wood.

But he had nearly lost his mother today. He would not lose her
again. For a moment, just a moment, he understood his brother.
Understood his brooding, his brief storms of temper. Understood
the strain he felt, protecting their family.

Bar Cheleph's shoulders were tense. He kept his gaze lowered.
Her face stern, Rahel turned and walked back into her atrium.

Before he could either follow or shut the door, Koach was
startled by a cry in the street. He saw Yohanna striding down from
the direction of the synagogue and his father's house. In his arms
he carried a lean figure in a white robe. His face was strikingly like
Yohanna's, only folded up into wrinkles, his hair and beard the
clean white of foam on the night sea.

He was Yesse.

The priest's father.

Behind them came a great crowd of people—men and women,
fishers carrying baskets, and even a few boat people at the back,
their faces slack with fatigue and grief and the awareness of the
heavy tread of despair stalking the street behind them.

"*Navi!*" Yohanna cried. "*Navi!*"

They turned and saw Yeshua standing in the middle of the
atrium, his hair hanging about his face, lank and sweaty, half concealing the darkness of his eyes.

"Little time," he said. "Little . . . little time. The dead . . . I can . . .
can hear . . . All of them, all of them coming."

YESSE

"WATCH THE shore." Yeshua's voice was as calm as though he were mentioning the color of the sky. "They are coming."

Bar Cheleph cast a wild glance at his adopted brother and grandfather, and then turned and bolted from the doorstep, racing down the narrow street. The others looked on with wide eyes. Koach swallowed, realizing suddenly what the man's words might mean—if he were indeed the *navi*, if he indeed could see the things God could see.

Yohanna didn't seem even to have heard. He simply carried his grandfather over the threshold, his gaze on the stranger's face. "Help him, Bar Yosef," he said. "Help him."

Yeshua was staring after Bar Cheleph, and he didn't answer. Rahel glanced from his face to Yohanna's. "Bar Zebadyah," she said softly, "will you lay your grandfather by the olive?"

He nodded quickly, and carried him past. Rahel joined him, laying out blankets by the tree.

"I need to be there," Yeshua murmured. "I need to be there, there at the heart of it . . . but for what . . . what do I need to do, what do I need to do . . ." He let out a groan of frustration and lowered his head. For the briefest moment, his hands seemed to *burn*, as though he were holding them before a hot fire and the light was shining through his flesh. Koach's eyes widened.

"*Navi*," Rahel called.

Yeshua was breathing hard, as though he'd been straining against a locked door. The light faded, and he glanced up. His face beaded with sweat, as it had been after he had healed Koach's mother. He walked slowly toward the olive in the atrium, where Yohanna had lain his grandfather gently down. Koach followed. Unnoticed behind him, the people in the street who had followed Yohanna began to step through the door, their faces troubled or awed.

Yeshua knelt by the old man, gazing at the ruin of the elder's leg, twisted on that night of destruction long past. Rahel sat beside him, while Yohanna stood anxiously by. Yesse gazed back at the stranger with a question in his eyes.

"Help him, *navi*," Yohanna said.

"I am already tired," Yeshua said softly. "Already tired."

"You are *Eliya*," Yohanna said fiercely. "You are the *navi*. You are the one who takes away the uncleanness from the earth. Ha Matbil said it."

"The door is too hot," Yeshua murmured. "And even if I can, even if I can step through, what I will see, whatever I will do, whatever power this is the father has put in my hands, I cannot heal the whole land, Yohanna, not the whole land . . ." He swallowed, and his voice dropped, and he hung his head. "Yet what else, what else? Listen to the screaming until I am mad? Until it drives me back into the rocks? Into the sand and the wind and the wind and the desert? I cannot do that. I cannot."

The atrium was filling now with men and women. Rahel cast them a troubled glance but kept her attention on the stranger who had called her back to life with a song and a touch. The others, and Koach with them, looked on silently, waiting, as they had waited to see God's touch on their town for years, but now their waiting had a sharpness to it, an immediacy. Yesse's eyes bore that same look. It wasn't hope. It wasn't exactly hope. Only the demand for an ending.

"Who wounded you?" Yeshua asked without lifting his head.

"It doesn't matter." Yesse's was an old voice, rough and full of memory. "He no longer breathes." Yesse wet his lower lip with his tongue. "You spoke of the dead, the unclean lurching dead. There was a corpse on the shore. I saw it with my own eyes."

"More coming," Yeshua whispered. "I hear them."

"Is it true, what my grandson tells me?" Yesse gripped Yohanna's hand with bony fingers. "That God has sent a *navi* into the land? When have we needed one more?"

"When have we . . . you have said it," Yeshua said softly. His shoulders straightened. Then he said, quiet and clear, "I was raised the *nagar*'s son, his son, in Natzeret on the hill. I take things that are broken and broken apart and I join them, I join them together again." Suddenly Yeshua reached for the old man's other hand and gripped it tightly. His gaze met the old man's, and his eyes burned with sudden, dark intensity. "This is the truth, the truth, the truth I heard in the desert: All the world is broken and broken and broken apart. But nothing is broken that cannot be remade. Nothing is ill that cannot be healed, nothing captive that cannot be freed. Do you believe this, do you believe it?"

"I do," the old grandfather whispered, held by his gaze. "Yes, I do. Today I saw nets full of fish. I believe you."

"Then I can believe it also. Stand, old father," he whispered. "Stand. Your faith . . . it has made you well."

Yesse stared at him, his hands shaking. A strange look passed over his face. His right leg shifted slightly. He glanced at his calf, and his eyes were wild. Yohanna let go of his grandfather's hand and stood, almost falling over.

Yeshua rose more slowly, bending over the old man, still clasping his other hand; Yesse clung to his fingers. After a moment, Yesse got stiffly to his feet beside the stranger.

Those watching gasped, an almost sexual sound.

Yesse's eyes were wide, his hair adrift about his face. "I . . . I . . ." He glanced about wildly.

"Yes." Yohanna's voice was choked. "You are standing. You're standing, grandfather."

Yesse stumbled—as though his legs were numb from sitting too long—and Yohanna leapt forward, catching his arm, but Yesse shoved him away with a furious and wiry strength. "No," he said. His grandson stepped back, and Yesse recovered his balance. He took another step. This one was stronger.

Yesse kept his gaze on his feet. Then he laughed, a short bark. He glanced up at Yeshua with watery eyes. "You *are* the *navi*," he breathed. "The *navi* who will save Israel. All my life I have waited for you. All my life."

Yeshua's eyes were guarded, as though he were holding up his last shield against the yearning in Yesse's eyes. "I want only to sit by a fire, by a fire, and eat fried fish and talk," he said. "Or work with the wood, the cedar and terebinth in my father's shop. Only I can't stop the screams. I can't, I can't stop my ears."

───

The house of Rahel bat Eleazar filled with people and with activity. Men lay baskets of fish about the olive tree, and others threw fish over the coals. Rahel herself crouched with a knife—a spare from her supplies, not the one she had used against the dead—and she slit open one of the fish and pulled out its heart. This she set on the scented fire, and then leaned back and closed her eyes a moment, breathing in the redolence of it and, with it, the hope of safety for her house.

The silent woman—the woman from the boats—slipped into the house last, her face pale and so thin. But Koach only looked away. He cast aside his small knife and stepped out through the door. He needed to breathe a moment, and the atrium was too full of people; he didn't dare slip through them to his secret place. It would be like revealing that place to the whole town. So instead he leaned against the doorpost, his back itching from dried sweat. He felt something against his shoulder and stepped away from the post, saw a hole in the wood amid a corona of splinters, where one of the iron nails had been torn out.

Koach touched it with his finger, felt the sharpness of the splintered wood. Heard again Bar Cheleph's cry, *Board up the house! Board up the house!*

"He is afraid," he whispered.

For years, Bar Cheleph had seemed a giant to him: a fierce and brutal man with heavy fists. But Koach was not so much shorter than Bar Cheleph now. And he had seen Bar Cheleph's eyes. The man was only afraid. Terrified. Trying to live in a world that had tried to eat him.

The thought troubled Koach. He glanced back toward the street. And so he was just in time to see Zebadyah round the corner, hobbling toward him at a pace quicker than most men stride. Yakob was behind him, a net slung over one shoulder, his eyes anxious.

But *Zebadyah's* eyes . . .

The old priest had a desperate look, as though he were staring over the edge of a sea-cliff a mere breath before plunging in a long fall toward the deep. He all but ran to the doorstep, his hair wild about his face, bringing with him the heavy scent of wood smoke from the burning of the boats. Before Koach could step out of the way or say a word, Zebadyah grasped his weak arm and with strength like a bear threw him to the side. The priest rushed into the house as Koach struck the ground with his hip, cried out in pain, and rolled into the street.

PART 7

KANA

HALFWAY UP the hill, Tamar's body—which at first had felt as light as a bundle of dry twigs—became heavy in Shimon's arms. The sun overhead burned hot, and sweat slickened his face; Shimon clenched his teeth and kept placing one foot before the other. Though he longed to stop and rest, he did not want to hold that defiled, coat-swathed body cooling in his arms even a moment longer than he had to. He wanted to be done with it. And—

And he could see, so clearly, the grief in his brother's eyes, the anguish as Koach gazed up at him and asked him to perform this duty that he could not. His brother, who had never asked him for help before. His brother, who always asked *to* help. His brother, whom he had always rebuffed, knowing he would be useless at the nets, at the oar, at the hauling of the boat down to the sea.

That look in Koach's eyes haunted Shimon. Tore at his freshly opened heart. Though he placed each step with care over the rocky ground, Shimon shut his eyes a few moments against the sun, shut his eyes against the turmoil in his heart. The sea wind blew at his back.

So he did not see anyone approaching, and no scent forewarned him. The first warning he had was the weight of a body slamming into his right side, carrying with it the sickly sweet smell of rot.

His eyes flew open; he cried out as earth and sky tilted. Tamar was knocked from his arms. Shimon had a confused glimpse of her hitting the ground, her limp body rolling free of the coat. Then the earth slammed into his back, a jagged rock cutting his shoulder. Everything above him went dark; the silhouette of a human head blocked out the sun. Hands clutched at his face and shoulder, the fingers so cold. Shimon shouted and kicked, his own hands scrabbling at the thing's wrists. The creature's weight fell on him. It snarled. Shimon stared up into the dull sheen of its eyes, like unpolished iron.

Shimon had a terrible flash of memory; he was on his back in the sand with his father's corpse looming over him. Then he pushed the memory away with a shout and drove his knee into the corpse's gut. It didn't even notice. It hissed just above his face, its breath on his cheek cold as the sea. He drove the heel of his left hand hard against its brow, his right hand peeling its fingers away from his face.

The corpse bit into his sleeve and worried at his arm like a wolf, trying to tear away the wool and get at the warm, vulnerable skin beneath. Shimon cried out and kneed the corpse in the groin. It just kept tearing at the cloth with its teeth, growling. Panic ran cold through Shimon, like ice water pumped from his heart out to every part of his body, freezing him more with each heartbeat. All the world constricted to that face, those dull, empty eyes, the snarls from its throat. It was stronger than him, and it was going to eat him. Only a thick woolen sleeve held away his death. He was shaking.

Shimon had a momentary sense of someone looming over him and the corpse. A large hand gripped the corpse's shoulder and pulled the creature off him. Shimon had just time to draw in a shocked breath before glimpsing a flash of bright metal, the curved tip of a knife catching the corpse beneath its chin and then sliding smoothly up until the hilt of white bone pressed against the thing's chin, sheathing the knife in its head. The knife tip emerged from the creature's brow. The corpse jerked once and then went limp.

The man who had stilled it rolled it aside, and the body lay in the grasses, unmoving. Bar Nahemyah—Kana—stood bending over it. With a grunt, he set his sandaled foot against the creature's collarbone and then gripped the hilt and wrenched his knife free of the dead flesh. As Shimon scrambled back, kicking himself away from the corpse, and got unsteadily to his feet, Kana wiped the blade clean on the tattered remains of the corpse's garments. Shimon watched the blade; it was easier to look at that than to look at the dead.

"That's a Roman knife," he breathed.

The curved blade was nearly the length of Shimon's forearm between the elbow and the wrist.

"They call it the sica," Kana said quietly, stepping away from the corpse. "You catch the bottom of the jaw with the point—or you catch the bottom edge of the helmet, if you are stabbing a Roman—and you set your palm against the hilt and shove hard. Drive it up through the jaw and into the face. All the way to the scalp. One swift strike, and the corpse falls still. Then you do the next. And the next."

Shimon gazed at him in horror. The name he'd heard Bar Nahemyah claim—the name *Kana*, the zealot—rang in his mind, a name of knives and dread.

Kana began cleaning the blade on a tuft of grass. "The *kanna'im* have taken to carrying these. The fighting priests. You can't imagine it, Shimon. What Yerushalayim is like now. The poverty. The stink in the alleys. The dead. The Romans keep them down. Sometimes. The other times, *we* do." His voice went hoarse, as though he were holding back some great torrent of feeling. "We are the People, Shimon. The people of Yehuda tribe, the last of the Hebrews. The other tribes are dead. On all the earth, only we know the Law and the Covenant. Only we can keep this land, our land, free of the dead. The Romans bring hunger and slavery, and finally a weary death for us all." Straightening, Kana gazed down at the corpse.

"I said I didn't want your help," Shimon said. "Why did you follow me here?"

"I needed to talk with you." Kana's eyes were intent. "It is coming, Shimon. A dark time. You could help stop it."

"Your killers in the hills don't need me," Shimon muttered.

"*I* need you. This town respected your father. Revered your father. Your father, who stood against both Rome and the corpses that walk."

"My father is dead."

"But you live. And whether you like it or not, Shimon, Israel needs you. All men who are still true to the Covenant in their hearts wait for you. You could lead the fishing towns of Galilee to rise up. You could do it. They know your father's name."

But as Kana spoke, Shimon gazed at Tamar's body where it lay in a fumble of limbs like a crumpled spider. The stink of that corpse was worse now. One hand lay bent, and something had fallen from the sleeve. The object drew Shimon's gaze: a small wooden horse, no larger than a clay cup, an object you could hold in your hand. The intricacy of its mane, the small eyes and mouth, the lines of its flanks—this was something his brother had made.

Shimon crouched beside the dead girl. He picked up the horse carefully, ignoring Kana's frown. The small wood-carving felt cool in his hand; with an inward shiver he realized it had been nestled against the cold flesh of the dead. Yet he did not drop it or hurl it away. He held it, looked at it—the first time he had really *looked* at one of this brother's secretive carvings. He suddenly felt . . . heavy. Old. The burden of his People, his Law, his God, his heritage a weight on his shoulders. He didn't want to worry about the Law; he didn't want to revere his God or the traditions of the father who had betrayed him by being so long absent. He didn't want to fight each night for scraps from the sea to keep his family alive, fighting alongside other men's brothers because his own was too weak. He certainly didn't want to seek trouble with the Romans, or even to acknowledge that they existed on days other than those on which Zebadyah collected what few goods the town had to send to the tax collectors in the Emperor's City. He wanted only to sit in his boat, cast the nets and pull them up, and be silent like the water.

But he had made Koach a promise.

He would keep that promise.

"My brother is strange," he said. "But he is my brother." He turned on Kana. His voice heated. "What you've said, Barabba has said all this before. And right after he said it, he rode down my brother in the street. My *brother*, Bar Nahemyah. He tried to drive a spear through my brother's body. So you tell me, 'Kana.' What place will there be for Koach, for my kin and my blood, in this new uprising of yours?"

Kana was silent, his face cold with remembered pain.

"I have devoted every night of my manhood to the netting of fish, to the boat, to bringing home food for my family. And you would have me throw them away? It is more important to see that my kin eat than it is to hate the Romans."

"The Romans hate you, brother."

"Let them."

"Your father hated them."

"My father is *dead*," Shimon nearly shouted. "I am going to his tomb. He is *dead*, and we here in Kfar Nahum are all fatherless sons. Get out of my way, Kana."

Shimon rolled Tamar's corpse gently back into the coat and lifted her from the earth. He made to stride past the other man. Kana stepped out of the way but said quietly, "You can't sleep forever, Cephas."

Shimon stopped.

"Someday the Romans will want more taxes than Zebadyah bar Yesse can send. Someday, there will be nothing left, not even what you have now."

"What did you say?"

Kana looked at him strangely. "I said—"

If Shimon had not been carrying a corpse, he would have shoved Kana violently in the chest. Rage surged hot and wild like the sea inside him. "I am *Shimon*. God of our fathers, what do you all want from me?"

He began striding up the hill. He could see the *kokh*, the tomb in which his many dead kin slept the long sleep. Kana called after him: "Cephas is *the rock*. We want you to be your father's son, the man our People need. The man you were born to be!"

HIS FATHER'S TOMB

ONCE HE reached the tomb Shimon did his work quickly, for that place forced memories on him that he did not want. He lifted the girl's shrouded body and slid her feetfirst into the empty shelf to the left of his father's. The sunlight in the entrance to the *kokh* was pale, but the dimness of the tomb was not creepy or unnerving, only quiet. This was a place where the wind did not enter, a place where no *shedim* shrieked or whispered or demanded entrance to the human mind and body. Shimon slid the girl into the hole in the wall, onto the long stone shelf inside the hill, until only her hair was visible.

In this very tomb, Shimon's brother had been born; here, Shimon as a youth had held and comforted his mother as she bled from the birth. Everything that defined their family was here. The birth. Their father's body. And now this girl Tamar had a place on these cold stone shelves. Shimon gazed down at her hair. In the synagogue, Zebadyah had said once that God spoke a word, a secret word, into the ear of each child at the moment of its birth. And that this word, which each of them forgot as children but remembered when they had grown into men and women—though perhaps they had to spend many nights listening for it before they heard it again, spoken anew—this word was God's hope for their lives. Shimon wondered what word had been spoken into this girl's ear. Surely that word, that hope, had not been that she would be beaten by her father or devoured by the dead. Shimon thought the word must have been his brother's name. If the dead had not come to Kfar Nahum that night, if their father had not died, if the town had not been destroyed, if the corpses had not been dumped into the sea, if Koach had been born with two strong arms like a man, then he and this girl would have been together. Shimon had heard it in his brother's voice.

But whatever word God had spoken into Tamar's ear, she would never hear again. And whatever word he had spoken into Koach's ear, hearing it now would only bring his brother the sharp misery of joys glimpsed and gone.

All his heart a growl of grief, Shimon stepped toward the door of the tomb. Hesitating, he glanced at the shelf in the wall on which his father lay. He wrestled with himself, part of him longing to go to the shelf and pull his father's body free of it and see his face. He imagined unwrapping the burial linens, imagined hesitating before peeling free the final layer, fearful of seeing those eyes open but unliving, fearful of hearing again that terrible moan. But no, the face within would be still and shriveled tightly to the bone, preserved like the mummies of Kemet, though not so well. His father's eyes would be closed. The Greek pig-eaters placed coins on the eyes of their dead, to pay the boatman to ferry their souls over the last river; the Hebrews brought to their dead only spices and song. At his father's burial, Shimon had had neither. He had stood shaking and silent while his mother sang the Words of Going, the memory of his father's lurching over the shore still fresh and vicious in his heart.

Shimon stared helplessly at that shelf. Out of some chasm in his heart, rage welled up, hot as fever, until he shook with it. Rage at his father for leaving him standing on that shore, leaving him alone to care for his mother and his infant sibling. Rage at that other father in heaven who had turned his back when the Romans descended on their town. When the dead came down from the hills. When the dead devoured or blighted the fish beneath the sea. His father who had left them all like children outside the walls of a house, to eat what scraps they could find. Rage at both his fathers, who had proven too weak or too disinterested to help. And neither of them had been there to tell him that he was man enough to handle what would come, or to teach him how to.

And, finally, rage at the newcomer, the fish-caller who spoke so glibly and easily of fathers, and who thought that filling the nets could erase the pain and death-cries of a People as easily as an incoming wave might erase footsteps in the sand.

Shimon turned and strode from the tomb, breathing hard. Outside, the day was aging fast and God's sky was empty but for a crane winging slowly northeast toward the high ridges of Ramat ha-Golan. A slight breeze stirred the grasses on the hill, but Shimon did not fear it. He gazed down at the town at the sea's edge and saw it suddenly as he had never seen it before: a cluster of ill-organized stone houses about a tall synagogue, but with no wall, no shelter from the wind or from strangers out of the hills. Vulnerable to the dead and the living alike. Zebadyah was right. They should cast this man out. And Kana too. They should wall everything out, forever. They had lost too much. Let them cling to what little they had left, though it be only rags, though it be only empty nets. When had anyone outside the small atriums of their houses ever cared for them? The Romans preyed on them—though now from a distance. Barabba would prey on them, in his own way. Threshing and Rich Garden and Tower pretended they did not exist. Maybe they *didn't* exist; maybe the apparent survivors of Kfar Nahum were only ghosts, *shedim* without bodies, but too recently dead to realize it.

GREATER THINGS THAN THESE

"RAHEL!" ZEBADYAH cried. "Rahel!" Forgetting in his panic that her name was not his to use or to call, he sprang through the door, hardly noticing that he'd hurled Koach aside. There was only the terrible thought of Bat Eleazar—of Rahel, oh Rahel—lying cold as stone in her house, as cold as his own dead wife so many long years before. His breath heaved; he had run through the ruined outskirts and past the tanner's shop and through the square of the synagogue, where some sat with baskets and were gutting fish, unaware of any shadow of the dead. Rahel, Rahel, beautiful Rahel. He had wanted only to keep her safe, to honor his lost brother, to . . . to hold her. To think that she might be gone. Worse, that she might come *back*. That she might rise to rend those about her with her teeth and nails. No. Not Rahel. Not her. God of our fathers, not her.

He rushed into her atrium and stopped short, for he could see Rahel bat Eleazar bending over a cookfire and prodding fish on the coals, calm and focused, as though she had never known pain. The air was rich with the smell of fried musht, mingled with the herbs from the scented fire. Rahel glanced up at him, and her eyes were full of life. So full of life.

"You are alive," he whispered. "Alive."

"Of course I am alive," she said, and straightened. There were others around them, other people in the atrium, but Zebadyah hardly noticed. He could see nothing but her face. She should have been shaken with fever, or dead, or . . . or worse.

After Yakob had led off his search party for Benayahu, Zebadyah had gone out to the old altar, the all but abandoned altar. There he had thrown himself to the ground and wet the soil with his tears, praying for a consolation that did not come. Natan El had found him there and had gasped out a story of Rahel bat Eleazar bitten by the dead. Zebadyah had found himself on his feet and running, running into the town.

And now she stood before him as full of life as when she had been young and he had been young, as when he had first seen her laughing as she walked alongside his brother. She was alive, she was alive. With a hoarse cry of joy, joy that wrenched everything in him, he leapt forward and seized her arms and pulled her to him, crushing her, his mouth finding hers, the heat and softness of her against him. So, so alive.

She stiffened. Then her hands beat at his shoulders, and he let her go. He took a step back and nearly fell, dizzied. She stood staring at him, a few strands of hair across her face, her cheeks flushed, her eyes wide with alarm. "Bar Yesse!" she gasped.

"Get away from her!"

The shout came from the door. The whelp, Hebel, stood there, his eyes cold with fury—looking so strangely, in that moment, like Zebadyah's brother Yonah. But the priest felt neither unease nor anger. He was too overwhelmed. He opened his mouth to apologize to Rahel, but only laughter came out. And then he fell on his rump and sat there in the middle of her house, laughing, his eyes squeezed shut, as though he were a small boy again.

"Zebadyah." That was an old voice, a rasping voice. "I don't think I have heard you laugh in a long time."

Zebadyah looked up. For the first time, he took note of the others in the house. The men and women preparing for a meal. The boat people, crouched back against one wall as though to communicate that they were no threat. The witch from Natzeret. And beside him—standing beside him—his father. Yesse.

Standing.

"Abba," Zebadyah whispered. "Abba."

Yesse walked slowly over and knelt beside Zebadyah, putting his arms around his son, pressing his lips to his hair. Zebadyah wanted to weep, but could not; so many mornings he had crouched beside his reclining father, holding him, comforting him, and always he had longed to be the one comforted, the one guided, the one fathered. Always he had felt his aloneness and his inadequacy, his guilt for hiding beneath the boats while his father was maimed.

Now his father was back. Consoling him. Lending him his strength.

It was as though the sky had fallen into the sea and the sea had become the sky. He was spinning, falling. He clutched at his father's arm. "Abba," he moaned, "help me to my feet."

A moment later, they were standing together. He faced his father, looking into those eyes old and gray as the voices of cranes over the water. His hand trembled where he held his father's arm. He tried to say with his eyes the words he had never voiced to Yesse, words of regret for that night.

I'm sorry.

The skin around Yesse's eyes crinkled. *I know.*

Drawing in a slow, shuddering breath, Zebadyah glanced about him, saw the pale and hungry faces of those gathered in the house: fishermen and a few of their wives, and boat people, and the bruised face of the stranger from Natzeret. This house was now filled with just such an assembly as he'd feared: a mingling of the clean and unclean, a collapse in the order he'd so carefully shored up against storm and wind, and no wall of fire or stone to hold it back.

Yet—

"I should thank you," he said, and found it difficult to swallow. He didn't know whether to laugh or weep or rage. Perhaps he was asleep and didn't know it; perhaps he was lost in the dream country. The world had stopped making sense.

Yeshua's face shone with sweat. "You will see greater things than these," he said. His voice was sad.

Zebadyah gazed at his face, trying to understand. His father's hand was strong on his shoulder. He choked back fresh tears, a tightness in his throat, and rubbed his eyes with the back of his hand. This sudden joy in him was running out at his eyes. Prophet or madman, he didn't know, couldn't know. But he had his father back. He turned his head at a sound and saw, through bleary eyes, Hebel still standing by the door, the boy's face white with wrath.

Koach didn't even notice the people gathered behind him on the doorstep. He felt he could tear down a wall, even one-handed, even weak, he was so angry. When the priest turned his face toward him and Koach saw his eyes wet with tears, it was too much. The priest *dared* affront his mother. That hateful old man who had denied him his *bar 'onshin*, whose son had beaten him in the street—he *dared*. He would *not* feel sympathy for this man.

"This is my brother's house," Koach said, his voice loud in the atrium. "And you are an uninvited guest."

Yesse frowned, and Zebadyah flushed—though whether with anger or embarrassment, Koach didn't know.

"Koach!" His mother rose to her feet. Her face was flushed, too, but her eyes flashed. Her tone cut through Koach's anger like a boat's keel through water, parting it.

"Bar Yesse," Rahel said, her voice cool though her face betrayed how shaken she was, "has done me no lasting harm. If I were to see my own father here, and strong, I would be wild with joy, as well. He is the *kohen* of our village and deserves your respect."

"How can you say that?" Koach cried. "He hates us."

"Koach!"

"He does! He always has. He acts as though he is the father of this house, but he is not!"

His mother straightened, and there was such fire in her eyes that he fell silent.

"Koach," she said, her voice sharp, "we have all said hateful things, and many of us have *done* hateful things. Because we are hungry, and we are tired, and none of us have slept well in many years. But there are fish, and we are sitting to eat. And we have this chance to make things right again." She glanced down, and for a moment her hands trembled as though she were fighting to hold in some tempest of emotion. Koach suddenly burned with shame, though he couldn't have said why.

"Help me make things right," she said.

"Amma," Koach whispered.

Rahel turned to Zebadyah, her tone tightly controlled. "Bar Yesse, I would ask you to atone for the insult to me by accepting my sons' hospitality and sitting at our fire for a while with your father."

Koach bit his lip, hard, to keep from opening his mouth and letting out the harsh words in his heart. He certainly didn't intend any hospitality to the priest—or to *any* of these people. His mother needed rest, and he . . . he needed time to breathe, privacy, a chance to retreat to his secret place and think. His hand itched to hold his carving knife. Finding beauty within the wood, he would find also some way to cope with the strangeness and the horrors and the joy of this day.

Rahel said, "Will you sit at my sons' fire, you and all these others, Zebadyah bar Yesse? It has been a long time since Kfar Nahum sat together."

Zebadyah stood as though struck—so long this house had been barred against him. But Yesse took his arm and drew him to the cushions that lay about the olive tree. "My son accepts, and so do I, Bat Eleazar. I have missed my grandson's house, and my daughter-in-law's cooking." And Yesse sat, seeming a little sore from age, but otherwise as able as any other man, as though his hip had never been twisted, his dignity never assaulted by Romans or the dead.

Rahel took charge, as though she were a queen in a palace of Shushan and not a fisher's wife. She knew all the names of those who had stepped into her house, all but the boat people, and she demanded theirs. Then she recruited helpers and seated others, and soon more fish were roasting, and a few women were helping her grind bread while others poured water for the ritual washing to the elbows before a meal. With a start, Koach realized the silent woman was among them, still clothed in his father's coat, its hem sweeping along the ground at her feet. She had already washed her hands and arms, for they were clean, and she sat down to grind bread as though she were any other woman of Kfar Nahum, dipping her finger into the meal and lifting some to her mouth as she worked. Rahel gave her a cool look but let her be; when there is an entire community to feed, a woman doesn't turn down help. Mordecai's sister and Natan El's wife carried platters and bowls around the circle that the seated guests formed. Yeshua stood alone, to the side, and for the moment none bothered him. The scent of food demanded the attention of those who'd been starving far more than any miracle of healing could. Zebadyah sat by his father, his face dappled by shadows and sun through the leaves of the olive, and his eyes were dazed. Yesse gripped his son's shoulder and leaned in to speak into his ear.

The bustle had sprung up so swiftly, Koach was left standing by the door. His stomach snarled at the scent of fish, but he ignored it. He couldn't join them at the meal, couldn't bear to be around so many people, his heart naked to their eyes. Breathing raggedly, he leaned back against the wall and lifted his hand to his face; he could smell death on his skin. Tamar's death.

Abruptly, he realized he wasn't alone. Yeshua was leaning on the wall beside him.

"Why don't you eat?" Koach said. "You are a guest."

"Eat," the man whispered. His eyes were a little glassy in a face that shone with sweat. "How can I eat?"

Koach wet his lips, not understanding. The man unnerved him, and the grief was so sharp in Koach's chest that he wanted no company. But this man had helped his mother, had . . . healed her. Brought her back. He blinked quickly against the moistening of his eyes.

"Your hands are shaking," he said.

Yeshua lifted his hands to look at them; his fingers were trembling. He was very pale. "There's a door, Koach," he whispered. "A door. I'm doing too much. Too much, too fast. Not ready, not ready for it yet, whatever is coming. I have to . . . have to be able to stand in that door, see what he sees, first."

"What are you talking about?"

"But how can I stand there?" His voice low. "I heard him, *heard* him weeping in the desert. Like all the world weeping, such terrible cries. Tore at my heart." He shut his eyes, the shaking in his hands worse. "How can I stand in that door, in that light, stand to see what makes him weep? Isn't the moaning in my ears enough? How can I bear any more? I can't, I can't bear it."

His shoulders shook and, startled, Koach realized Yeshua was sobbing. The man let no tears leak from under his eyelids. He let no sound break from his lips. He just shook. Koach stood awkwardly, unsure what to do. He was accustomed to his mother's comfort and to the indifference or hostility of others to his own pain, but he was not used to standing by another.

Except Tamar.

Except her.

The stranger drew in a ragged breath. "I am grateful to you," he said, opening his eyes.

Koach shook his head.

"You are the only one here, Koach, the only one who has made no demand on me. None. Though I hear your screams, too, and they are loud, they are loud. But the others. Prophet. Witch. Heal my grandfather. Heal Israel. Bury the Romans. You . . . you make me a guest in your brother's house. You didn't even bring me your arm, though you saw a lame man stand on his feet."

Koach went still. He had been so furious—at the priest, at Bar Cheleph, at the town and himself for letting Tamar suffer and die—and in such panic and then delirious relief over his mother, that he had not even considered that the stranger might . . . might straighten and strengthen his arm. He stared at the man in shock.

Koach glanced down at his right arm, concealed in its thick woolen sleeve. No, not concealed. He could never conceal it. Instinctively, he glanced at the people eating. Some of them kept looking up from their fish and watching Yeshua and himself by the door. Others were talking together in low voices. He listened to their talk for a moment, caught bits of it:

. . . *a lame man healed . . .*

. . . *the fish, and the fish . . .*

. . . *and Bat Eleazar. Signs, these are signs . . .*

. . . *signs . . .*

. . . *he's the* navi . . .

. . . *he must be the* navi . . .

. . . *no, he's a witch. You heard how he babbles, and he . . .*

. . . said the dead are coming, the dead are coming. A vision . . .

. . . end of our town, this is our last meal . . .

. . . over there with Hebel? Why is he with Hebel . . .

"Could you . . . ?" Koach whispered.

"I think so," Yeshua murmured. He was staring at those feasting, too. "But I know why . . . why you didn't ask. You have a worse injury. I know that injury. It is mine also."

"Your bruises," Koach whispered. He understood. Though this man had two arms, not one, somehow he had suffered as Koach had.

"I haven't eaten with my kin in . . . in some time," Yeshua said. "I tried to. After the desert, after that. I came back, slept one night in my mother's house, only one night before her neighbors lifted stones to throw." He looked down. "I miss that town, Natzeret. It is a small town, Koach, so small. Much smaller than this one. It is . . ." He swallowed. "It is lovely. There are olive trees and one press that still works, and in the morning, in the beautiful morning, I wake and I hear . . . the press creaking. And when the night . . . when it's night, I fall asleep to my father's hammer, tapping, tapping in his shop by the house. I miss that. Sometimes I am sleeping, in the lee of some ridge, and I wake, suddenly, quickly, so that the world tilts as though I've been spinning too fast, too fast, like a small child, all the stars wheeling around me like the gulls. And I hear it. That tapping. It sounds so real. I miss it. I miss it, Koach. He made beautiful things. I miss hearing him work. Miss helping him. I miss the old midwife's scowls and the way the weaver's children play stones in front of the well." He rubbed his hand quickly across his eyes. "Ah. I think I *will* eat." He indicated the gathering people with a small motion of his head. "You mustn't hate them, Koach. The priest, the others."

Koach met Yeshua's gaze, and then it seemed to him that this stranger who had healed his mother was gazing not only *at* him but *into* him. As though everything he had ever hidden, every secret place, every word he'd signed to Tamar, every time he had tossed in his bed, every time he had dreamed of taking her far across the sea to some new place—as though everything, everything, was laid bare before this man.

"They hate *me*," Koach said.

"No." Yeshua gave a vehement shake of his head. "No, they don't. They do not hate *you*. Because they . . . they have *never* seen you. They look at you and see only what they fear, only that." Yeshua's face twisted in pain; he closed his eyes and put his forehead to Koach's own, an uninvited yet comforting touch, as though they had a shared history. The stranger whispered a word in Hebrew too softly for Koach to hear. Then he said, "They do not hate *you*."

"I'm scared," Koach whispered back, startling himself. But now he'd spoken and the words could not be taken back. Tamar was dead. His mother had almost died. His brother loathed him. There might be no one who would really see him, ever again.

"We are all scared," Yeshua whispered. "Every one of us. Maybe even the father in the desert. We could all lose so much, so much."

Hearing a footstep, Koach lifted his head and found the silent woman standing before them, still in his father's coat, which enveloped her small body like a winter blanket. She held out a bowl of water cupped between her hands. Her eyes lifted for a single instant; Koach saw the flash of them before she lowered them again. As Yeshua looked on silently, Koach took the bowl unsteadily in his left hand, felt the smooth clay against his fingers and palm.

"Thank you," he said.

The water was cool and clear in his mouth.

The young woman offered the bowl next to Yeshua, who took it and drank in slow gulps, watching her over the rim. His eyes were not unkind. She blushed, which surprised Koach, who had seen her perform a small seduction at that cookfire on the shore earlier without any reddening of her face.

As though flustered, the woman turned back to Koach. She made a small sound in her throat, and from within the long coat, she brought out an article of wood and placed it in Koach's hand, lifting her fingers quickly so that her hand would not brush his.

He searched her face a moment, and then glanced down. It was a wooden horse, warm from her touch. Rougher than the one he'd carved over many weeks for Tamar. He'd made this one to practice. He must have left it in one of the long pouches sewn inside the coat.

His chest constricted. "Thank you," he whispered again.

Knowing the carving to be his, she must have meant its return to comfort him. Yet it made him think of Tamar. He dropped the carving carefully back into her palm. "But you keep it. Someone should have it."

"Cast it away," Zebadyah called. "Or throw it into the fire." The priest had turned where he sat, his back to the other guests, legs crossed, hands on his knees. His beard tumbled down his chest. He had begun to recover from his shock, but his eyes were anxious. Yesse beside him chewed gingerly on a bite of fish, watchful.

Koach bit back the words he wanted to say. "It's a gift to her."

Yeshua set down the clay bowl. "May I see it?" he asked.

The silent woman took a quick step back. For the second time, it occurred to Koach that this might be the first day since she was a small girl that she had been given a gift. In the past few hours she had been given a coat, fish to eat, and a wood-carving, a small thing of large beauty for one whose life held none—with nothing expected in return. It might break her to give it back. He wished he could understand the emotions, wild and dark, that he saw in her eyes. He wished that she could speak.

"It's all right," he whispered.

Yeshua held out his hand, with that quiet intensity in his eyes.

The woman's eyes were wet, and she hesitated. Then she placed the carving in the stranger's hand and jerked her fingers back quickly, fear in her eyes. Perhaps she'd been beaten in the past for an unwanted touch.

Yeshua lifted the wooden horse, looked at it closely. Then he walked away along the wall of the atrium, as though he'd forgotten them. Koach watched him, bewildered. He was so *strange*.

Zebadyah rose to his feet, but Rahel murmured without looking up, "He, too, is my guest, Bar Yesse."

"We are open to the sky," Zebadyah said, his tone urgent. "What we do here, God can see. You, stranger. You have given me back my father, and I don't know what you are, if you are a *navi* or a witch, if it is prophecy and vision that make you shake like a twig, or *shedim* from the lord of flies. But that is an idol you hold in your hand, one touched by a heathen slut—"

"She is no heathen," Koach said sharply. "And—"

"She has spoken no word of Aramaic, no word of Hebrew."

"She *doesn't* speak. At all." The fury from before came back up, scorching. "Can't you see she is suffering and alone?"

Zebadyah reddened. "How dare you speak. You who made that *thing* of wood. You who insult my brother's memory—"

"Bar Yesse!" Rahel cried.

"Son," Yesse said.

"I will not see our town distracted by small gods!" Zebadyah's voice rose, thick with contempt. "Gods you can hold in your *hand*, rather than a God who can't be held, who will not come at our call, for we come at his. That!" He threw his hand out toward the stranger and the wooden horse he held. "That is an evil, a distraction you shape with your hand. A crack in the wall, while the dead press against the stones. That is not safe; it is not *useful!*"

Yeshua turned on the priest, his eyes hot, the wooden horse clutched in his hand, his voice loud and quick. "The father who made you may not find *you* useful—or you—or you—" He took them all in with a sweep of his hand. "Of what *use* are any of you to the Holy One who shaped the earth and filled the seas? But I have been in the desert and I . . . I believe this: There has never been a day when the father has not found you beautiful."

There was silence. Even Koach was taken aback at the hardness in the stranger's voice.

Yeshua turned the horse over a few times in his hand, peering down at it. His face was troubled.

"I think it is possible," he murmured, "to keep every letter of the written Law yet fail to live a lawful life. And maybe it is possible to yearn, even to yearn for the father's heart and yet . . . yet miss him entirely."

"Bar Yosef . . ." Zebadyah began.

"Sit, my son," Yesse said behind him. "Eat. Our town has been unclean a long time, and the cleansing of it can wait until after we eat. Tonight we are guests in Bar Yonah's house. I'll hear no shouting in my grandson's house."

Zebadyah kept silent, his face drawn with old pain. But he did not sit.

Yeshua walked back to the young woman and pressed the wooden horse into her hands; she took it and backed away.

"Bury it in the sand, if you will," he said. "You do not need it. You do not need it, *talitha*."

———

As Yeshua stepped away from the woman, his face went white. For a terrible moment he stood completely still. Then, with a hoarse cry, he clutched at his ears, at his head.

"Bar Yosef?" Koach cried.

Others leapt to their feet, staring in horror or confusion. Rahel stood, too, her face lined with worry. Their shadows appeared long before their feet, with the approaching Sabbath.

It was a long moment before Yeshua spoke. When he did his voice was thick. "Just stop . . . just stop screaming . . . stop . . ."

"Witch," Zebadyah whispered. Yesse took his son's hand, squeezing his fingers.

Rahel was at the stranger's side in a moment, her fingers all but touching his shoulder, though he was neither husband nor kin to her.

"Water! Get him water, amma!" Koach said to her.

Yeshua stretched out one hand as though to push them all away. "No," he gasped. "I am all right . . . It is just sometimes . . . sometimes too much . . ."

His gaze fixed on the young woman who still held that wood-carving.

"You are the loudest," he said. "The screaming in your heart . . . without pause. What . . . what hurt you so?" He drew in air, his chest heaving. Then he staggered toward the silent woman. The whites of her eyes showed, as though in a moment she might turn and run from the house.

There was a desperate look in Yeshua's eyes.

"Don't hurt her!" Koach cried.

"It *might* hurt, *talitha*," Yeshua said. "It might. You lost this, and it may hurt, coming back."

Talitha, he'd called her again.

Little girl, little daughter.

He reached for her, and she stood, trembling, as he touched her hair. Koach stood tensed, unsure what to do. Rahel's eyes were watchful. All their eyes were watchful.

Stepping near to the young woman, Yeshua bent his head and did a shocking thing. He pressed his lips to the woman's throat, gently.

The touch was intimate and familiar and unsettling. Not because he appeared to *want* her, but because he was treating her as the very closest of his kin, as though anyone who looked up into his face with such naked need might *be* his kin. No one spoke. All of them—those seated at their meal, those standing—all of them just watched the stranger, this man who stepped over their People's traditions and their boundaries as simply and without regret as though these were only lines drawn in the sand.

Yeshua straightened and looked at the woman's eyes a moment; she gazed up at him in shock. Her lips parted; she released a sound like a sigh, like something leaving the body. She began to tremble.

Koach saw her take a breath. He went still, seized with sudden, fierce premonition.

She was shaking.

She sang a high, wavering note.

Her eyes shone with tears.

"It's all right," Yeshua said softly. His own eyes shone. "It's all right. The Sabbath Bride, she is here, even just outside the door. Will you welcome her in for us, *talitha*?"

She lifted her voice higher, and her eyes filled with tears. Other eyes moistened around her. She began to weep as she sang, and she laughed helplessly.

"Come!" Yeshua cried, spinning to face the others, his arms out, his hair wild about his face. "Have the waters worn away your hearts and your lives like Iyobh's stones? Does she need to sing alone?" He took the girl's hand and lifted it high, and he held out his right hand to Rahel, who stood nearest. "Take my hand," he said softly, and with wondering eyes, she did. "Everyone, please. Sing."

He lifted his voice in Hebrew, strong Hebrew words out of a desert so deep in their past. Then Rahel began to sing, too, her voice thin at first, then stronger. Old Yesse stepped near, staring at the young woman; Rahel reached for his hand, and without even seeming to notice, he took her small fingers in a firm grip that belied his age. And as if that one touch poured water from a cistern, they all began to sing, some taking hands, some not. The song was an ancient psalm and one they had heard recited in the synagogue, though without music. Dawid himself might once have stood at the entrance to the Cave of Adullam and sang that psalm to the morning air in that voice of his that had charmed the land's women and its men and even the six-winged angels of heaven.

The house sang. In ten, twelve, fifteen voices, they sang their love of the Shabbat Bride who brought with her a covenant of rest and peace between God and all living things for whom even the drawing of breath is a labor.

Then something happened that had never happened before in Kfar Nahum or in any village of Israel. Those who were seated because their bodies gave them pain rose shakily to their feet. Sinews reknit themselves. Limbs straightened and strengthened. One beggar's murky eyes cleared and gazed for the first time on a world of color and shape. The healing passed by touch from one person to the next, swift as a whisper, and the room filled with heat. Each face lit with a glow like that of flames on a winter night. The hair of the men and women crowded into the house rose as in a lightning storm, and wind swept against their faces. They heard the walls creak with the pressure of God's presence, the *shekinah* that had fallen on their fathers' tents in the desert, now filling this small house until the stone out of which it was made groaned. Then the heat rolled through the door and out into the street, and dust billowed in the sudden wind.

The townspeople and the boat people looked on each other in wonder, hearing each other's voices. Most of them hadn't sung in years.

Not in this silent town where even the synagogue knew neither music nor laughter.

Not in this place of grief.

Not in the house-shaped tombs of Beth Tsaida by the sea.

One of them didn't sing.

Koach took up a clay pestle, small and heavy, that his mother had dropped by the firepit, and then retreated to the doorstep. There he stood and gazed out at the dust blowing in the street. He was shaken. Singing and joy and that heat in the house were as alien as the fish flopping in their hundreds on the sand. He clutched his weak arm. The dust gusted up from the street as though stirred by the footsteps of the Sabbath Bride.

Whatever had killed Tamar was out there still, prowling the shore or the wild slopes like a roaring lion, looking for someone to devour. Likely the sound of song and feast loud over the shore would bring it back, summoning that lurching corpse like a guest arriving late.

Koach glanced down at his right hand, the hand that was thin and dead. He tried to make it into a fist. His fingers didn't even twitch.

His eyes stung.

What if that arm were to be healed? That would not make him a man, not make him whole. He had been denied his *bar 'onshin*. He had been barred from the synagogue. He had been struck, spat upon, thrown to the dirt.

You have a worse injury, Yeshua had told him.

The other young men—Yakob, Bar Cheleph, Bar Nahemyah, Yohanna—they were not in his mother's house feasting with the old and the women and the beggars. They were probably all on the shore, watching for the dead or searching for signs of Benayahu.

Even while he sat idle here.

He had only one arm, but he had two eyes; he could watch. He could shout. He could do his part. He drew in a breath. It was for boys to mope and men to act, he told himself. He'd had no *bar 'onshin*, but at least he could do his best to be like a man. Anything less would shame the woman he'd loved, who was dead. He thought of Shimon entombing Tamar, doing her the honor he could not, and his face burned.

The surge of heat and power within the house behind him faded, but he still heard many voices singing, his mother's among them, pure and beautiful as he'd rarely heard it before. He didn't know what was happening, what was changing within this town. He didn't know what was changing in him. But he knew what he had to do.

He might step inside again, find his carving knife. But no, *no,* he would not go to watch for the dead with that in his hand. He was a youth who carved things of beauty and fittings for boats; his blade would remain a craftsman's tool, not a zealot's knife. His grip tightened instead about the pestle his mother had used for grinding meal.

Koach took a breath. This was a thing he had to do. But he would wait for his brother's return; he wouldn't leave his mother alone in a house crowded with others.

So he watched the dust move with the wind's breath, and listened for the approach of his brother's feet.

PART 8

RAHEL'S STORY

IT WAS almost dusk before Shimon staggered back into the town. Even as he reached the outskirts, he heard the singing of women. He stopped, astonished. Listened. Strained his ears as though his ears were cups to fill with all that music. He drew in a ragged breath. How long—how long since he had heard music like that? The Sabbath Bride was walking across the water into the town, following the last footsteps of the setting sun, and for the first time since Shimon was a boy, the town was welcoming her.

The singing stopped about the time that Shimon reached his house. The door was open, but Koach stood at it like a doorkeeper, with a pestle clutched in one hand, and their gazes met. There was a question in Koach's eyes.

Shimon found he couldn't speak, so he only nodded.

He saw the relief and sorrow in his brother's eyes and was startled, for it was not the sorrow of a boy he saw, but a man's grief. Whoever this youth was, he was not *hebel*. Suddenly Shimon wondered if his brother had grown to manhood while he slept between the nights' battles with the sea. The thought shamed him. But there was also a warm flicker of pride for his brother, something he hadn't felt before.

"I have to go," Koach said quietly.

"Go?"

He lifted the pestle, and his eyes glinted with a hardness that Shimon had seen before only in the eyes of the fishers.

"Something's still out there. Zebadyah's sons have gone already to watch. They'll need help."

Shimon stood very still. He could hear voices within the house, but not their words.

"Be careful," he said at last. There was nothing paternal in his tone. It was just one brother's advice to another.

Koach gave him a grateful look, and then inclined his head respectfully. "You also," he said. He stepped past Shimon and began walking quickly around toward the back of the house and the stretch of shore behind it.

Shimon watched his brother go. He gripped his shoulder a moment; it burned where the rock had cut him. Maybe that corpse up on the hill had been the only one they had to worry about. But he didn't think so. From Koach's tone, he knew Benayahu had not been found. And there might be others. Sometimes, it was not just one corpse you dragged up in your nets. There might be three or four. Since his thirteenth year he'd known that any winter might be the town's last. Nothing was certain, nothing was safe.

He stepped inside his house, turned, and shut and barred the door by long habit. And stopped. Startled. There were new scents in the air. Fish roasted for food, and the sharper scent of spices. His mother must have placed a fish over the spirit fire to keep the *shedim* from the house. He hadn't smelled *that* in . . . so long. For the first time, it really sank in that there were *fish*. There was food. There were hearts to lay on the coals to keep the *shedim* away. And maybe, just maybe, everything was going to be all right.

He blinked, his throat tight, and stepped through to the atrium.

The beggar-stranger from Natzeret stood with his back to the olive tree. Perhaps twenty men and women of the town—and perhaps ten boat people—sat around him, their faces upturned, listening. Some of them, Shimon knew, had been broken in body. One had been blind. And that young woman had been mute, the one who appeared to be wearing his father's coat—his *father's* coat, but Shimon was too overwhelmed, too bewildered, for the coals of anger in his chest to flicker into fresh heat. He just stared. Those who had been broken now sat hale and whole, and he knew the singing he'd heard had come from this house.

Facing the others, Yeshua was drawn and pale as after great labor. He was talking in a low murmur; Shimon couldn't make out the words. The stranger looked completely intent on those sitting near him, and didn't glance up as Shimon looked on, bewildered.

This man stood in his house, in his *house*, with more than two dozen unexpected guests. He looked about for Rahel, but couldn't see her; she was not among the seated guests. She was not at the firepit, though there was evidence of a meal. A *vast* meal.

His belly growled so fiercely that some of the guests glanced up at him.

There had been a feast here, a feast of strangers. He stood outside their circle, unsure how to act, everything in him a wash of confusion and fatigue. He glanced about, saw that the rug was drawn across the door to Rahel's small room along the outer wall of the house. Had she gone to bed, with so many strangers in the house? Nothing here made any sense.

Too weary and his emotions in too great a turmoil to deal with the strange *navi* or the people pressed all about him, or even to throw them from his house, Shimon went to find his mother. Stepping into her room, he let the rug over the door fall back behind him to block out the sight and some of the noise from their atrium. There was a little light, very faint, from between the slats of the boarded-up window, and by it Shimon saw that Rahel lay in her bedding with her small hands clasped at her breast, her fingers curled around a tattered shawl. His father's *tallit*. Shimon's throat tightened. In this dim light, though he had seen them many times before, his mother's hands looked suddenly wrinkled and aged.

"Amma," he whispered.

She glanced up, and he saw that she had been crying. A day ago, when he had been numb, it might have wearied him rather than distressed him. Now he ached for her, and hurried to sit beside her, setting his hand on her shoulder.

"Amma, what is it?"

She just shook her head.

"Amma—"

"All our people," she whispered.

His face hardened. "I will get them out of the house, amma. And that . . . that man from Natzeret. I'll throw him to the dirt."

"No." She smiled up at him and took his hand in hers. They *looked* frail, but her grip was strong. "It's not that, my Shimon. It's only that I didn't know. I didn't know our town was so broken, so many of us ruined. How bad it had become. Your father—" Her voice caught. "He would have wept to see this, Shimon. He *believed* in Kfar Nahum. He believed not even the Romans, not even the dead out of the hills, could do this to us. Could *ever* do this to us."

"What happened, amma?" Shimon took a breath. "There are people out there who were ill, a few who were maimed. Now they . . . What happened?"

Her gaze strayed to her arm. Shimon followed that glance, but saw nothing there. Just her olive skin.

"The dead are coming back up," she said.

"Yes." His own voice caught.

"They're coming for *him*. Have you seen his eyes, my son? He burns with life. So much that it spills out of him and touches the rest of us. It's like fire, and the *shedim* are moths, Shimon. He's drawing them out of the sea, just by being here."

"Then we have to get rid of him." Shimon's voice was cold, colder than he would have thought possible. He thought of the stones he could lift from the street outside. Thought of the bruises that purpled the man's face and arms. Perhaps this was why he had been driven out into the desert, so that the dead might follow him where he went and leave the living alone.

"No," Rahel said. "I have no fever."

"Amma?"

"I have no fever, Shimon. I thought—at first I thought it might come back. But it didn't."

He sat back on his heels. "What *happened*?"

Fever? *Something* had happened. And Rahel was—different. Lost in thought. Lying here in her bedding as though utterly exhausted. That wasn't like her. And Koach—he was different, too. His insides went cold with dread.

"It's not important," Rahel whispered. "He's what's important. He's anointed, Shimon. Our *navi*, our messiah, our anointed one. I have to tell Zebadyah bar Yesse tomorrow; he has been so afraid. I have to tell him. This stranger—he *is* the one we've waited for." She closed her eyes. "Fifteen years. I've waited fifteen years."

Shimon kept silent. He sensed that she needed to speak, needed badly to speak.

"I prayed, Shimon. That night your father died. As I held little Koach in my arms. I begged God, in the silence of my heart, I begged him to send the anointed one, that I would see him with my own eyes. I told God, *My boys need me. And everything out there is burning and dying. I can hear it. I can smell it. Let me see Kfar Nahum healed before I die. Let me see my two sons together and strong.*" Her eyes glistened. "When I opened my eyes this day and saw him there, I knew. I *knew*. I had suffered enough, enough even for El-Shaddai Our God. He had chosen to answer my prayer, little Shimon. He would not let me die until I saw that man. With my own eyes."

"Amma," he murmured, but said nothing else.

She squeezed his hand. "You can break a family or a People even as you can break an arm or a clay bowl. Everything had broken that winter. When the Romans came. They broke the doors of the synagogue. They took . . . whatever they wanted, Shimon, whatever they wanted. To fill the tax debt. They broke us." A hiss in her voice. "They took some of the boats, all the food, all the fine clothes. They hurt our girls. Yonah your father . . . he hid me." Her eyes softened. "He was so brave, your father. He hid me out in the *kokhim*, among the dead. The one place the Romans didn't think to look for anything of value, and the one place no one else in Kfar Nahum thought to hide anything. I was so scared, Shimon. It was dark, and all about me the bodies and bones of our dead. Yonah brought food and water when he could, but I had to ration it so carefully. He couldn't always come, and he didn't trust anyone else to. We were all afraid, everyone.

"Most of the time I sat huddled against the wall of the bone chamber, just praying. My belly was so full with your brother. I didn't want to move or do anything but sleep. And I was hungry, so hungry." Her voice trembled. "I was terrified that something would go wrong. That I would lose the baby. I did rise once, and I explored the tomb with my hands, because I couldn't bear not knowing what was there. There was the great chamber, and the tunnels leading out from it, and the shelves where our dead are slid into the living rock. I touched a few of them, Shimon. I . . . I had to. I had to know they were still."

He touched her hair gently. "It's all right, amma. It is long past."

"Long past." She smiled weakly. "Nothing stays buried, my little one. Maybe nothing stays broken, either. I hope that's so."

Her little one. It had been years since she had called him that.

She hadn't called him that since Koach was born.

Since before his father died.

Shimon blinked and swallowed against a tightness in his throat.

"I heard them carousing. The shouts, the screams. I could hear it all, all the pain of the women I knew, the men. And I couldn't do anything." Her hands shook. "I couldn't even cry for them, Shimon, because my labor took me, and all I could do was breathe, just *breathe*, between the pangs. Breathe and hear. Such horrible screams." She closed her eyes. "Even the moaning of the dead wasn't worse than that." She drew in a breath. "For all I knew, Yonah was dying while I fought to push Koach out of my body. Oh, Shimon, I wanted to die. And I wanted to live. I cursed your father, biting my lip to hold in the screams. He wasn't there with me. I hated him, for a few brief moments." She shook her head. "I didn't know if he lived, or if you did, or if I would live, only that I had to *push* that baby out into the world. Even if there was nothing left out there, nothing but the dead. They moaned all around the tomb, and my heart—I have never felt fear like that. Or rage. Or—"

Her hands trembled.

"And then I had two sons," she whispered, and fell silent.

———

All his adult life, Shimon had stood with his back to the memory of that winter. That memory had stalked him at every waking hour, until its cold fingers touched his very shoulder, and when he lay down to sleep it sprang on him like a lion on a gazelle. Now, in his mind, he turned and looked into the cold eyes of his pursuer.

He remembered waiting on the shore, unable either to shout or to flee as the boat came in. With its scrape against the sand, his father's body had staggered into the gunwale and toppled over to lie half in the water, half on the moist land. Shimon had stared in fascinated terror at this human shape that looked so much like Yonah, the fisher, who in the last year had taught him to carve an oar, to gut a fish, to tack a boat against the wind.

He remembered his father's face turning to him, the eyes lifeless, the low hiss in the dark. Remembered scrambling away over the sand and loose shingle, stumbling, getting back up, falling again. Remembered kicking up sand, frantic to regain his feet, the corpse bending over him, dried blood on its hand. His father's blood.

And he remembered his mother's scream, a cry raw with fury and pain and grief, as she leapt between Shimon and his father.

Then Rahel had stood painfully straight, her tunic dark at her thighs with the blood of the day after childbirth, her hair sweaty across her face. Both hands whitened about the haft of a fishing spear. The iron point had gone through his dead father's eye and into his skull and there it was sheathed. His father's limbs hung limp. He no longer moved or moaned, but the spear held him up, so that he appeared to be standing there beside his wife, gazing at her with those eyes that had looked out, unseeing, on the water and that had looked across the sand, unseeing, at his child.

With a low wail, Rahel wrenched the hook free; it left his father's body with a quiet squelching sound not unlike the spilling of innards from a fish's belly. Yonah's body toppled to the sand and he lay still. The wound was dark in his brow, a wound that didn't bleed. Rahel stood over him, breathing hard, the fishing spear held at her side. The hand that gripped it shook violently.

A wind came in off the sea, and her hair blew across her face, hiding her anguish from her son. Shimon felt the chill of the wind on his brow, which was damp with sweat.

"Abba," he gasped, "abba."

"No," Rahel whispered. She swayed on her feet.

Leaping up, Shimon caught her as she fell, a woman weak from horror and loss of blood from her labor; even as Shimon threw his arms about her and held her tightly, the spear slipped from her limp hand and sheathed its point in the sand.

———

That moment, and others, flashed through Shimon's heart like a school of fish. Rahel between him and the corpse of his father. Or leaping before Barabba's horse. Even Koach his brother, standing over the body of his beloved, that blunt rock in his hand. For so long Shimon had thought his entire life was but the last rattle in a corpse's throat—a last fight for air that was without meaning or hope of victory. His failure to bring in fish enough to feed his kin had always shamed him; now his days of despair shamed him more. While he'd sat in his grief and his gloom, his mother, who'd once given birth in a tomb even as the *shedim* moaned on every side, had stood constant, had never stopped hoping and believing in her sons. The waters may wear away the stones, but no matter how the waves crash against the shore, some hearts can never be worn away, can never be crumbled, can never be pounded into sand.

"How did you do it?" he asked suddenly. "When father came back. How did you do it, amma? How did you find the courage?"

Her face showed her pain. "I did it," she said slowly, "because I loved him. I loved him, Shimon. Most wives do not love their husbands, because most husbands do not love their wives. But I loved your father. I loved him from the moment he appeared at my father's door with a net of fish and a plea in his eyes, asking for me." She smiled faintly, her eyes wet. "I loved him, so I had to."

"Amma," Shimon whispered.

She reached up and grasped his hand again, tightly. Her eyes sought his. "Your father would be proud of you, Shimon. Never doubt it."

He choked. "I love you, amma."

"And I you, Shimon." Her face was tight with weariness. "Will you sing to me the way you did when you were a boy? After your father had kissed me, while he was gathering up his things for the boat, you would come sit by me and sing me to sleep. Do you remember?"

"I remember," Shimon said hoarsely.

"I am going to try to sleep." A faint smile. "I don't care how many people are here. You and Koach can care for them a while. Sing me to sleep, my Shimon."

Shimon drew up her wool blanket and tucked it around her chin. Long ago it had been dyed blue, but its color had faded away with time, like so many other things. Behind him, Shimon could no longer hear the *navi* and others speaking; it was quiet out in the atrium. Outside the house, his brother and the priest's sons might be watching for the dead, but he could not hear their footsteps or their fear. For the moment, there was nothing in the world but mother and son. Rahel squeezed his hand and he returned her grip, and sang in a low murmur, for her. A song he'd heard her sing once in a tomb, far away, on the other side of time.

> *Though the fig tree does not flower,*
> *And no grapes are on the vines,*
> *The olives give no oil*
> *And the fields no barley*
> *The flock does not come home to the fold*

Nor the herd home from the field,
Yet I will cry out in joy.

God is my strength;
He makes my feet like the deer's;
He makes me walk in high places.

THE LIGHT SHINES IN THE DARK

LEAVING HIS mother sleeping, Shimon stepped out into the atrium. The house was nearly empty again. The people who had gathered there were gone, and Koach hadn't returned. Yeshua sat alone by the cold firepit, holding a small lamp in his hands; there was a little flame—he must've lit it before dark fell, before the Sabbath Bride settled down for her night's rest—and the scent of rancid oil mixed with the lingering smell of roasted fish in a way that did uncomfortable things to Shimon's stomach, though it also made him aware that he hadn't eaten since the morning. The town had feasted, yet he had not.

He crouched across the firepit from Yeshua, giving him a wary look. Two fish still lay on the coals. Shimon snatched one up in his bare hands; it had cooled long before, but when he lifted it to his teeth and bit, the oil and flavor of the fish ran into his mouth, and his hunger roared in his belly. He tore at it in urgent bites.

A small sound made him glance up, and he noticed the beggar woman—the one Koach had helped—leaning against the olive tree, in its shadow.

Shimon cast the bones of the fish down over the coals; he would clean out the pit in the morning. He considered Yeshua. Madman or *navi*, was this man a blessing or a threat to the town? His mother trusted the stranger and thought him a holy one—*the* holy one, the *navi*. The bruises on the man's face were dark in the lamplight, his face thin. Shimon wondered whether this stranger in his house had eaten much, either.

"There were . . ." Shimon glanced around. "People."

"Gone home for the Sabbath," Yeshua said quietly. "All of them. Or to what shelters they could find or that those who feasted here would . . . would offer. All gone. I am alone." Anguish in his face, he didn't look up from the light. "Still alone. I'll always be alone, won't I, even if I feed a house, even if I feed a town, even if the lame walk and the mute sing. I am still alone. I am still standing in the desert, listening to the screams."

Shimon grunted. Earlier in the day, the stranger had been almost *furious* with energy. He had moved with a hastiness and an urgency that was entirely alien to the slow, exhausted men and women of Kfar Nahum. But now a hush had fallen over him; he looked faint. Worn. Shimon realized, startled, that there were wrinkles about Yeshua's eyes that had not been there in the morning. Now he looked more like the men Shimon knew. Even his voice, the way he talked, had changed. He no longer sounded frantic, desperate, dangerous.

Only sorrowful.

"You have the hospitality of this house." Shimon's voice was gruff. He would honor his mother's wishes and her hope.

"I would . . . I would like that," Yeshua said, a flicker of gratitude in his eyes. He stared at the small flame.

"Well," Shimon muttered. "I will bring some bedding out here."

"My mother lights a lamp," Yeshua said, as though he hadn't heard. "A small lamp, much like this one, a *lot* like this one, every night. *Every* night. Though oil is costly in Natzeret." He glanced at the fish bones on the cold coals, such grief in his face that Shimon had to look away. "I suppose it is here, too."

The flame wavered; the stranger glanced at it and then stilled the shaking of his hands. He took a breath, then set the lamp carefully to the side. "They are so loud. I hear them, Cephas. I hear them whether I rise or whether I lie down. I hear them always. Every hour, every day."

"Hear who?" Shimon peered cautiously at the man's face, but his eyes held a cold, clear intelligence. There was no madness there. Only thought and pain.

"The cries," Yeshua answered. "Their moans of hunger."

Shimon's breath caught. "The dead?"

"The living," Yeshua said sharply. Then he pressed a hand to his eyes. "The dead. Both." His voice was calm, though thick with fatigue—as though his raving had been a thicket he'd broken through and now he was in the open again, but sweaty and weary from his work. "All of you eating alone, and not together. So many closed doors, so many windows shut. So many of you dying alone in your lonely houses." He sighed. "Kana is wrong. Zebadyah is wrong, too. We can't avoid our past, its violence. Can't deny it, not ever. The screams in our desert. Nor even atone for them." His eyes were distant. "Only forgive."

Suddenly, a scream pierced the air. Shimon gasped. Yeshua's face hardened. Outside, a few doors slammed; wooden slats rattled shut over one window.

The murmur of the sea, the sigh of water on the sand.

Then they heard it.

Low, wavering moans. Distant yet loud in the stillness.

"You did this," Shimon said, his insides numb and cold. "You brought the dead back up."

"Yes." Yeshua's voice was quiet and sad. "And the fish also. But by this time tomorrow it will be over, I think."

Shimon stood. "We have to bar the door," he breathed.

"No." Yeshua's face hardened, and he stood, too. "Let others hide. You and I, we will do the father's work."

Shimon turned on him in horror. "Don't you hear?" Hardly daring to speak above a whisper. "The *dead* are coming."

Those strange eyes of Yeshua's were bright and fierce in the light of the lamp. "No matter how the door burns, Cephas, I have to step through it in the end. I can't flinch back from it anymore. Whatever the father wishes me to do, the weeping father, it's time I did it." He gripped Shimon's arm. A hard, tight grip. A workman's grip. A *nagar*'s grip.

His voice was clear and calm.

"Don't be afraid, Cephas."

When Yeshua stepped past him to the door, Shimon followed, still meaning to bar it. But instead, Yeshua took hold of the door and threw it wide. Shimon could see the shadow-shape of the house that leaned just across the narrow street from his own.

Then he sucked in his breath, for in a stab of cold dread, he remembered.

Yakob and Yohanna. And Koach.

His brother was out there.

A PESTLE, A MENORAH, A SHOFAR, A SICA, AND THE HEAT OF A SUN

BAR CHELEPH saw them first, and when the others—Koach, Yakob, Yohanna—turned their heads, it was as though Bar Cheleph's shriek had split the night open and let the *shedim* tumble out of nightmares into the real world, the world of time and suffering. The corpses stumbled up the shoreline toward them, lurching, their arms lifted, their moans muted by the surge and song of the sea, but no less terrible. There were perhaps ten or twelve of them, their eyes glinting in the faint light off the water. A few boat people, having lost their shelters, had erected hasty windbreaks of driftwood draped with lake-weed and had huddled behind them against the cold of night. Now they leapt to their feet and sprang, shouting, across the sands, fleeing the oncoming ghouls. The same wind that had brought the Sabbath Bride to Beth Tsaida with the dusk swept up, bringing to Koach's face this time the reek of the dead.

"God," Bar Cheleph gasped, "oh God."

Yakob and Yohanna went very still.

But Koach's face hardened, and his grip whitened around the pestle he'd taken from his mother's house.

The dead came trailing sea wrack and weeds from their arms. Sometimes the town saw straggler corpses from the hills, but these dead had risen from the sea, somewhere north along the shore. Benayahu was not among them.

"So many," Yakob breathed. "Why? Why now?"

"It doesn't matter," Koach said. "We have to stop them."

"No," Bar Cheleph whispered. "No." He glanced wildly at the faces of his companions, then broke and ran across the grasses.

He fled *toward* the houses of Beth Tsaida.

"You fool!" Yakob cried, his voice loud over the sand.

Three of the corpses turned their heads, their attention caught by Bar Cheleph's scrambling run, their mouths gaping. That *moan*, that sound without words or thought that made the blood move cold and sluggish like mud in the hills. The three lurched away from the group and slouched up toward the tideline, following Bar Cheleph. Koach's breath hissed out through his teeth. Bar Cheleph would lead them *right* into the houses of the fishers. To his *mother's* house.

Koach whispered a prayer, a bitter, desperate prayer, under his breath—*If you are a father, El Shaddai, El Shaddai, if you are what the stranger says you are, help us*—and then he ran along the grasses, leaving the others behind, pursuing the dead who pursued Bar Cheleph, though he felt out of breath, felt as though he might faint. He called out Bar Cheleph's name, but the other man didn't stop. Nor did the dead turn from their chase of him; they could not run, yet Koach closed the distance only slowly. He felt the fear, the fear eating his mind, trying to make him into a small, shivering animal who might drop into the tidal grasses to quiver and hide. It was more overpowering than when he'd faced Tamar, for then his fear had been crushed under a weight of grief. Now he could think only of cold fingers grasping, cold teeth biting into his arm or his throat or his belly.

He shoved back the terror, kept staggering toward the houses of Beth Tsaida.

———

The rest of the dead lurched after the boat people, who stumbled up the sand toward the priest's sons. Earlier Yakob had led a small search party north along the shore, searching for Benayahu and finding blood in the grasses but no sign of where the man had gone. He'd thought—for a moment—that he heard a moan in the hills, distant, barely audible. He had shivered and started back, his heart full of dark thoughts and darker fears. Now his fears were enfleshed.

"Shit," Yakob breathed. "Shit!"

He ran toward the boat people, gesturing wildly with his arms. "You! All of you! Follow me!"

They turned to him, their eyes fearful, desperate.

"Come *on*!" he shouted.

Yakob thought quickly. He could lead the boat people down the shore, away from the town, trailing the dead behind—then circle up into the hills, in the hope of losing the dead in the wild. Some of the boat people would falter and collapse, some would be eaten. But his brothers, his father, his grandfather, they would be safe.

He *could* do that.

Instead, he got his shoulder under one of the haggard women even as she stumbled. Half carrying her, he began walking up toward the houses of Kfar Nahum, toward whatever sanctuary the broken town could offer.

A moment's choice, a moment's decision.

His brother fell in alongside him, his face twisted with fear. Yakob met his gaze. "We are all kin," he said.

Yohanna nodded, pale.

The woman coughed faintly. Others ran past. Yakob refused to glance back at the moaning dead. "It's all right," he murmured to the woman. "Just come with me. It's all right . . . Yohanna, run. Run ahead. Warn father."

"And leave you to face this alone?" Yohanna choked.

"Hurry, brother. God will keep me."

Yohanna whispered, "God had better."

The wailing behind them drew nearer. The boat woman began whimpering almost too quietly to hear. Yakob gave his brother a strained smile . . . or something he meant to be a smile. He clapped Yohanna on the shoulder. "Go!"

Once again, Koach ran through the stone houses and decayed shelters of his people, with lives at stake. The stone pestle was cold in his palm. The sound of his breathing was loud in his ears, and sweat stung his eyes. He was not made for running, had done little of it. But there wasn't far to go.

Bar Cheleph had already strained his hip throughout the day, and Koach caught up with him as he was panting past the houses of the fishers. As they ran near, Natan El threw open his door, and he and his young wife stood at their doorstep across from Rahel's house, gazing out with horror in their faces. They could see Bar Cheleph stumble and catch himself; they could hear the moans of the dead, coming up from the shore behind their house. In another moment, the door across the narrow street swung open, and Rahel looked out, her face haggard, newly wrenched from sleep. Her face went white as she gazed out; even as Koach closed the distance with Bar Cheleph, calling out his name, the three corpses lunged from around the corner of Natan El's house, right in front of Bar Cheleph. One grappled him, its gray hands seizing his arms, its weight bearing him beneath it to the ground. The second staggered across the street toward Rahel. The third lurched past, toward Natan El's door. A shrill scream—from Natan El, not from his wife; he sprang back, and his wife swung shut the door even as the corpse reached it, slamming it against one grop-ing arm. The door rattled hard, the corpse hurling itself against the wood. Across the street, the other corpse threw itself against Rahel's door.

Koach let out a cry and sprang on the nearest corpse from behind, swinging his pestle. But the creature turned, hearing him, and its hand caught Koach's arm just above the elbow, a grip fierce and strong. Koach felt himself pulled from his feet toward the thing's mouth; its head snapped at his arm, the teeth closing on the thick wool his mother had woven for him. He felt the pressure of its bite and screamed, kicking wildly, thrashing in the thing's grasp. Those horrible, dead eyes looked at his for an instant as it worried his arm like a wild dog. Nothing in its face but hunger.

Then the door wrenched open. There was a sickening crunch of bone and a spatter of necrotic flesh as an iron shaft was driven into the thing's cheek. The corpse didn't release Koach's arm, but it turned, pulling Koach with it, its jaw still grinding, trying to dig into Koach's flesh through the wool sleeve. Koach fought to bend his hand and the pestle toward its head, but he had only one arm, and the creature held it. He caught a glimpse of Natan El's wife, Bat Abner, in the door, her face a grimace of terror. Both hands whitened around the haft of her husband's fishing hook. She was tugging at it wildly, trying to free it of the corpse's face, to thrust or swing it a second time, but the hook had caught on the creature's jaw and she couldn't free it. The ghastly face tore at Koach's arm and it growled against the wool. The scent of its decay was too much; Koach vomited, the fish of his brother's catch surging up his throat and out of his mouth in a hot, steaming rush, fouling his chin, his clothes.

Helpless.

Again.

Always.

No.

Vomiting, shaking, furious, Koach swung his body, lifting his left leg and slamming his sandaled foot against the corpse's groin. It didn't feel the pain, but the impact drove it back, even as Bat Abner's pull on the spear tugged hard in the other direction. The iron hook tore the creature's jaws free from Koach's arm, tearing the sleeve with it. Koach's arm slithered free of the thing's grip, unsleeved, and he fell, smacking his chest hard against the stone doorstep. Ignoring the stab of pain, Koach rolled hard. He'd dropped the pestle; it fell near him and he scrambled to it, lifted it in his hand, and turned to see the corpse biting wildly at the hook as its cold hands reached for Bat Abner. It shoved itself through her door, thrusting her back, the two of them, the living and the dead, separated by only the length of that small spear of iron. Shouting wildly, Koach surged to his feet and rushed the corpse, swinging the pestle; the hard stone drove in the back of the thing's head. He heard it spit and snarl, and he swung the pestle again, again, crushing in the creature's skull, until its legs crumbled and it hung, a silent, limp weight on the end of Bat Abner's spear.

Less than three paces away, Bar Cheleph struggled for his life. The thing he wrestled had been corpulent in life, and its dead flesh was massive and held him crushed to the grit of the street. The rage he'd felt when he speared Bat Benayahu's corpse had deserted him, leaving only stabbing, wild terror and hot shame, hot urine wet on his thighs. His fingers gripped the thing's face, holding its jaws back from his throat, and he panted and wept. The corpse's eye gave beneath Bar Cheleph's fingers, but the thing didn't shriek, didn't rear back, just kept biting at the air above his collarbone.

Then the corpse's jaw slackened and gray matter sprayed outward from the back of its head; its grip on Bar Cheleph's shoulders loosed. Glancing up, Bar Cheleph saw standing over him Koach, a clay pestle clutched in his left hand, the end of the pestle dark with gore. Gasping, Bar Cheleph just shivered beneath the corpse, staring up at his rescuer in shock.

The youth who stood over him was grim-eyed and fierce. And not in the least *hebel*. Yakob bar Cheleph did not know this boy.

Koach cast the pestle aside; bending, he wrapped his hand in the hem of his wool tunic and gripped the corpse's arm through the fabric, his fingers protected from the touch of skin against unclean skin; a heave, and the corpse was rolled aside. Bar Cheleph scooted out from beneath it, kicking. Then he stopped, his chest heaving.

Koach freed his hand of the wool and offered it.

Bar Cheleph swallowed. "But I . . . I tormented you."

"I forgive you." The youth's voice was quiet. "Now help me. One of them is at my mother's door, and I need more than one hand. Help me."

Bar Cheleph gazed up at him helplessly. Then he took Koach's hand and felt himself pulled to his feet. He marveled at the strength in the youth's left arm.

"My brother," he gasped.

Koach's eyes went cold, but he nodded. "Brother."

———

There was a moan behind them, and then a sharp crack. Turning, Koach gasped. The other corpse had stood facing his mother's door, its back to him, but now it swayed to the left and fell. Rahel stood at her open door, her hair wild about her shoulders, her husband's *tallit* drawn over her like a woman's shawl. Her face was gray, and she held tightly in both hands a shard of pottery longer than her hand, its broken point dark with gore. Other shards lay shattered about her feet, and there was a dark puncture in the head of the corpse. That sound they'd heard . . . Behind her in the doorway, the woman who had been mute gazed out with wide eyes.

Rahel glanced up from the corpse, and though she had no words, there were a thousand in her eyes, and memory dark as the sea—unburied memory of a night of the dead.

"Amma," Koach breathed.

Bar Cheleph, still panting, bowed his head slightly in respect. "Bat Eleazar," he murmured.

"My son. Kinsman." Her eyes flashed in the dark. She let the gory shard fall from her hand; it rang against the stone beneath her feet. She bent and spat on the corpse, then straightened, her face flushed. "Help me get this thing off my doorstep."

The boat people fled like deer between the old houses of Kfar Nahum, the empty houses that sat quiet as desert stones farther in from the shore, their doors and windows long since boarded up against squatters living or dead. Yakob was near the rear now, carrying that ragged woman who could hardly stand, let alone flee. The dead followed, lurching against the houses and scraping along the stone walls, but ignoring the structures, intent on the fugitives from the shore.

The vagrants broke out into the open space before the synagogue, its white basalt luminous in the rising moon. For a moment they stopped, their eyes round in the dark, glancing about, uncertain where else to run. Even as the first dead lurched into the space after them, the door to the synagogue was flung open, and a man in the white robes of a priest burst out onto the polished steps, a great menorah held in his hand, its eight candles new-kindled. His eyes burned as with fever. In an instant, a single beat of the heart, he took it all in: the pursuing dead, the sickly stench of them. The sobbing, stumbling boat people. His son Yakob half carrying one of them, risking his body and blood for these heathen and half-heathen poor.

Yohanna stepped out beside him, his face tight with fear.

"Go, son," Zebadyah said gruffly. "Warn the weaver and the other houses. All you can."

Yohanna gave a shaky nod. Then he sprinted; in a moment, he was gone.

Zebadyah wanted to slam the door of the synagogue against the boat people, but the old guilt coursed hot through his veins. He could not let others die before him, as he had long ago. The dead were within the town; whatever walls of fire or stone or will Zebadyah might have erected, it was too late. There was no time to sort out who were his kin, to protect, and who were not. And his oldest, by his act of carrying that woman and bringing all of them here, had already committed his house to sheltering these men and women. There was no wall here, and he was not Ezra.

He lifted the menorah high. "Into the synagogue!" he shouted. "All of you!"

His cry broke the stupor that had fallen on the boat people as sharply as a branch might crack beneath the blow of a man's heel. The vagrants rushed past him, stumbling up the steps and through the door, into the holy place at the heart of the town from which they'd so long been banned. Last, Yakob brought in the woman and laid her on the floor below the cabinet that held the scroll of Torah. Even as he glanced up from her, his eyes full of the intent to join his father, Zebadyah swung the door shut.

Zebadyah ran from the synagogue steps out into the open, wielding the light and hope of his People, like the knife-wielding *kanna'im* in the south, the grieving priests. Alone in that open space before the steps, he took his stand, thrusting the fiery meno-rah into the faces of the pursuing dead, their eyes glowing in the flames. His ears were full of the shrieks and moans of that other night, that terrible night, that night he had never woken from. Again he heard the whisper in his heart, *Run, little priest. Run. You are not Ezra or Moshe or Aharon. You cannot face this. You will be eaten.* That quiet whisper of the *shedim* waiting to take his heart and hollow it out and live inside its cold shell.

"Not this time," he growled.

The dead shied back before the stabbing flames, but only barely; and now the corpses closed in on either side. There were nine of them, their jaws snapping as they tried to press in on flame and priest. Though Zebadyah darted to the left and to the right, one man with a stick of candles, even a holy one, could not hold them all. He fell back but stopped when he heard the door of the synagogue thrown open behind him. Clenching his teeth, he swung the menorah in an arc of flame. Grasping hands, the growls of the dead—

"Father!"

Yakob at the door.

Run, little priest, run. You will be eaten, eaten, eaten—

To silence the drumbeat of his heart and the knife-sharp cut-ting of that whisper into his spirit, Zebadyah raised his voice in a desert scream of desert song, words invoking the strength and refuge of a desert God, ancient and severe, in whose presence all unclean things, whether mortal or immortal, withered like grass:

> *His arms are mighty,*
> *He shatters the foe!*
>
> *He is my tent*
> *My refuge,*
> *My rock and fortress . . .*

He trains my hands for battle,
And my fingers for war!

He drove the menorah into a corpse's face. It spat and hissed as it fell back, and then cold hands, so cold, grasped his extended right arm, and suddenly he was on his back gazing up at the stars in their sky and the dark shapes of the dead bending over him. Fingers dug into his flesh, into his arm, his shoulder. Then the touch of a cold face and the pain of teeth, more violent and sharp than he could have imagined or feared, peeling away his skin, tearing away a part of him, a part of his *body*. This was his death, his death . . . In a scream of agony Zebadyah cried out the life-prayer and death-prayer of his People, hoping that God, however distant, would hear his words: *Sh'ma Yisrael adonai eloheinu . . .*

———

Kana blew a long call on the shofar, desperate and loud. Then he dropped it from his lips and leapt into the crowd of dead at the synagogue steps, his sica flashing in the dark. He saw the priest tugged beneath the corpses and he howled in his rage, as he had once heard Barabba howl on the dusty pass of Adummim, the Red Way, the Way of Blood, when a pack of dead lurching out of the rocks took one of his most trusted warriors. Tonight Zebadyah had not hidden beneath any boat on the shore, leaving Shimon bar Nahemyah to stand in his place at the door of the synagogue. Instead, tonight the priest had stood in Kana's place, while Kana paced brooding on the slope of the hill of tombs. Hearing the moans, he had unsheathed his sica and run into the town, run fast until his sides burned. And yet he was too late.

As he drove his knife under the chin and up into the skull of one of the growling dead, he heard a cry from his left.

"Father! Abba! *Abba!*"

He knew the voice; without sparing a glance, he shouted, "Get him out of there!"

Another of the dead grasped at him; Kana caught the corpse's arm in a hard grip and pulled it in close—a wild glimpse of teeth—and he drove the knife in, then pulled it free just as swiftly, slamming his hip into the corpse to shove it aside and out of the way. Even as it fell, he had chosen his next target; he grasped the thing's arm to pull it near, but the soggy remnant of its sleeve came away in his hand, and he staggered back from the force of his pull. The thing turned on him, hissing. Its hands gripped Kana's shoulders, a grip fierce and cold, cold even through his cloak. With a shout, he drove the sica up through its chin and saw the thing's face go slack.

Others behind grasped at his shoulders, his hair. He dropped, had a confused glimpse of unsandaled feet all around him, pale and heavy with stench, as he let himself fall to the ground to roll away and back to his knees. A hop up to his feet, and Kana crouched with his sica ready. The corpses lunged at him, bending to grasp him, and then he was whirling and ducking and slicing in the dance of the fennec, the fox in the desert, the dance Barabba—damn his heart—had taught him in caves far from the sea, in ravines where the dry dust still carried the footprints of dead that had passed through years before. Fingers cold and damp brushed his shoulders, his arms, even his face, but none found a grip. He moved as quickly as the wind, for none know where the wind has come from or where it will go, they only feel the strength and the swiftness of its passing. On this wind there was a blade, with a bite sharper than winter or hunger itself. And when Kana slid the point and then the curved, cruel length into unclean flesh, he shouted, a hoarse bark like the fennec. Exultant, fierce, the cry at the kill, for he was alive and another was not. He danced, and another was still.

Memories crowded upon him as he spun and cut. That day of ambush on the high Adummim last summer; the sweat and heat of his long night's battle at the synagogue door fifteen years ago; the scream of Ahava, his beloved, dying as the teeth of the dead tore at her; his encounter with a dead child in the alleys of Yerushalayim, its empty eyes and wild hiss, a tattered doll still clutched in its hand. Kana shoved the memories away, hard; he had no time for them. Every bone, every beat of his heart, every breath had to be focused on this moment, on the slide and shriek of his Roman knife, on the lurching, groping movements of the enemy he faced. On killing.

The call of the shofar rang in Shimon's ears, a blast of sound like the roar of some beast, except deeper and clearer than any beast's cry in all the world.

Following its call, Shimon stumbled into the space before the synagogue, gasping for breath. Yeshua was there already, walking toward the knot of dead about Kana, and for an instant, Shimon stopped, breathless, seeing the other Hebrew dance among the dead, seeing his face and the efficiency of his movements, as though he were a Roman trained to kill. In that moment Shimon glimpsed what it must have been like in the wilds about Yerushalayim with Barabba the Outlaw. He wondered if this was what Yehuda tribe would become, in this generation or the next, or the one after. Caught between the Romans and the dead, both intent on devouring the People. Driven to the sica and the fever of killing, until they visited distant fishing villages and taught even the youths there to kill—as Barabba had sought to do.

Then Shimon saw Yakob pulling his father free of the corpses, and he let out a cry. Stooping, he took up a small stone from the street and ran at the dead.

But Yeshua was there before him. He walked into the dead, and his face and figure shone as though Shimon were gazing at a sun; he put his hand up before his eyes to shield them from the harsh light. Bars of fire flared across his vision. There was pressure against his chest, and he stumbled back with a shout.

Then the light was gone, and he was blinking against a blaze of color, his heart pounding. He made out Yakob drawing the priest up onto the steps, and Kana crouched with his knife in his right hand and his face red as though baked by the sun's heat.

And Yeshua.

The stranger stood with his arms out, the dead silent and still on the earth about his feet. Not one of them moved or twitched. Not one of them rose to its feet. Not one moaned in that hunger, cold and empty as the dark between the stars.

A BILLION STARS

SHIMON'S HEART was a storm on the sea. All these years, the dead had been his nightmare, his horror. And this man—this stranger he'd feared and hated—had just *walked* into the corpses and they had withered before the heat of his presence like leaves in a drought. All that he feared and all that he had known was as nothing to this man. Shimon fell to his knees on the hard earth.

"*Rabboni*," he whispered. *Rabboni*: My teacher, my master.

"On your feet, Cephas," Yeshua said quietly, without looking at him.

Everything in him shaken, Shimon rose and followed Yeshua toward the synagogue steps, where Yakob held his father's head in his lap. Kana stood near, his head bowed, his sica held at his side, the blade dark with gore.

The priest's shoulder and part of his neck had been torn open like cloth, and ragged strings of sinew and muscle had been pulled out of him. Shimon saw the glint of white bone. Blood had pulsed out over Zebadyah's chest and belly, dark and slick, running over his skin like olive oil. Yakob had stripped to his loincloth and was pressing the woolen tunic he'd worn to his father's wound.

"Zebadyah," Yeshua whispered, sitting down beside Yakob.

"He's dying." Yakob's voice was choked.

Zebadyah opened his eyes. "Yakob," he gasped.

"I am here, abba."

"Is Bat Eleazar safe?"

Yakob cast a glance at the *navi* and Shimon, and these were not the calm eyes of the fisherman Shimon knew. There was panic there. Shimon only nodded, his heart wrenched with pain for his friend.

"She is safe, father."

The priest's eyes glazed. "Tell her. Tell her that I love her still. As I did when I first saw her. That no man . . . that no man has ever been so jealous of a . . . a brother. That I hope her sons live long and good lives. Tell her that I am . . . that I am sorry."

Yakob's face crumpled.

Yeshua crouched beside him, his own face twisted in sorrow. As Shimon stood near, the stranger set his hand on Zebadyah's chest, as though blessing him. "You are not what I thought you were," Yeshua said softly. "*Shalom, kohen* of Israel. Whatever it is, this thing that burns in your memory, your shame, it is melted away like water."

Shimon stared at Yeshua. The stranger did not speak as he had earlier that day. His voice carried a quiet, clear authority.

Zebadyah's face tightened. "Only God can forgive or forget . . . evils," he panted. "Take your . . . hand . . . from my chest, Bar Yosef."

"Abba," Yakob whispered, pleading. "This man might heal you. He healed grandfather."

"No, Yakob. *No.* Not worth . . . I will die clean. If I must face . . . face our God at last, I will do it clean. I do not know whether this man's healing . . . whether it is a sign from El Shaddai, or some witchcraft . . . but I know that he has come . . . he has come to our town and the *shedim* have . . . have come up with him." He gripped his son's hand; his own shook. "I have made mistakes, terrible mistakes," he rasped. "But I have lived to keep my town clean . . . and . . . and faithful and *safe*, and I will die so."

The light had gone from Yeshua's face. His eyes were troubled. "So be it," he said softly. He rose slowly to his feet.

Yakob pulled Zebadyah close against his breast, his father's blood running over his hands.

"Keep our People faithful," Zebadyah whispered. "And safe. Follow no stranger. For me, Yakob. Ezra. Remember . . . Ezra. . . . Until the true *navi* comes."

Then he shuddered, and his face went slack. His chest rose and fell, shallow, for a few moments. Then stilled.

———

Shimon stood silent. Yakob's face was wet with tears. He clutched his father's body to his chest.

Kana crouched beside him, his sica still unsheathed in his hand. "Do you want me to do it?" The words came out gruffly.

Yakob shook his head quickly, and squeezed his eyes shut, his breath shuddering.

"I understand." Kana took Yakob's hand in his and opened his fingers gently. Then he pressed the hilt of the sica into Yakob's hand. "It's cleanest if you place the point beneath the chin and thrust up," he said quietly.

The look Yakob turned on him was a stab to Kana's heart. A look as though Yakob were gazing at a Roman, at a killer of his kin, at a man utterly strange and alien to their People. Swallowing, Kana closed the other man's fingers around the hilt and stood, turning away, leaving father and son alone. Staring down at the silent dead, he traced his thumb over the thin cuts on his arm, his lips moving. Counting.

"You were right," Yeshua said to Shimon. "I came to you too late. I hesitated at the door, and it . . . it is all wrong."

———

After that the night went thick and sluggish; they each moved as if in the midst of a fever. Yakob sat with his father's head cooling in his lap. After a while he took his hands from his father's face and was careful not to touch the skin that had lost its warmth, lest he be unclean. His pain was written on his face as dark and irrevocable as the words of God on the scroll of Torah.

When Yohanna returned to the synagogue after warning all those in Kfar Nahum to shut their doors and not open them, no matter what they might hear, he found his brother and his father like that. He stood over them, stricken.

Yakob lifted his head. "I waited for you, brother."

Yakob's tears had been silent, but Yohanna let out a long, low wail, as though something had been ripped out of his heart and he could not believe it.

As Yohanna wept, he and his brother lifted their father from the steps and carried him away into the dark. An empty shelf waited beside their mother's in a tomb on the hill.

———

Shimon walked to his house, found Rahel and Koach there, and embraced each of them fiercely. Then he took up a small shovel from the stack of tools he kept by the outer door and left without a word.

He began to carry the dead out behind the town—not to the old midden, but to a stretch of dirt near it, where he dug fiercely at the hard earth. To his surprise, some of the boat people, using rags torn from their own bodies for gloves, helped carry the corpses out to this fresh grave, helped him lay the bodies within it. The vagrants' eyes shone faintly in the starlight. Then, when the dead lay in the ground in a silent heap, they shoved the dirt back in over them and packed it down. They gathered stones, the heaviest they could find, and covered the grave, as the Hebrews had done long ago when their people had only just left the desert and were still uncattled and living in tents. They made a cairn over all those dead, a cairn taller than a man, perhaps the largest that had ever been made in the land, or the largest that ever would.

When the last of the rocks had been set atop the cairn, Shimon leaned his back against it, breathing hard, and several of the boat people leaned against it, too. He listened to the waves. After a few moments, gruffly, he asked their names. Obed, Philippos, and Xanthippos. One Hebrew, two who were Greek.

He would remember their names.

———

When the moon came up high over the water, Kana found the *navi* standing near the edge of the sea, gazing at the water, troubled. Kana was so weary he could barely stand; he had been checking to make sure no dead had broken into any of the abandoned and empty houses to remain a lurking threat that might fall upon the living later. He'd found none, but it had been dark and uneasy work.

Yeshua kept his gaze on the sea. He spoke softly as Kana approached. "I've been thinking about what you said. About the Romans. When they walk by and strike you across your face."

"It doesn't matter," Kana said bitterly.

"Kana, there . . . there may be . . . a way to face a man, an enemy, living or dead, without a knife in your hand. There may be. When a Roman strikes you across your face, turn your other cheek."

"My other . . . ?"

Kana's eyes widened.

When a Roman struck a Hebrew across the face, he did so with his left hand, and always with the back of the hand. To turn the other cheek to him . . . that would be a challenge; the Roman would have to strike with his right hand, or at least with his open palm. To do so would be to acknowledge that he was striking an equal. Then the Roman would owe a debt of honor to the man he'd struck, the man who was *not* his inferior and who had as much right to strike him and yet had chosen not to.

For one dizzying moment, Kana stared out over the waves in the dark and glimpsed what such a resistance could do.

What if a hundred, five hundred, a *thousand* were to behave so? The rulers of the land could not feed them *all* to the dead in the ghoul pits. The Romans needed men to work, women to warm their beds. If every man and woman in every town were simply to turn the cheek, or to do any of a dozen such acts, acts that involved neither cowering nor lashing out, but simply *insisting* that they and the Roman facing them were akin . . . could such a thing work? Or would the Romans not burn this land to ash, to keep such an insurrection from spreading across their world?

"God," he whispered, a prayer that was one word, one gasp.

"Don't you have eyes to see?" Yeshua said, his face sad. "Ears to hear?"

Kana's own words, turned toward him. Their original meaning had been peeled away, like that dying woman's rags by the boat, to reveal stark ribs and emaciation beneath, something that could not be unseen or avoided or forgotten. It seemed to him suddenly that he had lived his life fleeing from one violence to the next. He remembered the pale corpses dropped into the water like so many stones. He remembered the heat of the dust on the Red Way. And more than that, he recalled a girl sleeping, a Roman girl in a Roman bed. Recalled his own hand shaking in the dark, his palm slick with sweat about the hilt of his knife as he stood over her.

For a moment, he could only breathe.

"We are all screaming," Yeshua said. "We are all suffering. We are all kin. We must . . . we must gaze in our enemies' eyes and . . . and see our kin gazing back at us."

Kana didn't answer. He tossed his sica into the sand. It was all too much. Too much, too much. He bowed his head and struggled to shut his memories away.

He lifted his head when he heard footsteps in the sand. Koach was coming down the shore toward them, a ragged figure with one sleeve torn away and his other arm limp at his side. He stopped a few feet from Kana.

"You're back," he said tonelessly.

"I'm back," Kana said.

Koach glanced at Yeshua, then at the cairn. The boy had changed. He was still short and his right arm was still useless, but he *stood* differently. There was a hardness in his face that was not cruelty. Kana tried to recall where he had seen such a face before. He only knew that whatever man young Koach was growing into, he'd be a man others could trust. And Koach was not likely, Kana thought, ever again to need his protection against others in the town.

"Is it true?" Koach said after a moment. "Bar Yesse is dead?"

Kana's lips became a thin line. "It's true."

Koach gazed at the cairn a moment, then at the stone houses behind, and something flickered in those hard eyes.

"Then I will grieve for him," he said.

———

For a while the three of them stood together in a world without any speech but the crashing voice of the sea. Koach watched the shimmer of moon on the water and gazed at the horizon where sea and sky faded into endless dark. He thought of his fantasy of rowing Tamar, one-handed, over that sea in a boat. Of finding some far village that would not mind a cripple and a fatherless woman making a home beside them. A child's fantasy. He could not have given her that. He had not given her freedom. Only a release from her pain.

His thoughts were broken by a distant moan. Glancing up, he could see the corpse approaching over the shingle from the north, dragging one leg behind it. In the moonlight he could see that its bad leg was bare of cloth; it had been torn savagely just above the knee, as by an animal. Near the hip was a great gash, straight and sharp, as though the man had tried to cut his bitten leg away before he died, but had failed to complete the task—fainting perhaps from horror, or loss of blood, or the onset of the fever that brings the walking death. Koach sucked in his breath. A footstep warned him a moment before Shimon stood beside him; the boat people stayed by the cairn, watching.

Watching it approach.

Koach knew this corpse.

It was Benayahu.

Koach felt a sickness of fear moving like cold, sluggish water through his body, yet flame burned on the surface. The corpse's face was Benayahu's face. The same cheekbones, the same fleshy lips, the same scar by his eye. This man he'd hated, this man in whose shop he'd worked.

This man who'd beaten Tamar.

Part of him wanted to run out to that corpse and deliver some blow, some swift vengeance for the woman he'd lost.

And part of him wanted to bend over and be sick in the grass.

The *reek* of it.

Koach stooped to take up the sica Kana had thrown to the ground; one needed two hands to wield it as Kana did, but only one to stab with it.

"No, Koach, no." Yeshua pressed a hand to Koach's chest, stopping him. His eyes seemed very dark, pools that might swallow up stars, or pools out of which stars could be born. Before Koach or Kana or any of the others could argue, Yeshua stepped out over the sand to stand in Benayahu's way.

He put out his hand and the corpse halted as though pressed to a wall of stone. Its mouth opened and closed soundlessly. The air shimmered with heat.

"This is what I had to remember," Yeshua called to the others. "I am sure of it, almost sure. We must see the living and the dead as our father sees them, even if that sight burns us away like . . . like candles, because nothing else, nothing, will ever suffice. Our father, he sees all of us who are here and all of our children unborn and all of our fathers and their fathers and *their* fathers, all one People, in every moment that has been written or will be written, and we must leave not one behind and starving, not one of our People living or dead, not . . . not if we can do otherwise."

The corpse took no step forward, but it interrupted Yeshua with a low, quavering moan—such an agony of hunger. Koach barely held back from covering his ears. He stared at this corpse of the man who had been his enemy, though perhaps that man had never known it.

The sica was half-sheathed in the sand, yet Koach did not touch its hilt, and Kana did not reach for it, not yet.

"What are you going to do?" Kana called.

That haunted, desert look returned to Yeshua's eyes. "Try and find the man who was starving, the man the father lost."

The corpse leaned forward as though into a high wind. Its jaw worked as though it were chewing open-mouthed. It hissed at the living.

Yeshua straightened, his voice thickening with grief. "Benayahu, I see you. I know what you have done. I know what you did to your daughter. I can hear them all now, all the voices, all the words that before were lost in the moaning." His eyes shone with unshed tears. "I hear her, and I hear you. I hear Koach there behind me, and Kana, and Cephas, and all of them, all of them, and it hurts. It hurts." He sucked in a breath, and took another step toward the corpse. "And I know that somewhere in that rotting flesh you wear, somewhere deep, even now, your self-hatred and despair eats at you. I hear it loud as wind, as locusts in the crops. You can devour a hundred of your kin, a thousand, to fill that emptiness that not even your beating of your daughter could fill. And it will never be enough. I tell you the truth. Benayahu, it will *never* be enough."

The corpse growled, its eyes staring sightlessly ahead, and tried to slouch forward a step.

"No," Yeshua said. Koach could hear the tears in his voice, and even his mother's voice had never sounded like that, never sounded that hoarse with sorrow, that raw with pain. "It doesn't have to be like this," Yeshua said, pleading. "There's a choice. Everything we do is a choice. Everything. I *know* this. I hear us all, all, in my . . . in my *head*," he choked. "How could I not know this? I will not let you walk into that town, Benayahu. Nor any other corpse that may come. I promise. I promise. Not one. I can send you away." The heat made the air ripple like water, and the corpse staggered back one step.

They all did. Koach held a hand before his face.

"You can turn around," Yeshua said, his voice quivering. "You can walk away in that corpse you wear. No one will drive a blade into your head. I promise it. But you will not feed again on your kin. Not ever. If you leave, you will walk this earth always, hungering, thirsting, unsatisfied, in a misery whose origin you cannot even remember, until that body has crumbled away at last and is only soil, only that, only the dust it was in the beginning. And yet . . . and yet you will *still* suffer, famished, in an eternity without sleep, though no other will ever do you harm. If that is what you choose, Benayahu, my kin." Yeshua turned his hand, presenting the palm to the corpse, as though to invite it near. The heat abated, though the night was still warm, too warm for the shore of the sea. "Or let it go. All of it: the hunger, that body you wear, your fear and bitterness. Let it go." His voice dropped to nearly a whisper. "I hear your pain. And it is *my* pain. I am standing in the door, Benayahu, and I am burning, I am burning." Tears on his face. "The door of my father's house. And it hurts. God, it hurts. Take my hand. I'll help. I'll help you step through. We can't flinch away. Our father in heaven still loves you, Benayahu. He still finds you beautiful . . . as the day he made you. You think he won't welcome you, but he will, he will. Do you know what is on the other side of this door? His house . . . his *house* has so many . . . so many rooms, Benayahu. I wouldn't say this if I didn't see it. I *see* it. I see what he sees, and I am weeping, weeping like him." He touched his face. "These are his tears. That house where there is finally, finally no . . . no screaming. So many rooms. One even for you. And you can't even imagine it. It's that beautiful. So beautiful."

The corpse's head swiveled from Yeshua to the others. It *screeched*, making Koach start, his heart violent in his chest. He found himself staring at Benayahu's bloodied teeth in terrible fascination. All day Koach had grieved; now he was intensely grateful that Tamar was not walking the shore in just such a reeking corpse as this. Trapped like this, hungering like this, her mouth full of blood. He felt ill, unsteady on his feet.

"No," Yeshua said. "You look at me, Benayahu. At me. And choose. Please. Everyone chooses. Please."

The corpse faced Yeshua, and stood still. Something very strange began to happen. When he lay in his bedding later that night, Koach would not be entirely sure he had really seen it, had not imagined it. The life, the spirit, the person that Benayahu had been—all of that came back into the corpse's eyes. It came the way a great fish rises from the deep, murky and indistinct at first, and then gradually nearer until it was clear as a flash of sunlight on scales. Koach looked away swiftly, for all of Benayahu was in the corpse's eyes—all that he had ever loved or feared or craved, every moment of pain or regret. Koach didn't want to see that much of the man he'd hated, or that much of *any* man, all in one shattering instant. He kept his eyes averted.

Yeshua's face and hands began to burn with light, the way the sea does when it reflects the sun's fire. As Moseh's face must have when he lowered his hands from his eyes and gazed upon God at Har Sinai. As though all this shore was covered with God, with the fire of his presence, and only Yeshua could see it. The rest of them saw it reflected on his skin, and felt it in the heat that now scorched hot as the desert in the month of the lion. In a moment, all the sweat had been burned away from Koach's face, leaving behind only the taste of salt on his lips.

Yeshua's hand trembled as he held it out. "Please, Benayahu."

Benayahu staggered toward him, dragging one foot. His jaw slack. He reached for Yeshua, and his fingers, tentative as an old man's, touched the stranger's palm. The corpse's eyes filled with regret and pain so fierce, it hurt to look at them.

The corpse let out a slow sigh, a last exhalation like the world coming undone. Then its eyes emptied. Its knees gave way, and Yeshua caught the dead man in his arms and held him, the weight carrying him to his knees. He lay the body down on the wet sand.

Without knowing why, Koach found himself by Yeshua's shoulder. He stood over the corpse, the last of Tamar's kin. But he also remembered the misery in this corpse's eyes. And the way the *nagar* had stood staring at his wife's name on the wall of his shop. His hate was doused, for the pain in the man's eyes had been such that it could only inspire sorrow and regret, a regret deeper than the sea. Slowly, his throat tight, Koach leaned over the body. With his left hand he closed Benayahu's eyes.

"I'm sorry, Tamar," he whispered. "I didn't help you, and now you are gone, and your father, too. I'm sorry."

Beside him, the light faded from Yeshua's face as quickly as it had come. He fell to the side, but Koach caught him against his hip, breaking the fall. In a moment Shimon and Kana were there, helping him lower Yeshua gently to the sand.

Silent tears. Yeshua blinked them back. "Abba," he whispered. "The door is open. And the light, the light, the light . . ."

"*Navi*, are you all right?" Shimon asked hoarsely. He and Koach exchanged a wide-eyed glance.

"I looked into his eyes," Yeshua whispered, the tears running from the corners of his eyes down to his temples, tracing a path in the day's dirt and sweat on his face. "And he looked into mine. And I could see, oh I could see. Myself, reflected in his eyes. I remembered." The smallest shake of his head, his eyes glassy with pain and wonder. "I could breathe out a billion stars. All that life and beauty. Everything so beautiful—and so fragile. Everything dying and being born. And the sky, always getting bigger, always bigger. Too small to hold all the things I love. Cephas, I remembered." His hands were shaking, and Shimon caught one, squeezed it. Kana took the other, and cushioned Yeshua's head on his arm.

"It's slipping away now," Yeshua breathed. "All the suns and all the worlds and all their peoples. A moment ago, I could see them. See all of them. For just a moment—" He closed his eyes, but the tears still escaped him. His hands still shook as the men of Kfar Nahum held him.

"It's gone," he whispered. "I am Yeshua bar Yosef, a son of man, the *nagar*, of Natzeret on the hill."

PART 9

SIGN OF THE FISH

THE NIGHT was aging and Shimon staggered when he reached the doorstep of his own house; he hadn't slept since the day before this past one. Through bleary, bloodshot eyes, he peered down at the object that awaited him on the stone step, small and white in the starlight. He took it up in his hand; when he saw what he held, a shiver ran through his entire body and his entire heart. He didn't know how long he crouched there, holding the object, but his legs felt stiff when at last he lowered himself and sat on the step.

It was a fish carved from driftwood. A tail but no fins. A small, empty eye, just a circle carved into the wood. A simple thing carved by a child. Shimon held the small, precious thing in his hands and his cheeks were wet with tears. Glancing up, he found through the blur of his vision Bar Cheleph leaning against the house across the street, watching him.

"I took that from him, Bar Yonah," he said. "Years back." His eyes were dark with memory, his voice slow as though burdened with sleep. "He called me brother, tonight. That is his."

Shimon stared at him, mutely.

Bar Cheleph folded his hands uneasily behind his back. "I troubled your house. I regret it."

Shimon closed his hand around the small fish and rose, turning to his door.

"I'll watch your house tonight," Bar Cheleph called out quickly.

Shimon stopped, his fingertips just brushing the wood of his door.

"More dead might come. I'll keep watch."

Without turning, Shimon said, "You want to atone for striking my brother. He may forgive you; I don't. I don't need your atonement, Bar Cheleph." And he opened his door and stepped within, shutting it behind him.

WHERE THE WAVES EAT THE WORLD

SLOWLY, HOLDING her breath, Rahel walked out onto the sand, hearing bits of driftwood and the bones of fish crack beneath her naked feet. The world gray with the approaching dawn. Her husband's old prayer shawl was rough against her arm where she had tucked it into her sleeve. She kept her gaze on the man ahead of her, a man whose clothes were tattered, his face and arms dark with bruises. She had come down to the water to mourn a dead priest and a long-dead husband, and to be alone with the sea, but she found Yeshua there before her.

He stood where the land ended with the breakers wetting his feet, his arms extended, his hair tangled from a night walking in the wind without sleep, and without comb or basin to wash in. Though her sons had returned to the house in the late hours, and Yakob with them, as though he were unwilling to go back to a house now bereft of his father—Yeshua had not. All through the hours of the dark, he had been out here. Glancing to the left and the right, Rahel saw a few others here on the shore. Kana sat with his back to the cairn. Bar Cheleph stood leaning on an oar, a little way down the shore from Yeshua; Yohanna was at his side, a hand on his shoulder, his lips moving with words too quiet for Rahel to hear. Yesse sat cross-legged on the sand a few strides from them, his face desolate.

Even as Rahel drew near, Yeshua began calling out in high, quavering wails as if he were God calling some new world into being. The old desert God of their fathers. The God Rahel had always revered and resented and feared. Yeshua's arms were lifted as though he were prepared to part the sea as Moseh the Lawgiver had done. Then she gasped. Forms were rising from the water at his call, shapes of men dark against the morning in the east, at least ten or twelve. Corpses streamed water from their lank hair and the rotted remnants of their clothing as they staggered out of the waves, strands of seaweed caught about their limbs and trailing behind. Their arms rose from the sea, reaching for the man they saw before them.

"Amma!"

A cry behind her. Glancing back, she saw Shimon, his hair wild about his face, his eyes bloodshot from anguish and lack of sleep. Behind him, Yakob, looking scarcely better after the dark hours mourning his father. Both of them were in the dirtied garments they had worn the night before last, out at sea, when they had pulled up the nets full of fish. Some distance behind, slower, Koach stepped through the tideline grasses. All her boys, and Zebadyah's. One of them must have wakened to find her gone from the house; she had strained to lift the bar over the door but had done it quietly enough, and had stepped out softly, her grief so deep that she had forgotten her sandals. But after the deaths of the past day and night, an unexplained absence might well be an occasion for panic.

"Amma!" Shimon called. "Get back!"

Yakob called out, "*Rabboni! Rabboni!*"

The man from Natzeret let out another piercing cry. The dead were walking out of the waves now, their mouths opening to moan, water pouring out from between their dead teeth. Rahel's heart pounded with anger more than with fear—always, these dead rose to take from her those she cherished—and she might have approached nearer, either to stand by the strange *navi* or to scream her grief at the restless dead, but at that moment her sons reached her. Shimon's hand settled heavily on her shoulder.

Yeshua stepped out into the water and took the first corpse by the arm, gazing into its eyes and whispering something none of those on the shore could hear. Then Rahel saw what her sons had seen the night before. She saw the rush of life back into the eyes of the dead, its last, exhaled breath, and then its fall back into the water. That was a shock to Rahel's spirit greater than the rising of the corpses had been—that a man could whisper some word that would give rest so complete and final. She gazed at Yeshua in wonder, as he strode knee-deep along the surf, gripping each of the corpses, one after the next, as though they were his brothers and he was welcoming them home after a night of casting the nets. One seized his throat in its long fingers and pulled him near to bite, but he simply placed the heel of his hand against its head and pushed, holding it back long enough to catch and hold its gaze.

"Amma?" Shimon reached her side, breathless. "Are you all right?"

Rahel couldn't look away from the falling of the dead. "I dreamed this," she whispered. "Last night. A figure, all in white. White fire. Corpses falling like old leaves. I couldn't see his face."

"His robes are brown," Shimon said.

"Yet it was he in my dream."

"Amma!" Koach reached them, panting.

"I am all right, Koach, Shimon."

The corpses lay still as dead fish in the surf. And Yeshua stood there, water to his thighs, gazing down at them. If only all of this had been a dream—not only this night but all the nights previous, all the past fifteen years. All the moaning of the dead. Yet as Koach stepped close, she smiled faintly. No. She would not give up the past fifteen years with her sons. Not though her husband and his brother had been torn out of her life, if not out of her heart.

"He needs us," Rahel said quietly. "Come on."

Yeshua knelt a moment by a fallen corpse that lay half out of the surf, then lowered his hand to its face, closing its eyes. Those eyelids must have long since gone stiff and cold, yet at his touch they slid closed as easily as though the corpse had died only a moment before. The thought of that touch, that unclean flesh, made Shimon shiver; yet the corpse, now that it lay still, with its eyes closed rather than staring in endless hunger, seemed . . . *clean*. Like one who had lain down the burdens of the night and given himself to sleep, and who might wake before sundown to cook fish over the coals and ready the boat again. It was strange, so strange. He repressed an urge to approach the corpse, to kneel by Yeshua and gaze at it, see if it was truly at rest.

"I must get out on that water," Yeshua said.

"What?" Shimon gasped.

"There will be too many to face on the sand, too many, too many, yet they must come up. They must all come up." Yeshua's voice was cold and calm. His face might have been one of Koach's wood carvings. "I must get out there, Cephas."

"On the water? It's the Sabbath."

"The Sabbath was made for man, not man for the Sabbath."

Shimon swallowed. "There's dark weather coming."

"The darkest." Yeshua's eyes were hard. "And when the dead come up with it, I must be there to meet them. Will you row me out?"

Shimon hesitated, glancing at the bodies at the water's edge.

Yeshua stepped near, lowering his voice so that only Shimon could hear. "Years ago, something reached into your town and tore out its heart. The *shedim* have roamed that hollow space it left, and their moans have filled your ears. And you hear it, I know you do, in your mind, even now, even as I do. But we can end it. We can *end it*. You've shivered in the wind . . . too long. Let your faith be as a rock, Cephas, to shield you. Let it be as the Ramat ha-Golan, like mountains that can . . . that can challenge the sky. I tell you, I tell you, on such a rock as that I will build a new town, and a gathering to live in it such as this land has never seen. And not even the shrieking wind of Sheol will prevail against it."

Yeshua's words stirred him; a hard glint came to Shimon's eyes. Whatever revelation had come to the stranger with the light and the heat as he faced the corpses, it had burned away much of his uncertainty, his dread. Yeshua's face was still bruised, his words still rapid and breathless, but he spoke with a fierce confidence and a demand for help to which there could be only one answer.

Shimon glanced at his father's boat. "I will take you out there," he said.

Yeshua gripped Shimon's arm below the shoulder and squeezed so hard it hurt.

"We can end it," he said again.

Then he let go and strode back down to the water's edge.

"Come on," Shimon muttered, and ran down the shore toward that other line of boats, those still seaworthy. Yakob stood, hesitating a moment, staring after Yeshua. Then he ran after Shimon, shells and other sea debris cracking beneath his sandals.

Rahel watched Yeshua walk down the line of the sea. He was different this morning, Yeshua. Harder, colder. All his formidable energy channeled into one fierce purpose, as though every breath he took before launching out on that sea was a breath taken at high cost.

Rahel stared at the bodies of the dead. With the fingers of her right hand she reached into her left sleeve and touched the old, woolen shawl she had tucked away there. Yonah's *tallit*. It brought her a smile of both remembered happiness and remembered grief. All those years ago, she had grieved alone. Most of the women she could have called friend or sister had died that night, violated and beaten by the Roman mercenaries and then eaten by the dead. Having none to turn to for comfort, Rahel had taken to carrying her husband's *tallit* with her while she cooked and while she slept, while she nursed her crippled child. It was all she had left of him besides their children, and for a while, the cloth still carried his scent. It was many months before she could bring herself to wash it, and she did so only after the scent was too faint for her to detect it and after she had forgotten what that scent had been like. She had waited until her infant was sleeping and Shimon was gone from the house, then had wept as she washed the shawl in her basin, scrubbing it until the water was browned with the months of oil and dirt, then wringing it out and scrubbing it again. When it was clean and beautiful (though less so to her eyes than it had been), she had draped it over its peg to dry, and then sat for most of a Roman hour by the basin, staring at the dirtied water. In her heart she had felt that the last of her husband's scent and the last of him was in that water, and she could not bring herself to pour it out. She thought of asking Shimon to spill that water out over the sand or over the sea when she could not see it done. But she had decided at last that it had to be her, and, asking Shimon to watch the baby after he came home, Rahel had carried the basin down to the sea.

Now she gazed on the bodies of the dead, wondering who they were, and whether men or women in Kfar Nahum had grieved at their death. Their faces had been eaten away by time and the sea and the hunger of fish. She couldn't even tell if they had been Hebrew. One of them might even have been a woman she had laughed with by the cistern. She couldn't know.

The back of her neck warned her she was being watched, and a glance behind showed her Koach's waif, the young woman who had been silent and then had sung. She was picking her way carefully through the grasses. The sight startled Rahel, and she realized suddenly that the girl must have slept the night in her house. She should have been angered, but strangely she felt only pity and a sense of kinship, though this bewildered her. She and that girl—they had both been touched by the *navi*. Both of them had been given back something lost, something resigned. Both of them had been, by that act, torn away from their old lives. Now they stood in the empty place, the place of waiting, where the waves eat the world and yet the world remains. She didn't know what was going to happen.

———

While Yesse stood some way up the tideline and watched, his face drawn with grief, the men drew Shimon's boat toward the water, the scrape of it against the shingle an oddly comforting sound, an ancient sound, one the People had heard night after night upon this shore for generations—the sound of their men leaving behind land and bed and security and setting out on the fragile surface of a terrible deep. The boat slid quickly, its bow toward the surf, for Yeshua lent a hand, and Bar Cheleph did also, though Shimon gave him a look of furious warning, a look that said as clearly as a shout: *Get your hands off my father's boat.*

Rahel reached the boat just as the men brought it down to the surf. She took the gunwale in her hands and sprang in, almost as though she were a young girl again. She winced when her feet struck the bottom of the boat, jarring her hip.

Shimon gasped and motioned for the others to stop. They let go of the gunwale and stared at Rahel.

"Amma! What are you doing?"

"Going with you," she said, her teeth clenched against the pain. She seated herself between the oar benches, using one of the nets for a cushion, her back to the hard wood of the hull.

"No, you are not."

Rahel met his gaze, her own as hard as winter. "What began with a spear through your father's brow—I want to see it ended."

Leaning against the gunwale, Shimon exchanged uncertain looks with the other men. Yeshua was staring intently at the sea, seeming hardly to have heard. Then Bar Cheleph spoke, his brow damp with sweat. "I am coming, too."

"*You*," Shimon said, "are not welcome in my father's boat."

Bar Cheleph smiled faintly. "I am the adopted brother of Yakob and Yohanna. I would have been casting the nets with you long before, if I had any bravery at all. But . . ." He looked down. "I had dreams. The same dream, each night. I'm out on the water, and we're casting the nets, and in the dream I always bring *them* up."

Shimon gave him a startled look. He knew such dreams all too well.

Bar Cheleph whispered, "I never knew if my father and mother were among those who were tossed in."

Kana looked away. Yeshua stood gazing at the waves.

Shimon hesitated, the incoming sea nearly reaching his toes. "You are blessed," he said after a moment. "Never to have seen your father risen, like that."

"Not knowing is worse." Bar Cheleph looked out over the chop of the water. "Not knowing if he found rest. Or if he is hungering."

"He found rest." Shimon's tone was harsh. "Fathers don't pursue their children across the sand to eat them. Whatever is down there, it is not him. Nor your mother either."

Yakob nodded to Bar Cheleph, his face drawn. "I put your father in a tomb last night, and mine. Our father had two Yakobs. Never forget that."

Bar Cheleph's eyes moistened. He whispered a word of gratitude, so quiet it almost couldn't be heard.

"I always disappointed him," Yohanna said softly.

Yakob gripped his brother's arm.

Shimon looked away to let the two brothers have that moment to grieve. "Let's get the boat out," he said gruffly.

"One moment." Bar Cheleph walked to where Yeshua stood behind the stern and knelt.

"Before we embark," Bar Cheleph pleaded, "baptize me, *Rabboni*. I . . . I have done evil. My own kinsfolk loathe the sight of me. Immerse me. Please. Make me clean. Then I can follow you even against the dead. I will go where you go, eat where you eat. I will not be parted from you. I promise it. El Shaddai witness it!"

"Do not promise." Yeshua's face went stern, as cold and hard as the face of a mountain. "Do not promise me," Yeshua said, "and do not promise God. Do you think God who promised the stars they would burn each night will wait on your promises? Or that the father who has written his promises into stone itself will trust the vows of men and women, who break them? Say only yes or no. Do not promise. Only do."

Bar Cheleph swallowed.

Shimon listened with disquiet. The Yeshua he had known the previous day had worried him because he seemed a vagrant and because his raving questioned everything that kept Shimon's town and his family secure. But this Yeshua, the one who had faced the dead, worried him even more. This Yeshua called for a boat, and received one. This Yeshua dismissed the Sabbath and spoke of God as though he had something to say about him. This Yeshua seemed more the *navi*. The prophets of their past had raised and buried kings, called fire from the sky, and torn apart cities with a word. What might this one do?

Yeshua stepped away from Bar Cheleph and gripped the gunwale as though to leap into the boat.

"*Please*," Bar Cheleph cried.

Yeshua stopped, his face stricken, as though some defense he had erected that night against the screaming in his mind was shivering. For a moment he stood at the gunwale. Then he turned back. He placed his hand beneath Bar Cheleph's chin and lifted his face. Something flickered in his eyes. "You are loved," he said, his voice quiet and firm, "you are, and the way you were hurt, it does not change that. It never has. It never will. What hurt you have done to others, the father has forgiven. He has forgiven it. Hurt no one else."

Bar Cheleph gave a small nod, though that yearning had not left his eyes. Yeshua turned again and leapt into the boat and seated himself against the gunwale—leaving the benches, as Rahel had, for those who would be rowing. After a moment, Bar Cheleph followed, with a grimace of pain much like Rahel's. Yohanna climbed into the boat as well. Kana sprang in, too, a gust of wind pulling his cloak aside to reveal that he carried, once again, the sica at his hip. But his face was pensive.

Then they had the bow in the water, and Shimon got behind the stern while Yakob pushed from the starboard, and Koach came running, splashing into the water, with the beggar woman wading in beside him. They reached the gunwale opposite Yakob, and Shimon looked at them in shock. Bar Cheleph rose and stood over the gunwale.

"She is coming, too," Koach said. "It's important to her."

Bar Cheleph didn't say a word. He just reached down, let Koach take hold of his arm just below the elbow, and lifted the smaller man into the boat. Then he and Koach turned and lifted the woman in, water running from her coat and from the ragged remnants of her dress beneath it. She stepped toward the stern, tripping over the nets, but Koach caught her arm and helped her down onto the short bench at the stern. Then he shrugged his thick-sleeved outer garment off over one shoulder and used his left hand to tug it off the other. He threw it into the bottom of the boat as though it repulsed him, this garment his mother had made to conceal his arm. In just his tunic, with his withered arm naked, bare for anyone to see, he sat beside the strange woman. His face had set in hard, determined lines as though he had carved it from driftwood, as he had carved so many other things.

Staring at Koach's right arm, Bar Cheleph muttered, "Didn't he heal you?"

"He did."

And that was all Koach said.

Shimon cast a pensive glance at his mother. "A storm is coming. I can't take all my kin out there. And what use are women in a boat?"

"I have been in this boat before," Rahel said quietly.

Shimon frowned, not understanding. Then he glanced at the sky. Definitely a storm. Worry clenched in his gut.

Yeshua watched his face from where he sat near the bow, but he didn't speak.

Yohanna slid one of the oars into the oarlock and held the oar blade up above the shallow water. "It is written," he said softly, "that when the anointed *navi* comes to deliver the remnant of Yehuda tribe, his coming will make hills into valleys and valleys into hills. That what was wilderness will be as a straight road. Ha Matbil spoke of this often." He gave Koach a thoughtful look. "Perhaps his coming will also make women into fishers and brothers whose bodies are broken into boatmen. We are only men. Who are we to argue with what God has written?"

That talk did nothing to settle Shimon's unease. But Yohanna had always been like this—speaking more like a priest's son than a fisherman. "We are all fools," Shimon muttered.

The hardness in Yeshua's face broke, for the first time, into a wry smile. "You speak the truth."

Still Shimon hesitated.

Yakob exchanged a glance with him, a dry look, as though to say, *We are a long row from where we were last night, aren't we?*

And Shimon's eyes answered back, *We are, and I am not sure how we have ended up here, or where "here" is.*

Every night for fifteen years—except for the Sabbath and that one winter when Shimon had taken ill—he and Yakob had slid the boat carefully down into the sea. Just the two of them—and in the last year Yohanna, after he'd tired of eating locusts and wild honey with Ha Matbil by the Tumbling Water.

Now the boat was full of people. Bewildered, Shimon glanced up the tideline toward Yesse, whose white hair streamed behind him in the rising gusts of wind. But if the elder did not approve of this break with tradition and Law and all good sense, he gave no sign. He only watched. Shimon blew out his breath, recalled Yeshua staring into the eyes of the dead, the wonders Yeshua had done before collapsing into his arms. With a mutter beneath his breath, he gave the craft a great shove, and Yakob with him, heaving with their feet planted in the sand, and they ran the boat down onto the water until the next wave surge lifted it and the water was cold about their knees, and then each of them gripped opposite sides at the stern and pulled themselves in.

ONE MORE PROMISE TO KEEP

BEING OUT on the water is an isolating experience. The world is gone, the land barely visible, if at all. There are only the people in your boat, only the sound of your own breath and the lonely cries of gulls or the loud calling of cranes echoing over the water. The sky is wider and deeper than any sky over any town or village on the earth, and you glance up at it cautiously, knowing that at any moment it might crack open and unleash the wrath of God over your small, bouncing craft.

The sky was heavy. Shimon found that he and the others spoke in hushed voices beneath it. Even Yeshua's voice was soft. "I feel that I could sleep until Pesach," the *navi* murmured. "I have never been so weary, so weary. All of you, I see your eyes, I see them; you are too scared to rest. Don't be. Whatever . . . whatever happens on this sea, don't be afraid."

"I have lived most of my life afraid," Kana said, after relieving Yakob at the oar. "But I am not afraid today. I am here because I have seen *your* eyes. I know you have seen what I've seen. More than that. You've seen things I haven't. Things that would break my mind if I did see them."

Yeshua was silent for a bit. He leaned against the side of the boat, his head against the gunwale, and though he could not have been comfortable there, his eyes were lidded as though he might fall asleep in another breath. His face was still pale. "We are the same age, Kana," he said at last. "And we have both seen too many things. Too many."

"That is the truth," Kana said grimly.

"A dark time *is* coming," Yeshua said, and Kana breathed in sharply, hearing the echo of his own words. "But the father can take that time and make . . . make of it something different. Have faith in that." More softly, Yeshua added, "As *I* must."

"Where are we going, *Rabboni*?" Yakob asked.

"Out there," he said, with a nod toward the middle of the sea.

"Yes, but when do we stop? We can't row all morning, not with that storm coming."

"We will know when to stop," Yeshua said. "For now, keep rowing, keep rowing, and wait. You will need to wait . . . often, if you come with me."

"Come with you?" Shimon said, his throat tight. "With you, where? We haven't said we're coming with you."

Rahel smiled faintly, as if at some memory of his father, but said nothing.

Yeshua smiled too, a different smile, as though he wanted to laugh but was too fatigued. He opened his eyes slightly. "All your life you have fished for barbels and musht, Cephas, all your life. Come with me, and we will fish together for the hearts of men."

Shimon heaved at the oar, and wrestled again with the strangeness of this man. He remembered the man gasping for air, after . . .

after what he did with Benayahu. After those words about stars and memory, the night before. *I am spent*, Yeshua had whispered, gazing past Shimon's head at the night sky. *I have to go, have to go. Just for a while. Into the hills, to some quiet place, some place where the screams are not so loud, not so loud as this. There are so many, Cephas, so many, so many. The cries, the cries I hear. I need to be away. Just the father and the stones and the wind.* Yeshua had sucked in a breath, and his body had trembled as though with fever or great pain. Yet Shimon had no longer feared that there were *shedim* in him, that he might be unclean or a witch.

But not yet, the man from Natzeret had whispered. *Not yet. One more promise to keep.*

Shimon stared at him now, in the boat. Yeshua's face had settled into hard lines, as though he'd set his body against some great boulder and was bracing himself to push. One more promise to keep. Shimon didn't know what Yeshua meant to do, but he knew what promise was meant.

But because the riddle of this man could not be answered, Shimon turned to one that could. Kana was watching the sea, and he didn't look up when Shimon spoke. "Why did you come back, Bar Nahemyah?" His voice was rough. "It wasn't to recruit me, or others, not really. You were running. Hiding. Why? And why did it take you a year to return?"

Kana's face went tight with pain.

The others hushed, listening.

"The way you fought," Yakob said after a moment. "The way you moved with that knife. I've never seen anything like that."

"One of the things I spent that year doing." A bite in his voice.

"You almost saved my father." Nearly a whisper.

"Almost." Kana lowered his head.

Shimon had heard the memory beneath Kana's words, and knew the memory to be a bad one. He frowned. He had always thought Bar Nahemyah had thrown in with Barabba, that he had never come back because he had chosen not to. That, and the dead rising from the water in ever greater numbers in the year since— dead that Kana had dropped into this sea—had done little to endear his memory to Yonah's oldest son. Now Shimon wondered.

"Why *didn't* you come back?" he asked, more softly.

Kana's face darkened with shame. "At first, Barabba kept me bound in a cave, and men came—" He paused, then glanced at the young woman in the stern huddled beneath Koach's water-coat, the coat that had been Yonah's. Kana stared at her for a long moment, and then, as if deciding suddenly that if a woman who had seen horrors could bring herself to sing, then he could at least speak, he went on. "Men with blood on their hands," he said. "Not that you could see it, but you could smell it. They came to the cave and spoke with me, one night and then another and another. Told me what Barabba was doing in the land. Not his plans, but their effect. And stories of what Rome was doing. In the long days in the cool of that cave, bound and naked, I craved their return, their words. I can't explain it to you." His right hand trembled; he stilled it, and his face became distant, the secrets of his heart buried deep, drifting like restless corpses far below the reflective surface of his eyes.

"They took everything from me. My coat, my strength. I was thirsty and weak and shaking when the nights came. But they left me with the shofar, at least." His fingers touched the ram's horn where it hung at his breast. "And then, when I thought I would live the rest of my life in that hole in the rock, Barabba came to me. He looked bigger, somehow. He said, *I need men who will blow the shofar even in the streets of Yerushalayim itself. The dead and the Romans alike will devour us all, if I haven't such men.*" Kana was silent a moment, and then he glanced not at any of his kin but at Yeshua, the stranger. "He took me there. To Yerushalayim. Showed me how our People suffered. Not in Kfar Nahum, not in Natzeret, not in any ruined village of our land, but there, in the very heart of the land God promised us, where people rot where they stand

and the moaning fills every street and our people die between the cold stares of the priests and the Roman walls." His voice went hard and cold. "You don't know what it is like. You can't know. What it's like in Yerushalayim."

"I know," Yeshua said, his eyes unfocused as though he were listening to distant voices.

And then Kana's control crumpled.

The *anguish* in his face. Shimon swallowed. He wondered if his own face had looked that way, sometimes.

"You don't have to tell us any more," Shimon said. "You are home." He took a hard pull at the oar.

"Home." Kana gave a small laugh, hardly more than a breath. "I haven't been home in fifteen years. Since that night. I am an outsider, in my own town."

"We've all been that," Shimon murmured.

Kana nodded, took a breath. "I fought for him for a while. After what I'd seen. Because I *had* seen, and I couldn't look away. I couldn't just run back here or steal some Roman's horse. Not after what I'd seen. So I stood before Barabba in the hills and he put the sica in my hands. The very knife he'd used to cut my bonds. And I made the first of these." He brushed his hand over the cuts on his arm, his face still raw with emotion. "I fought with him. Killed. But—" He struggled a moment. "There was a . . . a woman, and her husband, their daughter. Roman. The man was some petty official under Pontius Pilate. It was . . . a test. So Barabba would know if each of us could do what had to be done, if we were in truth to rise against Rome and drive the Romans back to the sea. There were four of us; we went into that city. I haven't seen the other three since, because I left that night and kept moving until I reached this shore." He met Shimon's eyes, and Shimon wanted to look away from the pain there, but he couldn't. "That family, that Roman family, was given into my hand. I was to kill them. In the night, as they slept. With the sica I carried. All three, Barabba said, and any slaves in the house." He wiped the back of his hand across his eyes. When he continued, his voice was hoarse. "I thought I could do it, Shimon. I thought: They were Roman. I could do it. I was in their house, I was standing over their daughter's bed. The sica in my hand. And I . . . I couldn't. She was young. I just kept thinking of the dead I'd seen. And Ahava, my betrothed. I hadn't thought of her in so long. Do you remember her, Shimon?"

He nodded, though he had rarely spoken with her as a boy. She had been tall for a girl, he remembered that, and she used to sneeze tiny sneezes that sounded like laughter.

"Now I see her, every night. Every time I close my eyes." Kana looked away, his voice unsteady. "I couldn't do it. We can be torn from our lives so easily. Can be left grasping and moaning for what we've lost. All my life I have loathed and feared the dead, and now I don't."

"*I* fear the dead," Bar Cheleph muttered.

Kana said, "I pity them."

For a moment there was only the splash of the oars, the chop of the waves against the boat, the duck and roll of their path out onto the uneasy sea.

As he heaved hard on the oar, Shimon glanced at the *navi*. His eyes widened.

The stranger rested in the crook of the prow, his shoulders against either gunwale. His head was bowed almost between his knees, as though he was at the end of his strength after facing the living and the dead. Heedless of the roughness of the sea.

He was asleep.

SKY FULL OF DARK

It was day but the sky darkened, clouds piling onto and over each other, the wind whipping the waves into white fury, until the boat ducked and spun. The storm came on quickly, relentless, as though whatever *shedim* shrieked over the sea meant to crush this fragile boat carrying Israel's *navi* out over the water.

The boat tossed and heaved, and the hue of Bar Cheleph's face went green, though the pitching of their craft did not wake Yeshua. The silent woman drew her coat over herself, looking very small in the stern, a bundle someone had tossed there and forgotten. Koach, who had listened pensively to Kana's story, went to sit by her, his good hand resting on her shoulder.

Rahel, who had been out on the water only once in her life, stood straight on her bench at the stern, her face cold and controlled; if she felt ill, she revealed no sign of it. At last, she reached grimly for the rope that waited, coiled, beneath her bench. She took it up in her hands and, bending, she reached for the silent woman's ankle. The woman gasped and drew back.

Koach touched her shoulder. "It's all right," he said softly by her ear.

"You're thinking the boat may sink." Rahel gave the younger woman a stern look. "If the boat sinks on this sea, none of us will see the shore."

The girl gazed at the chop and surge of the waves, and shivered. Koach squeezed her shoulder, and she gave a small nod. Rahel's lips compressed into a thin line; she bent again, took a firm hold on the younger woman's ankle, tied a loop around it. The other end she fastened to one of the iron hooks set in the bottom of the boat, hooks meant to secure items against a storm.

"Bat Eleazar is right," Yakob said. He took up another coil, and began cutting lengths and passing rope to each of those in the boat.

Rahel fastened a harness of rope about her own waist, and then Koach's. For a moment he sat quietly while her small, sure hands knotted the rope. His face burned. It was embarrassing to be seen cared for in this way; though she had helped him dress each morning, that had been in the privacy of their house, before no other eyes. Yet it would be more humiliating by far to be seen fumbling one-handed with the rope himself, laboring with careful attention at a task that any of the other men in the boat would have found simple. He especially didn't want the woman in his father's coat to see that.

With a pang of sorrow, he recalled standing naked on the rooftop, with Tamar's gaze on his body, his every weakness visible to her. He blinked quickly to make the world less moist and blurry. Maybe he would never again feel so safe with any woman. Or maybe he would. He didn't know.

"Are you all right, son?" Rahel whispered.

"No," he said. He took her hand, stilling its work at the rope. "No more hiding. I'll do this, mother." His name must be a lie no longer.

Rahel searched his face. Then her eyes filled with both pain and pride. Biting her lip, she nodded slightly and backed away.

While Koach wrestled awkwardly with knotting the rope, Rahel took up one of the curved wooden blades that the fishers used for bailing from its place in the bottom of the boat, holding it ready in her hand. Kana relieved Yakob at the oar, and Yohanna tried to relieve Shimon, but Shimon gave a firm shake of his head and heaved at the oar, his shoulders tensed. His face was set, as though he were hunting something over that water and would not give up the chase, not though the day ended and the world grew dark.

But in fact it was not yet noon.

The beggar woman looked away from the growl of the sea, and after a moment she pressed her fingertips to Koach's tunic, at his shoulder. He glanced at her, his face twisted in the effort it took not to cry.

"Miriam," she whispered.

He looked at her. The others did also.

It became very quiet in the boat.

"Miriam." She was pale, her face twisted in anxiety, and she held his gaze, her hand at his arm, as though they were siblings or lovers. Her eyes shone with her reawakened desire to speak, to be known.

"Miriam," Koach repeated.

"My name. It's . . . my name. Miriam bat Elisa. From Tower. From Magdala."

Koach stared at her a moment. She had been silent so long; now the giving of her name seemed a gift of great trust. "Don't be afraid," he said.

Miriam's eyes were serious. "I *am* afraid." Her voice was halting, betraying how unaccustomed she was to making words rather than hearing them. "Father. Mother. They were eaten. In our house in Magdala. When I lost my words." She moved her hands as she spoke, touching her belly when she said *eaten* and placing her fingers at her throat when speaking of her long silence. Her eyes moistened as she searched Koach's face, then the others' faces, though whether she was pleading for empathy or forgiveness or only an acknowledgment of kinship, they could not have said—only that her eyes demanded some response. Seeing their own faces reflected in her eyes, they each saw the smallness of how they had treated her and others like her.

Koach took her hand and gripped it. After a moment, he felt her fingers curl around his and grip back.

"Need to be here," she said, her voice so soft it was almost lost in the cry of the wind. Her hair blew about her face. "Need to see. Need to . . . not be afraid."

"Shimon bar Yonah," Kana interrupted. He was staring up at the wild growl of the sky.

"I know," Shimon said, loudly over the wind.

A moment before, the wind had been only the first roar of a gale; now it was tempest, now it was the sky ready to tear their boat apart. The waves became walls that rose and crashed, and the boat pitched violently.

The others roped themselves quickly to the iron hooks. Yakob and Yohanna secured the mast and its small sail; Shimon slid the oars under the benches by the fishing spears. He should have tied them down also; they would be no use in this storm, which could only be ridden out, not argued with. But Koach saw the whites of his brother's eyes and knew his brother did not want to be without spear or oar, something he could lift in his hands.

"He still sleeps," Rahel shouted.

Koach looked and saw that it was true; the man from Natzeret's face, which had been pale, was now ashen, and his bruises were dark shadows—as though this was not sleep but the first touch of death. Koach shuddered.

Then the storm buried the last of the light out of the sky, as though a lamp had been covered with earth, and Yeshua was only a silhouette. They all were. What light remained was ghostly, showing the white edges of the waves. Koach's hand tightened about Miriam's fingers. She squeezed his hand again. Yet he didn't know if she meant to seek comfort or to give it. He felt her pressed to his left side, and he wished that he might put his arm about her, but he would not let go of her hand.

"Don't be afraid," he kept whispering. "Don't be afraid. Don't be afraid."

"They're coming," Shimon shouted.

The water frothed—not just from the storm but from what was coming up *with* the storm. Koach gazed over the gunwale into the crashing dark, a small noise of fear in his throat. The sea was full of faces, and there was moaning in his ears that was not wind.

SILENCE OVER THE WATER

THE DEAD were rising—not just one, not just a few.

All.

They surged and fell back, white as foam on the waves. Already some of the corpses were driven against the boat, their hands beating the hull as the waterborne dead had beat at the sides of the Ark in the old story.

The sky was dark like the ending of the world, and the air and the sea were black. There was only the dull sheen of their eyes and their silhouettes against the water. And the moaning, a sound that merged with the wind to become the wailing of all the *shedim* that had ever hunted in the lonely places of a broken land.

Koach and all the others and their entire town were but a tiny boat, a chip of wood on the wild thunder of the sea, and so many pale hands out of the past were grasping that fragile chip to drag it beneath the waters. These were the old dead, thrown into the sea fifteen years before. The cords about their wrists had parted long since, and their bodies were bloated with water. Some were without eyes or face, sea-eaten. The waterlogged flesh peeled back from their fingertips even as they grasped the gunwale. Their weight began to pull the boat down, down, into the dark, the water sloshing over the side. More of the white dead climbed over those first corpses, clambering over their backs to get at the warm life in the boat. The reek of them was stronger than the smell of the sea, covering that ancient scent the way slick, sickly oil covers the surface of the water. Miriam screamed, shrill and piercing over the moans of the dead, and Koach found he was screaming with her. He had only one hand, only one; he let hers go and snatched up the cold metal of a fishing spear to defend her, and himself, and his kin.

A horn call rang out, clear and deep, a challenge to sky and sea and everything within them. Those few notes, music raised in defiance of the dead like the voice of all the living deepened and strengthened. The sound woke the others from their horror.

Kana let the shofar fall from his lips. Then they were all on their feet, taking up hook, oar, or net, whatever they could grab. One of the dead, fat as though it had swallowed the sea, came up over those clutching at the gunwale and slipped into the boat, sliding into the bottom on its belly like a swollen fish, spewing water from its mouth. Shrieking, Rahel threw a net over it. Koach leapt onto its back and drove a fish hook, one-handed, down into the back of its skull. Vaguely, Koach recalled Yeshua's words about the dead, but in this darkness on the sea with the dead surging into the boat, he had no faith in his ability or anyone else's to stare the dead in the eyes. His insides were cold and weak with panic. As the corpse beneath him went still, he caught glimpses in the dark, all around him: Yakob and Yohanna thrusting the points of the other two fish hooks into the shoulders and faces of the dead with little effect. Kana with his sica, the pale sheen of it, driving it up through a corpse's chin, and then another, implacable as the *malakh ha-mavet*, the angel of death. Each of the corpses jerking once, then going still. Rahel beside him, with a knife out, slashing across the fingers of the dead, cutting away their grip on the boat, so that the dead slid back, pulled down by the grasping hands of those surging up behind them. Water rushed in over the stern. Then the boat righted itself, barely. Miriam took up one of the heavy nets, and Shimon lent his strength; they cast it out over the dead, entangling several.

Lightning, sharp against the eyes, revealed for one frantic heartbeat all the dead in the water, all of them climbing over each other toward the boat, all of them surging on the wildness of the waves. Koach saw one of the dead half over the other gunwale, its hands gripping Bar Cheleph's storm coat. Even as Bar Cheleph struggled, flailing, to shrug away the garment, another corpse climbed up over the first, its fingers gripping the first corpse's face, digging into its left cheek and its right eye, hissing as it fought for purchase. Koach screeched like one of the dead himself. Stepping to the side of that man who had once assailed him and beaten him to the grass, he brought the fish hook down and sliced neatly through one of the dead wrists clutching Bar Cheleph's coat, half-severing it. The fingers slackened, and Bar Cheleph pulled his coat free of the thing's other hand and fell across the boat, shouting wordlessly, his eyes white. But the corpse grabbed Koach's spear with its good hand and moaned. The weight of the corpse behind it pulled it back, and both slid down into that water teeming with pale bodies, pulling Koach over the side.

With a cry, Koach released the spear, but too late, he'd been pulled right over the gunwale toward all those faces beneath him, all those faces white as rotting fish, their mouths gaping. The rope harness about his chest went taut; their fingers brushed his arm, his hair, and he screamed. Then something pulled him back, something had his belt and he was yanked fiercely back into the boat. Then Bar Cheleph's arm was around him. Koach screamed and screamed, kicking wildly as the dead came up over the gunwale after him. A flash of lightning, and there, stark against the shadows, a corpse with only one eye, its belly balanced on the brink of the boat, its legs in the water, its hands reaching for him.

The blade of an oar smacked into its face, hard, the sound of the blow lost in thunder that cracked the roof of the sky. Shimon stood there, bellowing against wind and storm, sudden rain lashing his face and hair.

———

That thunder had been right above Shimon's head, so loud it must have cracked open the world and all the water would now pour out. And it had cracked open time, for Shimon stood with his oar raised, gripped in gloved hands, the rain sharp against his face, and before that oar came swinging down, he stood in a single moment that held an eternity of thought and terror. Then a flash of lightning, the whole world light and dark; as Shimon brought the oar down, his heart wild in his chest, for an instant he could see the others in the boat, all their terrified faces, all of them about to die together. The woman from Tower, weeping as she bent to haul up another net, with Yohanna stooping to aid her in Shimon's place; Rahel driving her knife into a corpse's brow even as it clutched at her left breast like some nightmarish lover, seeking some hold to pull her toward its teeth; Yakob swinging the point of his spear hard against the grasping hands, breaking fingers; Kana wrestling with one corpse that had grappled his knife arm, then tossing the knife deftly to his left hand and sliding it up beneath the corpse's chin and through its head as though it were made of butter and not flesh and bone. Bar Cheleph falling back into the bottom of the boat, clutching Koach to him with one arm, Koach's rope tangled about his legs. And Yeshua, still, silent, seated in the bow, his face stark like a skull's in that flash of wild light.

All of them about to die.

And in that moment, in all their faces, Shimon saw himself, saw the horror that had eaten away all his life and left him only a husk. Between one beat of the heart and the next, he saw himself, and forgave.

He forgave Zebadyah the priest for hiding beneath his boat.

He forgave Kana his rage and his tossing of the dead into the sea.

He forgave his father for dying, for leaving him to raise his brother alone and to fish on the sea without guidance or aid.

He forgave himself.

For every moment he'd wakened shivering from the dream country. Every morning he'd brought home not enough fish. Every night he'd sunk like a stone beneath the water of his anger, his help-lessness.

Because neither the priest nor the zealot nor his father nor he nor all the town together were enough to put their dead to rest. To hold in his heart the bitterness of so much wrath, and not forgive—it was as though a puddle of water were to hate itself for drying beneath the sun's heat in the month of the lion, the month of desert. The pool of water was not sufficient to withstand the sun that would devour it, and he was not sufficient to withstand the rising tide of the town's dead, of so much unforgotten history and pain and hunger.

In the next moment he might die, or not. But he could no longer hate himself, or his brother, or his people.

Shimon dropped the oar and flung himself to the floor of the boat beside Yeshua. He grabbed the man's shoulders and shook him, screaming, "*Rabboni! Rabboni!*"

None of them were sufficient.

But he had seen the stranger from Natzeret call a dead man back into his body and give him rest. If they had any hope, any chance of burying the dead, that chance was with Yeshua.

"*Rabboni*, my master, wake, or we perish!" Shimon cried. "Please!" He screamed his plea, desperate for the need of one small man on a small boat to sound louder than wind or water or the shrieking past. How was it that God heard prayer? Or that any human being heard another's cry for help or for love, when each day, every hour, every moment our minds are deluged by the cries of everyone around us and the cries of those in our memory, the thousand cries screaming within us?

"*Please!*"

Yeshua opened his eyes and blinked back water from his lids.

"Master!" Shimon shouted. "How can you sleep! The dead! The storm!"

Yeshua swept his lank and soaked hair out of his eyes, then reached for Shimon's hand; Shimon took it, and Yeshua surged to his feet. He looked out into the storm, his eyes dark against the night, though whether with fury or grief, Shimon couldn't tell. He released Yeshua's hand. There was a shriek, and a moving shadow that must have been Miriam throwing a net over one of the dead that was clambering into the boat. Yeshua stepped past her. Wood cracked behind him, and a spar swung loose from the mast toward his head; he lowered his head without glancing back, and it swung by. He placed one foot firmly against the gunwale, standing even amid the pitch and heave of the boat in the storm, even as the dead grasped at his ankles, his shins. His hair flew about his face, dark in the wind. Shimon gazed up at him in wonder and dismay.

Screams from others in the boat.

Then the sun's heat was all around him and passing through him, and this time there was no light but only heat, heat, *heat*, as though the world might burn away and leave nothing but flakes of ash beneath the cold stars. Shimon cried out and heard the others' cries and the wailing of the dead and the howl and crack of the storm. He saw the empty eyes of the dead all about him glinting in the dark, their hands reaching for him. And pressing on his body and his heart . . . the weight, the *kavod*, surely the same glory that the *kohannim* taught filled the Temple at times and made its pillars creak. The unbearable weight of God, the lightest press of whose fingertip might crush the land.

Shimon cried out, falling back.

Yeshua spoke, and his voice was soft as wind in the grass, soft as sunlight on still water. Yet Shimon could hear it in his very heart, hear it above all the noise of the world's wreck.

"*Shalom*," Yeshua said. "*Shabbat shalom*. Be at peace."

———

Zebadyah the priest had taught that the land had always had history, even before there *was* land. God had not made the world from nothing, as idle thinkers among the Greeks taught, but from the turmoil and wrack of the *tohu vavohu*, the whirling chaos, the dark materials that were without form or shape, the great waste of the sea upon which no light shone and in which drifted the debris and detritus of uncounted things that had not yet been shaped into anything living or beautiful. Sundered pieces that made up no whole, drift that clashed and crashed in the dark.

And because peace, because any bringing together, any settling of history's chaos into a new and meaningful story begins with words spoken and words heard, in the beginning God had whispered a few words into the rush of that primeval sea. And there was land amid the waters, and light.

———

The sky broke into pieces. Spears of sun pierced the clouds and fell into the cold sea, each of them doused in the water with a hiss so quiet only the *malakhim* could have heard them. For one wild moment, the eyes of the dead shone in the sudden light, so many sightless eyes, so many empty faces on the dark waves. All their mouths were open, their jaws slack. Shimon found that he was weeping, and he didn't know why. Only that, in this light, with the heat and the weight of Yeshua's power pressing him back against the opposite gunwale, all those staring faces were no longer a thing of terror but of sorrow. His face was wet with his tears.

Then all the eyes filled. He was looking out at so many of his dead rocking on the sea. The midwife he'd seen eaten on that night of the dead, she was there. And the eyes of young mercenaries who had rallied to Rome for coin or glory from far ends of the earth, and the eyes of young men and old men, and of women who had known men and women who hadn't, and of those who had borne children and those who had recently been children. All of them were there, all of their dead. Their spirits looked out of their white faces for one last instant, all those souls peering out as if in second birth. Harrowed from the dark waters, the dark fields of the sea.

Bar Cheleph whispered, barely more than a breath, "They aren't there. Amma, abba. They aren't there. Oh God, they aren't there."

The eyes closed—one pair, then another—and the dead slipped back into the water. All of them falling back into the crash of the waves. The last to go were the ones clinging to the gunwale, but their grip slackened and then they slid away, too. Shimon saw one hand remain for a moment, ghoulish and pale. Then it was gone.

All of them, gone.

The wind stilled, the rocking of the boat slowed. A quiet creaking where the broken spar still swung from the mast. Then even that went still. The Sea of Galilee went quiet as a pool in the rocks. Shimon glanced over the side, his hands shaking. The water was clear as the first water ever made. He could see far beneath the boat. Not to the bottom, but for just a moment, he thought he could glimpse the pale shapes of the sinking dead. Then nothing.

Silence over the water.

"*Shalom*," Yeshua whispered again. "My peace I give to you. Not as the world gives do I give. My peace I give to you."

Peace.

Gazing out over that still water, Shimon realized for the first time that a hunger for peace could raven the body and gnaw the heart almost as sharply as a hunger for fish could chew at the belly. That hunger could waste you away, day after day after day, until you were thin and empty as a corpse, though you still walked and moaned, grasping for something you needed, though you didn't know what it was.

Peace was more than stillness. More than sleep. More than numbness, more than the absence of conflict.

Peace was consolation and wholeness. Peace was two men breaking bread together, forgiving an old quarrel. Peace was a mother holding her infant up to its father for the first time, or a mother opening her eyes to greet her child after long illness. Peace was two lovers in each other's arms after a long, good night. Peace was an open door and a wall torn down. Peace was a *cephas*, a rock lashed by the waves yet unmoved. A rock people could stand on.

Kfar Nahum had starved for peace. *He* had starved for peace. He looked at his brother's face and saw the same shock of recognition there. His mother sank down to the bench and put her face in her hands. Yohanna and Yakob—their eyes were wet. Kana was gazing at the water as though he were looking at the face of God. The girl Miriam stared at Yeshua where he stood, her face bathed in awe. Bar Cheleph was looking at the others' faces, even as Shimon was, and their gazes met.

How strange, that they were all in this one boat. The son of the town's most renowned fisherman, his crippled brother, and the man who'd beaten him. Two women, one of them an outcast. A priests' sons and a trained killer and a stranger who could call up out of the water the living and the dead. All here, on this little bit of wood on the surface of the sea. *Shalom.*

Yeshua stood still while the boat rocked on water older and deeper than the dreams and the yearnings and the breathing of human beings.

His voice was soft above the waves, and sad as rain before dawn.

"So little faith," he said. "All of us have so little faith."

He turned to them then. His face burned briefly, and glancing at his eyes was like looking into the sun. Yet Yeshua's hands shook, and after a moment he sat slowly against the gunwale, tucked his knees against his chest, and closed his eyes. The light went out. His chest rose and fell.

The men in the boat and Rahel and Miriam of Magdala watched him sleep, their faces awed and troubled. Silent, but their silence no longer that of the fishers on the lifeless sea. And beneath their boat, the dead drifted at last in that same silence. All of them still beneath the irrevocable weight of a glory that could not be understood or named, only witnessed. So many bodies carried beneath the waves on currents no men knew, drifting to final sites of sea-burial marked and noted by none living, and whether God might remember them where they lay or whether their souls had gone to great rooms in God's house, none could tell. Unless perhaps that one man resting now against the gunwale, that man of sorrows whose eyes burned with a fire that consumed his memory to ash and whose coming had tumbled the houses of their town and all their lives into an architecture new and unpredicted. Yet perhaps not even he could tell, not even he.

FINIS

SETTING OUT ON THE WAVES AGAIN

This is the most difficult novel I have ever written, and I am not the same man I was when I began it.

As I wrote of Rahel's illness and her healing, and of her child's disability, my own infant daughter took ill. She was diagnosed with epilepsy and cortical blindness. She spent two of her first twelve months hospitalized for seizures.

I sat in that hospital by her bedside, in the cold of winter. It was warm enough in that carefully sterile place, but I *felt* cold. I felt angry. I felt exhausted, and determined. The wind that rattled the windows one night seemed to hurl against the hospital glass all the moaning horror and shrieking of the *shedim*.

Now my daughter is improving, and we are on the other side of that time together. Yet those nights by her bed are recent in my heart, and they hurt. I don't know what this past year has meant, only that the love I now hold for those I call my own is fiercer than anything I have ever felt. I have learned that hope, which I had thought small and delicate like a moth in the night, can be hard as steel, a blade with which you cut your way through a press of moaning and hungry foes.

Without the help and encouragement and quiet strength of a great many people, I would have made it neither through this past year nor through this novel. I name them here, because they were with me in the boat when the sky went dark: Ever Saskya, Andrew Hallam, J. R. West, Tim and Susie Grade, Brian and Lara Hedberg, Max and Tamara Siler, Jan and Jim Buntrock, Bill and Dottie Amann, Roxanne Herbert, and many, so many, in my community and my workplace. My editor, Alex Carr, did not blink an eye when I told him that I was staying up nights with my daughter and that this novel would be longer and harder to write than I'd thought. Jacque Ben-Zekry and many of her friends at Amazon Publishing—including many I know only by name—were there to encourage me. My house is filled with children's books that they sent to my family by the box, to let us know we were loved. Novelists Rob Kroese, Elisa Lorello, R. J. Keller, and Sarah Paquette sent my daughter what must surely be the world's largest pop-up book. Don McQuinn sent me the kindest note. Kevin Kientz grieved with me, and Amit Mrig had my back. Clarence Haynes read my novel with compassion and insight, and encouraged me. Aunt Dee, who I think had rarely let a day pass in the last few years without grinning, called often with words of hope or joy. She passed away the same week that I finished this manuscript, and we miss her. And we will always remember her.

My wife Jessica went through the storm with me and I with her, both of us lashed to the gunwale and howling our defiance to wind and sky. Little River gave me her laughter and her shrieks of joy, and hours watching *Doctor Who* together. And Inara, my youngest, faced needles, medical tests, medications, and sleepless nights with a grin on her face that could cure even Shimon bar Yonah's despair. I am a blessed man.

To all of you, my readers, I offer this book, with my thanks for casting the nets with me. Let us see what comes up. Whether scant fish to feed us or teeming millions to break the nets, in either case this life we live is our fathers' sea, and ours. Each night we will take our boats down to that water knowing that whatever happens, the night is ours to live.

Stant Litore
August 2013

THEY FACED THE DEAD

YOU'VE MET them before, or you think you have. You have seen their faces in stained glass, or in prints of da Vinci's *Last Supper*. You've heard their names recited in children's nursery rhymes or in your fathers' prayers—Jesus of Nazareth and his companions, who in the first century AD changed forever the way our world confronts the recurring threat of our restless and ravenous dead.

Yet if you who read this are to remember those who stood against the walking corpses—if you are to do more than remember, if you are to know what they knew, grieve as they grieved, burn with fury at what angered them, or smile at what warmed their hearts—then you must know them by their own names, not our English ones. And you must meet them in their own boat, the wood of the oars cold even through your gloves. Or on the shore with the fierce wind off the sea in your face. They are:

In Hebrew or Aramaic	In English
Shimon/Cephas	Simon/Peter
Koach	Andrew
Yohanna	John
Yakob	James
Shimon bar Nahemyah/Kana	Simon/The Zealot
Yakob bar Cheleph	James, son of Alphaeus
Miriam of Magdala	Mary Magdalene
Yeshua	Jesus

There they are, the first of them. And this is the first of their stories.

Koach

Entire libraries have been written about Simon Peter, but relatively little in recent centuries about his fierce brother. Yet the apostle Andrew has often been a figure of fascination. Today he is held to be the patron saint of nations as diverse as Scotland, where he brings victory in battle against overwhelming numbers; Malta, where he is associated with a rich harvest of fish; and Russia, where he is recognized for farsight and prophecy. The third century devoted an apocryphal text entirely to him: *The Acts of Andrew.* Other texts describe him, late in life, traveling among the nomadic tribes north of the Black Sea, teaching them the sharing of bread, and leading them to stand against the dead that in the later part of the first century lurched out of the Caucasus in great numbers. Overshadowed in history's eyes by his brother Simon Peter, Andrew yet possessed courage and compassion every inch as deep as his older brother's heady mix of loyalty and guilt. And he, no less than his brother, changed the world.

No Hebrew or Aramaic name is remembered for the apostle we know as Andrew; "Andrew" is from the Greek, and it means strong or manly. It means vigor. In reconstructing the events of AD 26, I have chosen to use the Hebrew word for strength and vigor— *koach* (the first syllable rhymes with the archer's *bow*, the second with the Scottish *loch*)—as Andrew's original name, speculating that the Greek recorders may later have translated it.

Koach was of course a physically weak man, and the vigor that others saw in him was a strength of the heart. The Hebrews regarded physical illness and weakness as a sign of evil, a blighting of the People; the Greeks and the Romans saw it as the outward sign of an inner malformity of the soul. Yet even in these cultures, the man Koach was able to achieve such stature through the strength of his heart—for he did not believe that the condition of his body was an impediment to his mission—that even the Greeks who loved beauty and feared its opposite consented to call him Andreas, the Manly. In this story we encounter him as still hardly more than a youth, though even then, he was a formidable youth.

The only irremovable impediments are those we shore up within our own hearts.

ABOUT THE AUTHOR

STANT LITORE doesn't consider his writing a vocation; he considers it an act of survival. As a youth, he witnessed the 1992 outbreak in the rural Pacific Northwest firsthand, as he glanced up from the feeding bins one dawn to see four dead staggering toward him across the pasture, dark shapes in the morning fog. With little time to think or react, he took a machete from the barn wall and hurried to defend his father's livestock; the experience left him shaken. After that, community was never an easy thing for him. The country people he grew up with looked askance at his later choice of college degree and his eventual graduate research on the history of humanity's encounters with the undead, and the citizens of his college community were sometimes uneasy at the machete and rosary he carried with him at all times, and at his grim look. He did not laugh much, though on those occasions when he did, the laughter came from him in wild guffaws that seemed likely to break him apart. As he became book-learned, to his own surprise he found an intense love of ancient languages, a fierce admiration for his ancestors, and a deepening religious bent. On weekends, he went rock-climbing in the cliffs without rope or harness, his fingers clinging to the mountain, in a furious need to accustom himself to the nearness of death and teach his body to meet it. A rainstorm took him once on the cliffs and he slid thirty-five feet and hit a ledge without breaking a single bone, and concluded that he was either blessed or reserved in particular for a fate far worse. Finding women beautiful and worth the trouble, he married a girl his parents considered a heathen woman, but whose eyes made him smile. She persuaded him to come down from the cliffs, and he persuaded her to wear a small covenant ring on her hand, spending what coin he had to make it one that would shine in starlight and whisper to her heart how much he prized her. Desiring to live in a place with fewer trees (though he misses the forested slopes of his youth), a place where you can scan the horizon for miles and see what is coming for you while it is still well away, he settled in Colorado with his wife and two daughters, and they live there now. The mountains nearby call to him with promises of refuge. Driven again and again to history with an intensity that burns his mind, he corresponds in his thick script for several hours each evening with scholars and archaeologists and even a few national leaders or thugs wearing national leaders' clothes who hoard bits of forgotten past in far countries. He tells stories of his spiritual ancestors to any who will come by to listen, and he labors to set those stories to paper. Sometimes he lies awake beside his sleeping wife and listens in the night for any moan in the hills, but there is only her breathing soft and full and a mystery of beauty beside him. He keeps his machete sharp but hopes not to use it.

http://stantlitore.com
zombiebible@gmail.com
@thezombiebible
www.facebook.com/stant.litore